THE SQUARE

Peter Garth Hardy

Gotham Books

30 N Gould St.
Ste. 20820, Sheridan, WY 82801
https://gothambooksinc.com/

Phone: 1 (307) 464-7800

© 2023 *Peter Garth Hardy*. All rights reserved.

No part of this book may be reproduced, stored in a retrieval system, or transmitted by any means without the written permission of the author.

Published by Gotham Books (November 18, 2023)

ISBN: 979-8-88775-590-8 (P)
ISBN: 979-8-88775-591-5 (E)

Because of the dynamic nature of the Internet, any web addresses or links contained in this book may have changed since publication and may no longer be valid.

The views expressed in this work are solely those of the author and do not necessarily reflect the views of the publisher, and the publisher hereby disclaims any responsibility for them.

DEDICATION

*This book is dedicated
to my wife, Meng,
and the beautiful life
we share.*

TABLE OF CONTENTS

CHAPTER 1
    Paxton 1
    Intake Day 6

CHAPTER 2
    Eden 17
    The Mexicans 24

CHAPTER 3
    Jazelle 34
    Friday Night 40

CHAPTER 4
    Elizabeth 58
    Initiation 61

CHAPTER 5
    Rachel 73
    The Horse 81

CHAPTER 6
    Barbara 97
    Maggie's Farm 101

CHAPTER 7
    Jonas 113
    The Ranch 116

CHAPTER 8
    Paxton 134
    War Plans 139

CHAPTER 9
    Wallace 154
    Saying Goodbye 158

CHAPTER 10
    Abraham 173
    Into The Desert 178

CHAPTER 11
    Marty 194
    Elizabeth's Escape 200

CHAPTER 12
    Grace 220
    The Vagabonds 225

CHAPTER 13
    Bill 238
    Eating A Dead Horse 242

CHAPTER 14
    Valerie 258
    Guadalupe Mountains 263

CHAPTER 15
    Richard 286
    The Tribe 290

CHAPTER 16
    Mukwooru 305
    The Comanche 310

CHAPTER 17
    Shi Li 328
    Antigravity 334

CHAPTER 18
Eden 353
Sweat Lodge 357

CHAPTER 19
Nantan 373
Suicide Mission 378

CHAPTER 20
Nicholas 391
Ground Zero 393

CHAPTER 21
Eden 414
On The Road 420

EPILOGUE
Paxton 435

CHAPTER 1

PAXTON

What I miss most about the way things used to be, is having a beer on my porch, in the slanting sunlight of a late, Friday afternoon with the whole weekend stretching out before me. I had not a care in the world during those few minutes, except possibly to wonder what I could rustle up for dinner. That wasn't a major problem either, because if the leftovers in my refrigerator weren't to my liking, I could just jump into my car and drive five miles to the grocery store. There I could get almost every food imaginable, and more beer to boot.

Oh, the choices we had! Beef, pork, lamb, turkey, chicken, fish and eggs for our protein. One side of a whole aisle was devoted to different flavored breads, with all manner of shapes and sizes of pasta and rice if you'd rather get your carbohydrates that way. I was always partial to bread. Any fruit or vegetable you could imagine was there for the picking, although some were more costly than others depending upon whether they were out of season or had traveled from another continent. All manner of processed food from crackers and potato chips to cookies and cakes and chocolate bars were as easy to procure as plucking them off the shelves and shelling out a little cash. Hell, we didn't even need cash. Most everyone had little plastic cards that you could swipe into a card reader and the money would be taken directly out of your bank account with no physical exchange whatsoever.

I couldn't even make it through the beer aisle in under ten minutes if I had a mind for browsing. There was imported beer from Germany, England, Canada, Mexico and Australia, beer with fruit in it, wheat beer, stout beer,

The Square 2

India pale ale, American pale ale, lagers and pilsners, and microbrews in colorful six-packs with catchy names. If it was summertime, I might not even be averse to the purchase of one of those watered-down, mass-produced American standbys like Budweiser or Miller Lite. Here we only have cactus beer, which is exactly what it sounds like, and I'm pretty sure it's eating a hole in my stomach.

We were at the apex of nature's ten-thousand-year-old experiment in humanity and yet we took it all for granted. We acted as if we had somehow earned it. We treated ourselves and our world as if we had unlimited time, unlimited resources, unlimited future. Then they let the whole fragile house of cards come crashing down on all our heads.

I say they as if I was outside of the whole affair, when in truth, I did more than my fair share to bring about our demise. Most of us were complacent, but I was also complicit. I gave them gravity. I gave them anti-gravity for that matter, no pun intended. And then they used it against me when they came to claim me, you have to appreciate the irony there. Someone has got to appreciate it, or we really have lost all of our humanity.

Back then we had it made, everybody lived on easy street, even the poorest among us. We had cheap electricity running through cables to just about every home in the country, our country of course, not every country. It did much of our household work for us. It washed our dishes and clothing, dried our clothes, too, and our hair, cooked our food and cleaned our floors. It powered our lights and heated our homes and our water for daily bathing. Hell, it cooled our homes, too, in the summertime, and kept our food from spoiling too quickly. We actually put ice into our drinks. I haven't seen ice in so long now.

It's been even longer since I've seen snow. We used to sing carols, dreaming of White Christmases, now that's all we can do, dream about them. It all seems so far-off and quaint to me now. There's still snow somewhere, I've got to believe that it's not all gone, somewhere in Scandinavia, or the Canadian Rockies or Russian tundra, Iceland for God's sake. There's no more snow in Maine, or at least there hadn't been for five or six winters, even before I got Squared.

We used to complain about having to drive in it, and shovel it off our driveways, but we also had a hell of a lot of fun in it. We went skiing and sledding, we built snowmen and snow forts and had snowball fights. The snowflakes themselves were a mathematician's dream-come-true with their hexagonal, crystalline structures that you could see right there on your glove if you caught a big enough one. It was so beautiful, to wake up to the new-fallen snow, blanketing everything and glistening in the morning sunlight. I sometimes imagine I see snow here, when the sun is glinting off the sand and the wriggling heat waves play tricks on my old brain. I guess that's what they call a mirage.

We had other ways to entertain ourselves, sedentary ways powered by those tiny electrons traveling networks of copper capillaries – giant television screens attached to the wall, video game consoles, stereo systems and virtual reality modules, because reality itself wasn't a compelling enough reason to get out of bed in the morning. Everyone, even small children, had their own personal computers. Our computers had gotten so small that they could be held in the palm of your hand and also used as telephones to communicate with anyone in the world instantly, if only you knew the right buttons to push.

We no longer had the need to commit anything to memory. The vast knowledge amassed by the human race throughout time was at your fingertips on the RepNet, processed by a company called Google. The mathematician in me always appreciated that name, though I'll wager that fewer than one in a million people knew it was derived from the term 'googol' which stood for ten raised to the one-hundredth power. Which, incidentally, is more than all of the atomic particles in the universe. I think that number is something like ten to the eightieth power, but I'm not sure if I remember that correctly. I'd google it if I could get some Wi-Fi in this All-forsaken place!

Not only could you look up any piece of information you could possibly want to know, but we used the RepNet for everything. We streamed TV shows and movies and music, read books and booked hotels and flights and did all manner of shopping. Anything that could be reasonably shipped to your home could be purchased with a computer and a RepubliCard, from food and clothing to furniture and appliances. If you could also work at home from your computer, you would literally never have to leave your home at all, ever. That was part of our problem, you see, we forgot how to interact with each other socially, other than what could be written or sent or received electronically.

The computer was our crowning achievement, but also our downfall. I'm not talking about some science-fiction world where we created artificial intelligence and the computers decided they didn't need us anymore, either. We did this to ourselves, human to human, but the computers played a big part. Once the government took control of the RepNet, they controlled what we could see and hear, how we communicated with each other and what information was shared with the masses. More importantly, they knew everything about us, every cell phone call and click on the computer. Click, click, click. Once they controlled the RepNet, freedom was nothing more than a catchphrase.

We still got our votes, on Election Day, sent in electronically from our laptops and cell phones, tabulated by computer algorithms in Washington. Soon the Republicans were winning every close election. Later they began to win elections in Democratic-leaning districts and states. There were mass protests everywhere which were met with an ever-increasing show of force from the government. I flew out to San Francisco myself, the weekend after we were told that California voted for a Republican president. Thousands of protesters were gunned down by the Republican Guard that Saturday.

I was one of thousands more that got arrested, but they had nowhere to put us all. That was back before they were putting common protesters in the Square. They had us all corralled together in Golden Gate Park for a day and a night, but the next morning the soldiers allowed us all to escape in a gap between two tanks and we spilled out onto Fulton Street.

I probably would've been fine if I could have kept my mouth shut at that point. I could have watched the decay of the great American Democracy and the rise of the Republic from my comfortable little home in Farmington, Maine. I could have taught my mathematics courses at the university and retired peacefully, sipping my cold beer on the porch, in the slanting afternoon sunlight of those carefree Friday afternoons. The problem is, I've never been good at keeping my mouth shut.

Oh, but what I wouldn't give for a nice, cold Samuel Adams right about now, on my Farmington porch, with a rocking chair to sit and drink it on.

INTAKE DAY

Paxton peered through the binoculars, lying on his belly on a small hillock overlooking the arid plain before the concrete, monolithic Wall. A raven was pulling meat from a carcass not twenty feet from the Wall, oblivious to the chaos, and the bounty, about to be unleashed upon it. Paxton thought immediately of wrestling the meat away from the bird, but decided it was problematic for many reasons, not the least of which that it was probably human flesh the bird was tearing apart with its big, black beak.

An air raid siren rent the still morning and the bird took off laboriously, squawking all the way. Even with his ear plugs stuffed firmly in his ears, the noise from the sirens was deafening. It would not be long before the big motor on the other side of the Wall burst into life to turn the cogs and open the heavy, iron gates.

Every Friday morning at nine-o'clock, without fail, the siren would wail and the doors would open so the emigrants could be let in. For the outside world it was like flushing the toilet, eliminating the waste of society before the weekend's pursuits. To those inside it was known as Intake Day, the day that new blood arrived on their side of the Wall; the day that brought news from the outside world; the day that brought workers and slaves, and fresh meat.

The air-raid siren was sounded so that no one inside or out could mistake what was about to happen. Heavily armed soldiers would march through the gates first, and everyone on this side of the Wall knew not to fuck with them. One day, about a year ago, a ruckus broke out between the Newts and the Collectors. The soldiers opened fire on the whole crowd, killing everything that moved. Fifty-four people died that day. Ever since then the Collectors wait patiently for the soldiers to retreat before descending upon the Newts.

The gates suddenly began to swing slowly inward followed immediately by soldiers in desert fatigues. They marched onto the dusty plain in two long rows. An officer on a horse cantered down the center of the line and then wheeled around to look back at the gate and the broken human beings in bright, orange jumpsuits, now moving tentatively through the gauntlet.

"Shit! There are a lot of them!" came a female voice from Paxton's right. He turned to see Jazelle's sinewy, brown body crawling up next to him.

"There's gonna be trouble," he agreed. "Gotta be more than a hundred of them down there!"

Paxton passed her the binoculars and scanned both left and right of their position to get a bead on the other interested parties. The Mexicans were the closest to him on the left, but he didn't worry too much about them. They mostly took in their own and mostly didn't mess with anyone who didn't get in their face. They were apt to take a few white slaves with them, but the Newts were so much easier prey than were other Collectors.

There was more than one raggedy-ass group on the right, all of them wild cards as far as he was concerned. He pointed to a stand of cottonwood about half a mile away and said, "I think we should head down to that copse as soon as possible."

"You got it," she said, handing him back his binoculars and walking at a crouch toward a handful of men.

You never knew exactly how Intake Day was going to go down, but Paxton surmised that more than half of the Newts now emerging from the other side of the New Great Wall of Texas would be dead by tomorrow morning.

If they survived the initial carnage on the plain, they were rewarded with the savageries that awaited them on Friday Night. The wounded on the plain would be taken by the scavengers as meat that they could keep fresh for days to come. Many of the Megiddans would die out there on the plain as well, and Paxton wanted to make damn sure that no one from his posse was among them.

Friday Night there was a general truce in Megiddo, one of the few laws they had in their country, if you could call it a country. There would be many debaucheries committed, gang rape of both men and women, competitions to the death and wanton murder and mayhem, but all of it directed at the Newts. Most of the inhabitants would get drunk on cactus beer and wind up passed out on the ground somewhere. Any of the Newts who survived that first night would join the clan that took them on Intake Day in one capacity or another, but they usually started out as slaves.

Paxton's captures were different. He offered his Newts an equal share of his farm, provided they were willing to work hard and obey the rules, because there were rules. Otherwise, they would devolve into the anarchy that was expected of them. Otherwise, they were no better than the cannibals waiting patiently to pick off the stragglers, the old and the weak, or just the unlucky. Even so, every Newt had to make it through their Initiation on Friday Night.

"Move out!" he heard Jazelle from behind him. Paxton fell into step at the end of the line behind the four men and one woman now jogging down the slope of the hill upon which they had been surveilling the Intake.

The soldiers' efficiency was the only blessing from this weekly funeral procession. They marched the emigrants into the Square quickly and purposefully, going no farther into the dooryard than was necessary for that particular group. There was always one soldier per prisoner, no more and no less. Once all the soldiers were inside, they called an abrupt halt and turned inward levelling their rifles into the space between them, almost as if they were about to shoot each other.

The prisoners were then herded through the gate, prodded by the bayonets from the line of soldiers behind them. The Newts shuffled forward in a shape-shifting flock, not sure what to do next. The siren stopped abruptly, but it would be a few minutes before the ringing in their collective ears ceased.

Paxton saw the general raise a megaphone to his mouth, but he couldn't make out the words he was now speaking to the emigrants, not from this distance and not with his earplugs still stuffed into his ears. Nevertheless, he knew the proclamation by heart. The general recited the prisoners' last rights, as in the last human rights they would ever have, at least as far as the Republic was concerned.

"You are hereby banished from the North American continent. Should you reenter it, you will be executed upon recognition. Within this facility, you have the right to life and to defend that life, unto your death."

Replacing the megaphone with a whistle, the commander blew one shrill note on it for not more than a few seconds. Immediately the soldiers performed an about face in unison and began to march out of the Square in two parallel lines with other soldiers providing them sub-machine gun cover from the top of the wall. The officer galloped between them so that he was amongst the first to exit The Square. A sobbing, middle-aged woman clutched at the jacket of the soldier last in line and was rewarded with a rifle butt to her face which sent her crumpling to the ground.

No sooner had the soldiers walked through the opening in the Wall than the motor whirred back to life and the giant, black doors began to close. Another prisoner made a break for the dwindling gap in closing doors and was gunned down from above. The gates met each other in the middle and a loud clang reverberated across the plain.

"Wait!" shouted Paxton to his small group when they had reached the relative cover of the cottonwoods. He crouched down on his haunches and took a look through his binoculars. He would go farther out into the plain if he had to, but he preferred to wait where he was and see what unfolded before making his move.

Some of the other groups were already pressing in and around the Newts. He saw six mounted cowboys from his own clan riding in from the east with Carl Johnson at the lead. Nearer to him was an advancing group from a rival Rancher clan. That in itself could spell trouble. They were primarily on foot but at their helm was a leather clad biker on a loud motorcycle with a human skull attached to the handlebars. The group of Mexicans to their left was larger than Paxton had earlier surmised, and well-armed by the looks of it.

The Mexicans controlled most of the South of Megiddo. They were not only Mexicans, but consisted of any and all Spanish-speaking exiles from Central and South America, but no one in the Square was too concerned with being politically correct. There were more pressing matters at hand, namely survival of the fittest.

The Mexicans were generally well-supplied as they were apt to receive arms and other aid from their families back home via catapult. It was a risky business, performed in the dead of night, because anyone on either side caught engaging in such an endeavor would be summarily executed by the guards atop the Wall. Many of the prisoners from the Republic had come a long way to the Square and could expect no such bounty from their loved ones.

Gunfire erupted from somewhere on the other side of the Mexicans and it was immediately answered from several other locations around the periphery of the orange throng. Several Newts went down and the others took off screaming and running in every direction. The Collectors closed in, tightening the semi-circle around the Newts, who were prevented from escaping to the north by the Wall they had just come through.

He watched Johnson's men as they singled out an orange jumpsuit breaking away from the pack and ran her down easily on horseback. They preferred to take their captives with a large net and then drag their screaming victims behind them until they could rendezvous and secure them to the backs of their horses, behind their saddles.

Any Newts that resisted were immediately gunned down, or hacked to death by the machetes which were stuck inside the belts of most of the Collectors, Paxton included. A particularly strong man might be worth the trouble of capture so that he could participate in the prizefights which took place all over Megiddo on Friday Night. The women were generally easier to corral as most of them did not put up much resistance once their initial sprints did not lead them to safety.

Paxton pointed to a group of five runners which had seemingly escaped from the various Collectors and were running almost directly toward their copse. He looked left and right at his brave but small group, nodded his head and yelled, "Now!"

All six of them took off at a run and Paxton was soon outpaced by everyone in his posse. As they neared the approaching Newts, a group of khaki-clad Vagabonds sprang up from the desert sand in a U-formation around the approaching runners. In one quick arc of his machete, the Vag nearest to Paxton's advancing group severed the head of the fastest runner, whose body took two more steps before pitching forward onto the ground.

The other four Newts stopped dead in their tracks and the Vagabonds closed ranks to form a circle around them, brandishing their machetes.

Vagabond, or Vag, was a term given to anyone not associated with a clan. They were nomadic and lived by scavenging and raiding throughout Megiddo. They were generally not cannibalistic unless they were desperate, but they were unpredictable and best avoided, if possible. Paxton quickly realized he was not going to be able to avoid this confrontation, as his small group approached the captured Newts.

"Go away!" hissed the man with the bloody machete, whom Paxton presumed to be the leader. "We were here first!"

"That may be," Paxton returned calmly, watching the man warily, "but I believe we have you outgunned."

He nodded his head at the two members of his posse looking through the sights of their shotguns. Jazelle had hers pointed at the leader's face while Carson was aiming at the man closest to him. Bill was also sporting a handgun, but only Paxton's group knew it had no bullets. Even the shotguns only had a few homemade shells each, and he hoped it would be enough.

As if he could read Paxton's mind the leader spat at him, "Those things probably aren't even loaded!"

"You want to try us?" Paxton asked, hoping the answer was no. "I wouldn't mind leaving a couple of more bodies here for the cannibals."

The man looked at Paxton with rage-filled eyes encircled by black eyeliner that streaked down across his cheeks. He bounced back and forth on the balls of his feet, turning with each step so that he faced Paxton directly. The other Vagabonds were now breaking away from their quarry and moving upon either flank of Paxton's posse.

A loud blast rang out near his left ear and Paxton flinched, even as the Vagabond's face exploded away from his body and he sank to his knees. Jazelle had already turned her shotgun on the next closest Vag, but was waiting to empty her second barrel. The other Vags screamed and waved their machetes but they stopped advancing on Paxton's group. One of the women threw down her machete and ran to their fallen leader, sinking to her knees so she could cradle his mangled head in her lap. He was still breathing, splattering blood in a maroon spray with every exhale.

"Put down your weapons!" Jazelle screamed at the remaining five Vagabonds. They looked at each other and then complied, tossing their machetes out in front of them. She gestured for them to move toward their fallen leader.

"Jesus, Jazelle," Paxton chided her, "I can't even hear out of my left ear anymore!"

"It weren't goin' to end well, one way or the other," Jazelle shot back in her southern accent. "At least we're all in one piece."

Paxton approached the four stunned Newts who were rooted to the ground upon which they had been ambushed. There were three women, two of them white and another Hispanic, and one enormous black man who towered over the women by a foot at least. The man stepped in front of the women as if to shield them.

"Come with us if you want to live!" Paxton exhorted them, sticking his machete into his belt.

"Come with you where?" asked the man in a deep voice, holding his arms back and around the women, who were now crowded together in his shadow, grateful for his protection. Paxton's group liked to try to guess where a Newt was from. It had become a game for his posse when they ventured forth to the gates for Intake Day, but he couldn't place this one, not from his accent, or lack thereof.

"Chicago?" asked Paxton.

"Detroit!" guessed Bill.

"New York," chimed in Jazelle, still pointing her shotgun at the Vagabonds.

"New York City is gone, man," said the big man, "they had to evacuate most of it 'cause of the flooding."

"What do you mean it's gone?" asked Bill, who had been living in Brooklyn at the time of his arrest.

"We don't have time for this, Paxton," broke in Jazelle. "We gotta move!"

"Paxton?" one of the women behind the black man poked her head out from around his protecting arm. "Did you say, 'Paxton'? Paxton Stevens?"

"What of it?" interjected Jazelle, now levelling her shotgun at the woman who had stepped out and around the big man and was walking toward Paxton.

"I've come here looking for you," she said. The woman was in her late twenties or early thirties and even though she was bedraggled and her long, auburn hair matted, Paxton could tell she was beautiful. Her bright green eyes held his own as she approached him fearlessly with outspread palms.

"It's me, Eden!" she exclaimed, continuing to advance upon him.

"Do I know you?" asked Paxton, taken aback more by the woman's calm demeanor than by any perceived threat to his person. Jazelle wasn't so sure about the woman's intentions.

"That's close enough," she said menacingly, jabbing the shotgun in Eden's direction while still somehow maintaining eye contact with the Vags.

"Lizzie is here, too!" the woman stated excitedly, although she stopped her advance. Beckoning behind her with a wave of her hand she said, "Lizzie, come here!"

Another woman disengaged herself from her protector and stepped out from his other arm to join the first. She had dirty brown hair, cut short and she moved with the grace of an athlete. She stood beside and a little in front of the first woman, pushing the smaller woman behind her own protective, encircling arm.

"We're Claire and Tucker's girls," Eden exclaimed as a matter-of-fact, peering from around her sister's shoulder.

"Beth?" asked Paxton incredulously, "is that really you?"

"Everyone calls me Lizzie, now," she answered, "or at least, they used to. It's only me and Eden, now."

"What happened to your parents?" he continued to question them.

"Paxton," Jazelle called to him again, pointing to the Vagabonds eyeing them hatefully from their kneeling positions, crouched around their fallen leader. "We don't have time for this!"

"She's right," Paxton agreed. He scanned the plain below them and saw that several groups were already returning in their direction with their spoils. "We need to get out of here! Will you come with us?"

Eden turned to the other two prisoners behind them and said, "It's okay. We can trust him."

The big man didn't seem so sure, but he advanced cautiously, the third woman in tow.

"What do you want me to do with them?" asked Jazelle, gesturing toward the Vagabonds.

"Take their machetes but leave them be," he said loudly enough so that they could hear him, "as long as they don't try to interfere or follow us."

"Are you sure?" Jazelle asked. She motioned for one of the men to collect their machetes.

"Move out!" Paxton yelled to his posse, ignoring her last question. He waved his arm and they immediately fell into step upon his flanks. Jazelle moved around behind their prisoners and jabbed the big man in the back with her shotgun.

"You heard the man," she said. "Move your asses!"

Soon all ten of them were jogging at a brisk pace back toward the copse of cottonwoods and the small hill behind it.

CHAPTER 2
EDEN

For as long as I can remember I have been able to influence people to do what I want them to do. As a child I always got my way, with my parents and my sister, Elizabeth. Lizzie knew exactly what I was doing, but she was always so sweet about letting me have what I wanted, from a second cookie to a victory in cribbage, and eventually to a boy we both had our eyes on, Eduardo. Not that I ever had much use for boys, Eduardo included. Lizzie could get boys to do what she wanted them to do, too, but not through the same mind games I play.

I'm not altogether sure why or how it works, but when I look deeply into other people's eyes I can read their minds, not their thoughts necessarily but their motivations and desires. I can read thoughts, too, but there are usually so many competing thoughts and ideas going on in someone's mind that I don't always get reliable information from thoughts. If I can figure out what a person wants, then I have some leverage over him or her and it's surprisingly easy to use that leverage to steer a person this way or that.

We lived on a small farm, about 100 kilometers southwest of Buenos Aires. Mom and Dad had expatriated themselves there, back at the turn of the century. I'm not sure where they got the money, because we never had much of it growing up, but they bought a small plot of land and built a house and a barn and started a farm. Mom was still pregnant with me when they moved so far south of their homeland. Lizzie was four.

We were off the grid. Dad had put enough solar panels on our roof to pretty much power the farm, except for the gasoline we needed to keep a few engines running. When the price of gasoline got too high for any of us to afford it, we relied more and more on the electricity we got from the sun.

Not everyone was so lucky and eventually people caught on that we didn't have it as bad as the rest of them. We were growing our own food, had a fairly consistent water source and electricity to power all manner of modern conveniences like a refrigerator, a stove, running water for flush toilets. We took in our neighbors and tried to establish rules for our growing commune, but eventually there were just too many starving people to feed. When my dad started to turn people away it got ugly.

A gang of mounted and armed gauchos came to the farm one day, ragged and hungry and spoiling for a fight. Dad didn't make it out of there. The paradise on Earth he had created for himself, for all of us, became his final resting place as well, most likely in an unmarked grave. Beth and I saw them both gunned down, before we fled into the corn fields with only the clothes on our backs. I wasn't able to influence the outcome of that confluence, as it turned out. I never could get close enough to any of the marauders to be able to read them. It all happened too quickly.

By some miracle Mom found us out there in the corn field, huddled together and crying in each other's arms. She was bleeding profusely from two gunshot wounds and we tried the best we could to dress her wounds. With Mom propped between us we made our way the couple of kilometers to our nearest neighbor, José Diaz. He had problems of his own and met us at the front door with his shotgun, but he let us inside when he recognized who we were.

Mom had lost too much blood and with no doctor in sight she didn't stand a chance. As she lay there dying, clutching each of our hands in hers, she told us to travel north, to the United States, as fast as we could get there, and find her former lover, Paxton Stevens. She said that he would know what to do next.

Lizzie and I had heard Paxton's name mentioned in the stories that Mom and Dad would sometimes tell when they had been drinking homemade wine. The three of them had experienced some sort of supernatural phenomenon on a mountaintop in Maine, and shared some love by the sound of it, but when we pressed them for more information, they grew reticent and said that we wouldn't believe it if they told us the whole story. No amount of pressure could sway them to elaborate, they were too bent upon keeping me and Lizzie safe from their past.

When I tried to delve into their minds in their drunken states, I got bits and pieces of a large tree in an open meadow. Someone named Thorn told them that I was destined for great things. There was always an undertone of sadness in their minds when they thought of Thorn, or Paxton for that matter, but I never understood why. I didn't try to read their minds very often. They didn't like it and I was reprimanded when they caught me at it. Lizzie never minded it though. We got to where we could communicate pretty well just through our minds, though it was always more one-sided, with me on the receiving end of her thoughts.

Lizzie had powers of her own. She could sometimes predict the future. Images came to her in her dreams. Images of future events which oftentimes came true. I think it scared her more than anything. She didn't like to share these prophecies but I could see them, in her mind, if I wanted to. That's how we knew Mom and Dad were going to die before it happened. Lizzie tried to warn them, but they brushed her fears aside. They were afraid of her powers too, and Lizzie did her best to hide them, but she couldn't keep that prophecy to herself.

They asked her where on Earth they were supposed to go. Everywhere things were falling apart. They reasoned that if it was their time to go, they'd rather be right there on the farm when it happened, and they got their wish, after a fashion.

That's also how we knew where to find Paxton. Lizzie saw him in a dream, while we were making our way north through Mexico. We argued about what we should do, but by the time we got to Mexico City we had settled on a plan. It wasn't too hard, really, to get ourselves thrown in the Square, two white chicas with no official papers, stealing food and clothing from the street bazaars and giving it to the homeless throngs.

The details of the story of our journey from Buenos Aires to the Square is better left for another time. It took us the better part of a year and we encountered many colorful characters and scoundrels along the way. We started off on foot, the day after we buried Mom in the wheat field next to José's wife and son. José was generous enough to give us two small backpacks filled with fruit and bread, some bottles for water and an extra pair of shoes each.

We couldn't travel in any official capacity to the United States, or the Republic, I think they're calling it these days, even if we could somehow get the money to do so. Argentina is not on their no-fly list as far as I know, tourists and migrant workers may still be welcome, but there is so much bureaucracy involved, even to get a tourist visa, that most people just give up. Plus, our Argentinian passports were forgeries, a fact that Mom saw fit to share with us on her death bed.

We just started walking, step after step, our hearts heavy with grief, and our legs heavy with an idleness that came from having too many hands and not enough chores to do on the farm those last few months when Dad took in every vagrant that wandered onto our property. Before this trek we had barely ever been off the farm or its immediate neighborhood. Mom and Dad had taken us into Buenos Aires twice on holiday, but that was about it.

Lizzie took care of me, just like she's always done. She's a bad ass when she needs to be. She practiced Brazilian Jiu-Jitsu under Luiz, the foreman of our farm, for as long as I can remember. I tried it, too, but I got bored of it quickly. Besides, I had other ways of resolving conflict, which also came in handy on our travels.

I'd love to tell you it was smooth sailing on our journey to find Paxton, but that would be a lie. Lizzie had to barter her body on several occasions for food or a place to stay. Ever the protective older sister, she made sure that I didn't have to do the same, and Lizzie and I were both able to use our powers of persuasion on several occasions when men tried to take us for free.

We worked on a coffee plantation for a month while Lizzie recovered from the cuts and bruises, she got taking down three grown men who attacked us in our sleep. I told you she's a bad ass. We smuggled cocaine for a Columbian cartel in exchange for a boat ride all the way to Costa Rica. We crossed most of the borders through jungle paths and our forged Argentinian passports held when we decided to chance a border patrol.

Lizzie and I can mostly pass as South Americans, which I guess I technically am, seeing as how I was born in Argentina. Both of us are fluent in Spanish and our skin is bronzed by the sun, especially since we no longer have access to the sun screen Mom would make us slather all over ourselves growing up. I wonder if anyone still sells sunscreen in those little plastic bottles. It seems as if there should still be a demand for it given how intense the sun's rays have become since I was a child.

The hardest border crossing of all was our last one, well, I guess it was second-to-last, if you count getting ourselves thrown into the Square. They took our fake papers away from us and threw us into jail in Tapachula when we tried to cross into Mexico from Guatemala. Some overzealous official made a phone call to Buenos Aires, only to discover that Lizzie and I didn't exist in any census, nor had we ever been issued Argentinian passports.

We languished in a jail cell for weeks, but at least we were together. Then one day the guards took us both out of our cell and brought us before a judge. He asked us some questions about our true identities and listened as we told the details of our shared upbringing on the farm in Argentina. I could tell that he had no idea what to do with us and did not relish the prospect of an expensive extradition to Argentina.

He wanted to know why we were in Mexico and we took pains to assure him that we were only passing through on our way to the Republic, at which point he laughed and laughed. In the end he told us we were free to go but that if we were ever arrested again in his country we would be taken to the Square.

They never did give us back our possessions but at that point we were pretty much living hand to mouth. We made our way on foot, and in the back of pick-up trucks when we could swing it, to Mexico City, all the time plotting how on earth we were going to get into the Republic. Everyone we talked to said that it was impossible to get over the Wall these days. Even the tunnels had been flooded and booby-trapped to the point of impassability.

We were living on the streets of Mexico City with thousands of other poor and homeless people, begging for food and money, accepting government handouts which were few and far between and doing whatever we needed to do to survive. Then one night, Lizzie dreamed that Paxton was in the Square, farming a plot of land just like Dad used to do.

It seemed so far-fetched, what with Paxton being an important scientist and all. He was even in the newspapers in Argentina! But I trusted Lizzie's dreams implicitly. She was rarely, if ever, wrong. The only time her dreams don't come true is when we take pains to change course to make sure something bad doesn't happen. In that sense we came to know that the future wasn't set in stone and the things she saw in her dreams could be avoided sometimes.

That's when we came up with the plan to get ourselves thrown into the Square. We weren't sure that they would really put us in there for something small, it had to be something clearly illegal but not anything dangerous enough to get ourselves or anyone else killed. We started stealing things, small things at first, but we got more and more daring as the days and weeks went by. We took food from the open-air markets, clothes from the kiosks and then we went for pretty much anything we thought we could get away with. We made a good team, Lizzie with her premonitions and I with my powers of persuasion.

I was in a bigger hurry than she was to get caught. We gave our spoils to the kids on the street, keeping just enough to feed and clothe ourselves, and I think Lizzie had found her calling. They never did catch us in the act, but one of those street kids gave us away, probably to cut some deal of his own. There were many people who could identify us as the Ladrones Gringas.

We were thrown into another jail cell, slightly more comfortable than our last digs, but not for long. Three days later we were handcuffed and sardined into the back of a moving van with twenty Mexicans and a half-dozen guards, all bound for the Square.

THE MEXICANS

All that day they moved steadily southeastward along the cracked and pock-marked asphalt highway, keeping the Wall within sight to the west. Jazelle preferred to travel straight through the desert east of the highway where they would be less prone to attack by bandits and foraging parties of cannibals, but the safer route was also the slower one, and today they were trying to make haste. Later, when the low rocky hills and meandering gullies gave way to the flatter scrubland of devil's grass and cactus, they could make a beeline for home.

The Intake had been well-attended, so the biggest threats to their safety were back on the plains of Megiddo. If they could stay out ahead of the rest of the gangs travelling back to whatever shitholes they called home, they might just get lucky and return to their own homey shithole in one piece. If they could just make it to Friday Night, they might be okay. But Friday night was a long, hot day away and a lot could happen between now and then.

After their initial two-mile sprint away from the gates, they had finally rested a few minutes while Jazelle verified that they weren't being pursued. The Newts were offered biscuits and water and they accepted them greedily. When Jazelle returned, she conferred with Paxton a couple of minutes before taking point as they all set off again, this time at a brisk walking pace which could be more easily sustained. It also allowed Paxton the chance to catch up with Elizabeth and Eden.

"Do you remember me, Beth?" he asked her. "You couldn't have been more than 4 or 5 the last time saw I you."

"I remember you, Uncle Paxton," she answered as enthusiastically as one can while trudging along in one-hundred-degree heat when God knew whom was chasing along behind you. "And I see you, sometimes, in my dreams."

"Dad followed your career," Eden asserted as well. "We found a shoebox full of newspaper articles in the toolshed, all about the amazing Dr. Stevens, the greatest scientific mind since Albert Einstein!"

"You were just Uncle Paxton to me," said Lizzie.

"But you know I'm not your real uncle, right?" he continued.

"Of course, we do," chimed in Eden. "But that's what they always called you, when they bothered to call you anything. Both Mom and Dad always seemed under some shadow of guilt whenever your name came up. What happened with you guys, anyway?"

"What did they tell you?" he responded cagily.

"They told us you were friends, but we always thought you were in some kind of love triangle, didn't we Eden?"

"I'm sure of it, now more than ever," she said, looking directly into Paxton's eyes. "It's all over his face!"

Paxton blushed, but said nothing and they walked along in silence a few moments. When he did break the silence, his words were slow and measured.

"We were good friends," he stammered. "Your mother and I were almost something more but it wasn't meant to be. I loved both your parents dearly. Tucker and I were best friends for a long time."

"So, you and Mom never…" Eden trailed off.

"Not at all, Eden," Paxton reassured her. "Tucker is definitely your father."

"And Thorn," added Beth.

When Paxton flinched, Eden followed up with, "So the stories they told us were true?"

"What did they tell you?" asked Paxton again.

"Plenty," answered Beth.

"Nothing," lied Eden in unison with her sister and they both giggled. It was music to Paxton's ears and something that he had not heard in a long time.

"Tell me what happened to your parents," Paxton deftly shifted the conversation away from Eden's conception and neither of the girls complained. They took turns telling him all about their life in Argentina and the environmental and societal degradation which led to the deaths of Claire and Tucker.

"She told you that I would know what to do?" he asked, when they had come to that part of the story. "What is that supposed to mean?"

"I don't know," answered Eden, "but she made us promise to come all the way up here and find you. I never thought it would be this easy."

"Easy?" her sister chided her. "You have a pretty selective memory there, Eden."

"You shouldn't have come here," Paxton interjected. "This place is horrible. You have no idea."

"Well, we didn't know you had gotten yourself thrown into the Square when we set out," argued Eden. "We were headed to the Republic. It wasn't until we got into Mexico that Lizzie dreamed you were in the Square. Then we had to figure out a way to get ourselves thrown in here as well."

"Wait," Paxton responded incredulously. "You two got yourselves into the Square on purpose? Are you insane?"

"Well what else were we going to do?" countered Eden. "There was nothing left for us in Argentina except for a slow death by starvation. Mom and Dad were gone and the farm lost."

"How did you get in here?" he asked.

"We were stealing things," explained Beth, "in Mexico City. And we had fake passports."

"We gave most of it to the street kids," Eden defended their actions, "kind of like Robin Hood."

"You probably don't want to mention that later, when we get your news," offered Paxton, "the part about you getting thrown in here on purpose. People will be suspicious."

"How did you get in here, Uncle Paxton?" asked Beth. "We thought we were going to find you at Harvard University or some government think tank in Washington, D.C."

"I was critical of the Republic one too many times," admitted Paxton sourly. "I thought my fame would protect me, not to mention my numerous contributions to society, but as it turned out, they wanted to make an example of me, to show the masses that nobody is above the law."

"They put you in here for that?" asked Eden. "I thought you Americans had freedom of speech."

"We used to," said Paxton sadly, "and that's not what I was officially charged with, but I'm convinced it's the actual reason I'm here. One day the Guard just showed up at my house and started looking through all my stuff. I was none too happy about it and voiced my displeasure in no uncertain terms. That got me hand-cuffed and thrown in the back of an armored car. They didn't even have a search warrant.

"They found my pot stash right away, it's not like I was trying awfully hard to hide it. Later on, they found my plants in the woods. I didn't have a lot, but it was enough to convict me of possession of controlled substances.

"I didn't think much of it, I smoked a lot of pot. It was legal in Maine for a brief shining moment and then they cracked down hard upon it again. I grew a few plants, for my own use, and I wasn't too flashy about it. I didn't help myself by railing against everyone and everything in the intervening weeks before my trial. The Republic News cast me as a subversive trying to bring down the government. It did not take much deliberation for a jury of my so-called peers to condemn me to the Square."

"How long have you been in here, Uncle Paxton?" asked Beth.

"That's a good question," Paxton allowed, looking down at his relentlessly moving feet. "Some people keep time in here but I'm not one of them. Jonas McDonough, the man whose land we live on, keeps a calendar in his house and checks off every day as it passes. I don't see the point. I try as much as I can to live day to day. What kind of a future do we have in a place like this?"

"But surely you must have some idea," pressed Eden.

"More than a year but less than two," Paxton surmised. "Probably closer to two years than one, I would guess. How long were you two, coming up here from Argentina?"

"More than a year," Elizabeth answered. "Wouldn't you say, Eden?"

"About a year," Eden agreed. "That sounds about right."

"You must have some stories to tell from that journey," Paxton observed.

"You wouldn't believe half of it!" said Eden excitedly.

"You would be surprised what I believe," Paxton returned. "Try me."

"There were warlords and drug smugglers," Elizabeth offered as a teaser. "Narrow escapes and ultimate capture. Lots of sex, in exchange for food or rides or shelter."

"And lots of walking," Eden reminded her sister. "Lots and lots of walking."

"So, this should be no problem for you," said Paxton. "It's only about a hundred miles to the farm."

"One-hundred miles!" exclaimed Eden.

"No problem," Elizabeth countered in exaggerated fashion. "If only it weren't so fucking hot!"

Eden and Paxton snickered at Elizabeth's vulgarity, just as Jazelle popped into their midst from behind them and scared the shit out of the two sisters.

"This might not be the best time for a family reunion, *Uncle Paxton*," interjected Jazelle from out of nowhere behind Paxton's left ear. "The Mexicans are almost upon us."

As she finished speaking Paxton could already see the mountain bikes on the ridge behind them. They could not avoid this confrontation. Paxton looked around him and then pointed to a small rise of boulders off the road to their east about a quarter of a mile.

"Head for those boulders!" he yelled loud enough for the whole group to hear him. "Run!"

A dozen or so mountain bikes came speeding down the inclined highway toward them as they took off at a sprint toward the cover the rocks would provide them. Paxton expected to hear shots being fired from behind him at any moment and was amazed when they reached the small hill without incident.

The few members of his posse found crevices and caves in the rocks where they could hide themselves and peer out at the approaching riders. Jazelle and Carson each took up a position lying flat on the top of a large rock outcropping with their shotguns pointed downward at the approaching bikers. Paxton, after verifying that everyone was safely hidden, turned to face the Mexicans from his position at the base of the hill. He did not have long to wait.

There were ten bikers in total and they each skidded to a stop in succession in a loose half circle around Paxton, who was standing with his arms raised in an unspoken gesture of truce. Four of the bikers had guns which were now pointed at Paxton as their leader got off his bike and approached him, his eyes scanning the rocks above for the rest of Paxton's group.

"Carlos," Paxton nodded at the man and extended his hand.

"Paxton," the man greeted him without warmth but he did accept the proffered hand and shook it twice before letting go. "What are you doing at the Intake?"

"Same as you," Paxton answered, "looking for workers."

"You got any of ours?"

"One woman," Paxton answered truthfully. "We only got four in total."

"You gonna give her up peaceably?" Carlos asked him, knocking a homemade cigarette against his palm before sticking it his mouth and lighting it with a match.

"How about a trade?" Paxton asked hopefully, nodding toward the captives now appearing atop the ridge. There looked to be more than ten of them tied together at the wrists with a long string of rope. Another five or six of Carlos' gang were herding them along the road on foot. They were too far away for Paxton to determine if there were any Caucasians amongst them.

"I don't think so," Carlos answered, taking a long drag from his cigarette while examining the rocks above him for an assessment of their situation. "You got the drop on us, I'll give you that, but we have rifles to your shotguns, *muchacho*, and more of them."

Paxton thought over his options in a logical sequence. They couldn't fight the Mexicans. There were too many of them. They could no longer run and hide. Negotiation was rapidly failing. Paxton came to a decision.

"You'll take her and be on your way?" Paxton asked more as a question than a demand. "And leave us to be on our way?"

"That depends," thought Carlos aloud. "You got anything else I might want? Let me see your Newts."

"C'mon, Carlos," pleaded Paxton, knowing that he must now take Carlos' terms or have a bloodbath. "The others are Republicans."

"Let me be the judge of that. Bring 'em on out here."

Paxton waved for someone to bring out the Newts and Carlos motioned for his men to stand down. They lowered their rifles so that they pointed to the ground but kept both hands firmly in firing position. Richie and Bill prodded the four captives forward with their machetes.

"*¿Como te llamas, chica?*" Carlos asked the only obvious Mexican in the group.

"*Elena*," she answered timidly.

"*¿Estos cabrones te estan tratando bien?*"

"*Sí, señor*," she answered. "*Ellos me salvaron.*"

"*¿Qué es esto?*" asked Carlos, striding forward to grab a handful of Eden's red hair and give it a slight tug. "*Seguro esta es una puta de verdad.*"

"*¡Quita tus manos de mi hermana!*" Elizabeth shouted, trying to step forward. She was being held back forcibly by Bill's grip upon each of her biceps.

Eden did not seemed fazed by Carlos' close proximity but rather looked directly into his eyes, even as he yanked her hair backward. Not a word passed between them but they continued to stare at each other over long seconds which stretched out for an uncomfortably long time. Suddenly Carlos dropped her hair and pushed her backwards.

"*¡Puta bruja del Diablo!*" he cursed under his breath, making the sign of the cross.

"*¿Qué piensa Xavier de todo esto,*" she asked him, "*si pueze tu que empezó la guerra aqui mismo, ahora antes que el esta listo? ¿Qué sera de ti?*"

Carlos looked horror struck for another long moment and then said to his men as he backed slowly away from her, "*¡Vamanos! Ven aca, Elena.*"

Eden looked hopefully to Paxton to intercede on Elena's behalf but he just shook his head and mouthed the word *no* as the Mexicans retreated slowly backwards, Elena in tow. Carlos was the last to turn his back on them and climb onto his fat bike. Elena sat on the seat of another bike while the rider jumped upward to kick the bike into motion before pedaling slowly away in a standing position.

"We'll see each other again, Paxton," Carlos said in English, before kicking his own bike into motion. "Next time you might not have your *bruja* with you."

Paxton did not respond but held his breath until they were clearly on their way back to the highway and the danger had passed. He exhaled forcefully and struggled for a few breaths until he found his normal breathing cadence.

"What did you just do?" he asked Eden. "Why did he call you a *bruja*?"

"Eden just scared the shit out of that guy!" Elizabeth answered him, shrugging off Bill's arms and joining her sister.

"I can read people's thoughts sometimes," she explained to Paxton in a whisper as the others gathered around them in twos and threes. "Can we talk about this later?"

"What the fuck just happened?" asked Jazelle as she burst into the center of their gathering.

"Who the hell knows?" returned Paxton, covering for Eden. "You know how crazy Carlos can be. We got lucky, is all."

Jazelle gave him a look that said he was full of shit, but she didn't challenge him in front of the rest of the gang. Instead, she set about the task of getting them all moving again.

"We best stay off the road," she said, "from here on out. And we need to get a move on if y'all want to get back to camp before nightfall."

"Jazelle's right," Paxton quickly agreed. "We'll have time for talk when we get back to camp."

They started off again, travelling east and away from Interstate 10. Jazelle instructed Richie to take point and she walked next to Paxton at the head of the rest of their group.

CHAPTER 3

JAZELLE

I am a murderer. That's what got me put in the Square. I killed my husband, the bastard. I stabbed him with a kitchen knife, twenty-seven times, while he was passed out in our bed. I had to use my left arm because he had broken my right. He beat me up pretty good that night, all because I asked him who he was sleeping around with.

He forced me to go down on him, after he stumbled up the flight of stairs to our apartment at one in the morning. I smelled her pussy on him right away, there's no mistaking that smell. I should of bit off his Johnson right then and there, but that probably would've gotten me killed instead of just beaten so badly I wanted to die. I guess this is better.

I just laid there on the floor, clutching my broken arm and sobbing, waiting for him to stop kicking me. He broke my nose and three of my ribs with his steel-toe boots. Eventually he grew tired and went to bed. I waited there on the floor and plotted my revenge. When his snores were good and loud, I got slowly to my feet and crept into the kitchen for our big carving knife. His eyes opened wide with shock when I plunged the knife deep into his liver. Then it was his turn to scream as I cut him again and again.

I was clumsy with my left hand and still in a lot of pain, but he couldn't do much to defend himself after the first few stabs to his gut. I cut his arms and hands when he tried to wrench the knife from me, but there was no way I was letting go of it! I only stopped when our next-door neighbor broke down the door and pulled me off of him. There was blood everywhere, all over him, all over me, the bed, the walls, the ceiling and my neighbor.

My court appointed lawyer tried to argue self-defense, but the jury wanted none of that. Every one of them was white, the judge and lawyers, too. And I had healed up pretty good in jail while I was waiting for my trial. They said it couldn't be self-defense because he was asleep and I had stabbed him so many times. I thought it would be the firing squad for me, but they put me in the Square instead. I guess this is better.

I've committed a lot more murders since I've been in here, but none as satisfying as that first one. The ones in here have all been in self-defense, for real, well, most of them. You can't stay alive in here unless you're willing to kill. I don't know anyone in the Square who hasn't killed at least once, except Paxton, of course. He somehow manages to stay above it all, but that wouldn't be possible without us protecting him. I guess this is better, or else I never would have met Paxton.

How do I describe my relationship with Paxton? That's a hard one. Mostly he is a father figure to me, to all of us, but we share the same bed. We make love, sometimes, not as much as I would like, but it's always nice. He don't have sex with anyone else, I'm quite sure of that, and he don't mind it when I do. A girl has needs, not that I'm a girl anymore at 32. Paxton looks to be in his seventies, but he has the strength and stamina of a man twenty years younger than that. He won't tell me when he was born, says he don't remember but I know he does. That man don't forget anything, he's the smartest man I ever met.

Paxton has been living a charmed life ever since his first Friday Night. He got taken by the McDonoughs too, about a year after they got me. Old Jonas recognized him right away and invited him right into the house. I was working as a house-slave by then, so I heard their whole conversation. Jonas was a big fan. He wanted to know all about Paxton's arrest and trial. He asked Paxton if he would come and work for him, as if he had a choice, but Paxton didn't know what was what back then, he was just a Newt on his first night inside the Square.

He had to go through Initiation, too, but it was nothing like mine. Old Jonas explained it all to him, said he had been to see an ancient Comanche shaman of some sort. They ate peyote together, had some sort of vision. Anyway, the Comanche convinced Jonas that a virgin will one day come into Megiddo and bring about its destruction, just wipe it off the face of the Earth.

Me, I would see this place destroyed, even though it would be the death of me, but old Jonas is better off than most, plus this is his land, been in his family for five generations, or so he says. His family used to own a hundred-thousand acres with ten-thousand head of cattle, long before the Square. He and a bunch of other rich mother-fuckers refused to give up their land to Eminent Domain. There were skirmishes with the Guard and the Texas Marshalls, but in the end the Feds gave everyone the same choice. They had to either give up their lands or be banished to them. I heard all about that on the TV news, long before I ever thought I'd be coming here.

Anyway, Jonas has a lot more to lose than most anybody, if this place comes crashing down around his head. His place is run just like a Southern plantation back in the day, complete with lots of slaves to do the heavy lifting. The McDonough territory isn't nearly as big as it was, he don't have the men to protect that much land. He's lucky if he has a hundred steer left, but he's still the most powerful man in Megiddo, not counting the Mexicans. That's why he made the law that every Newt has to lose their virginity on First Friday Night, with witnesses.

I'm sure it's different all over Megiddo, but on the McDonough Ranch, every new transfer gets tied naked to a tree with their arms stretched up and over their heads. First, they get the whip, to put them in their place. Jonas's boys are downright sadistic. Then all the McDonoughs and their crew get drunk and have a wild orgy with the helpless Newts to make damn-well sure that none of them is still a virgin come morning. Some of the Newts don't survive it, but no one gets too concerned about that. Life is cheap here in the Square. There is never enough food and the soldiers always bring in fresh Newts, every Friday morning.

The Initiation was going on outside in the paddock, the night they brought Paxton in too, while he and Jonas sat in the parlor sipping coffee and talking about it. Paxton winced every time he heard the crack of the whip or the agonized scream of a Newt getting tortured or raped, but old Jonas didn't even bat an eye. He offered Paxton a bed in his house, and me, to make sure he lost his virginity. Paxton wasn't fool enough to decline that offer.

He was gentle with me that first time, just as he always is, and embarrassed over the whole situation. I don't think he would have gone through with it if I hadn't begged him to, so I could avoid the whipping I would of gotten if he we didn't have sex. It was over quickly. What I remember most about that night was sleeping in that big bed, with clean sheets and a homemade quilt for a blanket.

Paxton and Jonas were thick as thieves after that. Old Jonas showed Paxton maps of Megiddo and the territories claimed by the various clans. He explained the few laws which governed the McDonough territory and which ones were pretty much accepted by all the clans. Paxton availed himself of the extensive library and was always hunched over his drawings and equations when not huddled in conversation with Old Jonas. I served in the big house a lot so I often caught bits and pieces of their scheming, not that I could understand half of it.

Jonas wanted Paxton to build something that would harness anti-gravity and Paxton had to continually remind him that he was a mathematician and not an engineer, let alone the fact that the odds of collecting the materials they would need from Megiddo were slim to none. In the end Jonas settled for an electricity generating windmill which kept Paxton and the McDonough boys busy for the next six months. After that they erected a water wheel in the stream so they could pump water to the main barn for the few remaining cows and horses.

Paxton could barely look me in the eyes after our first night together. He never did ask me to come back to his bed, or anyone else for that matter, even though he could have had his pick of the slave girls. He pulled me into his room once, after most of a year had gone by, to tell me that he had convinced Old Jonas to let him start a farm in the southwestern corner of the McDonough land. He wanted to know if I would come with him. I told him that Old Jonas would never let me go. He said he had already gotten the old man's permission, but he wanted the decision to be mine. He told me that on his farm I could be free.

Paxton is so naïve. As if anyone in this place could ever be free. His offer sounded too good to be true and I was suspicious, of course. I hadn't been able to make a decision for myself in so long, the thought of it brought tears to my eyes. I didn't answer him right then, because I couldn't believe it was a real offer, but I did reach my arms around him and kiss him on his lips before going back to my chores.

True to his word Paxton did start a farm, and he did bring me with him, along with another woman and two men, all of whom chose to go with him freely. I bet he would of had even more volunteers, but that was all Old Jonas would let him take. We go to the Wall from time to time, looking for Newts.

There are eleven of us on Maggie's Farm, now that Maggie has gone and got herself snake bit, the damned fool.

We enjoy the protection of the McDonough clan, but in return we have to give them half of everything we produce. This arrangement seems to suit Paxton, but I get a little more pissed off every time they come to collect the tribute.

Paxton and I get along, after a fashion, which is more than I could of hoped for in this hellhole. So yeah, I guess this is better.

FRIDAY NIGHT

They walked all afternoon in a southeasterly direction. No one spoke unless it was to bark directions at the Newts. Paxton did not get the chance to talk to either Elizabeth or Eden on this leg of their journey as Jazelle continually cautioned them all to keep quiet and to try to blend into the desert landscape. They took frequent breaks, but only long enough for someone to scout some unfamiliar territory before continuing onward.

The sun beat down relentlessly upon their backs and heads and radiated off the ground in rippling waves that made it hard to distinguish landmarks in the distance. Everyone in their party was drenched in sweat but they had precious little water between them to rehydrate their bodies. Paxton's group all had hats of some form or other but the Newts had no protection at all from the sun's heat. Paxton thought about offering his hat to either Beth or Eden but knew that it would provoke a tirade from Jazelle. In any event, all three Newts had darker skin than his own so he probably needed the protection more than they did.

They were exhausted and hungry when they reached the arroyo where they had hidden their camping supplies. As a result of their detour, they were too far north and had to walk along the course of the dry river bed for more than a mile until they found the stand of pine trees marking their cache. They had dug a well the night before and Paxton was grateful to see that it had a couple of inches of muddy water in it. He was the first to toss his pack, bend down and drink from the acrid water, using his cupped hand as a vessel.

As soon as everyone had slaked their thirst, Paxton and his group huddled together to divvy up the evening's chores. The tired Newts were prone on the ground in the shade of the western wall of the gully. Jazelle gave them each their assignments. Bill was sent to the lip of the twenty-foot gorge to keep watch lest they be taken by surprise by a raiding party. He grabbed a shotgun from Carson and began to climb the steep wall without waiting to hear anymore.

Jazelle reasoned that it was safe enough to make a cook fire as long as they waited until dusk when the smoke would be lost in darkness. They had forsaken a fire the previous evening because of the danger it posed and so that there would be no ashes to give away their cache when they went to the Wall. It would be safer to light a fire under the general truce of Friday Night, but Megiddans only honored the truce in inverse proportion to their desperation, so a fire was still risky. She sent Richie and Chuck in search of firewood and told them to take the female Newts with them.

"Get up!" she barked in the direction of their small group. "No one gets to sit on their asses around here!"

She took the few strides toward them until she was close enough to kick Eden's state-issued sneaker. Eden jerked her head up but otherwise reacted sluggishly to Jazelle's commands.

"C'mon, get up!" she repeated. "You two ladies are goin' to look for firewood."

"Sure," said Eden, laboriously rising to her feet. Beth stood up slowly as well, suspiciously eying Jazelle as she did so.

"You!" she pointed to the third Newt. "What's your name?"

"Abraham," he answered, looking up at her.

"You're going to help me get dinner," she told him.

Paxton and Carson were left to set up their three tents. Carson went in search of the hand shovels they had hidden in a hollow tree trunk while Paxton sidled up to Jazelle and put his arm around her shoulder affectionately.

"What are we having for dinner?" he asked playfully.

"Gruel," she answered, smiling at him briefly before shrugging off his arm. "What else? At least it'll be warm gruel. Now you get to work, too, mister man. Ain't no shirkers 'round here."

"I'm going, I'm going," he grumbled with good humor. They had survived the ordeal of Intake Day at the Wall and rescued three Newts as well. Paxton had reason to be in good humor, not to mention it was Friday Night.

He and Carson removed the thin layer of dirt from their camping gear and pulled it all from the hole. They handed the food and cooking supplies to Jazelle and then set about erecting the tents, one at a time in a tight triangle.

"How do you know those girls?" asked Carson as they fitted the poles into the third tent.

"I don't, really," Paxton answered truthfully. "I knew their parents, back in college, but that was a long time ago."

"What are the odds?" Carson surmised.

"Astronomical," Paxton concurred. "Especially since they lived most of their lives in Argentina."

"What are they doing here?" continued Carson.

"You can ask them that yourself," Paxton deflected his question, "when we get their news."

They finished the rest of their work in silence. Paxton glanced over at Jazelle and Abraham from time to time and it seemed that they were fast friends. It was obvious Jazelle was flirting with the big man, but Paxton was too old to be jealous of him. Jazelle was the most loyal member of his team, but she was still free to come and go as she pleased, and she did love to come. He may have been able to keep up with her in his twenties, but he doubted it.

Richie, Chuck and the girls came and went, delivering the armloads of dry brush and branches they had collected from the periphery of their camp. Eventually they deemed the pile big enough, but Jazelle wouldn't let them light their campfire until it was nearly dusk. When they did light the dry kindling, it began crackling almost immediately, shooting sparks upward into the darkening sky.

Abraham helped her to balance their cookpot in the center of the fire and everyone but Bill sat down around it. Chuck handed out three large canteens full of cactus beer which were passed around amongst the group for a few minutes before Paxton stood up to address them.

"Alright, let's get started," he began. Waving his arm at the two women seated to his right he continued, "I'll introduce Elizabeth and Eden, here, who just happen to be the daughters of some good friends of mine from college. They've been living in Argentina most of their lives."

"All of my life," Eden corrected him, "until now."

"How did you get in here?" Jazelle asked them pointedly.

"Our parents were killed by gauchos about a year ago," Elizabeth answered her. "Things are bad all over. We had been operating our farm like a refugee camp but we were overwhelmed by the sheer numbers of people needing our help. After the farm was lost, we decided to come to the Republic. I was born in Chicago, so I'm a citizen, not that I have the papers to prove it. We thought things might be better in the Republic than what's been going on in Argentina."

Paxton had cautioned the girls to share as little as possible when the group got their news, especially concerning their extrasensory perceptions and anything having to do with Thorn. He told them to be truthful, but to answer only the questions posed to them, with little or no elaboration.

"What's happening in Argentina?" asked Bill.

"The sea-level rise over the last decade made most of Buenos Aires unlivable, although there were people trying to turn it into the Venice of South America," Elizabeth continued to speak for the both of them. "Millions of people were displaced inland, but much of the fertile plains around Buenos Aires were awash in sea water as well. Our farm was intact, but we were dealing with a four-year drought at that point, which is kind of ironic when you think about it.

"Basically, there were a bunch of starving people with guns, it was bound to get ugly sooner or later. The whole of Argentina is under martial law now, just like every other country between here and there, but the military can only do so much. It's pretty much survival of the fittest, with people joining whichever warlord they think will feed and protect them."

"How did you get all the way up here?" Carson asked.

"We walked, mostly," Eden responded. "We got rides here and there when we could, but we took the border crossings on foot through the jungle paths by following the locals."

"And what did you do to get yourselves thrown in to the Square?" Jazelle reiterated her earlier question with a bit more clarity.

"We were living on the streets of Mexico City for a time," Elizabeth continued their story, "trying to figure out a way into the Republic. We were stealing food and clothing to survive."

"So, they're putting common thieves in the Square now?" Jazelle continued her interrogation, the suspicion obvious in her tone.

"We stole quite a lot by the time they caught us," Eden admitted, grinning sheepishly. "They were calling us the Ladrones Gringas. And we have no identification."

Jazelle questioned them for further details of their journey and their farm in Argentina and eventually seemed to be satisfied that they were telling the truth. After an unusually long pause, Paxton asked his group if they had any more questions for Elizabeth or Eden.

"Just one more thing," Jazelle stated. "What the hell happened back there, with Carlos, and the Mexicans?"

"Eden has a way of getting inside people's heads," Elizabeth responded.

"Like a psychiatrist?" asked Richie.

"Exactly!" Elizabeth answered over the response Eden had begun to articulate. "It's unsettling for some people."

"Show me!" demanded Jazelle, standing up and walking the few paces to where Eden sat cross-legged on the ground.

"Is this really necessary?" asked Paxton.

"If she can get inside my head, I wanna know about it!" Jazelle shot back. "Stand up, girl!"

Eden rose to her feet slowly and looked Jazelle full in the face. They stared at each other for ten seconds or so before Jazelle asked her, "Ain't you gonna ask me some questions? Ain't that what a psychiatrist would do?"

"That's not how it works," Eden responded, maintaining her eye contact a few moments longer before turning away. A flush came to her cheeks and she smiled sheepishly, looking over at Abraham.

"What is it girl?" asked an impatient Jazelle.

"You're thinking about Abraham," Eden turned back to her. "You want to have sex with him and you're wondering about the size of his, Johnson, I think you would call it."

The men seated around the campfire, with the exception of Abraham, burst out laughing and Jazelle turned to them with an evil glare. Abraham looked down at his sneakers with embarrassment, but they couldn't tell if his dark cheeks were blushing in the flickering firelight.

"Shit, girl, that one was easy," admitted Jazelle, refocusing her glare upon Eden. "I'm sure them two assholes was talking about me when you was workin' together."

"We didn't say a word," Chuck returned with his right hand upon his heart. "I swear to God."

"Then you're lucky God don't live here," she shot back at him. "Everyone knows I like a good roll in the hay!"

She shot Abraham a wink and a smile as she returned to her spot around the campfire. Paxton took this opportunity to steer their attention to the big, black man seated on the ground to Eden's right. Looking directly at him Paxton asked, "What is your name?"

"Abraham Cooper," he answered.

"Where are you from?" asked Richie.

"St. Louis," he answered, and Richie gave Bill a high-five.

"I called it!" stated Richie triumphantly.

"Originally," Abraham continued, "but I was living in Los Angeles when they took me. My wife and I were harboring fugitives, that's what the judge said.

We were trying to keep our Mexican friends from getting thrown in here is what we were doing.

"California was the last refuge for the Undesirables," he continued. "There was more widespread resistance back in the day, sanctuary cities they called them, Chicago and New York City of course, but others as well. The government systematically took them down, one after another. We were a sanctuary state, until they sent in the military. They say that they're only deporting the illegals and that only the criminals are being sent to the Square, but they get to decide who are the criminals and who are not. You can't trust a word they say anymore. Even the most diehard Republicans know that the RepNews is a bunch of horseshit."

"What happened to your wife?" asked Jazelle.

"I have no idea," Abraham responded. "She escaped out the back door with our two kids when the Guard came for us, at least I hope she did. They took me straight to jail just as soon as they found our neighbors holed up in my daughter's bedroom."

"What did you do for a living?" asked Paxton.

"Software engineer," he answered, "Same as everyone else in Southern California these days. My company worked on the code for the SmartHouse. I don't know why I'm talking in the past tense, it's only my life in California that is past tense. They work on the code for the SmartHouse."

After asking him a few more questions about his life, they turned to a more general interrogation for news of what was happening outside the Square. Paxton asked him, "Are we at war with China?"

"Not officially, but it won't be long," Abraham replied. "Seattle and Portland are gone, nuked by North Korea. Apparently, the ones meant for Los Angeles and San Francisco were shot down over the Pacific. That's what they told us, but it's probably true because the beaches are full of dead fish. We hit North Korea back hard, but everyone knows they are just Chinese puppets."

"What about Russia?" asked Carson. "Are they friends or enemies?"

"No one knows for sure," said Abraham. "One day they're telling us that Russia is our greatest ally and the next they're the devil's spawn. At least we haven't exchanged any nukes with them yet. That would be bad."

"What's goin' on in Europe?" asked Bill.

"Everyone's got their borders closed," answered Abraham. "There are just too many refugees. Europe's dealing with the Africans because Africa is mostly uninhabitable and they're starving to death by the millions. They were sending them food and supplies a while back but I think that's mostly dried up. Now they're just letting them die."

"That's awful!" interjected Eden.

"The same thing's happening in the Republic, to our own citizens," Abraham continued. "The coastal cities are flooded and everyone's moving inland, except that the inland is already overcrowded and not willing to share. There are massive refugee camps in lots of cities, Atlanta, Cleveland, Dallas, Boston, but they aren't being supplied well-enough by the government and people are dying left and right.

"The Christians are calling it the Rapture and the scientists are calling it the Great Die-Off. The Republic News is telling us it's a perfectly natural phenomenon when a population has out-stripped its resources. They keep telling us they're doing everything they can for us and that the Republic is well-positioned to be at the top of the food chain when human population comes back into some kind of equilibrium."

"What about the ice caps?" Paxton asked him. "Are there any left?"

"The RepNews keeps showing us images of beautiful glaciers and large ice fields, but they are stock photos from years ago. I have a buddy, I had a buddy, who knew how to surf the RepNet without being traced and he showed me current pictures of the Arctic and Greenland. Greenland is mostly ice-free. There were still icebergs floating in the Arctic Ocean in the last picture I saw, but who really knows?"

When it seemed like the questions for Abraham had run their course, Jazelle announced that it was time for dinner. She stood up and motioned for Abraham to do the same. He held the cookpot for her as she ladled out spoonfuls of gray porridge into plastic bowls and handed them out to the group. Carson took a bowl and the remains of one of the canteens up the side of the gully and five minutes later Bill walked into their midst, demanding his own portion of dinner.

Paxton swallowed his first spoonful of gruel tentatively, but soon decided it didn't taste as bad as he was expecting. Gruel was a catch-all term they used to describe a meal consisting of a combination of old canned food which was still being scavenged in abandoned houses throughout the Square and any fresh or more recently canned ingredients from the farm. This particular concoction looked like it had a baked bean base combined with their own canned green beans from last year's harvest and some type of mystery meat. Paxton had ceased to ask where the meat came from and just ate it gratefully. He had flirted with vegetarianism in his former life but he couldn't afford that luxury in the Square.

When they had all been served and Jazelle and Abraham had returned the pot of leftovers to the fire, Paxton turned to the three Newts in their midst and stated, "Now you get the chance to ask us some questions, three questions each, to be exact, so don't waste any. Let's go in reverse order, shall we? Abraham?"

"Who's in charge here?" Abraham asked immediately.

"Do you mean here in this group or here in Megiddo?"

"Both."

"I guess I am in charge of this group," answered Paxton, "when Jazelle lets me be."

A couple of the men snickered and Jazelle shot him a withering look.

"We're a small outfit, there's only eleven of us, now fourteen, counting you three," Paxton continued, "but we're associates of the McDonough clan."

"Associates, pah," spat Jazelle. "Slaves is what we are. Living by the grace of the McDonoughs. Those fuckers would shoot us and think nothing of it, exceptin' Old Jonas has a soft spot for Paxton. Don't know what's gonna happen when the old fucker's gone. I try not to think about it."

"Does that mean that I am slave?" Abraham asked his second question.

"Not to us you're not," Paxton answered, "but we're all basically serfs living on the McDonough's land. Jonas refused to leave, when the Republicans closed up the Square. He told me that his family would be giving up too much if they agreed to be relocated. We farm their land and we've got a couple of animals, but we have to give them half of everything. That reminds me of a song…"

Everyone in Paxton's party groaned when he started to sing, "Half of everything, how do you measure that?"

Most of them joined in on the next line, however, despite their protests, "Half of a Buick, half of a cat."

"They do give us protection," Paxton admitted, after his song had trailed off. "That's worth a lot in a place like this. They definitely have a better arsenal than we do, I think they've been hoarding guns for generations."

"What do you have for weapons?" Abraham asked his final question."

"We have a few guns as well," Paxton was careful not to reveal everything to this complete stranger. "It's hard to get ammunition, though, and home-made rounds have the tendency to explode before they leave the chamber every fifty rounds or so. Home-made shotgun shells usually fair better. We've got machetes, too, and an old samurai sword that Jonas gave us. After that it's just the usual assortment of garden tools, you know, pitchforks and torches. Okay, Abraham, that's your three questions. You're free to ask more tomorrow, but for now we're moving on to…"

"What do you grow on your farm?" interrupted Eden without waiting for Paxton to invite her to speak.

"A little bit of everything," he answered, "but our staples are corn and soy beans. I chose the best land I could find but it's tired land, and there's not enough animal poop to go around. We've started to recycle our own waste to use as fertilizer too."

"Paxton calls it humanure," Bill chimed in and a few of them chuckled.

"We've got a dozen chickens and three goats," Paxton continued, "but it's tough to justify their feed when it takes food from our own mouths. We keep the goats around 'cause they'll eat anything they can scavenge and they are acceptable payment to the McDonoughs in a pinch."

"What does everybody else in the Square eat? It looks pretty dry around here for farming," Eden continued.

"We're blessed with a water source and an irrigation system," Paxton continued, "but you're absolutely right, there aren't a lot of farmers in Megiddo. People are continually scavenging for anything they can find from the old days, canned food, dry food, Twinkies. Most of it has already been gathered and stockpiled but sometimes we get lucky at an abandoned homestead or convenience store. Most of the wild game has already been hunted but there again you can sometimes get lucky. We are constantly at war with each other and stealing each other's stuff, but the stuff is getting scarcer and scarcer. And then there's the cannibals."

"You have cannibals in here?" Elizabeth asked.

"It's not your turn, Beth, but we'll consider that your first question," Paxton answered her. "Yes, we have cannibals in here. Cannibalism is officially outlawed, and punishable by death, but that doesn't deter people who are going to die of starvation anyway. The cannibals live on the periphery of Megiddo for the most part, within sight of the Wall, but they continually raid into the interior looking for fresh meat."

"As we were setting up camp," Eden broke into the pause that ensued as Paxton's words sunk into the Newts' heads, "I could hear you all talking about Friday Night Initiation. Chuck and Richie were snickering about it when we were gathering wood. What does this initiation entail?"

"Friday Night is our only holiday in here," explained Paxton. "There is a general truce on Friday Night but there again, it's not universally accepted by all of Megiddo. Those of us who still draw breath celebrate the fact that we are still able to do so. We get drunk and we howl at the moon and we initiate the Newts. It's our one respite from the rest of our lives in here.

"The three of you are New Transfers. We call you New-T's or Newts. You will remain Newts until you get accepted into a clan. Newts come in here every Friday morning from two different gates, one in the east and one in the west. All of the Newts are either captured or killed. Everyone on this side of the Wall is risking his or her life to come to the Intake. You have no idea how dangerous it is. We don't come very often because we can't afford to lose anybody. If we are still alive on Friday Night, we live it up. If we were lucky enough to rescue some Newts, we initiate them into our group."

"So, are we talking gang-bang here?" Elizabeth asked as a joke, not realizing she had just used up her second question. The uncomfortable silence that followed was palpable.

"You are luckier than most," Paxton chose his words carefully, "having stumbled across our path this morning. But you wouldn't know that, you don't have any basis for comparison just yet. Many Newts don't survive their first Friday Night. We're probably the most peace-loving bunch of hippies you're likely to meet in the Square…"

"Which ain't to say that we won't put a bullet in your head if try to fuck with us," interjected Jazelle, sitting up straighter and looking each Newt fiercely in their eyes. Then she broke into a wide smile and added, "On Friday Night, we get to fuck with you."

"In the McDonough clan," Paxton continued, "Every Newt has to have sex on his or her first Friday night. I'm not making this up. By decree from Jonas McDonough himself, he's our overlord, I guess you could call him."

"Evil overlord," Jazelle interrupted him again and then spat in the dust between her crossed legs.

"Some might say," Paxton conceded, "nevertheless, the crux of the matter is that no one in here is allowed to be a virgin, so to make sure, every Newt must have sex. For the women it's vaginal penetration but for a guy it can be penetration or being penetrated. Many tribes treat it as an excuse to have a gang-bang and many Newts do not survive the experience."

"Anyone who tries to rape me better be prepared for a fight," Abraham warned them calmly, looking around at the men."

I'm sure it won't come to that," Paxton chuckled uneasily, "not with Jazelle here practically drooling over you!"

Jazelle shot Paxton a wounded look, but she joined in the general banter and catcalls from the men. Grinning broadly, she granted them, "Yeah, I might have a use for him."

"But I'm a married man!" protested Abraham amidst their guffaws and cheers.

"You were a married man," Paxton corrected him. "You are never going back to that life, Abraham. This is now your life. The sooner you accept that the better. You will never again see your wife, unless by some miracle she gets thrown in here with us and stumbles upon our little commune, and the odds of that, my friend, well let's just say you'd do better to worry about getting struck by lightning.

"You'll soon learn that life in the Square is not worth as much as what you might think it should be worth. We never have enough to eat or drink, and we are always fighting each other over what we do have. The more new people we let in here, the more spread out our few resources become, so no one gets too concerned about what happens to any given Newt on Friday Night. People around here see it as mercy killing, kind of like when you cull a herd of deer to keep the rest from starving through the long winter.

"We're offering you a chance, at a semblance of a life, but life nonetheless. Life always struggles to perpetuate itself, to propagate, to proliferate. Life never gives up. This is a shitty kind of life compared to what you were used to on the outside, but it is still life, and that always beats the alternative."

"Life on the outside is not so rosy these days, either," interjected Abraham."

"Perhaps not, but I'm gonna say that it's better than what we've got in here," continued Paxton. "I've seen Newts literally raped to death. They are sometimes pitted against each other in bare-handed battles that don't end until one has beaten the other to death. Have they resorted to cannibalism in the outside world yet?"

"Not in L.A.," answered Abraham, "but I don't know about the rest of the world."

"Our world is dying," Paxton pronounced, with a far-off look in his eyes. "Civilization and society are crumbling around our heads and those who cling to privilege and power are trying desperately to hold onto it, deluding themselves into believing that they don't share the fate of the common folk."

There was a general silence after this declaration and Jazelle broke it by informing Elizabeth that she still had one more question she could ask. She seemed deep in concentration for a long time before turning to look Paxton in the eyes.

"What are you all still doing here, Paxton?" she asked him directly. "You should be well on your way to Washington, D.C."

"I already told you why I'm here, Beth," Paxton answered, his confusion evident in his tone. "What do you mean?"

"You told me why they threw you in here, but not why you've stayed," she continued. "Contrary to your little speech, you've got no life in here. You've got bigger and better things to do. I've seen you speaking to hundreds of thousands of people, with the Washington Monument in the background!"

"I've never spoken to a crowd that large," he responded, "and definitely not at the Mall in Washington!"

"Then it has yet to come," she responded calmly. "You need to devise a plan to get us all out of here. Put that big, amazing brain of yours to good use!"

"It's never been done," Paxton stated emphatically, "not to anyone's knowledge, though we have heard many stories about failed escape attempts. And you can see the bodies hanging from the Wall, if you get close enough, but who wants to get close enough to risk running afoul of the cannibals?"

"Last one I heard," ventured Chuck, "somebody built a homemade catapult and started throwing dead bodies up on top of the Wall. It took a lot of experimenting but they eventually got a live one to the top of the Wall and he tossed down a ladder made out of rope. Everyone who climbed up that ladder was hanging from the Wall the next morning."

"Tell me more about these dreams, honey," Jazelle pressed Elizabeth, but it was Eden who answered her.

"Lizzie can see the future in her dreams."

"It's not anything I can control," Elizabeth elaborated, "but many of the things I see in my dreams come to pass, unless I try purposefully to prevent them from occurring, and even then, they usually come to pass anyway."

"I'm sure that might come in handy later, Beth," interrupted Paxton, anxious to change the subject. He cut off further conversation with his next pronouncement, "It's time for the Newts to choose."

"Choose what?" asked Eden.

"Choose whom you want to initiate you into the McDonough clan," Paxton explained. "Abraham has already made his choice perfectly clear. How about you, Beth?"

"I don't know," Elizabeth answered, getting to her feet. "Do any of you boys know how to dance?"

She raised both arms into the air and began to sway her hips back and forth seductively, dancing to a tune that only she could hear. Richie rose to the occasion immediately, passing off the cactus beer gourd to Bill and standing up opposite Elizabeth. Taking hold of one of her hands and placing his other at the small of her back, he began to twirl her slowly around the perimeter of their campfire.

"What about you, Eden?" pressed Paxton. "Does anyone here strike your fancy?"

"I choose you, Paxton," she answered looking him straight in the eyes.

"Me?" he stammered, taken aback. "I'm old enough to be your father."

"Grandfather!" Jazelle chimed in, looking daggers at Eden. "Weren't you two calling him, Uncle Paxton earlier? That's perverse!"

"Since when is anyone in here above perversion?" Paxton shot back, amused by Jazelle's jealousy. "Anyway, I'm not their real uncle, just a family friend. Eden, are you sure?"

"If it really is up to me, then I choose you," she answered with conviction. "Do we get to have some privacy or are we going to do it right here in front of everyone?"

"We can go back to my tent," he offered, standing up and extending his hand to Eden. "I trust you all to carry on without me!"

As they were turning to walk toward the tents, Paxton caught Jazelle's eye and she did not appear amused by this turn of events. He shrugged and raised his eyebrows as if to say, "What am I supposed to do?"

CHAPTER 4

ELIZABETH

I have been playing second fiddle to Eden for most of my life, ever since she was born, I guess. But I don't mind, really, I don't. Mom and Dad had plenty of love for the both of us, and we were never wanting for much of anything that mattered growing up. I consider myself lucky to be a part of her life, let alone her sister!

Eden is special. I don't mean it in the way that 'everyone is special.' She really is special. Eden is the culmination of thousands of years of spiritual striving, of humanity's search for God, for purpose, for meaning. She's the last hope we have of saving our planet, of saving humanity. Eden is the next Messiah, foretold by the prophets of so many different religions. Only she doesn't know it, which is the most frustrating part of all of this!

Mom and Dad knew, though they forbade me to talk about it. They sat me down once, when I was probably six or seven years old and Eden was just beginning to be able to hold a conversation with us. I told them about the dreams I had been having. We talked about what I had remembered from my previous life back in Maine. They admitted what I already suspected about Eden, but made me promise never to speak of it again.

They wanted Eden to have a normal childhood, they said. They were afraid that if the truth came out the bad men would come to kill us all. They never did explain who they thought the bad men were, but we went all the way down to South America to escape them. They told me they were protecting Eden and me, which was fine when we were kids, but why didn't they tell her later on, when everything started to go to hell, before it was too late?

Why didn't they tell her when the ice caps melted and the Atlantic Ocean rose up to swallow Buenos Aires? Why didn't they tell her when we lived through drought after drought those last few years of their lives? Why didn't they tell her when the petroleum dried up and everyone started to starve to death, or when martial law was declared and the mass killing started? Why didn't they tell her before they got themselves killed?

I tried to talk to her about it, on our journey up here. I figured I was released from my promise now that Mom and Dad are gone. She didn't believe any of it, thought I was pulling her leg. She says she doesn't believe in God, not with everything that's going on in the world, and Mom and Dad were never big church-goers, either. But I believe. I've seen God and talked to Her. And Thorn still comes to me in my dreams, not very often anymore, but he still does from time to time.

Why doesn't Eden remember any of her past lives? How can she not know who she is meant to be? I keep waiting for her to have this big revelation, to see God like I did or something, something which jolts her out of her constant complacency. I swear, the whole world could be burning around her and she would still have a smile on her face!

And why shouldn't she be smiling; she's gotten her way her whole life! We let her have everything she wanted growing up, even before we realized that she could make people do pretty much anything she wanted them to do for her anyway. And that's not all she can do. Things happen inexplicably when she feels something strongly - anger, fear, love. I've seen objects move of their own accord and a thunderstorm blow up from out of nowhere on a perfectly sunny day. Once, a boy who had been bullying her fell down the stairs all of a sudden and broke an arm and a leg.

I don't think she is quite aware of her abilities. They just seem to happen, mostly in times of need, but she once 'found' an emerald necklace for me, for my birthday. She found it right there in the rainforest, under a giant mahogany tree. If she is aware of her powers, it's amazing to me that she doesn't lord them over the rest of us mere mortals.

It has always been my job to protect her, though no one expressly told me to do it. I try to keep her safe and as happy as possible in a world crumbling around the edges. It has never been hard to keep Eden happy. She is so full of life, of wonder, of love, for everyone and everything. She cheers up everyone around her rather than the other way around. I love spending time with her and we've been inseparable for most of our lives. We share everything, well, almost everything.

There's one experience we have yet to share. Eden is a virgin. I'm not even sure why she has yet to experience the pleasures of the flesh. She could have had her pick of boys growing up and she could have her pick of men now. I really think that just an inviting look from her would be enough to entice all but the most strong-willed of men. I've had some experience at that myself. Men are so easy to captivate.

I am no virgin, haven't been for a long time. What's more, I love the pleasures of the flesh. There's no substitute for the feeling of a hard cock, deep inside, as long as it's on my terms. It's usually on my terms, but I have also had to barter my body to survive the journey to the Wall and I have learned that sex is not always pleasurable.

Still, I have one thing I can hold over my sister, not that we ever talk about sex much. When we do, she asks me questions about where and how I feel it in my body and how deep an emotional bond I form with my partners. She has been studying sex with her intellect but she has yet to feel it and until you feel it, you don't know what sex is. Eden may never know.

INITIATION

Eden and Paxton sat cross-legged, facing each other across a disheveled sleeping bag which had been spread out over the floor of the tent. Their knees were touching and at Eden's insistence they had clasped hands and were staring deeply into each other's eyes.

Paxton was finally able to get a good look at her features. She had Claire's green eyes for sure, but he could also see Tucker in her strong jawline and the dimples that formed when she smiled. Her long red hair was dirty and matted, but served only to make her look wild and wanton. She was beautiful and sexual and Paxton found himself aroused despite the awkwardness of the difference in their ages and his close relationship with her parents.

"You want me!" Eden broke their silent staring contest with a giggle. Paxton blushed and looked away.

"Am I that obvious?" he asked. "How can I help wanting you, you're gorgeous!"

"Then I guess you're the one," stated Eden enthusiastically.

"The one for what?" he asked, confusedly.

"The one to take my virginity," she answered. "I wasn't sure when I chose you out there by the fire, I just wanted to get you alone. But I'm okay with you being my first."

"You realize that when we say we're taking the Newts' virginity we're speaking metaphorically. No one really thinks you all are virgins, it's just an excuse to have some fun with the Newts, and obey the letter of the law, of course."

"But I *am* a virgin, Uncle Paxton," Eden responded evenly. "Do you mind that I call you Uncle Paxton?"

"I do if we're about to have sex!" he answered. "What do you mean you're a virgin, like, an actual virgin?"

"I've never had sex before. Isn't that the textbook definition of *virgin*?"

"How is that even possible?" Paxton asked incredulously. "Just look at you!"

"I've never met anyone that I wanted to share that kind of intimacy with," Eden explained. "I've come close, on several occasions, but when I give them the same test, I just gave you, I always balk. It's not a blessing to be able to see someone else's deepest desires and motivations, believe me. Once I open a window upon someone's soul, his or her outer shell is no longer that appealing to me, at least not in any sexual way. At that point I just convince them that they don't really want to have sex with me either!"

"How am I any different?"

"You don't want anything from me," Eden answered immediately. "You are only here with me to spare me a worse alternative with the other members of your gang. And I sense such goodness in you, Paxton, more so than anyone else I've ever met, except for Lizzie. Nobody is as good as Lizzie! You truly care for the rest of your people out there and you put their well-being above your own, it's such a rare trait, you have no idea. What's even more rare, you seem to care about everyone, all of humanity and the fate of this planet, not just what happens to your little group."

"You got all of that, just by looking into my eyes?" asked Paxton, embarrassed. He added, as if suddenly remembering something important, "Speaking of Beth, is she going to be okay out there? Is she a virgin, too?"

"Not for a long time," Eden laughed. "Lizzie can hold her own, both in and out of the bedroom. You don't need to worry about her. They're not going to team up on her, are they?"

"They had better not!" Paxton asserted. "I made it clear to everyone how important the both of you are to me, but you both still need to be initiated."

"Okay then, let's do this thing!" Eden exclaimed, springing up off her crossed legs abruptly and pushing Paxton backwards onto the sleeping bag. She pressed her lithe body onto his and began to kiss his astonished mouth forcefully. Pressing her pubis against his groin she coaxed him to full hardness quickly, defying Paxton's advanced age.

With all the resolve he could muster Paxton pushed her off to one side and rolled over to look once again into Eden's dreamy, green eyes. Both of them were breathing heavily and it was several moments before Paxton could find his voice.

"I can't do this," he said, shaking his head.

"Your body says otherwise," Eden chuckled, reaching a hand between his legs.

"I can physically do this," Paxton agreed, rolling his eyes and removing her hand from his crotch, "but it's not happening. Don't you get it, Eden? You're the one!"

"The one, *what*?"

"You're the one from the prophecy, the one that's going to put an end to this awful place," he explained. "You just told me that you're a *true* virgin. I've seen you read minds and I know where you come from, you're the one."

"So, Lizzie keeps telling me," said Eden, propping up her head with her right hand. "She thinks I'm the reincarnated soul of some prophet from Maine, or some such bullshit."

"It's not bullshit," interrupted Paxton. "I was there. It was so long ago, now. Honestly, didn't your parents tell you anything?"

"They were pretty close-mouthed about their past," answered Eden. "Anything I know about it comes from Lizzie. She says she was there, too. She says that a bolt of lightning hit an old oak tree, on the top of a mountain in Maine, and the tree collapsed. Lizzie says that everyone who watched it fall to the ground had a vision of God."

"It wasn't a bolt of lightning," Paxton corrected her, "but a sudden microburst of wind, like a mini-tornado. You don't remember any of this?"

"How could I? It was before I was born!"

"So, you don't remember *anything* from before you were born?" asked Paxton. "Your parents seriously never talked to you about all this?"

"No, they did not," confirmed Eden. "Do you remember things from before you were born?"

"It's not that I remember them, exactly," Paxton said, thinking out loud, "but Thorn helped me to figure out some of my past lives. I might be able to help you figure out some of yours."

"Really?" Eden sounded skeptical. "How?"

"You'd need to be in a deep state of meditation," Paxton. "Have you ever meditated before?"

"Do you mean, like, pray? Not really. Mom and Dad were not at all religious, and certainly not Catholic, like the rest of Argentina."

"It's not praying," Paxton hesitated, "not like you're thinking of praying. It's more like sitting quietly and emptying your mind of all thought. It's easily enough stated, but not so easy to actually accomplish."

"Well, it's not anything I want to try right now," admitted Eden, once more pushing the palm of her hand into his crotch. "We have more pressing matters."

As if on cue they heard a loud moan coming from one of the other tents and they both burst out laughing.

"Who was that?" Paxton asked. "Beth or Jazelle?"

"That was definitely my sister," Eden asserted, and her guess was confirmed moments later when Jazelle's Southern accent came from a slightly different direction.

"Holy Jesus!" she exclaimed. This proclamation was soon followed by grunts and groans of both male and female timbres which caused another round of laughter to erupt from their own tent.

"We'd better at least make a show of it," decided Paxton, moving over and on top of Eden but making no effort to remove any of his clothes. "We need the rest of them to believe you've been initiated."

Eden did not respond verbally but she spread her legs and pulled his face down to her expectant lips. Soon they were kissing passionately and Paxton began to grind against her despite his resolve to the contrary. Eden pulled her lips away from his and began to emit loud, theatrical moans. Paxton was sure they wouldn't fool anyone, but he found himself becoming more and more aroused nonetheless. Soon he was rock hard and pressed firmly into the crease of her pants while she locked her legs around his thighs and grabbed his ass in both hands.

Paxton did not know when Eden's play acting turned into the real thing, but at some point, Eden was moaning and gasping with real pleasure and it seemed to Paxton that she was building toward a real orgasm. This in turn fomented his own passion and he was right on the edge of orgasm himself when Eden's washed over her and she pulled him closer, emitting a long, loud scream.

"Oh, Paxton!" she said throatily, when she had recovered enough of her breath to speak. "You're so bad!"

Flustered, he disentangled himself from her encircling legs and whispered his apology, "I'm so sorry! I don't know what came over me!"

Eden just laughed, but otherwise made no move to stop him as he pulled away from her. Staring over at him from those impossibly wide eyes she gushed, "I know what came over me. That was a good one."

"Was that your first?" he asked her.

"Don't be silly," she chided him, reaching out to stroke his arm lightly, her giddiness beguiling. "I said I was a virgin. I never said I didn't partake of the pleasures of the flesh. Did you come, too?"

"No, but I was a hair's breadth away," he admitted.

"Too bad," she winked at him, "but the night is still young."

"And so are you," Paxton shot back, pushing her wandering hand up against her own thigh. "Way too young for me."

"What about Jazelle?" Eden asked.

"What about me?" Jazelle asked from right outside the door of their tent. "Ain't you two finished yet?"

"Yes, we are," Paxton replied, grateful for the diversion from Eden's sexuality. "Come on in!"

In the next instant the zipper of the tent was pulled forcefully downward and Jazelle stuck her head through the ensuing slit in the thin mesh fabric. "Don't you worry about me, honey child. I ain't the jealous type."

A strange look passed between Jazelle and Paxton, but he couldn't quite read her expression. Was she upset with him? She had no right to be. She slept with whomever she pleased while he had been faithful to her since she started sharing his bed. Was she disappointed in him? In any event, he could not hold her stare for more than a few moments before looking down at the floor guiltily.

"Was it good for you, sweetie?" she asked Eden with exaggerated sweetness as she pushed the rest of her body through the opening in the tent.

"Definitely," Eden answered with a big smile on her face. She stretched her arms languorously over her head.

"Good!" Jazelle's tone had suddenly become perfunctory. She kicked Eden's foot playfully and instructed, "Then you can get your skinny ass out of my bed. I'm exhausted."

"She's gonna need some real clothes," Paxton declared as Eden pulled herself up to her knees, "now that she's been initiated. What did you bring?"

"They're all in this backpack," she said, picking it up from where it slumped next to the entrance and tossing it to Eden. "Give some to your sister, too. From what I heard she's gonna need some street clothes, too."

Eden left in a hurry, muttering her goodnights and clutching the backpack to her chest.

"Good night," Paxton called after her, even as Jazelle zipped the door closed. She plopped down upon the sleeping bag opposite Paxton in much the same position that Eden had just been in.

"So how was it, Paxton?" she cooed, even as she reached out to clutch a hand forcefully into his genitals. The sudden motion made him flinch but he did not try to escape her grip. It did not take long for Jazelle to realize that Paxton was still hard.

"What's going on here?" Jazelle asked him playfully, before another realization dawned slowly upon her face. "How're you still hard? You ain't never good for more than one go 'round a night! And then you need a few days to recover!"

"It's just that you're so sexy," he tried to con her, reaching for her breast.

"Bullshit!" she shot back, unzipping his pants and pulling them down to mid-thigh in one swift motion. He wore no underwear so she could immediately push her nose into his furry balls and take a long whiff. Next, she sniffed along the length of his erection.

"You didn't do it!" she accused him, before a broad smile erupted across her face. "You didn't fuck her!"

"Shhh!" he shot back, lifting a finger to his lips reflexively. He continued in a whisper, "No, we didn't do it. I couldn't bring myself to do it. She's practically my niece!"

"No big deal," she assured him, grinning like the Cheshire cat. "I'll just get one of the other guys to…"

"No!" Paxton interrupted her, more loudly than he would have liked. "She's the one, Jazelle! She's the one who's gonna make this whole shithole come crashing down."

"What do you mean?"

"She was a true virgin when she came here," Paxton continued, "and she still is. If Jonas' prophecy has any teeth at all, then Eden is the one he's afraid of. There's so much more I could tell you about her. She's not like you and me."

"Do tell," Jazelle allowed, removing her hand from his erection and propping herself up on one elbow. Paxton pulled his pants back up before beginning his story.

"A long time ago, now, back when I was still in graduate school at the University of Maine, I encountered a very old soul trapped in an oak tree," Paxton recounted.

"Here we go," Jazelle teased him, rolling her eyes. "If you don't want to tell me what's going on, fine. I don't need you to tell me some bedtime story."

"I'm not making this up," he assured her, "but I'm sure you'll find most of it unbelievable, anyway. The tree was in a section of the forest that was about to be clear-cut and my friends and I were trying to prevent that from happening."

"Sounds like you were a real tree-hugger," she continued to poke fun at him good-naturedly.

"Pretty much," he conceded, winking at her. "Thorn, that was his name, contacted us through mental telepathy and we were able to converse with him for the two weeks right before he was cut down. That's what those books I wrote were about, you know, the ones you never read."

"I ain't never been much of a reader," admitted Jazelle.

"Don't feel bad, nobody else read them, either," Paxton said ruefully. "In any event, Thorn could trace his past lives back to Jesus Christ and beyond and he believed that his next incarnation was going to be the Messiah prophesied in many of the world's religions, the one that's supposed to come to Earth to save humanity from self-destruction."

"Okay, let's say I believe all of this," allowed Jazelle, "which ain't necessarily true, mind you. What has that got to do with our current situation?"

"Before Thorn was cut down, he traded places with my best friend, Tucker, for one night. He said it was so that he could feel what it was to be human again before he died. While he was inside of Tucker's body he seduced and impregnated my girlfriend, Claire."

"*Your* girlfriend?" asked Jazelle. "Where were you at the time?"

"I was in jail," Paxton answered. "A bunch of us got thrown in jail for protesting the clear-cut. Claire was infertile, but Thorn convinced her that he could give her a child if she would consent to becoming the mother of the world's next great spiritual teacher, a modern-day Mary if you will, but without the Immaculate Conception."

"And you were okay with this?" Jazelle asked him.

"Hell no! I was *not* okay with it. But there wasn't much I could do about it after the fact. Claire and I parted ways and she and Tucker escaped to Argentina to keep their babies safe."

"Babies?" asked Jazelle. "There was more than one?"

"Eden and Beth," Paxton stated as though it were completely obvious, "although Beth wasn't really a baby anymore, and she was their adopted daughter. She must have been three or four at the time. Beth was there, on the mountaintop, when Thorn was cut down. She could tell you all about it, if she still remembers it."

"So, you think Eden is the next Messiah?" pressed Jazelle.

"Yes!" Paxton answered excitedly. "But she doesn't seem to know it, or to have any inclination of her many past lives. That's the part I don't get."

"You're so funny, Paxton," chuckled Jazelle. "For a man of science, you seem to be pretty comfortable with all of this voodoo you're talking about."

"I know what it sounds like," Paxton admitted. "You had to be there to believe it, and even then, it was pretty fantastical."

"Well, what are you going to do about it? If this girl is who you think she is, she doesn't belong in here."

"I've been thinking about that," Paxton began.

"Of course, you have," Jazelle interrupted.

"I want to take her to the Comanche. He's the one who made the prediction in the first place. Maybe he will know what we should do next."

"That's crazy!" Jazelle interjected. "You ain't got no clue how to find him, or even if he's still alive. He's older than Jonas, if the stories 'bout him are true."

"I know," Paxton agreed with her, "but I still think it's our best move. I'll have to ask Jonas where to find him."

"Old Jonas ain't gonna give up that information easily. It's gonna cost you."

"I know," Paxton repeated, "and I'm going to have to pay his price, whatever it is."

"Why don't you sleep on it, sweetie?" Jazelle said, moving toward him on the sleeping bag and draping her body across his for a kiss. There was no hiding the fact that he was still hard as Jazelle ground up against him.

"We better take care of this first," she said, reaching between them to stroke him. "Otherwise, you'll be up all night!"

Paxton was surprised by his level of arousal and he didn't put up any resistance to her advances. Jazelle pulled his pants back down to his thighs and then pulled her own panties to one side, just enough for her to be able to mount him. She was louder than she needed to be, probably so that the rest of the camp understood that she was reclaiming her man, despite Eden's initiation. Paxton added his own throaty grunts to hers as they finished together. Afterwards, Jazelle collapsed on top of him and fell asleep with his softening penis still inside her.

Sleep did not come as quickly for Paxton, but it did come, because the next thing he knew Jazelle was shaking him awake and the tent was already heating up in the early morning sunlight.

CHAPTER 5
RACHEL

I was a mother, maybe I still am, I don't know. My girls were taken from me, while they were at boarding school, I'm sure of it. I didn't even get to say goodbye to them. I don't know if I should wish them alive or dead, not after what I've seen.

They don't put anyone younger than sixteen in the Square. They have a separate facility for minors. But Barbara was 15 going on 25, and a good-lookin' girl. I shudder to think what became of her. That was my pet project on the other side of the Wall, I couldn't really call it a job. I tried to get some of those orphans out of detention and into a job and an apartment if they were old enough to work, and a better place to grow up, if not exactly model homes, for the young ones.

I was a senator's wife, with all of the privileges and responsibilities of one. God, that seems like a lifetime ago, like a lifetime I viewed on some reality TV show. "Real Housewives of Washington, D.C." That immaculate house, those beautifully manicured lawns and those unbelievably long state dinners. All of that was taken care of by the Mexicans, of course, when we were back home in Sonoma. That's where the Guard took us, in the middle of the night, while Congress was in recess.

My husband was amongst the last hold-out Democratic senators from California, it was only a matter of time. He was probably executed and thrown into a mass grave somewhere. At least he didn't come in here with me. The people they take are never heard from again. They don't get a TV interview, or even their day in court, unless it's so the RepNews can put carefully edited clips of their trial in front of the masses as proof that the judicial branch is still functioning. They mostly show old photos and video clips of the criminals while rehashing their crimes hour by hour, photo by photo and video by video. Eventually they pronounce judgement and the corresponding punishment.

I was taken before a judge, in my orange prison jumper, with my hands cuffed behind my back. I'll tell you something about that experience you might not realize. Hand-cuffs hurt! They rubbed my wrists raw where all the bony parts protrude, and it's not all that comfortable to be carried around like that, with your arms bent unnaturally behind your back. It seems quaint to complain about such a thing, me with half a leg and all, but I still have scars from those hand-cuffs.

They read the charges against me – Treason! Plotting to overthrow the Republic. There were more charges, but I kind of stopped listening at that point. They took a lot of pictures and some video, got some good ones of me bawling my eyes out. They also took footage of the lawyers and the judge. The whole place was decked out like a movie set, with glaring lights and six or seven cameras, all of them pointing in different directions. There was no director in evidence, but they didn't need one. Everybody but me had their parts down cold.

The jury just sat there looking thoughtful, until the very end when an elderly gentleman, I can only presume was the foreman, rose from his seat on the bench and pronounced – Guilty. More footage of the judge sentencing me to the Square. Then I was in the back of the van again, with two Guards who had guns strapped to their belts, and probably other places as well.

I spent two nights and a day in a holding cell with about twenty other prisoners. Then we were all marched out onto a school bus painted with black, green and gray camouflage. It was the Republican Guard that took us in a bus to El Paso for our last night on American soil. They gave us breakfast in the morning, toast and coffee, and one fried egg. It was the last meal for many of the people in that room. The next morning, we were marched into the Square with the sound of that siren obliterating all thought. The only thing I could focus upon was the insistent tap, tap, tap, of the soldiers' marching feet.

I could barely hear it when they read us our last rights, with my ears still ringing from that damned siren. The soldiers high-tailed it out of there through those big, black doors. Somebody tried to run back through the gate as it was closing and they shot him at least ten times, right in front of me. Some of his blood spattered on my orange jumper.

There was blessed silence for a long moment, after the doors clanged shut. That bang reverberated through the stillness, which lingered long enough for us to hear the metal overtone run its course. Then all hell broke loose.

We didn't have any idea what was expected of us at that point, but our survival instincts kicked in pretty quickly when we heard more gunshots. There was also the clip-clop of horses' hooves galloping nearer and nearer and a loud motorcycle engine in the distance. Then we were beset upon from every direction by small groups of the most ragged-looking people I had ever seen.

We stampeded like a herd of wildebeest, with those at the edges being taken down or captured while the rest of the herd pushed mostly forward, away from the gate. I pressed myself into the middle of that sea of orange and prodded everyone around me, urging them to move.

We picked up speed as we began to thin out. I saw a woman to my left go down with a half-naked man on her back. Still, we pressed onward, running now. Soon enough I realized that I was by myself at the head of the pack. I looked back over my shoulder to see four or five other prisoners running behind me, followed by a motley crew who were thankfully also on foot.

I just kept on running, running as if my life depended on it, because it sure seemed to hang in the balance. The next time I looked back there were no more orange runners, but two men still pursued me on foot. They couldn't catch me. I was a runner in college, and I have finished several marathons, the latest one just last year. I ran until my lungs ached, mile after mile, afraid to look back again for my pursuers, even when I knew that I had left them far behind. I kept the Wall within eyesight on my right and ran as fast and as long as I could. Eventually I had to cross a gully and I decided to travel along the creek bed that had formed it, reasoning that at least then I wouldn't be visible to anyone scouting from above me.

It seemed to work for a while, until I rounded a bend in the course of the creek and almost ran headlong into the chest of a skinny, brown horse. There was a cowboy on that horse, with a rifle perched upon his lap. Three other men trailed out behind him on foot. They were just as surprised to see me as I was to see them. After a moment's pause, I made a break for it, back the way I had come, but one of the men on foot quickly grabbed hold of my wrist and tugged hard on my arm, almost to the point of dislocating my shoulder. They could not believe their good fortune, of course, and wasted no time in hog-tying me and tossing me across the rump of the leader's horse.

They debated whether or not to head closer to the gate, to sit tight and wait for more Newts to happen along or to consider themselves lucky to have taken me so easily and head home. The sun moved slowly across the sky as they waited. I remember the sweat dripping off my face and the blood rushing to my head. I was dizzy and disoriented. I must have dozed off because when I awoke it was mid-afternoon and we were on the move.

We did not travel far before we were back at their campsite. There was a low green tent already erected and wood for a campfire assembled into a conical pile in a makeshift fire pit. No sooner did we arrive in camp than they tossed me onto a bedroll in the tent and began to take turns raping me. It went on for hours. My hands remained tied behind my back the whole time and I was gagged so that my screaming wouldn't attract unwanted attention.

When their lust was sated, the men complained of being hungry. The cowboy told them to keep quiet, but they persisted, clearly trying to convince him of something. They wore him down to the point that he finally gave his consent and then two of the men came over to where I was sobbing in the tent and carried me bodily to a nearby tree.

They seated me up against the tree and untied my wrists long enough to bend my arms back and around the trunk and then retie my wrists. They pulled my legs apart and attached them by rope to two stakes hastily pounded into the ground. One of the men removed his belt and pulled it painfully tight around the top of my left thigh, right near my torn and bleeding vagina. The other man checked the rags that had been stuffed into my mouth before unsheathing a large hunting knife and brandishing it menacingly in front of my eyes.

He squatted down between my legs and inserted the knife right below my knee, removing the knee cap in a practiced cut that involved some back and forth sawing to get through the tendons there. I screamed at the pain, and the horror of what was happening to me, but he was just getting started. Clamping down hard on my thigh with his left hand, he positioned the sharp blade of his knife in the gaping maw where my knee cap should have been and began to lever it into the junction between my femur and tibia.

The pain was excruciating! I screamed myself hoarse into the rags they had stuffed into my mouth. The tourniquet upon my leg held and I didn't bleed to death, obviously, but I passed out at some point during his grisly operation because I never saw it to its conclusion.

I awoke to the smell of smoke and charred meat and I immediately became aware of my hunger. It took me a few moments to gain my bearings and realize that I was waking up into a nightmare, rather than escaping from one. I was still tethered to the tree with my right leg staked out before me, but my left leg, what was left of it, was free and jerking spasmodically. There was surprisingly little blood on the ground and my stump had been neatly bandaged with white rags and duct tape to hold them in place. The tourniquet on my thigh was also still in place and I couldn't feel any part of my leg below it.

The men were seated around a campfire sharing a bottle of something alcoholic, by the sound of it. They were talking as if I wasn't even there, apparently oblivious to the fact that I had come to, and I wasn't about to draw attention to myself. I tested the ropes around my wrists for slack and surveyed the camp without moving my head, lest I give myself away.

The horse was tethered some twenty feet from the fire and the light from the flames danced all over its smooth, brown flanks. The cowboy's rifle was propped against a folding camp chair in the dark opening to a large canvas tent. When I turned my gaze back to the fire, one of the men had moved off to the edge of the firelight to take a piss and I could see that there was something being turned on a spit between the men. I screamed involuntarily when I saw the five toes of my left foot, blackened and cracked along with the charred skin of my calf all the way up to my knee. I screamed and screamed into my rags until one of the men told me to shut up and then stumbled over to me and slapped me so hard across the cheek that I passed out again.

I was passed out, or I slept, in and out of consciousness all night long. I watched as the men took turns passing around my lower leg, tearing at the flesh with their teeth and pulling it from the bone. They made crude jokes at my expense and speculated whether or not the boss would keep me for breeding stock or let them continue their feast. They urinated on me, each one of them in turn. I remember the smell, of the alcohol in their urine, but something else as well, something sweet, but sickly sweet, to the point that it was overwhelming.

The cowboy raped me that night, after the others had filled their bellies and crawled their drunken asses over and around and into their bedrolls. The cowboy was keeping watch, stumbling around talking to himself, his speech slurred and unintelligible. He untied my good leg and loosened the ropes ever so slightly around my wrists so that he could shimmy my body up along the tree trunk and take me standing up. He had to spit in his palm to get himself lubricated enough to get through all of the dried blood. Soon enough there was fresh blood to make it easier for him.

He was fast and furious for five minutes and then he came inside of me. I was beyond screaming at this point but just sobbed into my gag. He dropped me afterward and I sagged into the tree but I still had my good leg under me. Afterwards he stumbled over to a camp chair and fell fast asleep, clutching his rifle in his lap.

When I was sure he was asleep I pushed myself standing and took stock of my situation. If I did not escape from there soon, I was either going to be eaten or mercilessly raped until I bore the children of my rapists. They had left me one good leg and a mind that still had some hold upon reality. There was a horse I could probably ride if I could get it untied, but I knew I couldn't get out of there without making a lot of noise. I was so tired and in pain, and all I wanted to do was to just lie there and let blessed sleep, even death would have been welcome at this point, take me into oblivion.

I started to saw my ropes up and down the rough tree bark as quietly as I could so as not to wake the cowboy. It took a long time to get through the rope and every scrape was painful in my aching wrists and shoulders and my phantom leg. Back and forth, back and forth, my leg pushing me up and letting me back down again and again. When the rope broke, I lost my balance and almost fell to the ground. Very gingerly I lowered myself down on my hands and one knee and began to crawl toward the horse.

I moved methodically across the grassy campsite, my eyes alternately on the cowboy and the ground directly in front of me. Two hands forward, then drag the leg, over and over again. Slowly, ever so slowly, I reached the horse. It was sleeping but it shook its mangy mane when I touched its nose with my open palm. I untied the horse and almost fell again when it started to walk away with me still clutching the reins.

I remember thinking there was no way I could do it, but then I was pulling myself up and onto the saddle somehow, flopping my body across it onto my belly. I lay there quietly, listening to the sound of the horse's footfalls through the brush and praying that none of the men would wake up. Eventually I just fell asleep there, draped across the saddle, and the horse just kept on walking.

THE HORSE

"It's so fucking hot!" complained Elizabeth as they trudged along in a long, thin line along I-10 in a southeasterly direction.

"Welcome to the Square!" offered Paxton from behind her right shoulder. "Here, take my hat."

He reached up and loosened the string beneath his jaw and removed his cotton, fishing hat. They had remembered to bring plain clothes for the Newts so that they wouldn't stand out like targets in their orange jumpsuits, but nobody brought hats and all three seemed to be suffering some heat exhaustion after their forced, morning march.

Just as he was plopping it upon her head from behind, Elizabeth stopped in her tracks and the hat almost continued forward and onto the dusty ground. Paxton bumped into her back and was about to complain when he stumbled-stepped around her and looked back at her slack face. Her eyes were glazed-over and she was staring fixedly at the horizon, as though she could see something far away.

Eden grabbed hold of her and shook her gently saying, "Lizzie, what is it? What's wrong?"

"This is the place!" Beth answered excitedly, shaking her head as if to clear out the cobwebs. "I saw this exact spot in my dream last night."

"Hold up everyone!" Paxton called out and then whistled as loudly as he could so that Jazelle would know they had stopped walking.

"It was right here," Beth continued. "I saw a woman, on a horse."

"You saw a woman riding a horse?" Paxton repeated.

"Not riding," Beth elaborated. "She was draped over the saddle as though she were asleep, or dead. The horse came walking right up over that ridge, right there, and then dipped back down into that dry creek bed. It'll come right down here and cross this road."

"When is it likely to happen?" asked Paxton. "Or has it already happened?"

"I don't know, Uncle Paxton," she answered him. "Most of my dreams about the future are about the *near* future, usually the next day or two. It'll be full sunlight when she does come this way, that's all I can tell you. That's what I dreamed."

Paxton saw Jazelle striding purposely toward him from the back of the line and he stayed put until she was within earshot. Then he caught her tirade full in the face, "Why the fuck are we stoppin' here? Move your skinny, white asses! This ain't no fuckin' parade! Move it!"

Paxton stood his ground, "I think we need a breather. The Newts are dying out here."

"Too bad," she shot back. "We ain't got time to stop."

Jazelle was clearly their leader out here in the desert, but she usually deferred to Paxton when their plans were at odds. She had seen Paxton in action and he had good instincts. But Paxton was mostly concerned with the bigger picture while Jazelle took care of more immediate concerns, like getting them home safely to the farm. She had barked out orders all morning, in short, succinct instructions only as loud as they needed to be. She continually walked up and down the line, her eyes upon the horizons, ever watchful for trouble, and there was a lot to be had out here in the wildlands.

"Hear me out," Paxton continued. "We're in the midday heat out here, let's take a break in that gully, over there."

He pointed in the general direction Elizabeth had indicated and continued, "I'll bet we can find some shade down there, have a drink and a bite to eat. We could all use a break."

"And you're sure this is the place?" Eden asked her sister, grabbing her gently by the elbows. Both Paxton and Jazelle turned sharply to look at the two of them.

"Yes," insisted Elizabeth. "We have to wait for her, she needs our help."

Jazelle caught Paxton, out of the corner of her eye, trying to shush the girls discretely. Looking directly up into Paxton's eyes she asked, "What's going on, chief?"

Abandoning their secret, he told her the truth, "Beth just told us that she saw a woman on a horse, in this exact spot, in her dream last night."

"That's lovely," Jazelle said dismissively, but with a softened tone. "We gotta keep moving, Paxton. It's not safe here."

"You don't understand," broke in Eden. "Lizzie's dreams are prophetic. If she saw this woman in her dreams, she will be here."

Paxton had witnessed Elizabeth's powers of prophecy when she was a young child, so he was inclined to believe her. Elizabeth had correctly predicted that Tucker would become her adoptive father, even though Paxton was romantically involved with Claire at the time. Even so, they had no idea when she might come through here and they couldn't very well wait around indefinitely for this woman and her horse.

Jazelle pulled Paxton aside to offer her advice in private, "We can't stay here! There's no cover and we still have a long way to go to get back home."

"No one from the road will see us in the shade of that gully," Paxton surmised.

"Ain't no shade in that gully, Paxton," Jazelle disagreed. "It's gotta be close to high noon out here, on one side or the other."

"I know it doesn't make sense," he agreed, "but I also know Beth. If she is sure this is going to happen, then it might be worth the risk. We could really use a horse on the farm."

Horses were prized in the Square as transportation and draft animals. Most of them had been slaughtered along with the cattle for food when they stopped sending supplies to the Square. Jonas still had a dozen or so, as did some of the other clans, and they were jealously guarded and pampered, as much as anything could be pampered in the Square. It didn't make sense that a horse would be out here on the plains of Megiddo, unattended and carrying a sleeping, or dead woman.

Having come to a decision, Paxton turned around and spoke assertively to the whole group, "Let's take a break."

"I don't like it," Jazelle whispered in his ear so that no one else could hear. "Not one little bit."

"One hour!" Paxton continued, knowing that he had won her over. "We move out again in one hour!"

As an aside, Paxton said to Elizabeth and Eden, "That's as long as we can wait, and we really shouldn't wait that long. If this woman doesn't show in an hour, we've gotta get moving."

"Fair enough," agreed Elizabeth. Most of the rest of their posse were straggling into their huddle when Jazelle took up the reins once again, urging them ever onward.

"We're resting for one hour, but not right here!" she instructed them, taking off at a trot for the gully. "Follow me closely!"

Jazelle was right about there being no shade to be had in the scant crevice this time of day. The squat cactuses were no help either and they had to avoid them as they sat their asses down where there was once running water. Paxton took a small beige tarp from his rucksack and gestured for Eden and Beth to join him under it. Two of the men were doing the same and soon everyone but Jazelle was seated on the dusty ground beneath three tarps that did well to camouflage them from afar but not so much if one got a closer look. She joined them a few minutes later, after ensuring that they could not be seen by passersby.

It was hot under the tarp and the four of them were sweating profusely and swatting at sand flies as they waited for Elizabeth's mystery woman. Paxton passed a water bottle around and they all took long draughts from it. He also shared the rest of his biscuits.

"What do you remember about Thorn?" Paxton whispered to Beth, between mouthfuls of biscuit. They had already been admonished by Jazelle once.

"Everything," Elizabeth answered. "I remember being up there, on the top of that mountain, with you and Mom and Dad. I remember he could talk to me, in my mind, and I remember what happened when he died, when *you* died."

In answer to Jazelle's questioning look he quoted Monty Python and the Holy Grail, in his best British accent, "It was just a flesh wound, really."

"He still talks to me sometimes," continued Elizabeth, "in my dreams. He's the one who told me to look for you in the Square. We were in a jail cell in Mexico."

"Wait a second, honey," drawled Jazelle for the first time since she had taken a seat beside Paxton. She jabbed a thumb at Paxton and blurted, "You came to the Square looking for *him*? You must be some kinda fool."

"Play nice," Paxton warned her, but he was smiling. "This is no chance meeting; it's all been orchestrated."

"By who? *God*?" Jazelle almost spat out the last word as though it were distasteful to her.

"Yes, no," Paxton responded in confusion. "Certainly, the All, but also Thorn by the sound of it, or maybe Eden. I don't know."

"Aren't they one and the same?" asked Elizabeth.

"What are you talking about, girl?" Jazelle asked her impatiently.

"Thorn was God, or at least, a prophet of God," she explained. "He was cut down and then reborn as my sister, Eden."

"Show us a miracle, then," Jazelle demanded. "I could really use one right about now."

"I can't perform miracles," Eden began, but was interrupted by her sister.

"Eden can do some amazing things!" Elizabeth's voice rose in anger as she sprang to Eden's defense. "Call it what you will. She can have you eating out of the palm of her hand if she wants to."

"That I would like to see," challenged Jazelle.

"I'll tell you what else…" Elizabeth continued but was silenced abruptly by Paxton, who was peering out into the gully as far as he could see in the direction opposite the road. The heat rising from the ground in shimmering waves made the dull, brown earth tones dance like genies tethered to the ground but nevertheless eager for flight. He pointed in the direction of a darker brown spot which seemed to be getting larger. Jazelle took the binoculars and peered out from beneath the tarp.

"Sheeeit!" she drawled out longer than its one syllable. "Now I've seen everything!"

She handed the binoculars to Paxton and he took a look for himself. Passing them on to Eden he said smugly, "Sure does look like a horse to me."

Soon they could hear the clomping of the big animal's hooves as it marched slowly but steadily toward their position. Paxton made a move to get up but Jazelle caught his arm and pulled him back down.

"Don't nobody go out there!" she hissed. "There could be more of them."

She finally relented when the horse was practically upon them and there was still no sign of any other humans. Eden was the first to pop up from the ground, startling the horse, which probably would have reared if it had the energy to do so. She quickly caught the reins and quieted him down with gentle words and an open palm on his nose. Jazelle and Paxton were on their feet an instant later and turned their attention to the woman draped across the saddle, her long black hair almost touching the ground.

She didn't make a sound as they gently dragged her across the saddle toward them. Eden gasped when she saw what remained of the severed leg. Only then did she notice the blood all over the horse's flanks.

"Is she alive?" Paxton asked, cradling her gently in his kneeling lap. "Get a tarp over here."

They stretched her out upon the tarp and Jazelle put a finger to her neck. She bent over her mouth and turned her head to try to feel the woman's breath upon her cheek. Looking up at Paxton she verified, "She's still breathing, barely."

"What happened to her leg?" asked Elizabeth.

Examining her wound more closely Paxton surmised, "It had to be cannibals. They like to eat their victims one limb at a time. They keep them alive as long as possible to keep the meat fresh."

The explanation was meant for Eden and Elizabeth and this proclamation, as much as the grisly sight of the dirty flesh and protruding thigh bone, were enough to turn Elizabeth's stomach. She heaved and crumbled and vomited a thin, brown paste that had once been hardtack.

"She's burning up!" Jazelle exclaimed with the back of her hand on the prone woman's forehead. "Ain't no way she's going to make it. We'd best leave her here, take the horse and get a move on. I'll bet the cannibals are not far behind!"

"No!" said Eden, bending down to drip some water from the canteen between the woman's parted lips. This caused her to sputter and choke and her eyes flew open in terror as she tried to sit up.

"Shhh," Eden soothed. "You're safe here. We're going to take care of you. What's your name, hon?"

She had to bend in close to hear the soft response, "Rachel."

"You're going to be okay, Rachel," Eden continued to comfort her, stroking the hair from her temple with one hand while clasping Rachel's fingers with the other. Indeed, the color had come back into Rachel's face and they propped up her head with a bedroll.

When she caught the gruesome sight of her missing lower, left leg she let out a shrill scream before Jazelle could put a muffling hand over her mouth.

"Hush up, girl!" Jazelle cautioned her. "We don't wanna let them know we're here."

"They…took…my…leg!" Rachel sobbed.

"They took a lot more than that," Jazelle commented, noticing the dried blood caked upon her inner thighs. "The bastards! Maybe we should wait for them to catch up to us! How many of them were there?"

"Four," she confirmed.

"How many guns?" Jazelle continued to interrogate her.

"I only ever saw one rifle," she said, "their leader, the cowboy. But the other three were decked-out in machetes and knives."

Jazelle and Paxton conferred as the girls continued to administer to Rachel. Jazelle was all for leaving the poor woman, or putting her out of her misery, taking the horse and putting as many miles between their party and the cannibals as they could before sundown.

"She's not going to make it, anyway!" she repeated.

"I wouldn't be too sure about that," Paxton argued, pointing toward the ground. Rachel was sitting up between Eden and Elizabeth and drinking water from a canteen on her own. "She made it this far. That tells me she's a fighter."

"Then put her back on the horse and let's skedaddle!" said Jazelle urgently.

"We could ambush them," reasoned Paxton. "I'm sure they'll be coming after this horse, if not their fresh meat. And they'll only be expecting one wounded woman to resist them. Let's make Megiddo a tiny fraction safer for the rest of us."

"What's four cannibals?" countered Jazelle. "There's many more to take their place. We need to escape while we can, before they catch up to us."

"Then we'll be looking over our shoulders all the way back home. Let's remove the threat of our pursuers, first!"

"You mean *her* pursuers," said Jazelle testily, before spitting on the ground. "They ain't comin' after us."

They went back and forth a few minutes longer before Jazelle gave in. She punched him good naturedly in the shoulder before spinning on her heels to look for the rest of the men in their group. She sent two each in opposite directions along the gully in search of a suitable place for an ambush. She left Abraham with the women and Paxton, they were all too green to be much use to her, and Paxton was about worthless in combat. He was too indecisive and reluctant to cause anyone bodily harm. He was learning, though. The Square was a harsh headmaster.

Jazelle scaled the steep, earthen side of the ditch for a better vantage point. She scanned the western horizon in the direction from which the horse had come stumbling into their midst.

Paxton collected the men's discarded tarp and pulled it over the three women on the ground before joining them beneath it. Abraham said he was fine for the moment and would tend to the horse, just outside their makeshift shelter. Apart from her severed lower leg, Rachel seemed to be doing much better and she was sitting up and eating a biscuit. Eden and Elizabeth had helped her to don a pair of dull, khaki shorts which now concealed her crotch but not the dried blood on her legs.

"What's going on?" asked Elizabeth aware that the others had left their group.

"Jazelle is looking for a place to ambush your pursuers," Paxton said directly to Rachel. "We're assuming they're coming after you, or the horse, or both. How did you escape?"

"I guess I just got lucky," she began, and then filled in the details of her last harrowing twenty-four hours. "They all got stinking drunk and just left me tied to that tree. They must've thought I couldn't get myself free, much less get very far away from them with just one leg."

"They were still sleeping when you left?" asked Paxton.

"Must've been," Rachel confirmed, "or I wouldn't be here."

"What time of night was it?" asked Paxton.

"You think I've got a watch?" snapped Rachel, showing some of the spunk that had gotten her away from her captors. "It was still full dark, that's all I can tell you. I was unconscious, or sleeping in fits and starts before I managed to cut my bonds, so I think it must've been well on toward morning."

"So, there's no telling how far behind you they might be," Paxton mused, "but I venture to say they were travelling faster than that plodding horse once they woke up and realized you were gone."

A moment later a volley of shots rang out to the west in support of Paxton's claim. There was a brief silence followed by three or four more shots in rapid succession. Paxton jumped up from his cross-legged position and said to Abraham, "Stay here and cover up! I'll be right back."

He took off at a run along the creek bed in the direction from which the horse had come. In no time he stumbled upon his posse, huddled around three bodies lying in the dirt. He immediately looked for Jazelle and her eyes locked onto his own from where she was squatting on the far side of the carnage. He ran straight up to her. She stood and they embraced briefly before Paxton started asking questions between his belabored intakes of breath.

"What happened?" he panted.

"We didn't have time to get set up before they came trottin' through here," she said, "but it didn't matter. They were right surprised to see us. Didn't even get off a shot before Carson and I took 'em all down."

"Is everyone all right?" Paxton asked, concerned for his friends.

"Everyone but Bill!" she answered, and Carson sniggered. "And these three fuckers!"

"What happened to Bill?"

"Nothing," he muttered with chagrin. "I tripped comin' down here from the rim, up there. I think I sprained my ankle."

"Have a nice trip," Carson teased him. "See ya next fall!"

"Wait a minute!" Paxton suddenly remembered. "Three? I only see three bodies here! Rachel said there were four of them!"

Just then they heard a scream from back where they had left the Newts. Everyone but Bill, who limped along behind them, took off at a sprint toward the sound of the screaming. It ended almost as abruptly as it had begun and long before they could reach the spot of their disturbed afternoon siesta. Of all of the images running through Paxton's brain for what they might find upon their return, he never would have conjured the scene that awaited them.

The tarp had been thrown off the women and was caught on a low cactus behind them, fluttering in the slight breeze. Abraham and the horse were nowhere to be seen. Eden had her arms around her knees and was rocking back and forth, nodding her head and muttering to herself. Elizabeth was cradling

Rachel's tear-streaked face to her breast, whispering words of comfort to the distraught woman.

On the ground at their feet lay a man, face down and motionless, a long machete still clutched in his right hand. The machete looked well-used, but there was no fresh blood evident on the blade. Jazelle kicked him hard in the ribs to no effect and then she and Richie flipped him over. She kicked him hard again, this time on the opposite side of his ribcage and still he did not budge.

Paxton knelt down next to Eden and she suddenly threw her arms around his neck, sobbing into his shoulder and muttering, "I killed him, Uncle Paxton! I'm so sorry! I killed him!"

"Shhh, shhh," he comforted her. "You're all right. We're all okay. The cannibals are all dead."

"I killed him," Eden whispered in disbelief. "I've never killed anyone before."

"Tell me what happened," he whispered back, but it was Elizabeth who answered.

"It was my fault," she said. "I lifted the tarp, just enough to see where Abraham had got off to."

"Where *is* Abraham?" asked Jazelle.

"I'm right here!" he came running into their midst with Richie and Chuck trailing behind him. "Is everyone okay?"

"No thanks to you," Jazelle chastised him, with unmistakable anger in her voice.

"I heard something," Abraham explained himself between lungfuls of air, "back toward the road. I was investigating when I ran into these two guys."

"He was pretty far off from the gully," Richie remarked, looking at Jazelle meaningfully. "We had to shout for him to hear us."

"Well, we're all here now," she said finally, letting the matter drop for the moment. "One big, happy family!"

Paxton turned back to Elizabeth and asked, "So then what happened, Beth?"

"He had his foot in the stirrup and was just about to mount when he caught me looking at him," Elizabeth continued. He probably would've just ridden away if he hadn't seen me!"

"So, he saw you," Jazelle pressed her, "then what?"

"He disentangled his foot and came running toward us," said Elizabeth. "I threw off the tarp and tried to stand up but Rachel had her head on my shoulder and all I could do was to raise my hands up in defense. He had his machete out and was lifting it to strike when his eyes bulged in their sockets and he clutched at his chest with his free hand. Then he just fell face-first onto the ground and started twitching."

"I killed him," Eden repeated.

"What you talkin' 'bout girl?" asked Jazelle. "You ain't got no weapon!"

"I can't explain it," said Eden, pushing Paxton gently away from her and standing up. "He was just about to bring his machete down onto Lizzie's head! I panicked! All I could think was the one word, 'Die!' I threw it at him, with my mind, and he fell before he could use his machete. I think I burst his heart!"

There was a moment of silence before the men burst out laughing and Jazelle exclaimed, "Shit, girl! You expect us to believe that? What really happened?"

"Believe what you want," Elizabeth said, rising both literally and figuratively to her sister's defense. She took Eden's hand in her own and turned to face Jazelle, saying, "You have no idea what Eden is capable of. You wanna know how we got away from that Mexican gang? Eden got inside that guy's head and scared the shit out of him! You should be thanking her for saving your life!"

Turning to Eden she took her face in her hands and made her sister look her in the eyes, "I know you didn't mean to, Eden, but he would have killed me. He would have killed us all. You saved me. You saved Rachel. Everything's going to be okay."

She took Eden in a fierce embrace and they both burst into tears. Paxton came up to them and put a hand on each of their shoulders. He asked Elizabeth more than Eden, "Is this the first time she has ever hurt someone like this?"

"Eden can usually avoid direct confrontation by deflecting a person's desires," Elizabeth finally answered him. "She hurt a few kids in school, when we were kids, but that was before she learned how to control her gift."

"There was no time," Eden stammered.

"I know," Elizabeth continued to comfort her. "You did the right thing, sis."

"Paxton," Jazelle said with uncharacteristic gentleness in Paxton's ear. "We'll have time to get to the bottom of this bullshit back home, hon'. We can't stay here. Everyone for miles around heard those gunshots. We've got to get a move on!"

"You're right, of course," he responded, turning so that he could kiss her lips briefly.

Jazelle's demeanor changed a split-second after their kiss ended as she yelled over Paxton's shoulder, "Get your asses in gear! We're leaving in three minutes."

It took three more days to get back to Maggie's Farm and the journey was mostly uneventful. The horse actually slowed them down as it plodded along beneath the weight of both Rachel and Bill. They left I-10 briefly at what used to be McNary and traveled secondary roads for twenty miles or so before rejoining it farther east. The Interstate was still the fastest way home, even though you were more likely to meet up with unsavory characters on the highway.

Richie managed to snare a rabbit the second night, while they were sleeping, and Jazelle let them cook it in the morning for breakfast, since they were fairly close to home and most likely now under the protection of the McDonoughs.

They came straggling to the gate of Maggie's Farm at sunset of the third day. The others were eating dinner and did not come out to greet them until they were in the courtyard right outside the dining room window. Then it was bedlam as everyone tried to answer shouted questions at once.

Barbara bellowed when she caught sight of Rachel. She grabbed Eden and Elizabeth, both of whom had flanked Rachel for the whole journey to the farm, to help her get the patient down to their makeshift infirmary in the cellar.

Even amidst the cacophony of noises, Paxton sidled up to Jazelle and slipped his arm around her waist.

"We're home," he said, smiling down on her.

"Home, sweet home," she agreed sardonically, taking his hand in her own.

CHAPTER 6

BARBARA

I was a nurse, back in the day, and a damn good one. Still am a good nurse, truth be told, and Lord knows these people need one. I don't have the same energy I once had, but I still have everything I need to know right up here in the old noggin.

When I started nursing, in the Dark Ages, medical care was available to everyone. There were problems with it, of course. The cost for the procedures and medicines and hospital fees skyrocketed over the years, and the doctors had to cover their asses with malpractice insurance. Our patients would never be able to afford their medical bills without health insurance. Then they started messing with that, too, fixed it so only the rich could afford proper health insurance. And to think that we had come so close to universal health care for everyone before it all came crashing down.

We didn't turn anyone away when they came looking for help in the Emergency Room back then. We didn't always get paid for our services, but we had all taken an oath to heal the sick and tend to the injured and we actually tried to do just that. When I left Phoenix General, involuntarily I might add, in handcuffs, we had become very selective about who we let come through those doors.

We lived on the outskirts of Phoenix, in a nice little home with a nice little yard in a nice little gated community. Randy and I raised two strapping boys, identical twins, Jessie and Jarrod. Football stars they were, and local heroes. They were the apple of my eye. They both had scholarships to play for the

University of Arizona when they were finished with their Service. They were going to be roommates, those two were inseparable.

Service has been mandatory in the Republic for years now, but the boys were drafted when the program had just been passed into law. Two years of service to the Republic, on the day you turn eighteen, regardless of whether or not you've finished or even gone to high school. Education was being phased-out anyway. Two years of mandatory Service, except of course, if you were granted an exemption from the Republic. Exemptions were expensive in lawyers and court fees, believe me, I looked into it.

You can't buy anything on credit anymore, either. RepubliCard is strictly a debit card and if you don't have the money, you don't make the purchase. Citizens receive RepubliCards for their fetuses just as soon as the pregnancy is verified by a medical professional. I've done my fair share of those procedures. The RepubliCard has become the only thing we need to carry in our wallets these days. It completely identifies each citizen and grants privileges or imposes restrictions according to his or her status in society.

By the time I left Phoenix General we weren't admitting anyone lower than a level six, and to think that I had complained when we started turning away patients who didn't hold valid RepubliCards. That was my first strike as far as the hospital administration were concerned, the first of many.

My boys died fighting for the Republic, fighting over uranium mines in Kazakhstan, together even in death. There were no purple hearts or gold-medals given out, although I became a Gold-Star Mom, for whatever that was worth, there were a lot of us by then. A colonel or some such came to the house to tell us, gave us their dog-tags and phones. Eventually we buried their bodies in an Army graveyard in the godforsaken desert.

Randy was never the same, but he still kept getting up every morning to go to work. It was a shitty job in the Electric Plant, it really was, he cleaned the toilets. At least he wasn't producing the electricity, riding the damn bicycles with all those poor souls who were incapable of finding any other gainful employment. I kept going to work, too, but I was on autopilot, for a long time. I'm not the same anymore either, and not just because I'm in the Square. I got pretty damn lucky to end up here on Maggie's Farm. I don't know what became of Randy, but spouses don't fare well when their significant others are convicted of treason against the Republic.

I started treating the homeless throngs outside of the locked and heavily guarded hospital doors, discretely at first, before and after my shifts at the hospital. Soon I was taking the supplies I needed, little things in the beginning, but I grew more brazen over time. They caught me dead to rights on the hospital security cameras with a duffle bag full of gauze pads, bandages and a dozen shots of penicillin. Then they tricked me into admitting I had been performing abortions. It was true, I was giving those poor ladies abortions, in pretty squalid conditions, but I hadn't meant to tell the Guard anything about that.

It was just one more way for them to cull the herd, just like taking away their health insurance and access to medical care. They made it illegal to have a baby without first being granted a permit from the Republic, said it was necessary to curb rampant overpopulation. If someone did have an unauthorized pregnancy, the baby was taken from the mother at birth and raised by the State. The mother, and the father if she named him, were both thrown into the Square. The ladies I helped were frantic for me to end their pregnancies before they started to show. I never thought very kindly on abortion or abortionists, for that matter, but I became one nevertheless.

That's what got me thrown into the Square, Gold-Star Mom or not! The fact that I have some skills in the healing arts has been what's kept me alive since then, especially given my acid tongue and proclivity to speak my mind. The McDonoughs captured me at the Intake and gave me to Paxton just as soon as they learned I was an abortionist. Now that I'm on Maggie's Farm I feel like my life has purpose again, miraculous as that might sound. Paxton has something special going on here. Paxton is something special. Anyone can see that just talking to the man for five minutes. This story, my story, is my gift to him.

There you go, Paxton, I wrote in your damn book. Please don't ask me to do it again.

MAGGIE'S FARM

"Good morning, y'all!" Jazelle called out as she entered the busy kitchen with a smile tugging at the corners of her mouth.

"What are you so happy about?" asked Barbara, handing her a cup of hemp tea. "You get laid last night?"

"And this morning," said Jazelle, sidling up to the bigger woman. Just then Paxton entered the room wearing the same shit-eating grin on his face. Barbara offered him a cup of tea as well and he accepted it gratefully.

"You old dog," she whispered in his ear when their hands were still touching. Paxton's eyes met Jazelle's briefly and then he looked down at his bare feet in embarrassment.

"Are there no secrets around here?" he lamented good-naturedly. Changing the subject quickly he asked their resident nurse, "What's the good word on Rachel?"

"I think she's gonna make it," Barbara answered excitedly. "I got her stinking drunk on tequila last night, not the good stuff, and I cleaned out her wound. I had to cut back some of the flesh that had begun to turn necrotic."

"Ugh, too much information, but it's good to hear she will live." Paxton commented. His mind made a few forward leaps and he mumbled mostly to himself, "I'm going to have to build her a prosthetic leg."

"The two new girls have been great," Barbara offered, bringing him out of his head and back to the kitchen. "They haven't left Rachel's side except to go to the bathroom and they've done everything I asked them to do to assist me."

As if to refute this statement, the basement door swung suddenly inward and Eden and Elizabeth stepped into their midst.

"Good morning!" said Paxton and Elizabeth in unison before the sisters strode across the kitchen floor to embrace him warmly, one hanging upon on each of his shoulders. Elizabeth smiled demurely at Barbara and Jazelle, but Eden didn't look up from her bare feet, a palpable sadness swirling about her being.

"Paxton, you are on fire!" Barbara teased him some more, unperturbed by Eden's melancholy.

"No, it's not like that," he defended himself.

"I know," she admitted, handing the two girls their hemp tea. "They told me all about it in the wee hours of the morning as we fixed that poor girl's leg. What are the odds?"

"Very slim," Paxton answered, "which is why this cannot be mere coincidence. We were reunited for a purpose."

"And what purpose is that?" asked Barbara.

"I'm going to wait and tell everybody at breakfast," he answered, "and that includes you. What's for breakfast?"

"Your guess is as good as mine," she answered. "I'm on clean-up duty this week."

"I think Rachel would like to join us for breakfast," interjected Eden.

"Really?" asked Barbara skeptically.

"She's doing so much better," Elizabeth agreed. "She'll need some help getting up the stairs, though."

"I'll grab Bill," Paxton announced, disentangling himself from the girls.

"Better get someone else," Barbara instructed. "Bill's ankle is still pretty swollen."

"I'll help you," Elizabeth offered.

"Alright," Paxton agreed. "Let me dump my mug first."

He helped Eden into a nearby chair and then told Elizabeth he'd be right back. Paxton then proceeded to walk to the other end of the kitchen to greet the breakfast crew as he peered into pots and pans and eventually made his way to the sink to deposit his now empty coffee mug into the standing water there. He and Elizabeth then disappeared through the basement door.

They returned a few minutes later, carrying Rachel awkwardly up the stairs. Elizabeth came up backwards with her hands in Rachel's armpits and Paxton followed below her with his hands under her buttocks and her legs straddling his waist. She was wearing a pair of jeans cut on one side to expose her freshly bandaged leg.

Wallace had been sent to ring the bell for breakfast and the loud tones reverberated through the small farmhouse. No one slept in on Maggie's Farm, regardless of one's chores for the week. Early morning was the coolest part of the day. If you didn't get your chores done first thing in the morning, you would be sweating your ass off doing them in the godawful heat of the day.

After getting Rachel seated somewhere in the middle of the long table, Paxton took his customary seat at its head and waited for everyone else to arrive. He gestured for Elizabeth and Eden to sit on one side of him, but had to correct Eden when she tried to take Jazelle's usual spot on his right. It was only a matter of minutes before the whole commune was seated around the table and waiting expectantly for Paxton to say the blessing.

"Dear All," he began, "Thank you for this food, thank you for this farm, and thank you for this new day."

There was a scattering of "Amen" from the assembly and a few people made the sign of the cross before Richie and a young woman with a crewcut got up and began to walk around the table with a big pot. Richie held the pot while the woman ladled out large dollops of what turned out to be oatmeal with some diced asparagus in it.

When most everybody had been given their portion, Paxton looked up from his oatmeal long enough to say, "Why don't we start by introducing ourselves? I am Paxton, the oldest and most sensible person on Maggie's Farm."

"Sensible, huh?" Barbara jibed him. "Like putting up that windmill so far from the house, because the wind was better on that hill? There was nothing left but the foundation in three days' time!"

"Mostly sensible," he conceded, chuckling. "This is Eden and Elizabeth and before you all start gossiping and wondering, I knew them on the outside. Or at least I knew their parents, a long time ago."

"I'm Elizabeth," she said, raising up her hand as high as her cheek. "My sister, Eden, and I come from Buenos Aires, Argentina."

Eden raised her hand but did not say anything, for the moment. They proceeded around the table one by one, some more loquacious than others.

"I'm Abraham," he said, "from Los Angeles. I was thrown in here because I was hiding my Mexican friends from the Republic. I had a wife and two children. I don't know what became of them."

"How old were the kids, hon?" asked Rachel, and all eyes turned toward the other side of the table where she was seated just like everybody else.

"Tamara was six and Jason three," he said, and their eyes bounced back to Abraham.

"They'd be wards of the Republic," Rachel said with a mouthful of oatmeal. "They're young enough that they might be trained as soldiers."

When all eyes ping-ponged back to her she put her bowl down, wiped her mouth with a cloth napkin and said, "My name is Rachel Martin, wife of Senator Edward Martin from California. I was put in here for being a liberal. I'm sure that my husband is dead and I can only pray that my two girls are wards of the State and not the alternative. I'd get up and shake your hands, but you know."

They all looked down at their soup bowls, not sure of what to say next. Bill soon broke the silence, hobbling back from the sink with a pitcher of water. He set the pitcher upon the table and knelt down next to her, grimacing at the pain it caused his hurt ankle to do so. Taking her hand in his he said, "My name is Bill. I'm one of the ones that found ya."

"Thank you, Bill, and all of you," she said sincerely, looking around the table at them. "I lost my home and my family and half of my leg and I will never be the same, but you all saved my life."

"You got Elizabeth to thank for that, girl" Jazelle spoke up. "I'm Jazelle."

"The Enforcer," Richie added in an ominous tone of voice to a few accompanying chuckles. He then looked over to Rachel and said, "Richie."

"Chuck."

"Carson."

"Wallace," a bespectacled and balding middle-aged man said from right next to Rachel and offered his hand to shake. "I was an analyst, for the National Security Agency, for the Republic. I stumbled across something I wasn't supposed to see, something that should have been buried a lot deeper than it was. I'm lucky to still be alive."

"Aren't we all?" asked Barbara. "Rachel and I are already well-acquainted. I'm the one that stitched you up. Barbara Sullivan."

"My name's Marty," said a man who looked older than Paxton. "I've seen too many winters, but I'll not see another one!"

"None of us will, Marty," said Carson, throwing his napkin at the old man.

The two women who had been whispering to each other during this entire exchange, now looked up at the lull in conversation only to realize that all eyes were on them.

"I'm Jillian," said the younger woman who had helped Richie cook this morning's breakfast.

"And I'm Grace," said the middle-aged woman next to her, completing the circle. "I hail from the once lovely state of Nebraska and I had the weirdest dream last night!"

There were groans from around the table and Paxton explained to the newcomers, "Grace is always having strange dreams. She's our resident storyteller."

"I'd like to hear your dream," said Elizabeth, followed by another chorus of groans.

"Last night I dreamed I was seated around a campfire. Jillian was there too, and Paxton and Jazelle and the Newts. And there was an ancient Indian man, American Indian, seated just like the rest of us. He was speaking in a different language, but I could understand him perfectly, in my dream. Only now, that I'm fully awake, I can't remember a word of it. It was something like an invitation, to come and see him."

"I had the same dream!" said Abraham, looking across the table at her.

"Me too!" said several others around the table.

Paxton looked meaningfully at Jazelle and whispered, "That settles it. We need to go talk to Jonas."

He listened to them talk amongst themselves about the similarities in their dreams for a few minutes. It seemed that half of them had dreamed something akin to Grace's dream, including Paxton, though he was not forthcoming to the group about his own dream. Instead, he changed the subject asking, "What went down on the farm while we were away? Anything I should know about?"

"The water table is still dangerously low," Wallace commented. "We could use some rain."

"What else is new?" asked Paxton, but it was more a referendum on the status of their water supply than an actual question.

"The tomato blight is getting worse," said Grace. "I've been harvesting the green ones before they go rotten and trying to ripen them on the kitchen counters."

"Jazelle and I need to go to the Rockin' M today," Paxton finally announced, but decided immediately to cover up his real motivation for going. They would cross that bridge when they came to it. "We have to report in to Jonas and see what he wants for a tribute."

"Probably take the horse," predicted Chuck.

"And a Newt," added Richie.

"There's no use speculating," said Paxton. "We'll know what it is soon enough. Perhaps some of you can give the Newts a tour of Maggie's Farm before it gets too hot. We're going to need to put them into the work rotation right away."

"It's already too god-damned hot!" said Chuck.

"I can show them around," said Jillian.

"Me too," added Grace from beside her.

"While we're away," Paxton continued, "I would love it if you Newts could take some time to write in the Book."

Paxton pushed his chair back and reached behind him to a small shelf beneath a window with its shades drawn against the already oppressive sun. He pulled an overstuffed three-ring binder from the lowest shelf and caught the heavy tome with his other hand as he turned back to the table. He plopped the book down in front of him with a loud thud.

"We call this simply the Book," he began to explain to the initiates, "and it contains the personal histories of everyone you have met around this table. It's sort of a pet project of mine and I would really appreciate it if the four of you would add your own stories to the Book."

"To what purpose?" asked Abraham.

"So that we don't let those fuckers wipe us off the face of the Earth!" Paxton exclaimed excitedly. "We'll show up in their history books only as criminals sent to the Square. I think we deserve better than that. I don't know who might read the Book, or when, but I want someone, anyone, to know that we lived and to hear the injustices heaped upon us by the bastards who usurped the American Dream and turned it into a Republican nightmare!"

"Let me see that," demanded Rachel, and Paxton shuttled it across the table to her. She began to flip through the pages of hand-written words before asking, "Is it okay to read what's already been written? Is any of it secret?"

"Yes, it's okay, and no, it's not secret," answered Paxton. "You can read any of it you want, and it'll serve to introduce you to the rest of the gang here on Maggie's Farm. If you are lucky enough, or unlucky enough, to survive for any length of time in this place you will have ample opportunity to read at your leisure, but first I want to make sure I get your stories, all four of you, just in case we become separated by circumstances beyond our control."

"Circumstances beyond our control?" asked Rachel, looking up from the Book.

"He's talkin' 'bout dyin', girl," explained Jazelle. "Your life expectancy just got a hell of a lot shorter when you got yourself thrown into this pit!"

"We need to get a move on," Paxton said to Jazelle, putting a hand on her arm as if trying to dissuade her from elaborating upon her last admonition. Pushing himself and his chair backward he stood up.

"I want to go with you to talk to this Jonas," said Elizabeth suddenly. The others had already taken Paxton's lead and were rising from the table. Marty and Grace began to clear the dishes and put them in neat stacks in the sink to be washed.

"Out of the question," was Paxton's immediate response, as Jazelle looked on with interest.

"If Lizzie's going, then I'm going too!" Eden chimed in. They were the first words she had spoken since coming up from the cellar. Paxton sat back down and reached across the corner of the table to take each of the girls' hands in his own.

"I don't want either one of you anywhere near Jonas," he began, intending to educate them on the finer points of Megiddan law. "As our landlord …"

"Evil overlord," Jazelle cut into his explanation.

"As our landlord," Paxton repeated, "Jonas is owed rent and that can take many forms in here. Essentially, he takes half of everything good that comes our way."

"That means he'll want two of us," calculated Abraham, listening intently.

"Maybe," Paxton mused, "but I'm going to argue that there are really only three and a half of you. No offense, Rachel."

"None taken," she said absentmindedly, looking up briefly from the book. "Can someone get me a pen?"

"That still means he'll want one of us," Abraham persisted.

"Unless I can get him to take the horse instead," Paxton countered.

"It's more'n likely he'll take the horse, as well as a Newt, or even two!" Jazelle said sullenly. "And there's not a damned thing we can do about it."

"It should be me," Elizabeth reiterated. "If he's going to claim one of us, it should be me."

"What are you talking about, Beth?" Paxton asked.

"I dreamed of Mukwooru last night, too!" she answered.

"Moo-war-who?" asked Jazelle.

"The old Indian man," she explained. "Like the others, I could understand him perfectly even though he was speaking in his native tongue. He told me that Jonas would know where to find him. He told me that I was the only one who could get that information from him."

"It's too dangerous," Paxton objected.

"You don't want to ignore Lizzie's dreams," advised Eden. "Something bad will happen. And you need to take me with you. Lizzie and I haven't been apart in more than a year."

"No!" Paxton and Elizabeth spoke in unison for the second time that morning.

"I'm not letting Jonas sink his claws into you, Eden!" Paxton continued. "You're staying right here on the farm."

"Did you even dream of the old Indian last night?" asked Elizabeth.

"I can't remember," hedged Eden. "Maybe."

"You would remember," Elizabeth informed her and then looked back to Paxton. "What about you, Uncle Paxton? You never said what you dreamed about last night."

"I dreamed of the old man, too, but it was different," he began. "We weren't around a campfire but underground, in some vast cavern. Both of you girls were there, and someone else I didn't recognize. We were walking deeper and deeper into the cave and I could feel the sadness, like we were on a funeral procession. I don't remember how it ended."

"Sorry, sis," Elizabeth said. "You didn't dream of Mukwooru, you don't get to come."

"That's ridiculous!" countered Eden. "I'm a grown woman. I'll do what I want."

"You'll stay here, fool!" Jazelle interjected. Putting both hands on the table so she could glare down at Eden. "We're not gonna parade you Newts out in front of old Jonas like some damned smorgasbord."

"You're going to have to sit this one out, Eden," said Elizabeth, rising from the table. "You gotta trust me on this one."

The two sisters disentangled their hands from Paxton's and threw their arms around each other in a short but fierce embrace before Elizabeth turned back to Paxton and asked, "When do we leave?"

Paxton looked at Jazelle, who just shrugged her shoulders at him noncommittally. Turning back to Elizabeth he said, "Immediately. I hope you know how to ride a bicycle!"

CHAPTER 7

JONAS

I was fucked over by my own government. After all I did to keep those sons-of-whores in power all those years, they were gonna take my land. Eminent Domain my ass. This land has been in my family for five generations. James McDonough was amongst the first American settlers in the great state of Texas in 1821. His cousin, John McGregor, was killed at the Alamo.

We McDonoughs have raised cattle on this land ever since, just north of Van Horn, Texas. The ranch had grown to more than 100,000 acres by the turn of the millennium. Those bastards said they would pay me for it, fair market value, determined by them of course. As if any amount of money could ever compensate me for the loss of my land.

Where could I even begin to start over again? They were never going to be able to relocate all of us to comparable ranches elsewhere. They talked about shrinking the National Parks. They had already shrunk the National Monuments as small as they dared, got rid of a bunch of them completely. They must've taken the Parks, too, where else could they find the land, they needed to give the landowners that took the deal? They talked about pushing around the Indians again, but everybody knows the Indians already got the most godforsaken lands available to man or beast.

"Keep Texas Republican!" they said, and I believed 'em. I bought it hook line and sinker for years and years. I gave millions to their campaign funds. Cheered 'em on as they forced out the Democrats and prosecuted the Liberals. We took complete control of the country. It felt like we had really accomplished something, like we had finally arrived, until we were no longer in the "we."

"Lock them up!" they said of the protesters, and they arrested so many of them that they had to start repurposing government buildings as jails. Too many for the courts to try them all. We believed 'em when they told us they were all domestic terrorists and weren't afforded the same rights as the rest of us law-abiding citizens of the Republic. I was glad to see 'em all go to prison, until the prison became my home and my land. Now I've got a bunch of them liberal types working for me here on the ranch and they ain't no better or worse than any of the other god-forsaken souls in this place. Everyone in here's just trying to survive, one day at a time.

All of those damned slogans, all of those long years. I wore the hats, posted the signs and repeated them ad nauseam at Millie's dinner parties. "We gotta save those babies!" we said. "Homosexuality is a sin! Protect our borders! Build a wall!"

Then they built that god-damned wall around me and mine. It's all still mine, as long as I can keep it, and I can still draw breath. After that it'll go to Bobbie, if he can still draw breath. He's the only boy I got left, now. Dougie got himself shot at the Intake and the other two took the deal. Not that I can blame them, they had their wives and children to consider, but that didn't stop Dougie from stickin' with me. His wife up and left him and took the kids, too, but they got nothin' for their capitulation. Dougie wouldn't cede over any of his land to them so that they could sell it to those jackasses.

Jackie and Charlie sold off what land they had been given as their birthright, not that it matters much, it all still belongs to me in here, whatever the Mexicans haven't already encroached upon. The Republic doesn't much concern itself with us anymore, except to put more bodies in here every Friday at the Intake.

I haven't heard from my sons since they left. I have no idea where they are or what they're doing outside these walls. I offered them both my blessing the day they joined the long caravan headed toward the newly constructed gates in El Paso. I watched them drive away with a mixture of sadness and rage, but the rage wasn't directed at them or their families. I hold them no ill-will to this day, though I do still miss 'em a bunch, especially my grandchildren.

We weren't the only ones that decided to stay. The Harrisons to the West of us and most of the Wilcox family to the North stayed put. We're all allies now, for the most part, 'cept for a squabble here or there. United against the Mexicans, for now. Most of the other riff-raff know better than to mess with us, and the cannibals don't come in this far from the Wall as a rule, though they're becoming more brazen as well.

The Mexicans were content to live and let live for a long time, until they realized they outnumber us two to one. Now they taunt us at every opportunity, lookin' for an excuse to start a war. Who knows what kind of fire power they got comin' in from over the Wall? I'm not at all sure we're going to be able to defend ourselves, but we most certainly will defend ourselves. Those smug fucking Congressmen didn't take away our guns, and we Texans know how to use 'em. The Rockin' M may be our Alamo, but we're gonna take just as many of those Mexican bastards down to hell with us when we go.

THE RANCH

The four of them sat at one end of a large mahogany table in what must have been the formal dining room of the house back in the day. Jonas sat at the head of the table and Paxton, Jazelle and Elizabeth sat in that order in a line at his right side. Jazelle had been replaced by a younger girl, also African-American, who served them coffee and cookies before retreating back into the kitchen.

"Frannie's nowhere near as good as you were, Jazelle," Jonas said with a mouthful of cookie crumbs. "You sure you don't want to come back here to the ranch?"

"I'm happy right where I am, thank-you just the same" she offered, grasping Paxton's hand in hers and looking meaningfully at him before returning Jonas' gaze.

"How's the farm doin'?" the old man asked Paxton. "Your latest shipment of vegetables was a little light."

"We sent up everything we could afford to give you," Paxton answered. "The tomatoes all have dry rot and we've been having a hell of a time keeping the Japanese beetles off everything else! Every year there's more of them!"

"Used to be the only insects we needed to worry about were the cicadas every seven years," coughed Jonas in a gravelly voice before spitting some phlegm into his napkin. "Now we got every plague imaginable we gotta contend with. Is there anything I can do to help?"

"Not with that," said Paxton, "not unless you want to give me some more bodies to help pick 'em off the crops."

"How many Newts'd you get at the Intake," questioned Jonas. "Carl told me he saw you there."

"We got three women and a man," admitted Paxton reluctantly, knowing that Jonas would demand a tribute. "The Mexicans took one of their own on the way home. We were lucky to escape from them unscathed."

He deliberately left out the part about the cannibals and the horse and the fact that the lost Mexican had been replaced by a half-legged woman. It was a lie of omission, but he felt sure Jonas would find out for himself in the due course of time.

"The god-damned Mexicans grow braver with every passing day," spat Jonas excitedly. "They've been stealing cattle again. Bobbie got shot up pretty bad night before last trying to stop 'em."

"Not Bobbie, too?" Paxton asked sympathetically. "Is he gonna be okay?"

"Too soon to tell," answered the old man. "He was gut-shot pretty close-up with a shotgun. Carl's still trying to get it all out of him. He's a tough son-of-a-bitch, though, he'll pull through. Then he's gonna want to go after those greasy mother-fuckers. I'm afraid it's going to come to an all-out war this time, before it's all said and done. I need to know I can count on you, when the time comes."

"We're farmers not fighters," argued Paxton. "We've only got a few guns between us."

"You're not going to have the luxury of that distinction once we're overrun with Mexicans. Don't you worry about the guns. We've got a stockpile here at the ranch. We'll be ready for 'em when they come."

"They're coming tonight," Elizabeth broke into the conversation, looking distractedly at a landscape painting on the wall with a far-off expression on her face. "I dreamed it last night. There were five or six of them, huddled around some sort of a pump."

"A water pump?" asked Paxton.

"It was bigger than a water pump," answered Elizabeth. "It looked like a giant bird dipping its head down and back up over and over again."

"An oil derrick!" Paxton and Jonas said together.

"They put something explosive on it and ran for cover," Elizabeth continued. "The flames shot a hundred feet into the air!"

"Who is this?" asked Jonas, eying her suspiciously.

"This is Elizabeth," Paxton offered, "one of the Newts we picked up the other day."

"Has she been initiated?" asked Jonas, involuntarily running his tongue across his lower lip.

"They all've been," Jazelle lied to him and then bit her tongue when Paxton squeezed her hand in warning.

"She gets these premonitions," offered Paxton, and then looking directly at Elizabeth he continued under his breath, "*at the worst possible times*!"

"How do you know it's going to be tonight, sweetie?" asked Jonas.

"It's a full moon tonight, isn't it?" asked Elizabeth. "It was almost full last night. In my dream I could see the full moon low on the horizon, before the explosion."

"And what makes this a *premonition* instead of just any old dream?" he pressed her.

"I can tell the difference," answered Elizabeth matter-of-factly.

"She's been right about other things," Paxton interjected, coming to her defense. "She saw a woman on a horse, in the middle of nowhere, on our way back to the farm. We waited for over an hour at the spot Beth recognized, and sure enough this half-dead, half-*eaten* by cannibals, woman comes strolling into our midst on the back of a half-dead horse."

Paxton had not intended to mention the horse, but now that he had let it slip, he did his best to down-play its significance lest Jonas claim it as tribute. The horse would definitely come in handy on the farm, once it was fed and watered back to good health.

"Surely you did not come all of this way to warn me of a sabotaged oil-well," opined Jonas. "What is it you want, Paxton?"

"There will be a much bigger explosion!" interrupted Elizabeth before Paxton could answer. "It will be big enough to obliterate us all!"

"What is she talking about?" asked Jonas.

"That's why we're here," offered Paxton. "Elizabeth has been dreaming of a nuclear explosion, here in Megiddo. We want to go and talk with the Comanche, to find out more about the prophecy, to see if there is anything that can be done. These things that Elizabeth sees are not set in stone, they can be altered. Perhaps there is a way we can save ourselves."

Jonas sat silent for a long time before responding, "Such a thing is not possible. Let's say that I believe you, with absolutely no proof at all, and I'm not saying that I do. The Comanche was ancient when I made the journey to meet with him, and that was nearly a decade ago. There's no way he's still alive. You'd be going on a wild goose chase, and a dangerous one at that!"

"We're willing to take that chance," Paxton responded. "If he *is* still alive, perhaps he can help us find some way out of this."

"If what you say is true," surmised Jonas, "then there is already someone in Megiddo who hasn't been initiated, the virgin from his prophecy."

"I don't know anything about that," lied Paxton, "but the Square is a big place. It's certainly possible that a virgin Newt escaped everyone's notice on one of the bigger Intake Days. He or she could be hiding out somewhere in Megiddo."

"Tell you what I'll do," said Jonas, stroking the white whiskers at his chin. "Let's see if there's anything to this oil-rig explosion tonight. If what she says is true, I'll tell you where to find the Comanche. Hell, I'll even send you with provisions and some of my boys to protect you. If she's wrong, and nothing out-of-the-ordinary happens tonight, I'm going to have to ask myself what the hell you're up to and what is the real reason you want to see the Comanche after all of these years."

"It doesn't have to be tonight," Paxton backtracked Beth's prediction. "She merely saw the full moon. It could be next month, or the month after that."

"It will be tonight," Elizabeth interjected, "but I can't tell you if it's dusk or dawn because I don't know which direction I was facing."

"What else did you see?" questioned Jonas.

"Nothing," answered Elizabeth. "There were no other distinguishing features. It was absolutely flat."

"That would be the derrick south of the corral, then. We only got a few of them up and running but that rig's out there in the middle of nowhere. It makes sense that they would target that one. It's farthest from the house and closest to their land."

"Frannie, get your ass in here!" he barked loudly and without warning. She was at his side in a few moments and immediately began to clear the table.

"Never mind that," he chastised her without even looking up. "Get Carl in here pronto. I need to talk to him."

The girl scurried off in the direction of the double French doors at the other end of the table and there was a moment of silence in the room after she had gone. Paxton took a sip of his tea, his eyes never leaving Jonas' countenance.

"What are you going to do?" he finally asked when it appeared as though Jonas would never break their silence.

"I'm going to have a surprise waiting for those *pendejos*!" he answered. "That is, if they show up at all. You're all welcome to spend the night here, of course. You can have your old room, Paxton. No one has been in there since you left. I assume Jazelle will sleep with you. As for this little lady over here, she can stay with me."

"What...?" Paxton stammered, looking meaningfully over at Elizabeth.

"Let's just say that she and I need to become better acquainted," he winked at Paxton. "I have a lot more questions for her and to be safe, I think I need to make sure that she's been properly initiated."

Paxton started to object but Elizabeth beat him to the punch saying, "I'd be delighted to make your acquaintance, Jonas."

Paxton looked at her sharply but she just smiled back at him warmly and then stood up and took the few steps to where Jonas was sitting. She grabbed his hand and held it in her own, standing a little behind and to his left side.

"Might I get cleaned up first?" she asked him sweetly. "I can't remember the last time I had a bath."

Jonas sent Carl and five others, all heavily-armed, to the only oil-derrick south of the main house. Jazelle, Elizabeth and Paxton ate dinner with Jonas while they awaited either the return of the men or a huge explosion signaling the demise of the derrick. None were forthcoming until well after dessert. Paxton and Jonas sat smoking cigars and chatting up the ladies when a lone rider returned with news akin to, "It's all quiet on the Southern front!"

Jonas was determined to see his defenses through until after the moonset in the morning and he sent the rider back to Carl with instructions to that effect. Shortly thereafter, he and Elizabeth took their leave, walking slowly arm-in-arm toward the old man's bedroom. Elizabeth seemed completely at peace with her role in all of this and she had been waving-off or completely ignoring Paxton's ugly glares all evening as she laughed at all of Jonas' jokes.

Paxton and Jazelle each took another shot of the old man's liquor, which tasted vaguely of tequila and not too badly either, before heading upstairs to the room Paxton had occupied for most of his first year in the Square. They had made love for the first time on the four-poster bed, which still dominated a dustier and more disheveled room than he remembered. He reminded Jazelle of this as they fell down heavily next to each other on the soft feather-mattress, his arm draped upon her hip.

"Don't get any ideas, mister man," Jazelle chided him, playfully punching him in the chest. "We gotta figure some things out."

"What's to figure out?" he asked, gently stroking a stray strand of her hair up and off her temple. "Nothing's gonna happen until morning. Let's hope that Beth is right about this raid, otherwise we'll be in trouble with Jonas."

"We've gotta figure out what we're gonna do if she's wrong and nothing happens out there," Jazelle responded, "and we've gotta figure out what we're gonna do if she's right."

"We're going to go and see the Comanche if she's right," Paxton assured her, "and with Jonas' blessing."

"His blessing and his boys to keep an eye on us," Jazelle pointed out. "You're gonna have to be careful what you say to the Comanche in front of 'em. But we got more pressing problems than that if she's right. If Jonas' boys get the drop on the Mexicans, don't matter if they kill or capture 'em, it's gonna be war with the Mexicans. You're crazy if you think you can be Switzerland!"

"We'll cross that bridge when we come to it," said Paxton. "Depending upon what we find out from the Comanche, we may have other fish to fry."

"What do you mean by that?" she pressed him, with her words and her body, snuggling a little closer into him and touching his cheek tenderly with her open palm.

"If Eden is the next Messiah, as I was told by Thorn all those years ago," reasoned Paxton, "then isn't it our duty to do everything we can to make sure she fulfills her purpose on Earth? What could we possibly do in the Square that would be more meaningful than that?"

"If she *is* the Messiah," Jazelle shot back, a sarcastic tone to her voice, "then she don't need our help. What can mere mortals accomplish that can't be done easier and better by God?"

"Either way," said Paxton, kissing her on the lips, "this is probably our last night in a comfortable bed for the foreseeable future."

"Then let's take advantage of it," she responded. Jazelle immediately flipped over onto her other side and pushed her back up against his chest and he enfolded her in his warm embrace. Any misconceptions he may have had for the rest of their evening were soon dispelled when she continued, "Spoon me to sleep, stud."

He kissed her neck and whispered in her ear, "I love you."

"I love you, too, sweetie," she responded. They were both sound asleep within the next five minutes.

They were awoken before daylight by the distinctive popping sound of gunshots in the distance. More than a hundred rounds were fired before the dawn silence was restored. Neither Paxton nor Jazelle could get back to sleep so they rousted themselves from the comfortable feather bed, got dressed and joined Jonas and Elizabeth, who were already drinking coffee at the big dining table.

"Good morning," Paxton said as he plopped down into the chair next to Elizabeth. "Any word yet?"

"Not yet," said Jonas, "but it won't be long, now, assuming we came out on top."

Not ten minutes passed before a couple of trucks pulled up in front of the house and their boisterous passengers emerged. Jazelle had gone to the window to see what was happening but the other three sat at the table awaiting news of the morning's events. The front door opened and they heard the loud footfalls of Carl Johnson's cowboy boots on the hardwood floor, complete with jingling spurs. He came into the room in a hurry but then stopped and took his hat off apologetically when he caught sight of the ladies.

"It was just as she said, Boss," Carl began his report, after nodding his hello to their assemblage. "Six Mexicans and enough dynamite to blow up five oil rigs! We were ready for 'em, though, been sittin' up all night. We shot 'em all to hell and back, got a couple nice rifles and a truck full of dynamite!"

"Did any of our boys get hurt?" asked Jonas.

"George took a slug in the shoulder, but he'll be alright," Carl answered. "They didn't even know what hit 'em, the sorry bastards, they didn't stand a chance. We brought one of 'em back still breathing, but I can't say for how long. You wanna talk to 'im?"

"In a minute," Jonas answered. "We've got some unfinished business to conduct here, first. String him up!"

"Sure thing, Boss!"

"Nice work, Carl," praised Jonas. "Make sure that the boys get extra rations this morning, both food and drink!"

"Thanks, Boss!" said Carl enthusiastically. He put his cowboy hat back upon his head and tipped it to them all before turning to leave.

Jonas reached over and took Elizabeth's hand in his exclaiming, "Your gifts are gonna come in mighty handy, little darlin'."

"Beth was right about the Mexicans," stated Paxton. "She saved your oil rig. Now it's time for you to hold up your end of the bargain. Just point us in the right direction and we'll be on our way."

"This little lady ain't going anywhere," Jonas said, lifting up their clasped hands a foot off the table before returning them to their resting positions. "She's much too valuable to send off on your wild goose chase."

"But you promised," Paxton began before being interrupted by Jonas.

"I promised nothing of the kind," Jonas stated flatly. "I said I would tell you where to find him and give you an escort. I never said all three of you could go. I'm keeping this one. We'll consider her your tribute and call it even."

"I have a much better tribute for you back on the farm," Paxton said hurriedly, his desperation making his voice crack. "A strapping young man, perfect for manual labor or a champion for the games."

Jazelle looked sharply at him, but Paxton's eyes never left Jonas' face. "Elizabeth is like family to me. She's the daughter of a long-lost friend."

"Why didn't you tell me this before?" asked Jonas, but he did not give Paxton time enough to answer. "Never mind, it doesn't matter. She's staying with me, and you need not worry about her safety. If she can replicate tonight's foresight, she's much too valuable to me to be tossed in with the other Newts. She'll bunk right here in the house and I won't let anyone touch her. Anyone but me, that is."

Jonas said this last with a wink at Elizabeth and she dropped her eyes demurely before looking up at Paxton, saying, "I'll be okay, Uncle Paxton."

"*Uncle* Paxton?" asked Jonas, raising his eyebrows.

"I'm not her real uncle," Paxton explained. "It's just what they call me."

"*They*?" Jonas continued to interrogate him as Paxton realized his mistake.

"Beth and her brothers and sisters," Paxton lied. "I was really good friends with their father."

"It's settled, then," Jonas declared. "Now go get my map of the Square from the living room."

Paxton found the open map of Texas on a small table next to a bay window overlooking what used to be the front lawn, back when it was possible to keep the grass well-watered and green. He looked out of the window as he was rolling up the map.

There was a bustle of activity around the two trucks. Two men were unloading bundles of dynamite from the bed of a beat-up Toyota Tacoma while another two were wiping blood stains off the Toyota as well as a slightly less beat-up Dodge Ram. A burly man with a thick black beard waved to Paxton when he noticed him in the window but Paxton didn't immediately recognize him. Nevertheless, he raised his hand in greeting as well.

In the brown grass at the center of the U-shaped driveway a man was tied by his wrists to two thick wooden poles mounted into the ground about six feet apart. His back was to Paxton but based on the thick crop of black hair upon the man's head and the dark skin of his arms, not to mention all of the blood dripping from his body and pooling in the dust beneath him, Paxton surmised he must be the captured Mexican. Although it would have been possible for the man to stand between the poles, he was slumped and dangling by the tethers at his wrists, his feet bent unnaturally beneath him and his head lolling upon his shoulder. Paxton did not give the man much of a chance of seeing another sunrise.

Returning to the dining room with the map, Paxton spread it out upon the table in front of Jonas. The boundaries of the Wall were clearly marked in black Sharpie pen, as were the boundaries of the ranches belonging to the landowners who had refused to leave when the Wall was completed. South of the southernmost ranch, two words were scrawled in capital letters with the same black Sharpie, 'THE MEXICANS.'

Jonas reached for his glasses and as he adjusted them upon his crooked nose, Jazelle got up from her seat to join Paxton behind Jonas where they could both examine the map over his shoulders. Elizabeth craned her neck to see better from her seat at Jonas' side.

"We're here," he pointed with his arthritic index finger at a large ranch labeled with a capital M on a semi-circle. Using his other index finger, he pointed to a dark green oval on the map nestled right up against the straight line that formed the northern border of the Square. "The Comanche is up here, in the Guadalupe Mountains."

"The National Park?" asked Paxton.

"It's not a National Park anymore," corrected Jonas.

"Damned straight!" Jazelle exclaimed when she saw how far they would need to travel on this fool's errand. "This is crazy, Paxton! We'd never make it there and back in one piece!"

"You will make it, there at least," Elizabeth contradicted her. "I saw you and Paxton and Eden, talking to the Comanche, last night in a dream."

"Yes, they say it is Eden, or as close as we're going to come in here," said Jonas, mistaking Elizabeth's words even as Paxton shot her a warning glance from behind the old man. "From what I hear, the Indians have taken over the whole place. Not even the cannibals will go there."

"Yeah, and anyone who goes there never returns," said Jazelle. "We've all heard the legends."

"Can you give us a better idea where to look?" asked Paxton. "That's a lot of ground to cover."

"He was here ten years ago," Jonas pointed to a thin blue line between mountain ranges, "in Pine Spring Canyon, but that ain't gonna do you much good. They were all living in teepees and the whole camp was mobile. You won't find him if he don't want to be found."

"Then I guess we're just going to have to trust in Beth's dreams and hope for the best," asserted Paxton. "You mentioned something about sending us on our way with some manpower and provisions?"

"I can't spare you much," Jonas back-tracked upon his earlier promise. "I'm gonna have a war on my hands within a fortnight. There's no avoiding it, now. I can't spare one of the trucks. I'd loan you a couple of horses but they won't do you no good in that country. There's no food and no water to be had unless you know where to find it."

"How about a dirt bike?" pressed Paxton. "It'll be loud but it'll get us in and out of there in a hurry. Jazelle and I can share one."

Jonas stroked his chin deep in thought for a moment before answering, "Here's what I'm gonna do. You can take two of the motorcycles, and enough gas to get you there and back. I'm gonna send Frank with you. I can't spare anybody else. You can each have a rifle; the boys took a couple of extras from the Mexicans this morning."

"That's more than generous, Jonas," said Paxton.

"If I were you," Jonas continued, "I'd hightail it right from here to there without stoppin' for nothin'. If you're lucky, the cannibals still give the Indians a wide berth, but that don't mean the Indians aren't gonna shoot you on sight when you get there. If you by some miracle survive this quest, I want you to come straight back here to the ranch and give me a full report."

"Deal," said Paxton, shaking the old man's wrinkled hand. "We need to head back to Maggie's Farm first, though. We gotta pick up a few things and give the rest of them some instructions in our absence."

"You'd better *instruct* them to come on in to the ranch," Jonas advised. "It won't be long before all hell break's loose and I won't be able to protect them when it does. We can use all the help we can get right here."

"I'll tell them," Paxton promised. "Now where is that pump you wanted me to take a look at? I'll tackle that while Jazelle and Frank get us packed up and ready to go. Beth, why don't you give me a hand?"

"Toss me a screwdriver, please," Paxton directed Elizabeth. They were alone, for the moment, in a barn that stabled what remained of the Rockin' M's horses. The broken pump sat on a table in one of the unoccupied stalls. "Are you going to be okay here all alone?"

"I'm hardly alone, Uncle Paxton," Elizabeth replied.

"You know what I mean. I hate the thought of leaving you here with that lecherous old fool."

"I can handle Jonas," Elizabeth assured him. "He's become quite enamored of me."

"For the moment," Paxton responded, removing the pump's housing. "What's going to happen when he grows tired of you?"

"He won't grow tired of me in the time it takes for you to return."

"Did you two…" Paxton stammered, unsure how to finish his question, "last night?"

"Yes, we did," Elizabeth answered his unfinished question. "Jonas is a surprisingly gentle and generous lover, even if he didn't last as long as I might have liked."

Paxton immediately regretted having broached the subject and he took renewed interest in the innards of the pump he had been half-heartedly dismantling. He pressed onward without looking up at her, "Try to keep him happy until we return. Jonas is not a bad man, but I've seen him give in to irrational behavior and fits of passion. He's been in here too long. We've all been in here too long."

"You have to take Eden with you, to see the Comanche," instructed Elizabeth, changing the subject. "Something happened to her, in my dream, when she met him. The five of you were seated cross-legged around a ring of stones in a dark cave. There was some kind of steam or mist surrounding everything. Eden jumped up, as if she had just remembered something vitally important. Her astonishment was written all over her face."

"Five of us?" Paxton asked her. "Who did you see around the campfire?"

"You and Jazelle, Eden and Abraham, and the Comanche, of course," Elizabeth answered.

"What about Frank?"

"He wasn't in my dream," she admitted, "not that I remember."

"Well, there's only room for four on two motorcycles," surmised Paxton, "and that's going to be none too comfortable as it is. What's going to become of Frank?"

"I can only tell you what I've seen," said Elizabeth. "You're going to have to figure out the rest on your own."

There was silence between them for a few long moments as Paxton stood staring at the pump, deep in thought. Elizabeth broke into his reverie, asking, "Do you even know what you're doing with this thing?"

"Not at all," Paxton said, and they both burst out laughing. "Jonas thinks because I have a degree in Mathematics that I should be able to problem solve my way out of everything. Given enough time I can usually figure these things out, but time has suddenly become a precious commodity. You and Eden have made me realize how long I've been languishing in here. I guess I thought that this was it for me, the end of my story. You've given my life purpose again."

"When Eden finds out what's happened, she's going to want to come right back here and rescue me, I guarantee it!" said Elizabeth. "You need to convince her to wait a full day. Come back here the day after tomorrow, at dusk. Come from the north. I'll be in the garage, in a pick-up truck. The Mexicans are going to unleash holy hell upon this place at sundown, the day after tomorrow. I fear for the continued existence of the McDonoughs. Tell Eden I said she needs to be patient and heed my words and that I'm going to be just fine until you get back. Promise me, Uncle Paxton."

"Okay," Paxton agreed, "I promise. But we will come back for you, Beth. I'm not leaving you to the McDonoughs, Mexicans or no Mexicans. Are you sure this escape plan of yours will work?"

"As sure as I can ever be about these things. It's what I dreamed would happen," confirmed Elizabeth.

"That's good enough for me," Paxton replied. "We'll be here the day after next, at dusk."

"I have every faith in you, Uncle Paxton," Elizabeth exclaimed, smiling up at him. Paxton could suddenly no longer concentrate on the task at hand and he strode around to the other side of the table to give her a hug. They walked out of the stable hand in hand, apparently unconcerned about leaving the pieces of the torn-apart pump strewn all over the small table in the otherwise empty horse stall.

CHAPTER 8

PAXTON

The New Great Wall of Texas is a massive, concrete and steel barrier stretching nearly two thousand miles from the Gulf of Mexico near Brownsville, Texas all the way to San Diego, California along the Mexican border. It's thirty feet tall and thirty feet wide, with towers every mile. They say there's room for two vehicles to pass each other along the ramparts.

When the Wall was first proposed it was said that Mexico would pay for its construction, either directly or through increased tariffs on Mexican imports or reductions in foreign aid. This plan quickly became untenable and was scrapped in favor of a joint venture between the two countries, with the Republic providing the materials and heavy machinery and Mexico providing the unskilled laborers.

The public sector was no longer privy to such information, but it was speculated that the wall cost more than a trillion dollars, not to mention the lives of thousands of migrant workers, most of them Mexicans. It took more than a decade from start to finish, though the completion time was also hard to estimate because the wall was always in need of maintenance and repair. Shoddy construction, flash floods and tornadoes all took their toll on the Wall, as did the explosions from saboteurs on both sides of the smooth concrete.

Work on the Square began quietly, using the materials and laborers leftover from the Wall. It was months before the public even noticed that the construction equipment in West Texas was still rolling along and the New Great Wall, built to keep the Mexicans from entering the country illegally, had suddenly turned inward into the great state of Texas. Only then was an explanation offered and the plans for the Square revealed.

The idea was met with more than a little opposition, back when such a thing was still possible; back when we still had the remnants of a two-party government and an independent press; back when our government officials were more than nominally elected by the populace.

The Square was not a square at all, but a triangle consisting of two mostly straight lines and the natural meandering border of the Rio Grande River. The northern edge was formed by the border between Texas and New Mexico from El Paso to Kermit. The eastern edge traveled slightly southeast from Kermit to the western edge of Fort Stockton. From there it continued south along Route 385 but eventually left the road for a beeline through the desert to the nearest point along the Rio Grande. Basically, the western boundary line of the Texas panhandle had been extended southward in a mostly straight line to the Mexican border.

There were two gates into the Square, one near the city of El Paso and the other near Fort Stockton. That's the gate I came through. Prisoners from the Western half of the country entered through the West Gate and those from the Eastern half entered through the East Gate. Mexico was allowed to release its undesirables, some guilty of crimes and others guilty only of poverty, into the Square from the West Gate under the strict supervision of the Republican Guard. This arrangement was part of the settlement for the unpaid Mexican laborers who worked on the Wall from its southern side.

No one really knows why they called it the Square. I used to joke that the Republican brain trust that came up with the idea couldn't tell the difference between a triangle and a square. The mathematician in me now shudders at the thought that they have probably bastardized the English language to the point that a triangle is now commonly called a square, but if that's the case, what do they call a square? I suppose they could call it an equilateral rectangle. That is, if they're still teaching math and science in the public schools anymore.

I heard somewhere that they called it the Square because the original design was an almost perfect square straddling the border between Arizona and New Mexico. Both states pushed back on the idea and the terrain was deemed too mountainous, so it was decided to move the facility within the borders of Texas, a state which was willing to cede the government its land in return for several hefty political favors. Once some clever bureaucrat turned it into an acronym there was no going back. The S.Q.U.A.R.E. officially stood for the Sequestration and Quarantine for Undocumented Alien Resident Extradition.

The acronym changed as the justification for the Square evolved during the years it took to construct it, but it was originally proposed as a holding facility for the millions of illegal immigrants in the Republic as they awaited deportation. The majority of the undocumented alien residents were Mexicans, so it only made sense to build the Square on the southern border, making use of the recently completed wall.

The emergence of the plans for the Square was both cheered and jeered in equal measure, as was most every piece of news in those days. The political divide between the Republicans and the Democrats had reached its deepest point and there was no longer any attempt to find common ground. The Republicans eventually found a way to tip the precarious balance in their favor.

It started when the Republicans held both houses of Congress and the Presidency and were able to install a conservative Supreme Court. Congressional Districts were gerrymandered to ensure their majority and procedural rules changed to ensure the Democratic minority had little or no voice in passing or defeating new legislation. Over the ensuing years they set about systematically dismantling the Democratic Party to the point that to be affiliated with any group deemed "liberal" became a 'Squarable offense' in the eyes of the law. They had tolerated dissent, up to a point, at least until the Square was completed.

The Square soon became a part of the vernacular and all manner of new slang erupted around it. People started to say, "Get squared!" instead of "Get lost!" Those inclined to avoid the f-bomb could now say, "You're so squared, man!" Later, when they started putting Americans into the Square, it became common at political rallies for the crowd to yell, "Square the bastard (or bitch)!"

When it was about half-completed the government released the information that the Square was also going to be used as an alternative to the prison system. Rather than maintaining thousands of jails scattered throughout the country, the "worst of the worst" could all be housed in one giant Federal facility with little or no oversight and hence no cost to the state beyond the initial construction costs. A much smaller number of minimum-security facilities would still be necessary for crimes not involving life-sentences, but the burden upon society would be greatly alleviated, especially when they stopped feeding the prisoners.

The S.Q.U.A.R.E. then came to stand for the Sequester and Quarantine of Unlawful Americans and Resident Emigrants. And half the people cheered.

When the environmental collapse began, and more and more people wanted to get into the Republic, laws were hastily enacted to deter any and all immigration. We were largely responsible for what happened with the accumulation and consumption of more than our fair share of the world's resources, and we were going to make damn well sure that no one else was going to share in our good fortune. A new law was passed that anyone caught on American soil without a valid Republican passport would be thrown into the Square.

The S.Q.U.A.R.E. then became the Sequester and Quarantine of Unlawful Americans and Refugee Expatriates. And half the people cheered.

When they started putting prisoners of war in the Square, half the people cheered. Then political prisoners, protesters and liberals were being put into the Square. And still half the people cheered. Finally, the S.Q.U.A.R.E. became known as the Sequester and Quarantine of Undesirables, Aliens, Refugees and Enemies of the State.

And half the people cheered. They cheered and cheered for a decade or more. They cheered until they figured out just how truly fucked, they were, and by then, they were just good and truly fucked.

WAR PLANS

Everyone was already seated upon the living room floor when Paxton and Jazelle entered and moved toward their customary seats beneath a torn reprint of Georgia O'Keefe's *Light of Iris*. There were blankets and cushions and yoga mats spread across and completely covering the floor, but Paxton took his seat in a red bean bag chair that he had claimed early on as necessary for the comfort of his old bones. He and Jazelle sat facing the other ten expectant faces. Marty and Frank were in the garage and Rachel was resting in the infirmary.

No sooner had Paxton settled himself than Barbara, in her customary way of getting right to the point, burst forth with, "What is going on, Paxton? Why is Frank tied up in the garage? Where is the Newt who went with you to the ranch? Where did the motorcycles come from?"

"Hold on," Paxton soothed, sitting up as straight as he could in the bean bag and holding up both arms in a gesture of surrender. He waited for the general murmur of voices to die down before continuing, "I'm going to fill you all in on current events as best I know them and then you can ask all of the questions you want but you have to let me start from the beginning. Agreed?"

There were several begrudging assents from the group, some nodding heads and at least one echoed, "Agreed!"

"I've talked to most of you about my experiences with Thorn, back in Maine a long time ago," Paxton began. "A couple of you have even read the books. You may choose to believe me or not, but I stand by my account as one-hundred percent accurate, at least as far as my point of view is concerned. Some of it I had to piece together as best I could because Claire and Tucker had already skipped town."

"This is Eden," Paxton pointed to her with a flourish, "from the book, or at least she was foretold in the book. She is Claire and Tucker's daughter, and so is Beth, the other woman we brought home with us from the Intake. Beth has been claimed in tribute by Jonas."

"What does that mean?" interrupted Eden.

"It means that she now belongs to him," answered Paxton.

"You mean, like a slave?" pressed Eden.

"Exactly like a slave," Jazelle responded before Paxton could. "But I wager she'll get better treatment than the rest of them lot."

"We have to go save her!" Eden exclaimed, jumping up.

"Beth told me you would say that," confirmed Paxton. "And we will, just as soon as we come up with a plan and figure out exactly how we're going to do it. Elizabeth will be just fine for the moment. Jonas sees her worth as a soothsayer and won't harm her as long as her predictions keep coming true. There was nothing I could do, Eden. Jonas seems quite smitten with her."

"Of course, he is," Eden agreed, sitting back down upon the floor. "Lizzie knows how to get a man. It won't be long before Jonas is enslaved to her!"

"While we were at the Rockin' M," continued Paxton, "Beth correctly predicted a raid on one of Jonas' oil wells and his men were able to stop the Mexicans before they blew it up. I'm pretty sure this will mean war with the Mexicans. Every one of you will have to decide what you want to do about the upcoming conflict because I don't think we get to sit this one out.

"Jonas is expecting us to join him on the ranch and be his foot soldiers. If it comes to all-out war, our farm will no longer be safe, we don't have enough people or firepower here. You can take Jonas up on his offer of *protection,* or you can strike off on your own, but you probably shouldn't stay here. I'm not going to stay here."

"What are you going to do, Paxton?" asked a balding, middle-aged man wearing wire-rimmed glasses with one lens missing.

"Long-term I have no idea," Paxton answered. "In the short-term, Jazelle, Eden and I are going to take the motorcycles Jonas lent us and ride on up to the Guadalupe Mountains in search of the Comanche."

This pronouncement was met with incredulity from the assemblage and a cacophony of half-formed questions:

"What the …?"

"I thought he was dead?"

"The Comanche is real?"

"Why would you…?"

"We went to the Rockin' M to ask Jonas where we could find the Comanche," Paxton voice rose above the general clamor. "He not only pointed us in the right direction but he loaned us the motorcycles you saw us ride up on, and Frank to keep us company, but really to spy on us. I have him tied up now so that we can hold this meeting in confidence, but I have no intention of taking him with us to look for the Comanche."

"Jonas is not going to like this," Barbara stated the obvious.

"No, he is not," Paxton agreed, "but Jonas is going to have his hands full with the Mexicans in short order. Beth thinks an attack is imminent. I don't think Jonas has the firepower to hold back the Mexicans, not if they come at him full-force, but what do I know? Each of you will have to make up his or her own mind where to go from here because either way, I think our little experiment in communal living is coming to an abrupt end."

"Why can't we go with *you*?" asked Barbara. "I don't want to go back to the Rockin' M. I have only bad memories of that place."

There was a general murmur of agreement in the group and Paxton raised his arms to quiet it down. He had expected such a response from them, and he wasn't sure he'd be able to dissuade them of their folly.

"You're all welcome to come with me," he began, "but I'm not going to be able to get the lot of you on two motorcycles and a malnourished horse. We'll need to come up with a travel plan, but you need to think this through before you make your decision. My path is almost certainly more dangerous than taking your chances with the McDonoughs.

"I have no idea what lies between the northern borders of the Rockin' M and the Guadalupe Mountains. We'll probably run out of food and water along the way. We've all heard the legends of that place. No one who's ever gone there has returned, so it might just be a death trap. We'll be in cannibal territory so close to the Wall and if we somehow manage to elude them, I don't expect the Indians are going to welcome us with open arms. If the Comanche is still alive, he could be anywhere in the Park, so we'll need to track him down. And if by some miracle, we overcome all of these obstacles and get an audience with him, I have no idea what path he might set us upon."

"You make it all sound so romantic," Barbara teased him and everyone laughed, relieving the tension in the room momentarily. "Where do I sign up?"

"I just want you to know what you're getting yourselves into if you decide to follow me north," Paxton continued. "It's going to be a dangerous journey."

"More dangerous than fighting a horde of angry Mexicans?" asked Carson. "It's the Alamo all over again."

"Jonas has repelled the Mexicans before," chimed in a thin woman with mousy, brown hair. "What makes this attack any different?"

"It feels different," Paxton answered. "The Mexicans have been looking for an excuse to start an all-out war for a while now. But the most convincing argument to me is that Beth says the Mexicans are going to throw everything they have at the McDonoughs."

The group was silent for half a minute before Bill asked, "Why now, Paxton?"

"Why now? Because the McDonoughs just shot up a half-dozen Mexicans trying to blow up one of their oil rigs!"

"No," Bill corrected him, "why do you need to talk to the Comanche now?"

"This is where it gets strange," Paxton began.

"Really, Paxton?" Barbara interrupted him. "This is where it gets strange?"

"I believe that Eden, here, is the subject of his prophecy!" he proclaimed, pointing at her.

"Eden?" Carson asked in surprise. "I thought you initiated her yourself!"

"We were faking," Paxton admitted, to the astonished gasps of the men who had accompanied him to the Intake. "Eden is still a virgin!"

"What are you playing at?" Barbara asked him. "You've put the whole farm at risk, Paxton!"

"Perhaps I have, and for that I am sorry, but I think Eden is going to put an end to this shithole! Isn't that worth taking a few risks?"

"Why her?" pressed Barbara. "How can you be so sure?"

"It actually goes all the way back to my time with Thorn," Paxton admitted. "Thorn predicted that Eden would be the next Messiah, not just the Savior of Megiddo but a Messiah for the whole world."

"Lizzie has been trying to convince me I'm the Chosen One for years," commented Eden, "behind our parents' backs, of course. They never said a word about any of this. She thought I would somehow feel different after they died, that I'd see the light or something, but the only thing I felt was sadness."

"They probably didn't want you to know," Paxton commented. "They were trying to keep you a secret to keep you safe. That's why they took you to Argentina in the first place."

"Tell us more," demanded Carson, looking at Eden rather than Paxton.

"Yeah," echoed Barbara. "How can we believe that you're the Messiah?"

"I don't believe it myself," Eden began. "I know that I have certain powers. I can read people, not their thoughts exactly but their motivations. I can get people to do what I want them to do. I'm very persuasive that way. I have wished for things or events to go my way and they do, for the most part. Until I left home, I had no idea these traits were rare to nonexistent in most people, but that doesn't make me a Messiah."

"Don't forget how you laid your hands on Rachel and healed her," Paxton mentioned. If Rachel was awake in the basement, she could probably hear the louder outbursts from their assemblage.

"She'll never be healed," Eden commented.

"You saved her life, even if you couldn't save her leg," returned Paxton. Turning to the rest of the group he continued, "Eden is one of a long line of reincarnated prophets stretching back as far as Moses and beyond. She was Jesus and Mohammed and Buddha and Lao Tzu and Quetzalcoatl and Baha'u'llah and many more. She was also Thorn, the oak tree in Maine, the tree that I stood in as it was cut down around me, the one I wrote about in my novels.

"Show us something miraculous!" one of the men said.

"I don't think it works that way," Paxton interceded. "Something happens as the soul enters each new incarnation. We can't seem to remember any of our past lives. Thorn showed me how to do it through intense meditation, and we explored each other's past lives together. He thought he would be able to begin his next incarnation with this knowledge intact, a feat he had yet to accomplish, but it seems that he was mistaken because Eden is just as oblivious to her past lives as are all of you."

"Thorn did, however, reveal the circumstances for his next life. He told me he would be born as Eden, the daughter of Claire Harrison and Thomas Tucker. He told me they would raise her in obscurity in South America so as not to attract unwanted attention from darker forces at work. This is Eden, the daughter of Claire and Tucker, standing right in front of us. I believe her to be the world's next Messiah and I am no longer content to eke out an existence on this farm.

"Don't get me wrong. It's been my pleasure and my honor to create this oasis of sanity with all of you. I expected to live out the rest of my days right here, growing crops and writing memoirs, but I now have a new purpose in life. I will do whatever I can do to keep Eden safe from harm and to help her fulfill her destiny here on Earth.

"For that to happen, I believe we're going to need to break out of the Square, once and for all," Paxton continued, coming to his conclusion. This pronouncement caused a fresh outburst of incredulity from the assembly and the dam could no longer hold back the floodwater of their questions and concerns. It seemed as if everyone in the room was suddenly trying to talk over one another.

"Is such a thing possible?"

"It can't be done!"

"Have you lost your cotton-pickin' mind?"

"We're all gonna die!"

Paxton let it go on for a minute or two before he cleared his throat and raised his arms to quiet them down. Their individual conversations trailed off one at a time before Paxton resumed, "I have no idea how we're going to bust out of here, or where to go from there if we are successful. A lot depends on what we find out from the Comanche, if we even find the Comanche. He's the one that predicted a virgin would bring this place crashing down, so he seems as good a place as any to get started!

"Any of you that want to join us on this quest are welcome to do so, but there is a good chance it will not end well for many or all of us. The alternatives are to stay here on Maggie's Farm and hope for the best, to join up with the McDonoughs and their impending war with the Mexicans or to strike off on your own. One of the other families might have you, but I suspect they'll be swept up in the war as well before all is said and done."

"I'm goin' with you and Jazelle!" stated Bill emphatically, and there seemed to be general agreement with this sentiment from their group.

"I appreciate your enthusiasm, Bill," Paxton returned, "but let's sleep on it tonight and assemble here again in the morning, after breakfast. We'll take stock then. I will not think less of anyone who wants to join the McDonoughs. In fact, it's probably the sanest option I've given you. I'm sorry to have made this unilateral decision to travel north to see the Comanche. I know this is not our way, but our way of life, in all probability, is coming to an end.

"I'm going out to the garage now, to have a conversation with Frank. I want him to know that I am solely responsible for his incarceration so that none of you will be held in contempt by the McDonoughs should you choose to return to the Rockin' M. Let's pick up this discussion in the morning."

With that Paxton started to rise laboriously from the bean bag chair and Jazelle jumped up from her cross-legged position next to him to help pull him up. He started to leave but then turned back to face them, as if he had just remembered something important that needed to be said.

"We've made a good go of it here in this hell hole, haven't we?" he asked them on the verge of tears. "Better than any of us could have expected when we got thrown in here as Newts. I love you all and if this is goodbye for some of us, I wish you well. As for tonight, let's rock the house! Break out our stores of food and drink and we'll celebrate our success! Let's roast a goat! It certainly beats handing it all over to the McDonoughs, or the Mexicans!"

Paxton strode abruptly out of the room and did not stop until he was all of the way out of the small house they had commandeered at the inception of their commune. Jazelle and Eden were right behind him and they each grabbed one of his arms, forcing him to stop and turn around.

"You sure about this?" Jazelle asked him.

"Absolutely," Paxton replied. "Would you rather help Jonas fight the Mexicans?"

"Hell no!" she answered. "But breaking out of the Square, is such a thing really possible?"

"Anything is possible," he assured her, "if you believe it to be."

"You sound like fuckin' Walt Disney," she said, punching him playfully on the shoulder. "Aren't you just gonna make all my dreams come true!"

"You know it, darlin'," he returned with a smile and a wink. Turning to Eden he said, "Speaking of making dreams come true, Beth told me to come back for her the day after tomorrow, at sundown. She said that's when the Mexicans will attack. I guess that'll create the diversion we need to escape with her."

"And you're sure she'll be safe between now and then?" asked Eden.

"I'm not sure about anything, Eden, but Beth seemed to be sure and that's good enough for me."

"From what I seen she can hold her own, sugar," chimed in Jazelle, "as long as Old Jonas doesn't gum her to death!"

"I don't like being separated from her," admitted Eden. "Lizzie and I have been together our whole lives. We make a great team, but I don't think we'll be so strong, one without the other."

"In any event, we'll need tomorrow to get things packed up and ready to go here," Paxton observed. "I'm not planning on coming back. Regardless of who wins this war, we won't be welcome here. Let's just hope we're welcome in the Guadalupe Mountains!"

"What are you gonna do about Frank?" asked Jazelle.

"I don't know," answered Paxton truthfully. "I'm not going to hurt him, not unless I have to, but I also can't have him running back to warn Jonas of our plans. We can keep him tied up until we leave, and then toss him a knife to cut his bonds on our way out the door. We might just be saving his life to make him miss the battle at the Rockin' M. Should we offer to let him join us?"

"I'd never be able to trust him," Jazelle said. "He's too loyal to Jonas."

"We might be the only game left in town," reasoned Paxton.

"Yeah, but he don't know that, not unless he sees the Rockin' M go down for himself," she returned.

"I'll try to see where his head is at when we talk and I guess we'll go from there," Paxton decided.

"You want me to come with you?" asked Jazelle.

"Not really," Paxton answered truthfully. "You intimidate men, and I want him to speak freely."

"You intimidate everyone," Eden concurred.

"I don't intimidate your *Uncle* Paxton here," Jazelle countered, stepping close enough to give him a playful hip check. "Which just goes to show he ain't got the sense that God gave him!"

Paxton hip-checked her back and said, "Why don't you two go back inside and get ready to *party*! We're going to have a feast the likes of which Maggie's Farm has never seen!"

"Why do you call this place *Maggie's Farm*?" asked Eden suddenly. "I have yet to meet a Maggie."

"Margaret is no longer with us," Paxton explained. "She died early on, clearing land for planting, bit by a rattlesnake."

"It's our tribute to her," Jazelle finished for him.

"And to Bob Dylan," added Paxton.

"Who is that?" asked Eden.

"Are you kidding me?" burst forth Paxton. "You don't know who Bob Dylan was?"

"Somebody famous, I'm guessing," said Eden.

"Only one of the best folk singers of all-time!" said Paxton, bursting into song. "*I ain't gonna work on Maggie's Farm no more, no I ain't gonna work on Maggie's Farm no more...*"

"Enough!" groaned Jazelle. "It was bad enough when *he* was singin' it."

"Never heard of him," admitted Eden.

"Well, you grew up in Argentina," Paxton suddenly remembered. "And he would be a lot older than me if he was still alive. I'll guess I'll have to tune up my guitar later and let you in on the genius that was Bob Dylan."

"Not if I find that guitar first," said Jazelle good-naturedly.

The women turned to go and Paxton gave Jazelle a playful pat on her round rump. She winked at him before grabbing Eden's arm and pulling her back into the house conspiratorially. Paxton turned away and strode the few yards to the small side door of the garage. He knocked but soon discovered that the door was unlocked so he turned the knob and pushed his way into the oppressively hot and gloomy space.

"Paxton, what is the meaning of this?" asked Frank, raising his tied-up wrists as Paxton closed the garage door behind him. Frank was seated behind a small table with a glass of water and a half-eaten muffin upon it. Marty leaned against the far wall, a pistol pointing out from the crook of one of his folded arms.

"You can take a break, Marty," Paxton said. "Why don't you find someone else to spell you for a while?"

"Sounds good to me!" Marty said enthusiastically, pushing himself away from the wall into a fully upright and standing position. "I could really use a nap!"

"And you can settle down," Paxton said to the big man in the small chair. "No one's treated you badly, have they?"

"Well, no," Frank admitted in a Cajun accent. Raising his trussed-up hands he continued, "Except for this. What's goin' on?"

"Do you want the gun?" offered Marty on his way past Paxton.

"No, I won't need it, will I Frank?" Paxton replied, maintaining eye contact with Frank, who remained silent. "We're just going to have a little conversation."

Frank relaxed visibly and set his hands back down on the table, but his words belied his calm demeanor, "That all depends on what you got to say."

"Don't worry about it, Marty," said Paxton, waving him away. "Send somebody else back here in ten minutes."

Paxton waited for Marty to close the door before he bluntly began, "You're not coming with us to see the Comanche. I'm taking my own muscle. You'll be released unharmed just as soon as we head out, the day after tomorrow."

"The day after tomorrow?" blurted Frank. "You gotta be kiddin' me!"

"We have preparations to make," explained Paxton. "And I can't have you running back to Jonas to tell him our plans. You won't be missed for a few days because you're supposed to be traveling with us. After that it won't matter."

"It'll matter when you come back!" Frank predicted. "Jonas will have your hide!"

"Haven't you heard?" asked Paxton. "No one comes back from the Guadalupe Mountains. You gotta be relieved that you don't have to go up there with us."

"Hell, yeah!" Frank agreed. "But Jonas is gonna have *my* hide for letting you go without me."

"We captured you! There was nothing you could do. *I* captured you. This is all *my* doing. Make sure Jonas knows that. I want his anger directed at me and not the others. I suspect that at least some of my crew is going to join you at the Alamo to stave off the Mexican hordes. What do you suppose your chances are there?"

"We'll be ready for 'em," said Frank without conviction, "but we can use all the help we can get. Jonas will welcome them with open arms."

"I'll bet he will," Paxton agreed. "And then he'll put them right out there in the front lines."

"They're fucked any way you look at it," said Frank.

"Aren't we all?" asked Paxton rhetorically. "Aren't we all?"

"Why now, Paxton? What do you expect the Comanche's gonna tell you?"

"A way out of the Square," Paxton answered truthfully. "We're going to bust out of this freakish place!"

"Good luck with that!" sputtered Frank, after a moment's silence. "I think I'll take my chances with the Mexicans."

"We hold you no ill will and we'll make you as comfortable as possible under the circumstances," Paxton offered, "but we do intend for you to stay with us for a couple of nights, as our *guest*. You might as well make the best of it."

Just then there was a knock at the door and Richie poked his head in asking, "You ready for me, boss?"

"Yes, I am," said Paxton, standing up. "We're all done here."

CHAPTER 9

WALLACE

I was an analyst for the National Security Agency. No wife. No kids. Never had any time for socializing. I was consumed by my job, and I was good at it. I was mostly in charge of listening, we called it. Listening in on phone calls, reading emails, monitoring posts on social media. We had access to anyone in the Republic, anyone who used any type of electronic communication whatsoever, and in this day and age you couldn't make your way in the world without it.

I would be given a name and a photograph and off I'd go, full-on stalker into the private life of whichever citizen I was assigned. I almost always found something they could use, some law being broken, some dirty little secret the mark would not want to come into the light of day or some comment or post or tweet that could be construed as subversive or treasonous. I would report my findings, that was my job, and then I would wash my hands of the consequences to my mark. I had to, or I never would have been able to continue working and without my job I had nothing. And I had seen what happened to analysts who suddenly developed a conscience. They just stopped showing up at work one day and no one ever heard from them again.

Most of them wound up in here, I'd be willing to bet on it. I saw one of my marks, on my Intake Day, running from the chaos like the rest of us. Jennifer Clarkson, a reporter for the Republic News. She was secretly working on a story about a senator who liked to have sex with his interns, men and women alike. It would have been the end of his career, his life most likely, if any of it had ever come out, but I made sure that didn't happen.

Jennifer had been the editor of a very liberal publication, the Maam'zine, years ago at the University of Minnesota. She also had an abortion there, which is probably what got her Squared. Abortion is a Squarable offense in the Republic, applied retroactively by the courts to any time in a woman's past, even if abortion was legal in her state at the time. That one got me a pat on the back from my boss. It was a twofer, the subversive woman and the senator they now had in their back pocket. Not that I even know who *they* are anymore. Somebody is driving the bus, but it's certainly not the politicians we make a show of electing every couple of years.

There were only two people I was unable to smear in my ten years with the Agency. One of them was clean as a whistle, not so much as a parking ticket. They eventually took me off his case and he was charged with pedophilia. They made a big show of it in the courts, said they had found all kinds of child pornography on his computer. I didn't put it there, but somebody above my pay grade must have done it, because I would have found it if it existed. I was quite good at my job. The other one got me thrown into the Square, and to this day I'm not sure why they didn't just kill me and be done with it. Maybe there is still some loyalty left at the Agency, though I find that hard to believe.

His name was Frederick Douglas, just like the abolitionist. I don't know if he was African-American like the abolitionist, because they didn't have a photo of him, if indeed the mark was even a man. They were desperate to find him, his physical location, and that's what I was tasked with. It became my obsession, especially when it turned out that it wasn't going to be an easy or quick hatchet-job. This guy knew his way around a computer system. None of our tracking algorithms could trace his whereabouts. His anti-Republic blog rants bounced all over the world before they were ever posted.

Each time we thought we had him it turned out to be an elderly grandmother or young child, someone incapable of the havoc he was causing all over the Internet. Once the trail led to a venerable and ultra-conservative Supreme Court judge, who was immediately disqualified as the potential person-of-interest.

I'll never forget the first text message I got from him, "I know you're looking for me." He told me that he would only continue our dialogue if I just kept it between the two of us, said he had some information to pass along. We played a cat and mouse game all over the Internet for months. He'd send me tidbits about people or events that invariably turned out to be true. I didn't share the information with anyone but deleted everything as soon as I had read it. Six months into our correspondence he sent me a small computer file, no more than a Megabyte, but big enough to rock my world, and the rest of the world if it were ever to see the light of day.

Everyone in the Republic suspected the elections were being rigged by the Republicans, but not many dared speak openly about it. Such talk was considered treasonous and was shouted down by the political pundits as crazy conspiracy theories. It is one thing to suspect something and another to have proof. FD gave me the computer algorithms that were used to alter the votes necessary to skew a presidential election from the Democratic victor to the Republican contender, back before the Democratic Party was disbanded and outlawed.

I deleted the file immediately, as I had done to all of his other correspondence. What was I going to do with it, take on the Republic? But it was already too late. The watchers were being watched as well, and the Agency was well aware of everything FD had ever sent to me. I was picked up by the Republican Guard in an unmarked black van on the short walk to my apartment that very evening. There was no trial, nor was I ever allowed to talk to another human being until the bus ride to the East Gate of the Square.

I have done some terrible things. Lord knows I deserve to be here. Not directly, mind you, but the information I extracted from people's private lives was used to destroy those lives, and in some cases end them. Some of the jobs the Agency had me doing at the end of my tenure would have made me quit my job had they been given to me at the beginning of my career, but over the years the degree of my complicity rose so imperceptibly that it all seemed normal and just. I was helping to put criminals behind bars, until I wasn't.

I remember a parable from my youth, about a frog who gets put into a pot of room temperature water on a stovetop. Then the burner is turned on and the frog is slowly cooked to death without realizing the danger he is in. By comparison, the frog tossed into a pot of boiling water will immediately kick and claw and jump his way out of the pot as quickly as he can.

That's how it was for me, that's how it was for all of us. Things changed around us slowly enough that we didn't see the danger we were in until the behemoth that had become the Republic had gathered momentum and by then it was suicide to throw oneself in front of a speeding train. At first there was just a new law here and a presidential edict there. Then the independent news sources were discredited as fake news, and protesters to the new regime were deemed un-Republican. Borders were closed and illegals thrown out, until the Square was finished, of course, then they were thrown in.

Never in my wildest dreams would I have entertained the possibility that I would be thrown into the Square. I was a good soldier. I obeyed orders and didn't ask any questions. I never broke any laws, never had time to, I was always working for the Agency. My only crime was curiosity. The crime that killed the cat will be the death of me as well, damn you, Frederick Douglas! Damn you to hell!

SAYING GOODBYE

Paxton awoke in a sitting position, his guitar still perched upon his thighs, his ass planted firmly in his favorite beanbag chair in their assembly room. Eden was curled up next to him on a pile of blankets and cushions with a sheet draped mostly across her clothed body. He had a splitting headache and when he tried to stand up the room started spinning and he knew he was going to vomit. He lurched out of the soft chair and onto all fours, sending his guitar clattering across the floor. He managed to crawl out of the room and into the hallway before his stomach heaved and last night's feast came spilling out of his mouth and onto the floor in short, violent outbursts.

"Uncle Paxton," he heard from somewhere behind him. "Are you all right?"

"I've been better," he grumbled, but the worst of it was over. He dry heaved twice more before he pushed himself into a squatting position in preparation to stand. Eden came up to him and took his hand. With her help he managed to rise up to his full height causing his head to throb with renewed vigor.

"It must've been the sleep that did it," he joked. "I felt just fine before I fell asleep!"

"If it makes you feel any better," Eden said, slipping her shoulder up and into his armpit so that he might drape his arm over her and use her for support, "I don't feel very good either, and I didn't drink anywhere near as much as you did!"

They stumbled into the kitchen together and were greeted by a cheerful Barbara who gave them each a mug of steaming tea. She also tossed Paxton a white plastic bottle of Ibuprofen and said, "I hate to break into our stores for a hangover, but you're not the only one who's going to need these this morning."

"How are you so cheerful?" Paxton asked.

"'Cause I didn't make an ass out of myself last night like the rest of you yahoos!" she retorted. "We have a lot we need to figure out today!"

"Yeah," Paxton agreed, falling down heavily into the nearest chair. "Just as soon as my head stops pounding."

"I don't think we can wait that long," Barbara muttered and just then they heard a scream from outside, adding an exclamation point to her pronouncement.

Paxton was instantly alert but still moving hesitantly. He stood up laboriously and then followed behind the others out of the kitchen and into the harsh glare of the midmorning sun. There were five or six of their number already assembled in the courtyard when Jillian came running out of the garage door shouting, "Wally's dead! Wally's dead!"

Paxton ran toward the garage door but both Bill and Carson got there ahead of him. They all pushed past the astonished woman and into the dimly lit garage. Wallace lay face-up on the floor, his neck sporting a ring of faint, purple hemorrhaging typical of a strangling victim. There was no blood in evidence, nor any sign of Frank except for several pieces of the rope that had been used to tie his wrists scattered around the floor.

"Are we sure he is dead?" Paxton asked.

Bill knelt next to his head and checked for a pulse at his neck. Looking up at Paxton he said, "He's stone cold and already settin' up. He's gone all right."

"Any sign of Frank?" Paxton continued.

"If Wally's been layin' here as long as I think he has," said Bill, "Frank must be long gone by now."

Just then Jazelle burst into the room and shouted, "What's going on? Where's Frank?"

"Wally's dead and Frank is missing," stated Paxton simply. "We need to see if Frank is still hanging around or if he made a beeline back to Jonas. We gotta search the farm."

Paxton strode out into the courtyard followed by Bill and Carson. Jazelle had stooped to inspect the dead body but she soon followed the three men. Most of the rest of their commune were assembled on the shaded porch. Paxton walked under the protection of the metal roof and removed his hat.

"Wally is dead and Frank seems to be gone," he addressed the expectant faces with all eyes on him. "It appears that Frank somehow cut his ropes and strangled Wally. We need to verify that Frank is gone. We're going to search the grounds in groups and make sure to take weapons with you. We think he escaped hours ago, so he could be anywhere or he could be gone. Either way we need to know.

"Grace and Jillian, you go with Bill and Carson and check the house," Jazelle said to them from behind Paxton. "Look in every closet and behind every door. Barbara, Eden and Marty, you three make sure he's not still hiding out in the garage and see if he's taken anything. And get Wally out of there and into the house. We're gonna have to say goodbye to 'im and then burn 'im, we ain't got time for a burial."

"Can Abraham come with us?" asked Eden shyly. "I'd feel safer, no offense to Barbara or Marty."

"Shit, girl!" exclaimed Jazelle. "You're the biggest badass here!"

Abraham stood a little behind and in stark contrast to Eden. He towered over her, for starters, his skin providing a dark backdrop to her tanned but still much lighter shade of brown. He was yin to her yang, earth to her sky, Adam to her Eve. He took a step forward and put his hands protectively upon her shoulders.

"I'll go with Eden," he said, in a defiant tone that made it clear he was not asking for permission.

Paxton had watched the two of them together at last night's party. They were inseparable, laughing together like old friends, dancing and cuddling up on the couch. Paxton felt himself almost jealous of them, even though there was nothing sexual about their playfulness. It seemed more like they were brother and sister, or close friends reunited.

"Fine," Paxton granted. "Jazelle and Richie and Chuck and I will check the grounds and the barn. Let's meet back here at the house in fifteen minutes."

Paxton planted his hat back down upon his head before he turned and traded the shady porch for the light and heat of their small courtyard. Everyone else on the porch suddenly burst forth into motion as well, but Paxton did not bother to look back as he walked purposely toward the little shed that they had converted into a barn.

"Don't go out there by yourself, you old fool," Jazelle shot over his shoulder when she had caught up to him. "You don't even have a gun!"

"I have you!" he said. "I don't need a gun."

Looking back at her Paxton verified that Jazelle was armed. Not only did she have a pistol out in her hand, but a machete was tucked into the belt at her waist. Paxton reached over and plucked out the machete for himself, saying, "Now I'm ready!"

Chuck and Richie were not far behind. When they reached the barn, Paxton directed them to look around the back of it for the motorcycles while he and

Jazelle examined the interior. He immediately regretted the job he had assigned himself when a blast of foul-smelling, hot air escaped through the opened door. He let Jazelle take the lead and entered the stifling barn right behind her.

The barn was a twelve-foot square shed with a garage-style door on the front of it so that a riding lawnmower and wheelbarrows could be taken easily in and out of storage. Paxton had erected walls in the interior to make two stalls and a chicken coop with an attached run that could be accessed by a small hole in one of the corners. The only other door opened upon a make-shift pasture with a wooden and barbed-wire fence.

It appeared, without counting, that all twelve chickens were in their coop waiting to get fed. Paxton picked up a couple of corn cobs half-full of hard and dried yellow kernels and tossed them through a hole in the chicken wire onto their shit-covered floor. He picked up another double handful of cobs and threw them to the two goats huddled together in the far corner of their stall. The other stall stood empty and Paxton was immediately alarmed.

"Hey!" he remarked to Jazelle, without thinking it through. "What happened to Charlie?"

"You seriously don't remember the goat roast you ordered up last night?" she asked him, shaking her head. "Must've been a rough night for you, old man."

"Last night was just fine," he responded, "but this morning's not going so well."

They cleared out of the stinky, close quarters of the small barn as soon as possible and ran smack into Richie as he came around the corner looking for them.

"Both of the dirt bikes are still here, Paxton," he reported, "but the blue mountain bike is gone."

"I still have both keys," Paxton said, turning out his left pocket. "That must be why he took the mountain bike. I guess we should consider ourselves lucky he didn't wreak more havoc."

"Wally wasn't lucky," said Chuck, joining them under the blue tarp that provided a little shade for the goats.

"No, he was not," Paxton agreed. "What do you suppose happened out there?"

"Wally spelled me about midnight," Richie confessed. "Frank was still good and trussed up when I left him. We were playing cards but I didn't untie his hands for it."

"Do you think Wally untied him?" Chuck asked.

"Could be," Jazelle answered. "Wally was a big softie, but he weren't stupid. He probably passed out and Frank strangled him even before he cut his hands free."

"So, it's about three hours by bicycle to the Rockin' M," Paxton calculated. "Chances are that Frank's already there. What's Jonas gonna do?"

"If not for the Mexicans, old Jonas'd send a truck-full of his boys up here to teach us a lesson," Jazelle offered. "We can only hope that he's got his hands full and he'll leave us be."

"What's he gotta mess with us for?" asked Richie. "Frank got home to him in one piece."

"We've still got his motorcycles," said Paxton, "and he's gotta be wondering what we're up to. I think we need to leave here just as soon as we can."

"What about Wally?" Chuck asked. "We gotta to do right by Wally."

"Yes," Paxton agreed. "We need to say goodbye to Wally. Let's do what we gotta do and hope for the best as far as Jonas goes. Let's get back to the others."

None of the searches turned up anything out of the ordinary except for the missing bike, and Wally of course. Paxton told them to meet in their assembly room in five minutes and then he asked Chuck and Carson for help in carrying Rachel upstairs to their meeting. The room was already packed when the three of them came awkwardly through the door and deposited Rachel in Paxton's habitual beanbag chair. He sat down cross-legged next to her and raised his hands to quiet the noisy room.

"First of all, is everybody armed?" Paxton asked. "We may be getting a visit from the Rockin' M at any moment and we need to be prepared for that possibility. Richie is keeping watch as we speak, and he'll whistle an alarm if need be. I invite everyone to speak freely, but speak quickly as well because it feels like time is of the essence."

"Do you have a plan, Paxton?" asked Barbara.

"It's still forming," he admitted, "but I want to get on the road as soon as possible at this point."

"We've got to avenge Wally!" Marty shouted. "He didn't deserve to go out like that!"

"How you gonna do that?" interjected Jazelle. "You gonna start a war with the McDonoughs? Maybe join up with the Mexicans?"

"I don't need a war," said Marty softly. "I'm just gonna kill Frank."

"What do you think happened out there?" asked Grace, looking directly at Paxton.

"Your guess is as good as mine," Paxton offered. "Either Wally fell asleep and Frank was able to work himself free, or else he convinced Wally to cut him loose. Either way it didn't end well for Wally."

"What are you gonna do?" asked Bill.

"Well, I thought we were going to have today to pack up and say goodbye but it looks as though we need to get out of here in a hurry," Paxton answered. "I'm headed north to the Guadalupe Mountains and I don't plan on coming back. You all need to decide your own fate!"

It was no surprise to anyone when Jazelle affirmed, "I'm with Paxton!"

A chorus of "Me too!" came from several of the others including Eden, Abraham, Jillian, and Grace. Barbara soon followed saying, "I think this idea of yours is going to get us all killed, Paxton, but I'm not going back to the Rockin' M. Those assholes got no respect for women!"

"The boys and I have been talkin'," Carson spoke up, looking directly at Paxton. "We also think this is a suicide mission. We're going to take our chances with the McDonoughs."

"You all feel that way?" asked Paxton, looking from Marty to Chuck to Bill. "Bill?"

"I changed my mind," Bill spoke directly to Carson, a guilty look on his face. "I'm gonna throw in with Paxton and Jazelle."

"Suit yourself," said Carson noncommittally. "No skin off my back."

"Marty?" Paxton asked and all eyes turned toward him.

"I just want to kill Frank," said Marty. "That's my new mission in life. I don't care what happens to me after that."

"What about me?" Rachel finally spoke up. "Do I have a choice in this as well?"

"Of course, you do," Paxton started but he was soon interrupted by Jazelle.

"She ain't comin' with us!" she interjected. "She's only gonna slow us down!"

"She can ride the horse she stole from the cannibals," Paxton countered. "She's earned that much. It's not like we're going to need it here on the farm anymore."

"You don't wanna be a fuck puppet for the McDonough clan," Barbara advised her. "Trust me on that one. You're better off to spend the rest of your short life with us."

After a slight pause Rachel said, "You've all shown me nothing but kindness. You saved my life. I'd like to stick with you if you'll have me."

"That's settled then," said Paxton, ignoring the dirty look he was getting from Jazelle. "Pack your things if you're coming with me, we're leaving within the hour. Can I ask you boys to do one last thing for me? Can you make preparations for Wally so we can send him off properly before we head out?"

"Sure thing, Paxton," replied Carson, who seemed to speak for the rest of them. "You wanna burn him or bury him?"

"If we had more time I'd bury him," admitted Paxton, "but under the circumstances I'd say we make a bonfire they'll be able to see for miles! It's not like we need to conserve the wood anymore!"

"Will do!" agreed Carson, standing up. The other men followed suit and they all left the assembly room together. When they were gone Paxton turned to the others and gave them their marching orders."

"We're going to be traveling light," he began, "one change of clothes and one personal item for everybody. Barbara, you collect whatever medicine we still got. Jillian and Grace can round up our food. Take everything except what the guys'll need for a day or two."

"How we gonna carry all that shit?" asked Jazelle.

"Bill, Eden and I are going to make a travois for the horse to drag behind it," he answered. "You and Abraham can round up the weapons and camping gear. We're going to have to divvy up the guns between our group and the guys that are staying."

"Old Jonas will arm them," countered Jazelle, "I ain't giving up any guns."

"Well, I'm not going to leave them here defenseless when the McDonoughs show up," argued Paxton. "We can spare them a couple of guns."

Jazelle glared at him but didn't say another word as she stood up and gestured for Abraham to do the same, "Come on, big man. We got work to do."

Paxton stood up as well. Looking down at Rachel, he offered her his hands and she let him pull her into a standing position.

"You can help in the kitchen with the food," he instructed her. "Lean on me and I'll help you get in there."

Rachel put her left hand on Paxton's shoulder and together they hobbled out the door and down the hall. The others followed behind them slowly until the hallway opened up into the kitchen and then they pushed past Paxton on their way to their assigned chores. Paxton helped Rachel onto a chair and then turned to Eden and Bill saying, "Let's see what we can find in the garage for that travois."

It was more than two hours before they were saddled up and ready to go. The travois they had fashioned out of two-by-fours, rope and lawn-mower wheels looked rickety-as-hell and it was packed as high as the sled full of Who-presents in the old Dr. Seuss story *The Grinch Who Stole Christmas*. Like the dog-turned-reindeer in the same story, it did not appear as if the old horse attached to it had any hope of being able to pull it. Indeed, he seemed oblivious to the monumental task ahead of him and instead chomped lazily at the crabgrass beneath his hooves. The two goats tethered to the travois did the same.

Four bicycles and two motorcycles on kick-stands were parked a few yards away from the animals. Each of them were outfitted with make-shift packs and sacks that were also full to overflowing. It was painfully obvious that they weren't going to be speeding away from Maggie's Farm off into the sunset, but would rather be moving in the opposite direction at a snail's pace, with the single-track trails to complete the analogy.

When the preparations were complete, the remaining members of the soon-to-be-defunct Maggie's Farm commune gathered around the funeral pyre which had been erected hastily by Richie, Carson, Chuck and Marty. They had taken one of the wooden tables from the kitchen and laid Wallace out upon it in the button-down shirt and slacks that he preferred to wear as if he was still an analyst for the Republic. Dried tumbleweed and old newspapers had been placed beneath it with scrap wood and two-by-fours stuffed into every available space that remained.

The thirteen men and women stood together with joined hands in a loose oval around the table with Paxton at its head, directly behind Wallace's head. Barbara was able to locate a pair of crutches she had commandeered on one of their numerous scavenging parties and Rachel had them stuffed into her armpits as she held onto Eden and Grace's hands. Whether by chance or choice the women had separated from the men and stood on one side of the table, beginning with Jazelle on Paxton's right side and ending with Barbara, whose hands held tight to both Jillian and Bill.

"Dear All," Paxton began, "into Your hands we commend the spirit of Wallace Turner, who will be remembered with fondness by everyone here on Maggie's Farm. He was a loyal friend, a hard worker and a good person and we pray that he is in a better place than he left behind. Would anyone else like to say anything?"

"We'll miss you, Wally," said Grace on the verge of tears.

"Give 'em hell," offered Jazelle, "wherever you are."

"Go with God, you big stiff," said Carson.

"Hey! He resembles that remark!" joked Richie, quoting one of Wally's favorite sayings. Several of the men chuckled softly before the somber mood squelched their humor.

Marty broke the circle to step forward and put his hand on Wally's chest. He bent down to kiss his cold lips briefly and whispered, "I'm gonna take care of Frank for you, buddy. Don't you worry about that."

Paxton also disentangled his hands from Jazelle and Abraham and reached behind him to scoop his guitar off the dusty ground. He worked the strap over his head and pulled the pick from its resting place between the strings. He waited for the chorus of goodbyes to die down before he started to strum the most appropriate song he knew how to play. Before launching into the words, he nodded his head toward Bill to tell him it was time to light the bonfire.

"*Yes, I understand, that every life must end, uh-huh,*" Paxton began to sing the soulful Eddie Vedder tune, 'Just Breath', as the newspaper burst into orange flame. He was only half-way through the song before the fire had become fierce enough to force their little group backward to escape the searing heat. He finished the song for the small group which had retreated from the flames on his side of the pyre. Then he swung his guitar so that it rested upon his back with the strings pointing downward and caught Jazelle's eyes with his own.

"We gotta go," he told her, and she nodded her head once in the affirmative before shouting for the others to join them.

The four men who were staying behind stood staring into the flames as the others made their last preparations to leave. Only when Paxton and Abraham had boosted Rachel up into the saddle of her horse did they make their way around the bonfire and join the departing group. The men shook hands and the women gave hugs all around. Grace was crying by the end of their farewell and Jillian held onto Richie so long that it seemed she would never let him go.

"You could still come with us, you know," Paxton said to Carson as he shook his hand.

"I know," Carson admitted, "but the devil you know is better than the one you don't, you know?"

"I hear you," said Paxton, "but your devil's facing a thousand screaming Mexicans bent on dismembering your body parts."

"We've been talking over the pros and cons all morning," Carson admitted, "ever since we found Wally in the garage. We're going to take our chances with the old man."

"The other old man," Richie added, and they all laughed, dispelling the sad aura which had settled over their parting.

Marty walked up to Paxton and took his hand in a both of his own saying, "It's been an honor, Paxton. You have quite literally saved my life."

"Well don't go and squander it on the McDonoughs," Paxton returned. "Come with us!"

"No can do," Marty responded. "I'm a man on a mission."

"A mission that will get you killed," said Paxton.

"We all gotta go sometime," Marty returned. "I'm gonna go out in style!"

Paxton raised his voice so that all four of the men who were staying behind could hear him, "If things go south at the Rockin' M, you know where to find us. At the rate we're going to be traveling, you shouldn't have any trouble catching up to us."

"We'll take that under advisement," said Chuck, reaching over to clasp Paxton's hand. "You take care of yourself, old man."

"You do the same," said Paxton. Having completed his round of handshakes, Paxton climbed onto the dirt bike behind Jazelle, his guitar still slung across his back. She had earlier groused about including the bulky guitar in their exodus, but Paxton had insisted on carrying it as the one personal item he was allotted. He had argued that the Book belonged to all of them and shouldn't be counted as a second item.

She kicked the engine into sputtering life and Bill did the same with the other motorcycle. Barbara took a seat behind Bill as the rest of their motley crew, save Rachel, straddled their bicycles. Richie slapped the horse on its skinny rump and it started to walk slowly forward, dragging their mountain of gear behind it.

Paxton continued to look over his shoulder intermittently as they rode slowly northeastward toward Route 54, which would take them in a straight shot toward the Guadalupe Mountains. He half-expected the McDonoughs to come speeding toward them at any moment. It was only after he could no longer see the smoke from Wally's funeral pyre that he allowed himself to look forward, over Jazelle's shoulder, toward the uncertain future his course of action had created for all of them.

CHAPTER 10
ABRAHAM

It was only a matter of time; we knew our days were numbered. We were luckier than most, for the time we had together as a family. Maybe we should have taken the chance to go back to Africa, hopped on board the boats with all those poor bastards that didn't have a choice in the matter, but I don't reckon things are any better over there. Africans have been starving for centuries, but the last decade hit them really hard. I was afraid of the brutality of it, especially with us so accustomed to a certain standard of living.

My brother Darryl called me a 'house slave' when he got shipped away. He said those old, white men were happy to have me serving them just as long as I knew my place and I didn't get too uppity. I kept my head down, for sure. I had two kids and a wife to take care of, I wasn't going to make any waves. I just sat in my cubicle from nine to five every day, writing heating and cooling programs, one small cog in the vast machinery of the SmartHouse, a technology which is now mandatory in all new construction in the Republic.

It was pretty amazing technology, the SmartHouse, if I don't say so myself. It was designed to interface with the residents of any domicile and pretty much take care of their every need. The SmartHouse could cook your food, and do the dishes afterwards. It cleaned the floors and windows, washed and dried the laundry. It controlled the temperature and humidity, the lighting, sound and security systems. All it took was a text to have your bath water ready for you at the optimal temperature when you arrived home from work.

The SmartHouse also gave the Republic a way to monitor all of its residents. Each one could be accounted for, right down to his or her vital signs, from anywhere in the house. That's how they caught us. We didn't have SmartHouse. Our brownstone was too old and they were just starting to retrofit. But the second time they came to talk to us they had portable sensors, looking for heat signatures no doubt. The third time they came with the dogs and they were done asking questions.

Darryl would laugh his ass off, if he knew that I landed myself in the Square. He had been given that option as well, when they cleaned out the prisons. Banished from the Republic in either case, but he chose to try his luck in Africa, God bless him. He's no longer alive, I'm sure of that. Twins can sense these things. He didn't last much longer than the time it took the ocean liner to get from here to there, if he was ever sent across the ocean at all. I wasn't given a choice in the matter, but at least I escaped the firing squads.

I don't know what happened to Sarah and the kids. I think they escaped the raid; I hope to God they did, but where could they go afterward, with me in here and their black faces scrolled across the bottom of the RepNews with all of the other Deplorables? I don't think it ever took the Republican Guard too long to track down any of them, the faces on those endless screens changed every couple of days. Except for José and Lucinda, of course, they were with us almost a year. The News kept putting them on the screen, but only once a month or so, long enough for most folks to forget they had already seen them. The Republic would never admit they couldn't find someone.

It still amazes me that we were able to hide the three of them for eleven months. They lived in Tamara's room, with the shades drawn. They never came out of our house again, once they crossed that threshold, not until the Guard came for them.

They probably would've just gotten thrown into the Square if they had given themselves up early on. They didn't think it through and neither did Sarah and I. Now I'm sure they're in a mass grave somewhere, even little Juanita.

Juanita was the biggest reason we decided to risk everything to help the Gutierrezes. She and Tamara had been best friends since day care. How could we say no to those tear-filled eyes and her earnest six-year-old pleading, "We have to hide them, Daddy, or else they'll die!"

Truth be told, Sarah and I decided we could not, in good conscience, go along with it anymore. We could not just close our eyes and ears and pretend that everything going on was normal and necessary and just.

The changes were subtle and all seemed reasonable enough at first. There were terrorist attacks and violent criminals to be brought to justice, or put down as the case may be. There were a lot of people moving from coastal cities to the inland because of the sea level rise. All of the cities were overcrowded and massive refugee camps sprawled outward from too many of them.

The Republican Guard were given some latitude to keep the peace and to track down suspected terrorists and murderers and anyone intent on bringing down the government and destroying our way of life. Then we were at war with China and they made military service mandatory for all young adults. Each subsequent step brought us more firmly under Republican control, but no single change was audacious enough to cause a general uprising. Local uprisings were squashed with extreme displays of force, which never quite made it onto the RepNews, but weren't soon forgotten in the subjugated cities.

There was no definite marker in my mind, one single event, for when it all changed from normalcy to lunacy, from objectionable to downright scary. They closed the borders and started deporting everyone without a RepubliCard. The

Chinese were rounded up into detainment camps to be traded for Republican prisoners, until the camps were overrun with common prisoners, refugees and liberals. The Square alleviated some of that pressure and the firing squads took care of the rest.

They deported or detained the Hispanics before they started in on those of African descent. José and Lucinda had RepubliCards which protected them for a while, but in the end it didn't matter anymore. If their skin was too dark, how could I expect them to keep looking past mine? It was only a matter of time.

When we had the chance to do something, to stand for something, we took it, knowing full well it would end badly for all of us. We are Christians after all, not that religion seems to matter much to anyone anymore. It's all about the survival of the fittest. Nowhere is that more true than in the Square.

But these folks seem different, Paxton and Elizabeth and Eden, especially Eden. She's making me a believer, and that is no small feat. And to think I almost left them, in the desert, when I was a two-day old Newt and we had just rescued Rachel. What did I know about the Square?

I saw my chance to escape and I took it. I was fixing to ride off into the sunset on that old horse until I heard Richie and Chuck yelling to me, and even then, I thought long and hard about making a run for it. That would have been the worst decision of my life, probably would have ended my life, and some small voice inside me told me so. My absence almost got the girls killed that day and ever since then, I've made up my mind to make sure that doesn't happen, not while there's still breath in me.

I had a vision, the night that everyone dreamed of the Comanche. In my dream the Comanche told me to protect Eden with my life, that she is our last and best hope for saving some semblance of humanity from extinction. It has become my new purpose in life to protect her, and I have not let her out of my sight since, even though she seems to be quite capable of taking care of herself. As Jesus is my witness, I will give my life for her, if that is what it takes to keep her safe.

INTO THE DESERT

Jazelle had not called a halt to their slow escape until it was dinnertime and they had a clear view of Route 54 in the distance. She and Paxton had reconnoitered a small hillock with a deep ridge on its western slope that would shield them from every view except for the direction from which they had just come. Jazelle left Paxton and his guitar on a boulder overlooking the sunset as she backtracked to round up the rest of their posse.

No sooner had the sound of Jazelle's engine faded than another one took its place. Bill rode up to a waving Paxton five minutes later and dropped Barbara off before he too retreated back down the hill on his motorbike. Barbara joined Paxton on his perch and playfully bumped his shoulder with her own.

"Play me a song, cowboy," she demanded. "Something uplifting, for goodness sake!"

Paxton immediately launched into an original song that he had written a long time ago, before he had even finished graduate school, *"You think you're so clever, with your supersonic planes, artificial hearts and computer brains. You can see inside the atom, gaze off into outer space, and you can vanish in a moment leaving nothing but a trace."*

"Jesus Christ, Paxton!" Barbara chided him during a musical interlude. "I said *uplifting*!"

Paxton laughed and answered her as he waited for the next verse to come around on his guitar, "What? This has a good beat to it!"

"Yeah, as long as you don't listen to the words!"

"*You debate over abortion, homosexuality,*" he continued, undaunted. "*You can clone a human being, but is he just like you and me? Your greatest minds are busy creating plasma TV, as your greatest cities vanish in the rising of the sea.*"

Barbara joined in the chorus she had heard way too many times, "*Hey, Diddle, Diddle, Nero's tuning up his fiddle. Who cares about the burning we've got 'Malcom in the Middle.' The Pats are in the Superbowl, the new 'Survivor' is here. Just sit down on your sofa and grab yourself a beer.*"

When the song had run its course and none of the others had turned up, Paxton was contemplating which song to sing next when Barbara turned to him with a serious expression on her face and asked him point blank, "Paxton, do you believe in God?"

Paxton looked up at her and answered immediately, "Absolutely."

He did not bother to elaborate so she pressed on, "How could He let a place like this exist? How could He abandon this world, *His* Creation, and let us destroy it?"

"We brought this shit down upon ourselves," Paxton responded. "God had nothing to do with it. The All hasn't abandoned us. Think of all those prophets throughout the millennia, attempting to teach us spirituality, to give us a glimpse of eternity. We burn them at the stake, or hang 'em on a cross, or invent some other brutal way to silence them. We're very creative that way."

"I believe," Paxton continued, "that Eden is the next in a long line of prophets, here to try to save us from ourselves."

"She's got her work cut out for her," Barbara commented.

"That she does," agreed Paxton.

Barbara pointed her finger at the setting sun, announcing excitedly, "There's someone, on a bike! Do you see 'em?"

Paxton took his glasses out of the front pocket of his blue jeans and put them on his face. He still had to squint to see what Barbara was seeing.

"Ayuh," he answered in the accent of the Mainer he would never be again. "There's two of 'em."

"It's Eden and Abraham," Barbara identified them. "Thank goodness!"

They were followed by Jillian and Grace, in that order but each of them five minutes behind the previous bicycle. Paxton and Barbara greeted everyone in turn, and they all talked excitedly until they heard a motorcycle in the distance.

Jazelle and Bill rode up the small hill together, their motorcycles loaded with camp gear. They dumped out the tents and some food and turned right back around for another trip.

"We gotta take some of the load off that old nag," she offered by way of explanation, "else she ain't never gonna make it!"

"You want me to come with you?" asked Paxton.

"Don't sweat it, sugar," she said, winking at him. "Bill 'n' I got it covered. You get them tents set up."

"O Captain, my Captain," he saluted her and stood watching as she and Bill sped off down the hill and were soon lost in the slanting light of the sunset. Turning back to the others Paxton tossed a tent to Barbara, Jillian and Grace and then beckoned Eden and Abraham over to help him with a second one.

"How are you two holding out?" he asked them as he and Abraham pulled the nylon tent out of its sack.

"Alright," answered Abraham without enthusiasm.

"I'm exhausted," admitted Eden. "I could lay right down here in the sand and fall asleep."

"Let's get this tent set up then," offered Paxton, "so you don't have to sleep in the dirt."

Paxton tossed her a set of poles to assemble. They worked in silence for the next few minutes, raising the tent up from the sand. Paxton had been lucky enough to find a relatively flat spot for both of their tents on the bottom of their rocky ravine.

"I want to come with you," Abraham said simply, when their work was done.

"You are with us, Abraham," Paxton replied. "We're all in this together, for better or worse."

"No," Abraham continued, "I want to come with you to rescue Lizzie."

"Out of the question," Paxton responded immediately, and without thinking it through. "It's much too dangerous."

Elizabeth had seen Abraham in her dream, talking to the Comanche, but she had never said anything about him being part of their rescue operation. They only had the two motorcycles and they already had three passengers since Eden had insisted on coming along. They would need the fourth seat for Elizabeth, assuming they were successful in liberating her. He said as much to Abraham, and to Eden, who had come up beside him to slip her hand around his giant bicep.

"I've only been in here a few days," reasoned Abraham, "and I'm well aware that you all still consider me a Newt. But so too are Eden and Lizzie. They are the only people with whom I have bonded, maybe because we are all so new to this. I want to do what I can to help save Lizzie."

"Please let him come, Uncle Paxton," she begged. "Abraham is my friend. Lizzie wants him to come, too."

"How could you possibly know that?" asked Paxton.

"I talked to her last night," she admitted, "while we were all sleeping off the party."

"What do you mean, you talked to her?" asked Paxton.

"Well, it must've been a dream," she allowed, "but it was as real as you and I are talking right now. Lizzie told me to come at sunset, just as the Mexicans attack. She says that's our best chance of escaping unscathed. And she told me to bring Abraham along, that we need him."

"But it's Friday Night tomorrow night," reasoned Paxton. "They're not gonna break the Friday Night truce, are they? Jonas won't be prepared for that!"

"All the more reason to bring Abraham with us," Eden continued to plead her case. "Lizzie said something about meeting us in the garage, in a truck. Maybe we won't need the motorcycles to escape."

"She said essentially the same thing to me," Paxton concurred, "when I left her there, but she didn't say anything about bringing Abraham along. Can you even drive a motorcycle?"

"I used to own a Harley," Abraham replied, "back before I had kids."

"They're definitely not Harleys," said Paxton.

"No, they are not," Abraham responded, "but I think I can manage."

"Do you know how to use a gun?" asked Paxton.

"Please," Abraham drawled out the word, holding his palms facing outward. "I did my time in the Guard. Where do you think this body comes from? Not from sitting behind a computer all day. Of course, I can shoot a gun."

"Fine," stated Paxton, making a decision. "You can take Eden on one of the bikes and Jazelle and I will ride the other, that is, if you can convince her to take you with us."

"Abraham should have no problem there," Eden said, looking up at him with a smirk on her face. "Jazelle seems to like him well enough."

The two of them had been very vocally enjoying each other's company in one of the bedrooms during last night's party and had been the butt of more than one joke about their unabashed bacchanalia. Despite his dark skin, Abraham's cheeks blushed a dark red color and he looked uncomfortably at his feet.

"Speak of the devil!" exclaimed Paxton, as the sputtering cough of motorcycle engines once again came from the western horizon. He moved off in the direction of the sound, leaving the two Newts to their chuckling camaraderie.

The two motorcycles drove across the dimly-lit desert and up the slight slope to their campsite. This time they shut down their engines and found their quiet balance upon their kick stands. Jazelle came right up to Paxton and reported, "She's not that far behind us now, should be here in another hour."

"Another hour?" Paxton groused. "Should somebody go back for her?"

"That horse is slow as molasses," Jazelle complained, "but she'll be okay. I scouted things out between here and there. She shouldn't have any problems."

"Alright," said Paxton, putting his arm around her shoulder. "Come have some dinner."

Since they couldn't make a fire, they had to settle on fresh tomatoes and green beans for dinner, with cold oatmeal for dessert. They were already done eating and cleaning up their few dishes when Rachel rode up on her horse. Both looked exhausted as they walked slowly into camp with their heads down and bobbing to the cadence of the horses movements. The goats were slightly more lively, bleating their displeasure from behind the travois. Abraham reached up and scooped Rachel off the horse and helped her into a seated position next to Eden.

"My ass hurts," she said as Eden handed her a fresh tomato.

"Mine too," Eden agreed, putting her arm around her.

"Now that we're all here," Paxton said loud enough to bring everyone back to their gathering, "let's talk strategy for tomorrow."

Soon everyone was once again seated in a rough circle around what should have been their campfire. Paxton stood up and began to address the remaining members of their defunct commune, "Well, we made it through day one of our escape and we can be grateful for that!"

"Is that what this is, an escape?" asked Barbara.

"It felt like an escape when I thought the McDonoughs were going to drive up behind us at any moment all afternoon," Paxton elucidated. "If they haven't come after us yet, we're probably in the clear, from them at least. They're about to have their hands full with the Mexicans. How about we call it a migration?"

"More like a funeral march," Jazelle commented drily.

"Don't be such a glass-half-empty kind of gal," Paxton teased her. "We're all still drawing breath. We have food and water. We still have each other and we have renewed purpose in life."

"Well, I ain't ready to drink the Kool-Aid," Jazelle commented, "but we made it this far. What's the plan, chief?"

"Jazelle, Abraham, Eden and I are going after Elizabeth tomorrow. That'll take us in the wrong direction from where we ought to be headed. What's more, Elizabeth told me to come at sunset, so we're going to lose a whole day."

"Let's hope we don't lose our lives," Jazelle continued her commentary.

"The safest thing for the rest of you to do would be to wait right here for us," Paxton continued, ignoring her, "but that horse is moving so damned slow I would rather you keep heading north and we'll catch up with you, hopefully the day after tomorrow."

"I don't like us being separated," Bill commented, and the other members of what would become his traveling party seemed to agree.

"I don't like it either," Paxton admitted, "but we're going to be separated either way. We're not traveling en masse to the Rockin' M. You'd be vulnerable sitting here all day as well."

"Not as vulnerable as we'll be on the road," Barbara pointed out.

"We're gonna have targets on our backs from here on out," Jazelle offered. "We ain't on Maggie's Farm no more. It's only gonna get worse north of the ranches."

"You'll have guns," reasoned Paxton, "and bicycles, and it's a straight shot up Route 54, but you might want to stay off the road as much as you can. I'll leave it up to you to decide what you want to do and we'll go from there. If you'd all rather wait here for us to return from the Rockin' M, then we'll meet back here, but it'll still probably be the day after tomorrow. You can sleep on it, if you want. That's where I'm headed."

He left them all to discuss their options amongst themselves and walked the few yards to the tent that he would be sharing with Jazelle, Abraham and Eden. He was asleep almost as soon as he stretched himself out onto his bedroll, nor did he stir when Jazelle came creeping into the tent fifteen minutes later and sidled up next to his prone body.

Paxton was awoken before sunrise when he heard whispered voices and movement outside the thin fabric of their tent. None of the other sleeping forms around him seemed too concerned and he was going to let himself drift back down into their slumber before he heard his name whispered insistently from right outside their door.

"Paxton! Are you awake?" came the female voice he guessed to be Jillian.

"Yes," he whispered back. "I'll be right out!"

Jazelle opened her eyes as he disentangled himself from her draping limbs. He shushed her, shook his head and whispered, "Sleep."

"What's up?" he continued to whisper after climbing out of their tent and zipping the door shut.

"We're leaving," Jillian whispered back. "We wanna get some miles behind us before it gets too hot."

Paxton followed her back to her newly flattened tent and helped the others gather and pack their things onto the travois. He took a day's worth of food and water for four people but nothing else. When all seemed in readiness, he and Bill helped Rachel mount what had become her horse. Paxton gave hugs all around before issuing his last-minute instructions.

"Look for us the day after tomorrow," he said. "With any luck we'll still be on these motorcycles, or possibly a truck if we can swipe one. I plan on riding straight up 54 if it looks like it's safe enough. You take care of yourselves."

"You do the same, Paxton," echoed Bill. He climbed aboard his bicycle and the five of them took off at the slow pace set by the horse.

Paxton decided to take watch and let his tent-mates keep sleeping. He climbed to the top of their rocky knoll so that he could keep an eye on his departing friends. They had to descend the ravine toward the west, but as soon as they were clear of it, they turned northward. He watched their slow progress as they skirted the hill and adjusted their course slightly eastward to intercept Route 54.

As the sky began to lighten in the east, it became easier for Paxton to see them, but only for a short while. He watched as they crossed Route 54 and then turned northward to parallel the highway. He saw them disappear over a ridge, just as the sun's first rays peeked through the cloudy eastern horizon.

Once he could no longer see them, an overwhelming feeling of sadness washed over Paxton as his brain tried to wrap itself around the fact that he might never see them again. He was hopeful that wouldn't be the case, but there were so many wildcards to be played over the next two days that anything was possible. They could be ambushed and killed, or taken captive. He could be ambushed or killed, or thwarted in the rescue attempt they were planning to execute in the middle of a bloodbath.

They had managed to create some sense of normalcy in this hellhole, if only for a short while, but Maggie's Farm was no more. Regardless of the outcome of their rescue attempt and escape to the Guadalupe Mountains, he could see no way of going back there, no way of recreating the oasis they had once shared in the middle of Megiddo, near what was once the town of Van Horn, Texas.

Paxton had accomplished more than most in his lifetime. He was a mathematician and scientist; an author and musician and he solved the Unified Field Theory that had so vexed Albert Einstein for most of his career. In his own mind, however, his greatest accomplishment was the creation of Maggie's Farm and the living proof he and the others had provided that human decency was still alive and well, even when the powers-that-be had done their level best to destroy all vestiges of it. These people had become the family he had never had time to father in the outside world, and he was only now realizing how much he was going to miss the life they had been able to cobble together in this place where despair reigned supreme.

Now it seemed as if he had one remaining achievement to add to his long resume, one final act to complete his illustrious career. Thorn had told him long ago that he would become a prophet to herald the arrival of the world's next, great spiritual teacher, the Messiah who would save humanity from the brink of extinction. He had assumed that his role in this endeavor had been fulfilled by the books he had written about Thorn, but it was becoming ever clearer that the All was not done with him yet. Everything else he had done to this point in his life paled next to the importance of getting Eden out of the Square so that she could fulfill her destiny.

Paxton closed his eyes against the rising sun, put his hands palms up on his knees and began to focus upon his breathing. It seemed to him that it had been a long time since he had gotten the chance to meditate.

"*I was at home*", he remembered, "*before Intake Day. So, it's been a week.*"

Letting that thought pass through his brain and leave, Paxton brought his awareness back to his breathing. It became deeper and slower and soon Paxton was in a light, meditative state, a place he liked to call the 'realm of non-thought.' He remained there, more or less, until the sound of someone zipping open the tent door recalled him to body, to his space and time. He opened his eyes languidly and turned his head slightly to see who it was.

Eden was outside the tent, bent over so she could zip the door closed. She soon stood up and started looking this way and that. She cupped a hand over her eyes to look up the eastern slope into the slanting morning sunlight. As soon as she saw Paxton, she waved at him and then her legs began to propel her forward and upward, ascending the hill toward him.

Paxton quickly turned his body 180 degrees by spinning upon his tailbone and then he pulled his legs out in front of him to stretch them out and get the blood circulating again. Eden climbed the short distance in a hurry with her youthful, if a little too skinny, body. She plopped down beside him breathing heavily.

"Good morning!" quipped Paxton. "How'd you sleep?"

"Slept just fine," she answered. "I always sleep well, how about you?"

"I don't sleep as well as I used to," admitted Paxton, "the Square doesn't foster a good night's sleep. What about the other two, are they still snoozing?"

Eden looked up and found Paxton's eyes. She was clearly embarrassed, but she told him the truth, "They're awake, and starting to fool around. That's why I came out here, I don't need to see or hear that. Doesn't it bother you?"

"Not at all," Paxton chuckled, amused by her discomfort. "Jazelle and I have an understanding. We're both free to be with other people. I'm a one-woman man, and an old man at that. I can't keep up with her appetite and I don't mind if she takes some pleasure in this dreary, dreadful place."

"I'll bet she would mind," Eden teased him, running her fingers up is leg, "if you took another lover."

"Well, that's never been put to the test," Paxton admitted, brushing her hand away playfully. "She's the only woman I've been with in here. She was my first, in the Square, and she keeps me plenty busy! She's never had to contemplate me being with another woman."

"Did you notice how jealous she got when she thought that you had initiated me?" asked Eden.

"Yeah, I noticed," he agreed, before deflecting their conversation toward her. "What about you? Aren't you jealous of Jazelle right now? I've seen the way that you and Abraham look at each other."

"Me and Abraham?" she repeated, smiling broadly. "It's not like that for us. He's like my big brother, my protector. I know this will sound strange but I feel like I've known him for a long time, like he's always been there somehow."

"And how are you doing otherwise?" Paxton asked, abandoning the subject of Abraham for the moment. "You've been in here a week now. You've killed your first human being. What about *you*?"

"I don't know what's happening to me, Uncle Paxton," Eden said, looking at him earnestly. "It's like I have this power surging inside me. I seem to know things now, like what's the best course of action in any given situation."

"That's your survival instincts coming alive," Paxton surmised.

"No, my instincts kicked in just as soon as we left home," she contradicted him. "And they've been in overdrive this whole past week. This feels different. This is making things happen just by thinking them. I killed that cannibal, I know I did, but I never laid a hand on him. I just shot him a thought, just one word, 'Die!' with all of the venom I could muster."

"And his heart stopped beating," Paxton finished for her. "You had to, Eden. It was kill or be killed."

"I know," she agreed. "He was going to kill all three of us, I could see it in his eyes. I don't feel bad about it, not really, but it scares me, to think that I could kill someone with the power of my mind."

"I have the feeling that you're just beginning to scratch the surface of what you can do," said Paxton. "Don't knock it! I think you'll find these powers of yours pretty useful in this place. You've already found them useful, and we're going to need all the help we can get this afternoon."

"Tell me again what Lizzie said to you," begged Eden.

"She told me to come from the north at sunset," repeated Paxton. "She said she'd be waiting for us in a truck in the garage."

"And she told you to come today?" asked Eden.

"Yes," confirmed Paxton, "which I thought was weird because tonight is Friday night and all of Megiddo is supposed to be under a flag of truce on Friday night. I guess since Xavier's starting an all-out war with the most powerful clan in the Square, he's probably not all that concerned about honoring a well-established truce."

"Who do you think will win the war?" asked Eden.

"The Mexicans outnumbered us two to one the last time I estimated, but that was months ago. I don't know what kind of firepower they've got but if they come after the McDonoughs full-force, the Rockin' M will be overrun."

"We need to rescue Lizzie before things get too bad," reasoned Eden.

"I agree, but it's going to be tricky because we need to wait for the attack to start if we have any hope of getting in and out of there unscathed. The motorcycles will make too much noise unless there's already a heated battle going on!"

"Well, where are we gonna wait out the rest of the day?" pressed Eden.

"This is as good a place as any," said Paxton. We're protected from view in three directions and we've already got the tent set up. We can pass the morning and most of the afternoon right here."

"How far are we from the McDonough's ranch?" asked Eden.

"Less than an hour, I should think, on the motorcycles. We came a bit too far north to find this campsite and we'll have to backtrack, but it won't take us long. We can have a good rest and then pack up and head out after an early dinner. I'm sure Jazelle will want to talk strategy all afternoon, but I just wanna sleep."

"Speaking of Jazelle," said Eden, as the ebony woman emerged naked from the tent. Even from the distance separating them it was clear to see that Jazelle was a handsome woman, with full, round breasts and a muscular physique. She squatted and relieved her bladder and was about to reenter the tent when she caught sight of the two of them on top of the hill and waved.

"Let's go back down there," suggested Paxton, "before they get started again. I really could use some sleep."

"Why don't you go?" offered Eden. "I'll keep watch for a while. It must be my turn by now."

"All right," agreed Paxton, letting out a long, loud yawn. "I'll tell Abraham to come and relieve you after a while."

They both stood up and Eden gave him a fierce hug for a long time before she let him go. Paxton hugged her back and whispered in her ear, "It's going to be okay, Eden."

"How can you be so sure?" she returned.

"Because of you," Paxton answered. "You're going to save us, Eden, all of us."

He kissed the top of her head and then released her from his bear hug. Turning away from her, he began to descend the boulder field carefully without looking back.

CHAPTER 11

MARTY

I'm a gay man, and proud of it. At least I used to be proud of it, during the precious few years when it was possible to live out of the closet. Doug and I even got married, officially and legally, after we had been living together as a couple for more than ten years. He didn't need the piece of paper, but it was important to me, so we waited in line with hundreds of our homosexual brothers and sisters at San Francisco City Hall in the first wave of applicants vying for same-sex marriage licenses.

Those were heady times. It seemed like we were on the edge of finally being accepted, if not actually embraced, by our society. Laws were enacted so that we couldn't be discriminated against because of our sexual orientation. I even helped to put some of those laws into place. I was a lawyer, in my former life, before I got Squared. Now I guess I'm a farmer. There's no need for lawyers in here, not when the only law that anyone upholds is survival of the fittest.

I thought we would grow old together, Doug and I. We had another ten mostly good years as husband and husband before things began to go south, not just for homosexuals but for anyone on the fringes of society. The tide just seemed to turn, not in one big wave or any one event that I could put my finger on, but slowly we began to lose our acceptance.

I can't pin everything on the Republicans, if I'm being fair. They had half of America behind them, the ignorant masses. People are sheep. They're so easy to lead this way and that, especially if you have control of the media. But things didn't really start to go bad until the Republicans had taken over both houses of Congress and the Presidency. A fortuitous rash of Supreme Court retirements and an untimely death gave them control of the courts as well. Life has never been the same in America since then, for any of us, but especially for homosexuals.

The laws began to change, one case at a time. Soon it became lawful to refuse service to homosexuals based upon one's religious convictions. Same-sex marriage was taken from us, and then civil unions as well. The anti-sodomy laws were resurrected much later, but that's not what got me Squared.

People were being assaulted in the streets, not just gay men but the homeless, blacks, Latinos, women. And the police became uninterested in anything less than murder, and even then, only if the victims were respectable members of society. We heard of the violence, but we never expected it could happen to us, not in San Francisco, the safest haven for queers anywhere in America.

It happened to Doug, at a BART station, as we waited for the subway train to take us home from a Thursday night Giants game at AT&T Park. There were four of them, young kids, skinheads. We had just missed a train and were waiting for the next one. Doug and I were always very affectionate and we never tried to hide who we were. They surrounded us and got right up in our faces, calling us all of the usual names.

I offered to give them my wallet, hoping that would appease them, but they weren't interested in mugging us. The one facing me, with thorn tattoos growing up his neck and onto his scalp, suddenly punched me hard, right in the stomach. I doubled over and threw up the hot dogs and beer from the game. The train was approaching the station and I thought that it meant our attackers would scatter and Doug and I would be safe. I was dead wrong.

While one of them stood over me to make sure I was incapacitated, the other three grabbed hold of Doug and pushed him in front of the inbound train, just as it was screeching to a halt in the station. Then they scattered, but not before my attacker kicked me hard in the face, breaking my nose and knocking out my two front teeth.

The police were worthless. They sent a sketch artist to the hospital and he did a reasonable job at capturing tattoo-face, the only one of the four that I got a really good look at. Weeks passed and then months and still no leads. They told me the perpetrators must have moved on. I wasn't buying it.

I buried and mourned Doug and all the while, all I could think about was revenge. I bought a gun and learned how to use it. I took a leave of absence from my law firm and started hanging out at Embarcadero Station, looking for the skinheads. I would wander the neighborhood for hours, searching the faces of everyone I passed. I went to Giants games thinking that they might have been coming home from the game as well. It took less than two months for me to find them, which just goes to show the cops weren't doing their jobs.

There were only three of them that night, up on Market Street, leaning up against a building smoking marijuana. I saw the thorn tattoos from behind as I passed my attacker. I kept walking past them and took the gun from its holster beneath my trench coat. Turning around quickly I unloaded the full clip into the three of them. I just kept pointing and shooting, moving from body to body, until there were no more bullets and the empty gun just clicked when I pulled the trigger. I tossed the gun in the bushes and walked down the stairs of the same subway station in which they had murdered Doug and I took the train home and cried myself to sleep.

The police came for me the very next day. One of those fuckers survived, and he knew exactly who had shot him. He testified at my trial, months later, from a wheel chair. It was an open and shut case, two counts of murder and one attempted murder. It didn't take much deliberation for the jury to sentence me to the Square.

Sometimes I wish that I would have died right alongside Doug on that subway platform, instead of the long, slow death that awaited me here. But we humans cling to life, most of us anyway, and the life I've got in here could be so much worse.

Paxton saved my life, what's left of it, there's no doubt in my mind on that account. I would not have lasted very long with the McDonough clan. They just about killed me the night of my Initiation. I was told to pick a female slave with whom I was expected to lose my virginity. I tried to decline but I was told I had no choice in the matter. I chose the youngest, most frightened looking girl in the lot, thinking I was doing her a favor because I had no intention of bedding her.

We were afforded the privacy of a tent and she started to kiss me almost as soon as I zipped up the door. I tried to hold her at arms' length, but that only served to make her come at me with renewed fervor. It was not a sexual urgency, but she seemed rather to be afraid that she wasn't seducing me fast enough. She fumbled at the waistband of my orange sweatpants and I caught her hands in mine and told her that she didn't have to do this, that I did not want to have sex with her.

She was stricken at this pronouncement and she crumbled to the floor, sobbing loudly. She begged me to have sex with her. She said that they would punish her if I did not have sex with her and she showed me the crisscrossed network of ugly red welts all over her back. I gathered her into my arms and tried to soothe her, telling her not to worry, that I preferred the company of men. I don't know why I thought she might keep my secret, but that admission was almost the death of me.

She stopped crying and kissed me on the cheek before leaving the tent. Not knowing what else to do I stayed right where I was and stretched myself out on the bedroll beneath me thinking I would like nothing more than to sleep the night away and forget all about the ordeal of the past twenty-four hours. Little did I know that my ordeal was just beginning.

No sooner had she gone than the tent door was zipped back open and two pairs of hands reached in to grasp my ankles and drag me from the tent. They dragged me kicking and screaming to a nearby picnic table where they were joined by a third man who knelt upon my back and twisted my arms painfully behind me so that he could tie my wrists together.

They lifted me into a standing position and then tied my ankles to the slanted wooden legs of the picnic table. Someone grabbed my bound wrists and lifted them upward, forcing me to bend over the table until my face slammed against the sturdy wooden slats. A rope was then attached to my wrists and tied off to the other end of the table so that my arms were stretched unnaturally over my head. The strain on my shoulders was incredibly painful, but my complaints were soon silenced by a cloth gag that was forced into my mouth and tied behind my neck.

I was raped forcefully and repeatedly well into the night and they left me tied to the table all through the heat of the following day. I am no stranger to having a man ride my ass, but they left me torn up and bleeding and I wasn't able to sit down for days afterward. It was sunset when I heard Paxton's voice asking one of the McDonoughs what I was still doing tied up to the table. They told him I was a faggot, as if that explained everything, and then they left me there.

I recognized his voice right away and as I lay there wallowing in my misery, I wracked my brain to try to figure out where I had heard it before. It wasn't until much later, when I realized who Paxton was, that I put the pieces together and determined that Doug and I had heard him speak, at a rally in San Francisco, to protest the rigged elections.

Paxton returned twenty minutes later. He cut my bonds and helped me to walk slowly into the main house and lowered me into a tub of warm water in one of the bathrooms. He washed me and he held me as I sobbed uncontrollably into his shoulder and he told me that everything was going to be okay. For that kindness alone, I am forever in his debt.

When I was well enough to travel, he took me here, to Maggie's Farm, and I have been here ever since. It's not the life I had hoped for, that life was taken from me on the subway platform in San Francisco, but it's a better life than most have in this place. For that, too, I am in Paxton's debt.

ELIZABETH'S ESCAPE

After much debate, Paxton and his crew abandoned their motorcycles by the side of the road, underneath as much brush as they could find. They were only a mile north of the main house, and still the ranch was quiet. They couldn't very well ride right into the courtyard without a pitched battle to distract the McDonoughs and the motorbikes could be heard from a long way off.

Jazelle was worried they would encounter sentries so they advanced somewhat slowly until she could be reasonably sure that there were none. It seemed, for the moment, that all eyes at the Rockin' M were pointed toward the south. They eventually came to a small hill within range of their binoculars and Jazelle called a halt.

"Take a break," she granted them, before scaling the short slope at a crouch, the binoculars clutched in her hand. Paxton was right behind her and they both fell to their bellies at the top with only their heads poking out over the crest of the hill. Jazelle took a quick peek and then handed the binoculars to Paxton.

"What do you think?" she asked him.

"It looks deserted," he responded, handing her back the binoculars. "Where is everybody?"

As if in answer to his question, a shot rang out to the south of the ranch, followed quickly by the staccato outbursts of semi-automatic weapons.

"Shhh," said Jazelle excitedly, "it's starting!"

"Yeah," Paxton agreed, "but it sounds pretty far off."

"Can we be that lucky?" she asked. A sudden explosion startled them both into action. Jazelle bounded down the hill and almost ran head-long into Abraham.

"It's now or never," she informed the Newts. "Follow me!"

They took off at a run toward the building closest to them, which just happened to be the horse stables. Jazelle, Abraham and Paxton all had rifles at the ready but Eden had refused to carry the pistol Paxton tried to give to her. They reached the back of the stables without incident and Jazelle slipped through the sliding doors to see if there was anyone inside. Moments later she whistled and the three of them followed her into the dark and smelly barn.

"Ain't no one here," Jazelle informed them. "The horses are gone, too, all but one old nag in the corner. The McDonoughs are takin' this shit seriously."

"Course they are!" Paxton agreed. "This is life or death for them. I'm just glad we're not caught up in all of it."

"What do you call this?" Jazelle asked him sarcastically.

"We're just visiting on an old friend," Paxton joked. "In and out. No muss, no fuss."

They were looking out through a slit in the front barn doors while Abraham and Eden peered above the sill of a grimy window to their right. It was dark, but they could see well enough to know that anyone still left at the Rockin' M was holed-up somewhere out of plain sight.

Jazelle pointed to the house and whispered to Paxton, "Ain't no reason for us to go in the house if you think that girl's gonna be in the garage. We ought to get right on up to the foundation though, just in case someone's aimin' to shoot us from one of them windows!"

"Let's use the side door then," Paxton suggested. "We'll be less exposed!"

They started to move in that direction and Jazelle motioned to Abraham and Eden to follow them. Paxton was about to open the door when Jazelle put her hand over his on the doorknob.

"Let me go first, sugar," she drawled. Paxton knew better than to argue with her and stepped aside so she could push past him. They followed behind her in single file, moving as quickly as they could, bent over in low crouches. They reached the house and still no sound could be heard coming from within, although there was dim light filtering through the kitchen window from some source in the interior of the house. They moved swiftly and silently down the length of the house toward the detached, three-car garage on its eastern flank.

The garage was quiet as well and all three overhead doors were shut. Jazelle only stopped for an instant before she sprinted across the driveway and then pulled up short and slammed her back against the gray wall harder than she intended. When there was no response from either the house or the garage, she motioned for the others to join her. Abraham tried the handle of the side door between Paxton and himself, but found it locked.

Jazelle came around to stand in front of the door and she held out her fingers in a countdown; three, two, one. As she closed her fist into a zero, she lifted her leg and kicked the door hard with her heel. The wood around the doorknob splintered and cracked and the door burst open forcefully, banging the shovels stacked against the wall behind it. She was also the first one through, her rifle leading the way.

Paxton came through the doorway on her heels. He could hear Eden's gasp from behind him just as soon as he caught sight of Elizabeth. She was tied and gagged and struggling to stand upright by leaning into a man who held a pistol pointed up and into the soft underbelly of her jaw. At a second glance Paxton realized that her captor was none other than their recent guest, Frank.

"You're gonna wanna drop those guns," he ordered with confidence, "and tell that other nigger to get in here, too. We know there's four of you."

"Go ahead, Abraham," Paxton said, bending down to set his rifle on the floor. "Come on in here."

Abraham came through the doorway with his arms up and rifle pointed toward the ceiling.

"Put the gun down!" hissed Frank, now pointing his pistol at Abraham's chest. His other hand was entwined in Elizabeth's hair, pulling her head forcefully backward. Abraham slowly lowered his rifle and put it gently on top of the other two on the crumbling cement floor.

"Right now, all of you, hands on your head where I can see them!" Frank ordered. He ushered them together into the corner formed by the wall and the closed garage door by waving his gun and dragging Elizabeth with him between their small group and the truck parked in the second bay of the garage.

"Sit down, cross-legged," he barked. "Keep your hands on your head, Goddammit!"

It was only after Paxton was seated and looking up toward Frank that he noticed there was a person behind the dark-tinted passenger window in the truck's cab. No sooner were they seated than Frank flung Elizabeth headlong at them, toppling them all like bowling pins. He laughed as they struggled to regain their seated positions with Elizabeth in their laps.

"Hand's up!" he yelled at them again. "I'm warning you!"

To emphasize his point Frank abruptly rotated his arm forty-five degrees and fired a warning shot out of the still-open doorway. The noise was deafening in the enclosed space and had the desired effect of instantly bringing everyone's attention back to their present situation.

Elizabeth had landed sidelong with her ass in Paxton's lap and her head on Eden's bosom. Eden ignored Frank's command and cradled Elizabeth's head in her left hand while removing her gag with her right.

"Oh, Lizzie!" she whispered and kissed her sister's forehead. Tears fell freely down her cheeks and onto Elizabeth's already tear-stained face.

The door of the truck flew open at the sound of the gun firing and the gravelly voice of Jonas McDonough coughed out, "That'll do, Frank. Stand down."

Frank lowered the two-handed hold he had on his pistol only slightly, but he backed up far enough to clear a path for Jonas as he alighted laboriously from the truck. Reaching back inside for his cane, he closed the door and turned around to face their group.

"Paxton," he drawled the name out slowly, "what are you doing here? I thought you were headed up north to see the Comanche."

"We are," admitted Paxton, "but we had to come here first to rescue Beth."

"How's that going for you?" asked Jonas, clearly enjoying his victory.

"Not so well, I'm afraid," said Paxton, trying to get a read on Jonas' mood. He had seen Jonas change from calm to violence and back again in seconds, and he suspected their present situation was tenuous at best.

"I knew you were coming," Jonas explained. "Frank told me."

"And how did you know?" asked Paxton, looking up at Frank.

"Wally told me," Frank answered, "before he died."

"You bastard!" Jazelle spat at him.

"Don't get your panties all in a twist, Jazelle," Frank smiled down at her. "I didn't torture him or nothin' like that. The tequila you was all drinkin' loosened up his tongue just fine. Then he passed out. Fatal mistake."

"If he was passed out you didn't have to kill 'im!" accused Jazelle.

"Couldn't take no chances," Frank offered. "And I was pissed that Paxton tied me up in the first place! Don't think I've forgotten that, Paxton!"

The sound of gunfire was getting closer and Paxton looked nervously out of the open door. He turned back to Jonas saying, "We've got to get out of here, Jonas! The Mexicans are going to overrun this place!"

"I've got the drop on the Mexicans," chortled Jonas. "Thanks to this little lady on your lap. She told me exactly where and when they would attack. You didn't think I'd let a treasure like her go so easily, did you?"

"Then she's probably also told you how many Mexicans are coming for your ass!" Paxton said with urgency. "You don't stand a chance!"

"There aren't that many Mexicans in Megiddo!" contradicted Jonas. "Our defenses will hold. At least, you'd better hope so. We're in this thing together, now."

"I'm begging you, Jonas," pleaded Paxton. "Give this place up and come with us, while there's still time! We're busting out of the Square, one way or the other!"

"Frank told me that as well," Jonas replied. "Is that supposed to entice me to just give up what's mine without a fight, just so I can go and get myself shot by the Indians or the Republican Guard? I guess you don't know me after all, Paxton."

Jonas nodded at Frank, who advanced upon their group with his pistol pointed at Paxton's chest. Eden and Elizabeth were distracted, staring deeply into each other's eyes as though they were communicating telepathically. Abraham started to gather his feet under him for a lunge at Frank just as a deafening blast rang out, causing everyone in the room to flinch reflexively. A moment later Frank crumpled to the floor, his face and chest a bloody mash of torn and bleeding flesh.

"That was for Wally," Marty exclaimed as he walked slowly through the door with a shotgun on his hip. Levelling his gun toward Jonas he continued, "And this one's just for me."

"Marty, no!" Paxton screamed. He tried to rise but it was impossible with Elizabeth's weight pressing him down. A second shot-gun blast was fired and Jonas joined Frank upon the floor. Marty got down on one knee to reload his double-barrel shotgun.

Paxton pushed Elizabeth forcefully from his lap and stood awkwardly up. He took a step forward and said, "Marty, what the fuck?"

"There's no time, Paxton!" Marty exclaimed. "They're already here, thousands of them! You gotta get outta here, now!"

Indeed, they could hear shouting and gunfire from right outside their sanctuary. Marty stood back up and approached the doorway slowly, being careful not to overly expose himself to what awaited outside in the courtyard. Paxton shuffled over to Frank, trying not to look at the gore replacing his once meaty jowls. He rummaged around in his pockets until he had located the keys to the truck.

"Let's go everyone!" he shouted. "Get in the truck!"

Jazelle and Abraham grabbed the rifles and climbed into the bed of the Dodge Ram. Paxton directed Eden and Elizabeth into the oversized cab. Eden helped Elizabeth into her seat, but then turned away to squat down next to where Jonas was still coughing and sputtering upon the floor. She laid a hand upon his chest and he immediately ceased his struggle for breath and lay still. She then stood up and quickly took a seat next to Elizabeth.

Paxton sprinted around the front of the truck and was about to clamber into the driver's seat when he noticed that Marty hadn't moved from his sentry position at the door. He yelled at him, "Marty, let's go!"

"I'm not coming!" Marty shouted back. "I got nothin' left to live for. I died with Wally back on Maggie's Farm. I'm gonna cover your asses, now go!"

Paxton was about to try to reason with him when Marty fired his gun into the belly of a dark-skinned boy clutching a raised machete. The boy's momentum carried him into the garage where he tripped over Jonas' prone body and fell hard against the side of the truck. Marty shot him again to be safe and then bent over once again to reload.

"Get in and rev the engine!" Marty directed. "I'll get the door for you."

Paxton did as he was told and the old engine kicked and sputtered into life. Marty grasped the handle and lifted the garage door as rapidly as he could with his right hand, while still clutching his shotgun in his left. He jumped out of the way of the truck and immediately emptied both barrels of his shotgun into two different Mexicans running wildly across the courtyard toward them.

Paxton stepped down hard upon the accelerator and the truck jolted forward into the bedlam now overtaking the Rockin' M. Both the McDonoughs and the Mexicans were running and shooting each other in all directions and

Jazelle and Abraham had to be discerning at they shot from crouched positions over the lip of the truck's big bed. Marty went down as he tried to reload his shotgun and Jazelle shot the Mexican trying to decapitate him with his machete.

Paxton turned left almost immediately, forsaking the crowded driveway in favor the dusty path to the stables. Shots continued to ring out from behind him, even as bullets found their mark upon the steel sides of the truck. A bullet shattered the passenger side window but missed all of the passengers. Paxton used his right hand to push the girls' heads down lower behind the dashboard.

Paxton intended to use the stables to shield them from the thickest of the fighting. Soon they were behind the big barn and Paxton took an off-road tack to keep the stables between their truck and the pitched battle for control of the Rockin' M. Jazelle picked off a rider on a motorcycle who had given them chase and then it seemed as if they were in the clear. Paxton stepped on the gas and held his breath until the gunfire began to recede behind their speeding vehicle and he was able to relax his death grip upon the steering wheel.

He continued to speed away from the Rockin' M as fast as he felt he could comfortably push the old truck through the mostly flat desert. He knew that they would eventually cross Route 54 in this direction, so Paxton set his concentration to the ground directly in front of his windshield to avoid driving into any pitfalls or popping a precious tire.

When they did cross the road, Paxton was at a loss as to whether he should turn left or right to recover their cache of gear and the two motorcycles. He looked back over his right shoulder and snaked his arm behind Elizabeth's head to open the small window at the back of the cab.

"Which way from here to the bikes?" he asked Jazelle.

"Take a right," she advised. "They're further on up."

By the time they found the motorcycles it was full dark and the sky was alive in a plethora of stars. Paxton was exhausted and wanted to make camp right then and there but Jazelle convinced him to put a few more miles between themselves and the Mexicans, just to be safe, as if anyone could ever feel safe in the Square.

Paxton and Abraham manhandled the motorcycles up and into the bed of the truck and the five of them crammed into the extended cab. Jazelle took the wheel with Paxton and Abraham on the seat next to her and the two sisters looked at each other from the second-row half-seat where they rode side-saddle with their legs tucked up under them.

"We probably shouldn't get too far along," advised Paxton, still thinking about finding his bedroll. "We don't want to pass by the others in the dark."

"Won't they try to flag us down?" asked Elizabeth.

"I doubt it," said Jazelle. "They have no way of knowin' it's us. If I were them, I would just lay low and let us pass right on by."

"All the more reason to stop and hole-up for the night," reiterated Paxton.

"Just let me find the right spot," snapped Jazelle. "I'm not gonna park right next to the god-damned highway!"

Jazelle found what she was looking for a few miles farther along when the road crossed a bridge over a secondary road. She slowed down and pulled off the highway, but only after she had found a suitable place to turn the truck around and descend the slight slope to the desert floor below. She cruised slowly forward, scanning the ground in front of their headlights for any sign of danger.

"Keep that rifle ready!" she told Abraham, who pointed the business end of the gun out of his open window.

Paxton half-expected to find squatters beneath the bridge but it was empty of anything larger than the desert fox whose eyes glinted red in their headlights before it trotted quickly away from their intrusion. Jazelle pulled the truck completely under the bridge before killing the lights and the engine. She then shushed them all as she rolled down her window and listened carefully to the night sounds outside their metal haven. They waited for five minutes in silence before Jazelle allowed them to get out of the truck and set up their tent.

They passed the night without incident, taking turns at sentry every two hours. They were already packed and ready to go as the sun cleared the horizon the following morning and they plotted their next course of action over a breakfast of cold oatmeal.

"They ain't gonna be lookin' out for a truck," suggested Jazelle. "I told 'em to stay off the road. I'm gonna take a dirt bike on up ahead and see if I can't find 'em."

"I don't want you to go alone," said Paxton. "Take Abraham with you. Maybe they'll come out of hiding when they hear the motorcycles. We should've come up with a better plan to hook up with them."

"Shoulda, coulda, woulda," Jazelle recited the phrase from her childhood. "It is what it is. You game, Abraham?"

"I guess so," he answered, looking over at Eden. She nodded almost imperceptibly.

"We'll follow behind you in the truck," Paxton offered. "Let's get a move on. Xavier might send somebody up here looking for us."

"Them boys got their hands full cleanin' up the dead and dyin'," guessed Jazelle. "They ain't goin' nowhere!"

"You're probably right," Paxton agreed, "but the sun's already up and we need to find the rest of the gang. You wanna help me with these motorcycles, Abraham?"

A few minutes later Jazelle and Abraham were snaking their way through the cacti back to the main road, rifles slung across their backs. The truck could not maneuver through the scrub brush as easily and Paxton drove slowly behind their receding forms, being careful not to pop a tire on the uneven ground. Soon enough they had regained the road and Paxton opened up the throttle a little, but only until the truck was moving at a modest twenty-five miles an hour.

Paxton had charged the sisters with scanning the landscape on either side of the truck for any signs of either the rest of their group or of trouble. He kept his eyes pointed forward to navigate the minefield of potholes that had taken over the road since the Republic had ceased to maintain it. Certainly no one in the Square would have taken up that mantle. Soon enough they were cruising along and Paxton broached the subject of Elizabeth's two missing days.

"What happened back there, Beth," he asked, "after we left you with Jonas?"

"Do you want all of the gory details," Elizabeth teased him, "or just the abridged version? Jonas got hold of some Viagra from somewhere…"

"That's all right," interrupted Paxton, taking his right hand off the wheel so that he could gesture for her to stop. "I don't need to know about all of that! What happened when Frank returned? I was sure Jonas would send some of his boys around to Maggie's Farm. We took our time packing up and we had to say goodbye to Wally."

"What happened to Wally?" asked Elizabeth.

"Frank killed him," Eden answered. "He choked him to death and escaped."

"Jonas was livid!" Elizabeth confirmed. "He wanted to a send a posse over there for your head, Paxton, but I convinced him not too."

"How did you do that?" he asked. "Never mind, I don't want to know."

"I told him the attack was imminent," she answered, ignoring him. "I told him I dreamt that the Mexicans would attack at sunset that same day. Suddenly, he had more important things to do."

"He must've been upset with you when the attack didn't happen," Paxton surmised.

"He was," admitted Elizabeth, "but I was able to put out that fire. Plus, I told him that my powers of prediction cannot always pinpoint the exact day something will happen, that it was more than likely the Mexicans would attack the following day at sunset, and I was right about that one."

"It doesn't seem to have done him any good," Paxton commented. "The Rockin' M is lost!"

"He had the chance to set up a defense, but there were just too many of them," said Elizabeth. "I told him how it would end, that he should just pack up and leave, but he was far too stubborn to retreat. He said he had no place else to go and that if he lost the Rockin' M there was no reason left for him to live."

"So how did you come to be tied up in the garage when we got there?" asked Paxton. "I expected to find you there alone."

"Frank knew you'd be coming for me," Elizabeth answered. "Jonas probably already suspected as much, but Frank confirmed it when he came back."

"Wally spilled the beans to Frank," Paxton muttered to himself, "but how did Wally know we'd be coming back here?"

"You told him, Uncle Paxton," Eden chimed in. "Don't you remember?"

"No, I don't remember," Paxton admitted. "I was a little drunk."

"You were talking to me," Eden continued, "trying to reassure me that we'd go after Lizzie before heading north. But we weren't alone, Wally and another man were there, and Grace and Jillian, too!"

"Shit!" exclaimed Paxton. "Well, that explains it. I thought I was holding my cards close to my shirt. Fucking tequila does me in, every time."

"All's well that ends well," offered Elizabeth.

"Is this gonna end well?" asked Paxton, looking over at her.

"I wish I could tell you," Elizabeth answered. "I can't see past Mukwooru at the moment."

"It didn't end well for Jonas and Frank," Eden commented.

"Or Marty," Paxton agreed. "Who else came in with him?"

"There were three others," responded Elizabeth. "All men, but I can't remember anyone's name. Jonas was none too happy to see them but he sent them off to fight just the same."

"What's that?" asked Eden, pointing excitedly to a pinpoint of flashing light coming from the desert about a mile to the northeast.

"That's gotta be Jazelle," guessed Paxton. "She's got a little hand mirror she uses to signal."

"Are you sure?" asked Eden.

"Not completely," he admitted, "but there's only one way to find out."

Paxton searched for a viable place to take the truck off-road and he found it soon enough in the form of a dirt road which crisscrossed their path in an east-west direction. He slowed down and veered onto the side road, which turned out to be in better shape than the deteriorating remains of Route 54.

He drove slowly forward along the dirt road until he could visually verify that it was indeed Jazelle who had been signaling them with her mirror. Abraham was there as well and they both leaned up against their parked motorcycles waiting for Paxton to join them. He parked the truck with its bumper several feet from the rear tires of the motorcycles and climbed out of the driver's seat. Elizabeth and Eden did the same from the other side of the cab.

"What's up?" Paxton asked as he walked right up to Jazelle.

Pushing herself up and off the seat of the dirt bike, Jazelle motioned for him to follow her the short distance north of the road. She explained as they walked together, "We found their campsite, but somethin' ain't right. See the horse shit? And these are the holes from the tent stakes."

"In an octagon," Paxton interrupted her. "This must've been them. They didn't get very far. What is this, about twenty miles from the Rockin' M?"

"On a good day," agreed Jazelle. "They can't move any faster than Rachel's horse and that old nag's on death's doorstep! It looks like they broke camp and headed this way, following the highway."

"That's what we told them to do," said Paxton. "What's the problem?"

The other three had come up behind them and were now listening in on their conversation. Jazelle motioned once again for them to follow her as she took off in the direction the horse's hooves and bicycle tracks were leading them, away from the campsite.

About a hundred yards from their campsite, the tack they had taken crossed an old wash-out. They would have had to climb ten feet down the steep slope to the bottom of the gully and then back up the equally steep bank on the other side. Rather than risk the climb, their trail turned west toward Route 54 along the rim of the gulch.

In another hundred yards or so there was an easier entrance into the gully where water had once eroded the bank enough to soften the downward slope. They followed the bike tracks single file through what was almost a doorway minus the jamb and into the wider crevasse below. Paxton didn't like the claustrophobic feel of the gully almost immediately.

The tops of the banks on both sides were a few feet above their heads so that they had almost no visibility of the surrounding desert. The gulch itself followed the meandering course of the floodwaters which had created it so they couldn't see either forward or back for more than fifty feet. Paxton began to get a sinking feeling in his stomach.

"This is a great place for an ambush," he said to Jazelle's back. "I can't believe they came in here."

"That's exactly what happened!" Jazelle confirmed, looking back at him. "We'll be aw'ight, though, if we're quick about it. Abraham and I already scouted around, up top."

"It looks like they were trying to find a way across," Eden said from behind Paxton.

"The fools should've kept going to the road," said Jazelle, "instead'a comin' into this damn death trap!"

"Is that blood?" asked Eden, looking ahead of both them.

"Sure 'nough is!" answered Jazelle. "And a lot of it, but no bodies."

"What do you think happened?" Elizabeth asked as she came up behind her sister.

"They were hit from above," Paxton surmised. There were several bloodstains surrounding him. "See all the stones down here? That was probably the first volley. Maybe they had guns as well, but they could just as easily have jumped down in here with machetes, right upon their unsuspecting heads. After that they dragged everything up this bank here, you can see the scratch marks. Nothing gets left behind in Megiddo."

"Exactly," Jazelle agreed. "And there are no bodies down here, either."

"Isn't that a good sign?" asked Abraham from the end of the line.

"If they all lived, sure" quipped Jazelle, "but that ain't likely from all the blood down here. Only one reason to be cartin' around dead bodies."

"You don't think the cannibals did this?" Paxton asked her. "This far south? If that's true we're in some deep shit!"

"We gonna be in deeper shit if we stay down here," Jazelle pointed out as she poked Paxton in the ribs to get him moving. "Let's get on back to the truck!"

They all turned around and filed back out of the fissure with Abraham leading and Jazelle in the rear guard. They were quiet until they suddenly burst back into the light and heat of the desert and began to walk more or less side by side once again. Paxton's brain had not been quiet and he voiced his newest theory to the group.

"It doesn't have to be cannibals," he said. "Maybe it's just a bunch of Vags."

"If they keepin' the bodies then they barter with the cannibals," Jazelle stated. "Either way they're fucked!"

"We have to rescue them," Eden said immediately. "Let's go!"

"Hold on there," cautioned Paxton. "We don't even know if they're still alive, who took them or where they were going. We can't just go charging after them. They'll hear us coming a mile away."

"Grace and Jillian and Rachel are alive, at the least," Elizabeth offered. "I've seen them with us, when we meet Mukwooru."

"Of course, you have," marveled Paxton. "What of the others?"

"I don't know," she answered truthfully. "I didn't see Bill or Barbara in my dreams, but that doesn't mean anything."

"So put your big brain to work on this," interrupted Jazelle looking directly at Paxton, "and figure this shit out! Then let's get a move on. Every minute we sit here gabbin' they're another minute farther away."

"We should be able to pick up the tire tracks from the bicycles on the other side of that gully," reasoned Paxton, "but we're going to have to drive back out to the main road and double back to do it. The blood stains we saw down there were still wet. They can't be too far ahead of us if all of this just happened this morning."

"It they're cannibals they'll be headed north," offered Jazelle.

"And if they're Vags they could be headed anywhere," countered Paxton, "but they did come out on the north side of that washout."

"Maybe they have a hide-out nearby?" guessed Eden. Paxton and Jazelle both turned toward her as if they had just realized they weren't alone out there in the increasing heat of the steadily rising sun.

"Vags are nomadic," Paxton informed her, "but they could have a temporary camp around here somewhere."

"Maybe," Jazelle conceded, "if they Vags."

"The way I see it," said Paxton, "we have one of three options. We can stash the truck and the motorcycles and head out after them more stealthily on foot. Or we could take some combination of vehicles and make up some time but give up the element of surprise."

"Most likely they'd be surprisin' us!" Jazelle commented.

"What's the third option?" asked Abraham in his baritone voice.

"We could leave them to their fate and speed straight up north to see the Comanche like we planned."

"No!" exclaimed Eden and Elizabeth in unison. Eden continued, "We can't just leave them! They'll all die!"

"They most likely dead already, girl," Jazelle said. "And we gonna be dying, too, if we go after them blind, least-a-ways some of us."

"The girls are right," Paxton said to Jazelle. "If there's a chance, we can save some of them, as Beth seems to think, then we have to go after them."

"Well, I don't want to drive headlong into an ambush," conceded Jazelle begrudgingly.

"Okay, I guess we'll be hiking," agreed Paxton, "but we can still use the truck to pick up their trail and then find a good place to stash it. Does anybody else have anything to say? Are we all in?"

"I'm in," said Abraham immediately.

"Me too," said the sisters, though not in unison this time.

"Aw'ight," agreed Jazelle, "let's get on it!"

CHAPTER 12

GRACE

I'm not a lesbian. Let me just say that first off. Jillian and I, we take care of each other in here. And yes, it gets sexual sometimes, but she's more like a daughter to me than a lover. That may sound strange or disgusting to you, but then you never lived in the Square. There's nothing in here that surprises me anymore.

Now Jillian, she's as gay as they come. She was a bull dyke on the outside. I'm not sure what she is anymore after being gang raped so many times. She's a man-hater, that's for damn sure, but it's hard not to be in the Square. The only man she doesn't hate is Paxton. Even Jillian can't hate Paxton. He's not like the rest of them, not at all.

I was married once, living the dream in Tucson, Arizona. John was a lawyer, worked for the government. I didn't have to work, but I took work piecemeal, editing manuscripts that never seemed to get published. I was an English major at Arizona State University. That's where I met John. We were married just as soon as we graduated.

We were happy for a time, until John started cheating on me. There were all the telltale signs of his dalliances, in retrospect, but I didn't want to believe them at the time. Even after I suspected something wasn't quite right, I didn't confront him about it directly for a long time, and it went on for a long time after that. I guess I was just comfortable in our life together, and fearful of how I was going to make my way in a deteriorating world without him.

He said he loved me, that he would change, but he never did. I couldn't take the lying as much as the cheating. And I couldn't stop worrying about John giving me Hep-G. So, I divorced him. He didn't believe I would go through with it, not until he was served with the papers. He actually got pissed off at me! And he fixed it so that he got everything, everything except our apartment, which he apparently never cared for anyway, and my few personal effects. They had to leave me my computer so I could continue to work.

My editing never did make a lot of money. It made no money at all if you consider that it was all done electronically. I would receive the manuscript and instructions on my home computer, without really knowing who they came from, or where I was sending my edits. They advertised as Eagle Publishing and had a spot on the Web, but they could have been anybody. When the manuscript was done and returned, I'd receive credits on my RepubliCard. Worked the same as money, and I had control of its comings and goings up to a point, as long as I didn't get hacked or have the government put a hold on my account.

I never knew who the authors were. I would try to guess, that was the little game I played with myself, while I was working. This one was a man, that one a woman. He is Caucasian and she is a minority, possibly a Republican of African descent. I made up elaborate stories in my mind, what they looked like, their families, where they lived. The only one I ever met was Bill, but that came later, after I had edited his book and right before they threw us both in here.

John and I had no children, and I was relieved by that fact at the time, but now I'll never get to be a mother. Women are nothing but chattel in here, bought and sold and traded. They don't have any use for us as mothers, there's already too many mouths to feed. We do what we can to protect ourselves and failing that, we abort anything that grows in our wombs before we start to show. The men consider us a waste of resources at that point. Who wants to feed a growing fetus if you're only going to kill the baby just as soon as it comes out?

Jillian was with the Harrisons before she got traded to the McDonoughs, for a horse! I was taken by Carl on Intake Day, but Paxton bargained for me soon thereafter. He didn't have anything to give Jonas for me, except the promise of a harvest down the road, and he also agreed to lend his scientific mind to the Rockin' M, one day each week. I've been with Paxton since we began our little commune on Maggie's Farm. Jillian came later, by a year or so, I would guess.

She got thrown in here for protesting her government. To hear her tell it, she protested as often and as loudly as she could, and believe me, there is no shortage of reasons to protest the Republic these days. We've been stripped of most of the rights that the former United States Constitution afforded us, such as the right to free speech and assembly. Even attending a protest is considered treasonous, but Jillian and her friends had escalated things and had begun to target the Guard when they were inevitably called in to crush a protest. It was a Gay Pride rally, surprise, surprise, that finally did her in.

Jillian doesn't talk much. I don't know if Paxton will ever get her to write in his book. She is still seething with anger, you can see it right there behind her eyes, even when she's smiling. Maybe she's always been angry. It couldn't have been easy to be a militant, lesbian feminist in the Republic, but I'm guessing it was a hell of a lot easier there than here in the Square! I think she's going to explode one day and kill everyone in her path. I'm not worried for myself, we have a bond, but I wouldn't want to be a man when that day comes.

I continued to edit manuscripts, after the divorce. I dated, but not seriously. Mostly I just tried to keep my head down. I barely made enough money to keep my apartment and feed myself, much less than to spend it frivolously at a bar tying to hook up. Most of the men out there were so intense. Everyone in the Republic is tense these days. No one ever knows when they'll be called into account for this thing or the other, a black van waiting for them when they get home from work. No one who gets into one of those vans ever comes back.

I worked from home, and the Guard came for me while I was eating a tuna fish sandwich for lunch on a Tuesday. I saw them pull up to the curb, from the window in my kitchen, but I had no reason to believe they were coming for me. Not until I heard the knock at my door. Apparently one of the manuscripts I edited did get published, and they weren't too happy about it. They asked me for my name and citizen number and then I was handcuffed and escorted to the van, my cup of Earl Grey tea still steaming on my little kitchen table.

I got a trial, that's where I first met Bill. He was the author of "Economic Models for the New Republic." I remember editing it, but I was merely checking for typos and grammatical errors. I didn't really even try to understand it. It certainly seemed innocuous enough and it was full of praise for the Republic. Part of my job was to report anything I thought was too liberal, but this one didn't even raise a red flag. And I had him pegged to rights as a white male in his thirties from a privileged background.

His defense team tried to pin the blame on me, said that I had changed the text with treasonous intent. My court appointed lawyer made a show of proving that I didn't even understand rudimentary economics so that I couldn't have tampered with the subject material in the manuscript. In the end they threw us both in the Square, on the same Intake day, no less!

We saw each other, when they marched us in here. He was in the other line of prisoners, almost directly across from me. We huddled together after the soldiers left, drawn to a familiar face, I suppose. That's how it came to be that we both ended up at the Rockin' M. Carl snagged us together, in one of his nets.

Bill's been at Maggie's Farm as long as I have. He's a good man, or he used to be, before they put him in here. We've become friends, after a fashion, though we were never lovers. He's only got eyes for Jazelle and I seek the comfort of a woman now. If that makes me a lesbian then so be it. I could never cheat on Jillian, she's too fragile, and I don't have to worry about getting raped anymore, not on Maggie's Farm. I have Paxton to thank for that. We all have Paxton to thank, for a lot of things, but not getting raped anymore is high on my list.

THE VAGABONDS

The trail, consisting of four bicycles, deep hoof prints and at least a half dozen sets of footprints, had not been hard to find. They picked it up easily from the rim of the gully where it pointed in a northwesterly direction toward Route 54. They followed alongside the trail until it merged with the road and disappeared onto the cracking and pockmarked tarmac.

"*At least we're headed in the right direction*," Paxton thought to himself as he drove the truck slowly down the road. He scanned the western shoulder for their tracks even as he kept one eye upon the obstacle course of abandoned cars, washouts and potholes he was trying to navigate without destroying their boon of a vehicle. Abraham scanned the eastern shoulder from the passenger seat and Jazelle looked toward the horizon from between them. The two sisters were in quiet conversation in the cramped backseat of the cab.

"I feel different somehow, not quite myself," he heard Eden's voice from behind his head. "I don't know how to describe it."

"You *are* different, sis'," Elizabeth responded. "I've been telling you that for years!"

"Yes, you have, and I think I am ready to listen, but this is different than *that* kind of different. It's almost as if I can feel electricity gathering in the air all around me, as if lightening could strike at any time. It's a foreboding I feel, like something bad is about to happen."

"What's that?" asked Jazelle, but she was talking to Paxton and Abraham. She pointed out the windshield toward the western side of the road, partially obscuring Paxton's visibility.

"I don't see anything…" Paxton began, but then he did see it. There was something fluttering in the wind, low to the ground, most likely stuck upon a cactus.

"It looks like a black plastic garbage bag," said Jazelle, peering through her binoculars. "See if you can find a place to pull off."

"There's a house or some kind of ranch up ahead," Abraham observed. He put a hand over his eyes to shield the sun and added, "There are a couple of buildings, right there, in amongst those trees."

"Pull over," directed Jazelle in her usual brusque fashion. "Now!"

Paxton pulled to the side of the road instinctually, though it was hardly necessary on the deserted road. He turned off the engine and then he turned his torso toward Jazelle and asked, "What's the plan?"

"Here's what we're gonna do," she began. "When I'm done talking, Abraham here will open his door and step out to take a piss."

"I don't have to piss," Abraham countermanded her orders.

"Just pretend, then," hissed Jazelle impatiently. "Leave the door open and pretend you're taking a nice long piss. They'll never know the difference."

"Who won't know the difference?" asked Paxton.

"Whoever's holed-up in those buildings," she responded. "I'm gonna sneak out behind you, big guy, and come up on 'em from the south. Give me a two-minute head start and then drive up there, slowly. They'll be lookin' at y'all and ain't never gonna see me comin'. If you hear gunshots, duck down and wait 'til I signal the all-clear. If you don't see me, y'all are on your own!"

"Be careful," Paxton admonished.

"Is everybody ready?" Jazelle asked. "When you get back in the truck, Abraham, pick up this rifle and point it right at the front of that first building, you got it?"

"I got it," he replied.

"Let's go then!" she whispered urgently without any further preparation. Jazelle shoved her shoulder into Abraham's solid frame and he pulled upon the door handle forcefully. In the instant they were out the door, Jazelle flung herself upon the ground and crawled quickly away from their vehicle, gripping a pistol in her right hand. Abraham looked self-consciously over his shoulder at the sisters before unbuttoning his jeans to see if he was capable of expelling any fluid from his desiccated body.

Paxton timed two minutes from the dashboard clock, which he doubted was keeping the correct time of day. Abraham climbed back into his seat and slowly raised the rifle until it was pointing out of his open window. He rested his elbow on the door to steady his aim. Paxton began to drive slowly forward and then turned down the dirt road leading to the "Last Chance Ranch" as indicated by the broken sign dangling from a wooden post. Everyone in the cab grew tense as they continued to drive forward, bracing themselves for possible gunfire.

"Get down back there," barked Paxton and the two women did their best to crouch down in the already cramped quarters. They were just pulling up to what must have at one time been a garage, when Jazelle jumped out from behind the side wall with her hands waving back and forth above her head. Abraham fell back in his seat in relief, his gun still pointing out the window but angled toward the sky.

"Holy fuck!" he cursed, but there was relief in his voice. "I almost shot her!"

Paxton parked the truck in front of the open garage bay and turned off the engine. Jazelle came around the hood of the truck to speak to Paxton through his open window.

"Ain't nobody around," she reported. "These buildings ain't got a roof between 'em, ain't no place to get out of the sun. Been picked clean, too, but I bet we could hide the truck for a spell. I'm gonna go take a look at that flapper."

"Hang on, I'll come with you," said Paxton. He grabbed the binoculars off the dashboard and opened his door. Stepping out into the heat waves radiating off the tarmac, he took a quick glance inside the garage and then opened the half-door to the extended cab and spoke to everyone inside, "See if you can clear out the broken cement so we can pull the truck all the way in here. We'll be right back."

Paxton took Jazelle's hand and they hustled across the highway and into the dry and dusty plain beyond. A short jog brought them to where the plastic was still fluttering, caught upon the spiny leaves of a yucca plant. Even before they reached it, however, they came across the trail of the Vagabonds and their captives in the dust.

The plastic turned out to be a make-shift vest made out of garbage bags and duct tape. The bottom fringe was in tatters and one of the front pockets had been sliced clean through by a machete, most likely, judging by the dried blood caked on the spot where the pocket should have been. It looked to have outlived its usefulness a long time ago, but nothing in Megiddo was ever wasted. Paxton guessed that the previous owner no longer had need of clothes, else it would probably still be draped across his or her scrawny shoulders.

"You want it?" Jazelle asked, extricating the vest from the yucca's thorny leaves.

"I'm good," said Paxton, holding up both hands. She tossed it at him anyway and laughed when he jumped out of the way and let it settle upon the ground in a crumpled heap.

"Where do you think they're headed?" he asked.

"The trail leads straight into those hills," answered Jazelle, pointing toward the west. "Looks like there might be a pass, right there, between the two biggest ones. Gimme those binoculars."

He handed the binoculars to Jazelle and there was silence between them as she scanned first the ground leading up to the foothills and then the slopes beneath what appeared to be a saddle between two peaks.

"Hang on," spoke Jazelle softly. "I think I see somethin' movin'."

She peered out of the binoculars for another ten seconds before handing them over to Paxton and whispering in his ear, "Take a look in the valley between those two peaks and tell me what you see."

"That's our horse!" said Paxton, when he had focused the binoculars upon the spot Jazelle had indicated. "What's it carrying?"

"Looked to be a couple of bodies," said Jazelle, "but I couldn't tell if they were ours or theirs."

"How many of 'em did you see?" asked Paxton.

"Nobody but the Vag leading the horse and one other," she admitted, "but they was probably in the rear. I can't imagine that old nag movin' too fast with all them bodies on its back."

"They're not too far ahead of us," reasoned Paxton, hanging the binoculars around his neck by their cord, "if we get on after them…"

"Hold on there, big fella," interrupted Jazelle. "We don't know nothin' about these Vags, how many of them there are, nor where they headin'. If they see us trailin' 'em, they're gonna tear us to shreds comin' through that pass!"

"Then we leave the truck and motorcycles here and head after them on foot," offered Paxton, turning back toward the road and taking a few steps in that direction. He motioned for Jazelle to follow him with a wave of his arm. "We can stash everything in that garage and hope to hell no one finds it until we get back!"

"That's all well and good," agreed Jazelle, jogging to catch up and then falling into step beside him. "But we should wait until dusk to go through that pass."

"That's hours from now!" complained Paxton. "They'll be long gone by then!"

"Mayhaps," agreed Jazelle, "but that nag ain't movin' so fast and I'm not gonna risk the rest of our necks strollin' through that pass in the daylight. If they got the sense God gave 'em they'll post a sentry high in those hills as a rearguard. That's what I'd do. They'll see us comin' a mile away!"

"I don't like the delay," said Paxton, "but I won't fight you on this one. We've got to protect Eden at all costs. I'd leave her here with the truck if I wasn't worried about what would happen to her in our absence."

"It's settled then," she said, putting her arm up in front of his chest to stop him before they crossed Route 54. Jazelle held her finger to her lips and cocked her head to one side, listening for anything out of the ordinary. She peered down the ribbon of black tar in both directions before nodding to Paxton. They moved forward together and crossed the road a hundred yards north of the abandoned ranch.

There was no sign of movement in any of the crumbling structures, but they could feel eyes upon them as they got nearer to their destination. Jazelle whistled and Abraham raised his hand in the empty hole which had once held a glass window.

"What's that truck still doin' out there?" barked Jazelle as she crossed the threshold of the garage. "Get that thing in here!"

"We couldn't find the keys," answered Abraham in their defense, "but we cleared out a space for it."

Paxton held up the keys with a sheepish grin as he came into the garage behind Jazelle and said, "I got 'em! I'll pull the truck inside."

When Paxton pulled the truck through the gaping hole of the garage bay door, he immediately saw that the three of them had not been idle in his absence. A tarp had been strung up in one corner of the garage as protection against the sun and a makeshift meal of bread and raw vegetables huddled together in the center of a blanket upon the floor, assembled from the meager supplies remaining to them.

Paxton suddenly realized the full extent of his hunger and his growling stomach accentuated the point. He shut off the truck's engine and climbed down from the cab only to seat himself immediately beneath the tarp and within arm's length of the food. He tore off a hunk of bread and began to chew upon it lustily. Jazelle joined him and did the same with an oversized carrot. The others stayed at their posts, each of them staring out of windowless holes in the cement walls in three different directions.

"Have you seen anything out of the ordinary while we were gone?" he asked no one in particular.

"What would be out of the ordinary?" returned Abraham, reminding Paxton that all three of their companions were Newts.

"Movement out in the desert?" Jazelle answered. "Dust clouds? Fire?"

"Not really," answered Elizabeth.

"Abraham scared up a rattlesnake," said Eden, stifling the urge to giggle. "I've never seen someone jump out of his own skin before!"

"It's not funny," said the big man, though he was smiling from ear to ear. "Damn thing almost bit me! It was sleeping under one of the cement chunks we removed. I dropped it right back down on his head!"

"Well Jazelle and I caught sight of our party," Paxton informed them, "the tail end of 'em, anyway. They were just disappearing through a pass in those mountains off to the west."

"What are we still doing here, then?" asked Eden, making a move toward the front doorway. "Let's go get them."

"Take it easy," soothed Paxton. "Jazelle and I have talked it through and we decided it would be better to cross that plain in the dark. There's no telling what they will do to their prisoners…"

"Or to us!" interrupted Jazelle.

"Or to us," Paxton repeated, "if they see up trekking across the desert. We'd be sitting ducks, and hard to miss if they were smart enough to post a sentry high up in those hills."

"Them Vags ain't too smart as a rule," Jazelle conceded, "but we ain't taking no chances. We gonna wait until dark, or near dark, before we head out. Then we don't have to conceal nothin' and we can fly across that plain."

"I take it you all have eaten?" asked Paxton.

"Yeah," they each said in succession.

"Then let's rest up," he continued. "Only one of us needs to keep watch and I'll volunteer for the first shift. We may be walking half the night so you all should try to get some sleep."

They waited until the sun was well below the western mountains before starting out on foot from the Last Chance. Care had been taken to camouflage the truck as best they could with a tarp and the excess concrete blocks that were strewn all along the sides of the crumbling structure.

Jazelle would not permit them a flashlight, but the light from the half-moon was sufficient for their furtive movements, once their eyes had become accustomed to it. She and Paxton carried small backpacks and rifles. The others carried only one gun between them and the machetes that were tucked into their waist belts. Eden and Elizabeth were comfortable with guns, but neither of them had ever used one on a human.

They made good time crossing the plain before the small mountains, alternately jogging and resting between the available cover, which was scant. Most of the vegetation was stooped and stunted, with an occasional tall flower stalk from a yucca plant, but that wasn't something they could hide behind. There were some taller desert willows and mountain mahogany trees scattered across the desert plain and they used them as milestones and resting spots on their clandestine journey in the pale moonlight.

Jazelle was clearly the leader of their march, directing them this way and that, when to stop, when to start up again. In less than an hour they were already starting the climb to the pass between the increasingly jagged peaks. There was no cover at all in the foothills and Paxton prayed there wasn't a sentry watching them from above.

It was different in the pass. The sky wasn't as big, and it was darker in the moon shadows of those rocky spires. Sounds were amplified as well, bouncing around the walls of the canyon from who-knew-how-far-away. At first it was only animal sounds, the call of a hawk or night owl, or the howl of a coyote. As they crested the pass and crossed over to the western side of the range, they began to hear human voices and a flickering of dancing light to their south that could only be caused by fire.

Jazelle told the rest of them to sit tight behind a boulder which shielded them from the firelight and then she took off into the night after whispering in Paxton's ear and kissing him on the cheek. They waited for ten long minutes for her return, all the while listening for clues as to what awaited them further down the western slope of the mountain range. It sounded as if there were a lot of Vags having some kind of party, accentuated every now and then by the unmistakable screams of women in distress.

Eden wanted to go right down there and do something to relieve their distress, and it was all Paxton could do to hold her back and make her wait for Jazelle. He clutched her arm and told her stories of his wild college days with her father at the University of Maine.

"Tucker and I were inseparable the whole time we lived in the dorms," he began. "We actually met on the basketball court, one week into our freshman year. We didn't even realize we lived in the same dorm until we walked home together one night from the fieldhouse. Your father was voted the cutest boy in York Hall, but I was the most popular."

"He never told us any of this," Elizabeth complained. "He never talked much about his past at all, not anything from before Eden was born."

"He was probably trying to cut all ties to his past," Paxton explained, "to keep you girls safe."

"A lot of good that did," Eden remarked sarcastically.

"What are you talking about?" interjected Paxton. "You're here, aren't you? Against all odds, you're both still here."

"You won't be if you don't hush up, you fools!" hissed Jazelle, appearing suddenly in their midst.

"Jesus, you scared me!" said Paxton, nevertheless relieved to see her. "What's up?"

"I took care of one sentry," she said without compunction. "Mayhaps there's more, but I ain't seen one between here and the Vag camp. They's holed up in some natural bowl which hides 'em from all but the birds, but they's carryin' on so loud that everyone for miles is gonna know where they are!"

"How many of them are there?" asked Abraham.

"I didn't get close enough for a look," admitted Jazelle, "but from the sound of that great big party they throwin' I'd say there's at least a dozen!"

"It's not too late to abandon this quest," offered Paxton, testing the group's resolve.

"Uncle Paxton!" complained Eden immediately.

"We can't!" agreed her big sister at the same time.

"Abraham?" asked Paxton.

"I'm with them," said the big man, pointing at the girls with his thumb.

"You're all insane," scoffed Jazelle. "We ain't got the numbers for this, and we ain't got no idea what kind of heat they's packin'."

"But we do have the element of surprise," Paxton pointed out. "That's got to count for something."

"Well let's not lose it by jabberin' away like a flock of cacklin' hens locked out of the chicken coop!" suggested Jazelle. "Keep your mouths shut and your heads down and follow me!"

They moved slowly toward the source of light and sound, following Jazelle in single file along the clearly marked trail. Every step brought them closer to what sounded increasingly like a drunken bacchanalia and Paxton's adrenaline started pumping into his system causing his heart rate to accelerate as he prepared to respond to the unfolding situation with either fight or flight.

When they got right up to the lip of the depression, Jazelle made them lie down on the rocky ground and crawl the last few feet for a first glimpse of the Vags' raucous revelry. Two things were abundantly clear in that first glance – there were a lot of Vags in that clearing and not everyone down there was enjoying the party.

The fire they had going was a huge conflagration and Paxton's first thought was, *"Where did they get all of that wood?"*

His curiosity regarding their resourcefulness was immediately dispelled when he saw what they were doing to the remains of the other half of his posse. Grace was naked and splayed out across a nearly vertical buttress, her hands tied and secured over her head to some stanchion on its other side. She was alone and sobbing, her back a crisscrossed hatch of red weals from what must have been a vicious flogging.

Jillian and Rachel were both being raped, right there on the ground beside the fire, without so much as a blanket or sleeping bag to protect their backs from the rugged and rocky ground. Neither were tied and both were lifeless and looked as though they had endured this violation for a long time. There was no sign of Bill or Barbara.

A group of four or five Vags sat around a makeshift table playing cards and just as many sat next to the fire gnawing hunks of what looked like meat from a distance. Another one was tending to something roasting on a spit in the center of those flames and the smell of that roasting flesh suddenly came to Paxton's nostrils and made him salivate like a Pavlovian dog, despite the carnage he was witnessing.

Paxton had no idea how long they took in the scene, but it couldn't have been more than a minute. After he got over his initial shock, his analytical mind took over, noting the number and position of their enemy and already formulating a plan of attack. A quick glance at Jazelle verified that she was doing the same, nodding her head as she counted the Vags. When their eyes finally met, he was just about to ask her what she wanted to do when Eden made all of their strategizing moot.

Noticing a movement in the corner of his eye, Paxton turned his head to see that Eden was standing straight up and making no attempt to conceal herself as were the rest of their rescue party. Paxton reached toward her arm in the attempt to pull her back below the rim and out of sight but before he had even touched her, she screamed.

It was an otherworldly sound, full of lament and sorrow but laced with outrage and menace. It went on for several long seconds and it felt as if Eden was putting everything, she had left in her into that single scream, "Aaaaiiiiyyyaaahhhh!"

CHAPTER 13

BILL

My name is William Grayson, and I was a professor of economics at Arizona State University for most of my career. Paxton was a college professor too, but our jobs in higher education couldn't have been more different. Paxton was only nominally listed among the faculty at the University of Maine, more for the prestige of the institution than for his own. He is arguably the most famous living scientist there is, if you can call this living.

Paxton traveled all over the world to attend conferences, receive awards and collaborate with the best scientific minds of the times. When he did teach the occasional class in quantum physics or differential equations, he insisted that he meet with his students, face to face, in a real classroom, in real time. Very old school, but that's Paxton, and he could get away with it because he's Paxton Stephens. The rest of the world has moved on.

Arizona State was one of the first universities to embrace online education, and all but a handful of colleges followed suit. In the beginning, I really think an honest attempt was made to equate online education with the traditional model in terms of the quality of education we administered to our degree recipients. We argued that motivated students could learn in a variety of different settings and there was no longer any need for the antiquated style of classroom learning that had dominated education for millennia.

At some point it became a business, and maybe that was the intent all along, but you can't argue with the economic model. A university need only pay a professor up front to develop an online course, and then graduate students could administer several courses at a time for relatively small stipends. The professor would receive a small stipend as well, for attaching his or her name to the course and for fielding questions from the graduate students when their knowledge was lacking. As time went on, we had less and less contact, either direct or electronic, with the students actually taking these courses.

Online education was praised for keeping the cost of higher education affordable for most of the population. As long as you could convince everyone involved that the quality of instruction had not been compromised, it was a win-win all the way around. We patted ourselves on the back for giving our citizenry the highest level of education of any country anywhere in the world. The politicians liked it so much that they changed to an online model for high school education, back when it was still mandatory.

Paxton would argue, and we have argued, that it was not the same education. I'll grant him that we had some problems with academic dishonesty in the beginning, but we did our best to close those loopholes as they arose. He'll also say that students only put the information into short-term memory long enough to complete the online assessments, or worse yet they just looked up the necessary answers and didn't commit anything to memory. I would counter that observation with the fact that in this day and age, we don't need to commit anything to memory anymore since we have vast amounts of information at our fingertips on the RepNet.

Paxton likes to blame everything that's happened on the failings of our educational system, if not specifically online education. He will say it caused everything from the degradation of our environment to our failing infrastructure to the oligarchy that now calls itself the Republic. He may have a point about the Republic. It is certainly easier to control a population that rarely leaves their homes and communicates solely through an electronic medium that can be monitored and manipulated. We seem to have lost our ability to interact with each other face-to-face in a non-aggressive manner, but I'm not blaming that on online education.

It did free me up to work on my research, though, not that it ever amounted to much. I analyzed current economic models and tried to use them to predict future markets. I was always careful to heap praise upon the Republic, which wasn't really a stretch for me because I've been an avowed Republican my whole life. Perhaps I was too effusive in my praise when I wrote "Economic Models for the New Republic." Honestly, though, I don't know what I would have changed about it. I certainly didn't expect that it would land me in the Square!

In my paper I argued that we could replace all of the government's entitlement programs by giving every citizen a modest stipend upon which to live. Everyone would receive this flat, yearly payment, rich or poor, sick or healthy, saint or sinner, upon their indoctrination into the RepubliCorps and every year after that until death. If they wanted to earn more, then they would need to contribute something more to society. There would be no other financial assistance from their government in any form.

The government would pay for this program, and everything else a government needs to pay for, such as infrastructure and defense, by keeping a small percentage of every financial transaction, paid in some part by both the buyer and seller, as determined by the government. No other more complicated system of taxation would be necessary. There was more to it, of course, but I had all of the mathematics worked out in the paper. It seemed like such a simple and elegant solution to the behemoth our government had become. I had no idea the shit-storm it would create or I would never have published it.

The conservatives hated it because it was too close to socialism. The liberals hated it because it didn't go far enough to protect people on the fringes of society and it gave everyone an equal share of funding the government. Had they thought it through they would have realized that my system would have made the wealthy pay their fair share of government funding because there would be no more loopholes for them to use to get out of paying their taxes, and besides, the Republic had already been marginalizing those people on the fringes for years as our collective resources began to dwindle.

Some of the holdout liberal politicians did figure it out, and made my economic model a rallying cry for fixing a broken system of government. We all went down together, even though I had been a model citizen of the Republic my entire life. We're all going down anyway, everyone on this dying planet, though some of us will go down sooner than others.

This place is as good as any to make a stand and I lucked out when I hooked up with Paxton and Jazelle, especially Jazelle. I wasn't expecting to live out the rest of my days in some real-life version of "Survivor" but a man can make his way in here with his wits and his strength, and some help from his friends. I may die prematurely in here, but I have never felt more alive than this past year in the Square. Maybe this is better than the slow death by starvation and degradation that was probably going to be my lot on the outside. As Jazelle is always saying, "Maybe this is better."

EATING A DEAD HORSE

The Vag camp went completely silent in the wake of Eden's scream, for three long seconds, as all eyes turned to their suddenly unconcealed position. After that all hell broke loose. There was no longer time to strategize or prepare for this fight. Paxton's instinct for survival kicked into overdrive and he unloaded all five rounds from his bolt-action rifle in rapid succession, though he had no idea whether or not any of them found their marks. Both Jazelle and Abraham fired their guns from either side of him and Paxton's ears rang from the reports.

Eden started to climb down over the lip just as soon as her scream abated. Elizabeth jumped up and tried to grab her sister's arm but Eden shrugged her off and launched herself onto the gravelly slope where she alternately jumped and slid to the bottom. She immediately strode purposefully forward to where the two most recent rapists were struggling to zip up their pants and stand.

Paxton could only watch the scene unfold because he was too unsure of his aged aim to shoot into the group now containing Rachel, Jillian and Eden. Jazelle and Abraham continued to shoot into the periphery of their clan, but Paxton's gun drooped as he watched Eden deal with her attackers all on her own.

When she had reached a point directly between the two men, Eden's arms pushed forcefully outward from her chest, open palms aimed at the kneeling Vags. Both of the men flew backward as if they had been physically struck and then lay motionless upon the ground. Another one came at her from behind with a machete just as the rock next to Paxton's head shattered from the bullet which nearly ended his life.

"Shit!" exclaimed Jazelle. "Get down!"

She grabbed him by the shirt collar and dragged him below the edge of the lip. Abraham did the same to Elizabeth, who was still standing and staring at her sister with her mouth agape.

"Where's the shooter?" asked Jazelle, her eyes wide with surprise and fear.

Before anyone could answer they heard Eden give another blood-curdling scream, "Yyyaaaahhuunghhhaaiiyyy!"

Dead silence followed that scream, until the popping bonfire recalled them to their surroundings. The battle was over, though they wouldn't know that until they overcame their collective paralysis and ventured a gaze over the edge into the carnage below.

All of the Vags were down, without even the groans of the wounded and dying to break the silence. Eden knelt next to Rachel and was stroking her hair with one hand while the other rested upon her naked abdomen. The man who had just been about to slice her in two lay prone on the ground, his machete still clutched in his fist.

Jazelle was still scanning the rim of their encampment for the gunman when Elizabeth jumped up and over the edge and shinnied down the slope to join her sister. Jazelle, Paxton and Abraham joined them, but only after they verified that it was safe to do so.

Eden had already shifted to Jillian as they walked slowly into the camp, eyes darting this way and that for possible attackers. She had both hands upon her badly bruised abdomen and was whispering soothing words to the prone woman.

"You're going to be okay," she said. "Hush now, you're going to be okay. They're all gone. They can't hurt you anymore."

Jillian looked up at her with unfocused eyes and asked, "Who are you?"

"I'm Eden," she answered. "Paxton and Jazelle are here, too. We rescued you. You're safe again."

"Paxton?" she asked feebly.

"Come and help me with Grace," said Jazelle, poking Abraham in the ribs. They moved off in the direction of the stone slab where a sobbing Grace was trussed up like a sacrifice to some primitive god.

"Paxton?" Jillian repeated. "Is that really you?"

Paxton knelt down next to her and guided her head into his lap, saying, "I'm here, Jillian. We're all here. You're going to be okay. Where are Barbara and Bill?"

"Dead," she answered simply. "They're both dead. They got Bill in the ambush. He told us not to go down into that gulch, but we didn't listen. We even teased him about it. Girl power!"

She tried to raise her clenched fist to emphasize 'girl power,' but the effort clearly caused her pain and she immediately clutched at her ribcage. She explained, "I think I have a couple of broken ribs."

"Shhh!" continued Eden. "You're going to be okay."

"What happened to Barbara?" Paxton continued to question her.

"She needs to rest, Uncle Paxton," admonished Eden.

"She died after we got here," Jillian answered him, "loss of blood, I expect. Those fuckers cut her tongue out on the walk up here. They said she talked too much."

"You rest now," Paxton told her. "We'll talk more later."

He motioned for Elizabeth to take his place and he helped maneuver Jillian's head into her lap. As he was preparing to stand up, he glanced over at Eden and saw the blood on her shirt.

"Eden," he said with some urgency, "you've been shot!"

Eden looked down at her left arm and noticed for the first time that there was indeed a long, bloody gash on her bicep and blood was running down her arm and onto her shirt. She shook her head and exclaimed, "It's just a scratch. Don't worry about me."

Paxton took a closer look, turning her arm gently this way and that. Releasing her arm he said, "You were lucky, Eden. It looks like you were just grazed by a bullet. What were you thinking just walking down into their camp like that?"

"I wasn't thinking," she responded. "When I saw what they were doing to Grace, and Jillian and Rachel, I just wanted to hurt them."

"Mission accomplished," he agreed, shuffling the few feet over to where Rachel was attempting to sit up.

"Ouch!" she exclaimed, clutching at her back. Paxton took a look at her torn and bleeding back, but unlike Grace her wounds were caused by the jagged rocks she had been forced to lay down upon.

"I'm gonna go and look for some blankets and something we can use for bandages," said Paxton, unsure of how else he could help the situation and growing increasingly uncomfortable at the sight of the women's naked and tortured flesh. "We also have to make sure there aren't any more Vags hiding out in those tents."

"They're all dead," muttered Eden. "I killed them all."

"If that's true," Paxton commented, "then they got what they deserved. Don't beat yourself up over it, Eden."

Paxton gave Rachel a brief visual examination to verify that she wasn't in imminent medical danger and then he made a beeline for the largest of the tents. He approached slowly with the butt of his rifle upon his hip and the muzzle aimed at the zippered opening. Only the screen door had been closed and Paxton tried to peer through the black, gauzy mesh into the interior of the tent. Shadows from the flickering firelight bounced over all six walls of the hexagonal tent and Paxton stared at it for a long time before he convinced himself that it was unoccupied.

Setting his rifle upon the ground he remained on one knee and reached a hand forward to feel for the zipper. He pulled it from the ground to the apex of the doorway and looked into the half circle created by the drooping screen door. It appeared as though the tent contained nothing more than crumpled bedding and clothing. Tugging at the corner of the sleeping bag nearest him, he dragged most of the tangled hodgepodge toward him without having to cross the threshold of the tent.

Paxton gathered as much as he could of the soft bundle into his arms as though he were transferring a load of laundry from the washer to the dryer. He felt underneath him for his rifle, grabbed that as well and then stood awkwardly upright. He shuffled his ungainly but manageable load back to where he had left the women, turning his head sideways for a better look at his path as he moved around the large fire pit. When he had reach a spot between the two victims he opened his arms and let his bundle explode outward and downward, being careful to keep a grip upon his gun.

"Here are some blankets," he offered. "Let's make the girls comfortable."

Just then Jazelle strode into their midst with Abraham close behind. He was carrying Grace as one might carry a sleeping child, his hands cradled under her butt and her arms crossed behind his neck. In this way he needn't touch the raw welts upon her bleeding back.

Paxton spread out one of the sleeping bags and he helped Abraham to lay Grace down gently upon her side. He gathered a few articles of clothing and wadded them up into a pillow for her head.

"Paxton?" she whimpered.

"Shhh," he soothed. "Everything is gonna be just fine. Eden and Beth will take care of you. You're safe now."

"Where are we?" she asked him feebly.

"Shhh," he repeated and then turning to Abraham he continued, "Use one of these T-shirts to bandage Eden's arm. She took a bullet to the bicep."

Finding Jazelle's eyes, he motioned with a sideways jerk of his head that she should follow him. He stood up and announced, "We'll be right back. We need to have a look in the rest of those tents."

Abraham stood up as well and asked, "You want me to come with you?"

"You stay here," Jazelle answered for Paxton. "Keep your eyes peeled, especially out on them hills. If anything moves out there, shoot it!"

Paxton and Jazelle moved cautiously from tent to tent, peering inside each one to verify that there were no Vags waiting to ambush them. There was a dead man in one of the two person tents, which gave Paxton pause until he poked him hard with the butt of his rifle to no effect.

As they approached the last tent, they could hear noises coming from its interior and they stopped in their tracks to listen more closely. A whispered conversation was going on in there, but the door flap closest to them was shut tight and they couldn't see how many persons belonged to those voices.

They listened for several long minutes, frozen in their tracks, and the more they heard, the more it sounded as if there was only one voice in the conversation, a woman, muttering to herself. They could only catch a word or phrase here and there, but it almost sounded as if she were praying.

Jazelle caught Paxton's eyes and mouthed the words, "Stay here," before she took off toward the other side of the tent. Once she was in position, Paxton shuffled forward the few feet to the tent's front flap.

"We know you're in there!" he finally said in a deep, booming voice laced with all the menace he could muster. "We have rifles pointed at both exits! Come out of there slowly with your hands up!"

"Don't shoot!" a distraught woman's voice screamed from the other side of the tent's thin wall. "I can't move! I'm hog-tied!"

"How many of you are in there, girl?" barked Jazelle from the other side of the tent.

"Just me!" came the woman's earnest reply. "I swear! And two dead bodies. A man and a woman. I don't know who they are. I swear! I'm hogtied in here!"

"Can you move at all, girl?" asked Jazelle. "Can you open up this door so we can see you're tellin' the truth?"

"I can try," she said, and they heard shuffling movement from within the tent's interior. It went on for a long time and Jazelle grew more impatient with every passing second.

"What you doin' in there, girl?" she shouted in her nervousness. "Can you open the door or not?"

"Wait a second. I think I got it," the woman replied. The zipper nearest Paxton moved upward a couple of slow inches and then stopped.

"That's all I can reach," said the woman frantically. "I swear!"

Paxton nodded to Jazelle, who approached the opposite door slowly. She bent down to find the tent's zipper as Paxton moved the end of his rifle into the slit on his side. He caught Jazelle's eyes from over the dome of the tent and mouthed the words, "One, two, three!"

On three Paxton raised his rifle violently upward and the slit opened from floor to ceiling in an instant. Jazelle did the same on the other side of the tent and they both struggled to see into the shadowy interior of the tent.

A woman was indeed hogtied at Paxton's feet, her naked back to him and her hands right where the zipper had been before Paxton thrust it upward. She screamed, "Don't shoot!"

A quick look inside verified that she had been telling the truth. The only other occupants in the tent were two bodies stacked lifelessly one upon the other.

"It's Bill," Jazelle informed him, from her now fully opened doorway.

"And Barbara," Paxton concurred.

"How long you been in here, girl?" Jazelle continued, but the hard edge to her voice was gone.

"All night," she answered. "They found someone else to play with. More than one. I could hear them screamin' from here."

"I'm going to untie you, now," Paxton said, setting his rifle upon the ground. He knelt down next to where her ankles were tied to her wrists and searched with his fingers for the knots which would need to be untied before he could set her free. A quick pull on a dangling end of rope released her wrists from her ankles and she sighed in relief as her legs sprung back to a more normal position, parallel with the rest of her body.

"Don't untie her hands, yet," suggested Jazelle, "not 'til we know we can trust her."

"I'm not one of them," she assured her. "I'm just a slave."

Nevertheless, Paxton heeded Jazelle's advice and set to work on the ropes securing her ankles together. Once he had released them, he grabbed her biceps to help her into a sitting position.

"Ouch!" she complained, flinching as though she expected him to slap her. Paxton immediately released his grip and looked at her naked body for the first time. Her arm was black and blue where he had clutched it, but the bruises were there long before his contribution. As his eyes adjusted to the dim light, he could see that her whole body was covered in black and blue and straight crimson welts from what must have been a whip.

Looking down at the ground she commenced to whimper, "Please don't hurt me! I'll do anything you want."

"We're not going to hurt you, sugar," Jazelle comforted her. She had moved around the side of the tent to join Paxton. Bending over from behind the girl's back she gently but firmly cradled both elbows in her palms and lifted the woman into a standing position. "Can you walk?"

"I," she stammered. "I think so."

"We're gonna take you to someone that can help you feel better," Jazelle explained. She motioned with her eyes and head for Paxton to take one of the girl's elbows and together they helped her limp back toward the firelight.

"Who is that?" asked Elizabeth when she saw the trio appear on the other side of the bonfire. She jumped up and ran toward them to offer her assistance.

"I'm just a slave," the woman answered without looking up.

Elizabeth lifted up her chin and looked into her eyes saying, "What's your name, hon?"

"Valerie," she answered and immediately looked back down at the ground.

"Untie her hands, Uncle Paxton," Elizabeth ordered sharply. "Valerie is no threat to us."

Paxton ignored Jazelle's warning look and obeyed Elizabeth's command. He didn't feel threatened by Valerie either, the poor girl could barely stand up. It took a minute or two for Paxton to find a way to unfasten the knots, and when he finally succeeded her arms did not spring forward as her legs had done but rather hung limply at her sides.

Abraham had sauntered over to them as Paxton worked at the knots and he gathered Valerie up in his arms before she could fall over. He carried her the short distance to Eden's makeshift recovery room and laid her down on the blanket next to Grace. Eden immediately began to attend to her worst contusions.

"We gotta check out the rest of this camp," Jazelle reminded Paxton. "Before we do anything else, we gotta make sure that it's safe."

"Yeah, alright," Paxton agreed, grateful for the distraction from the victims of the Vags' bloodlust. He followed Jazelle back through the firelight and into the gloomy darkness beyond it.

A quick look through and around all of the tents yielded no signs of life. Jazelle was careful to check all of the fallen Vags for a pulse, but they were all good and dead. There were seventeen of them lying around the camp, with most of those near to the campfire. They found number eighteen, the one who had been shooting at them, when they searched the perimeter of the camp. Jazelle peered out onto the plain for several long minutes before she nodded her head and pronounced the all clear.

The Vags didn't have much to speak of save for their bedding and tents, and a few articles of spare clothing. They each carried some kind of knife, mostly machetes, and one of them had a watch. They only found the one rifle, and that turned out to be their own. The gear the Vags had stolen from their party was mostly intact, except that their food had been ransacked and devoured. Jazelle located their bag of medical supplies and she snatched it up before she and Paxton made their way slowly back to the flagging bonfire.

Paxton finally got a good look at the fire as they rejoined the others. There was a jerry-rigged spit over the center of the flames with a whole horse leg on the horizontal crosspiece. It was once being turned by the Vag that lay face down in the dust next to it, but now it was getting burned on the side that had been left facing the fire ever since his demise. Paxton turned the leg onto its other side and left it over a fire that was now incapable of burning anything not directly sitting upon its hot coals.

He found another horse leg already cooked and mostly eaten upon a greasy blanket that looked as though it had served many such meals. Two goat carcasses, also mostly picked clean, lay in the dirt not too far away. There was something alcoholic in a cooler next to the table. Paxton found a coffee mug and filled it halfway with the strong-smelling brew.

"Cactus beer," he cursed to himself, spitting out the acrid fluid almost immediately. He sniffed the cup, swirling it under his nose as a wine connoisseur would twirl a nice merlot to study its aroma. Shrugging his shoulders, he heartily drained what remained in the cup before setting it back down on the ground. He walked the few feet to where the injured women were being tended to by the others. Abraham had been sent by Jazelle to the perimeter to keep watch over the camp.

Squatting down on his haunches, Paxton began in a somber tone, "I'm so sorry for what happened, to all of you. I'm sorry for Barbara and Bill, they deserved better than what they got. We'll give them a proper good-bye tomorrow."

"I believe we're safe here, for the moment," he continued. We counted eighteen dead Vags, and one live one."

"I ain't no Vag," interrupted Valerie from where she lay upon the blanket. "I swear, I'm just a slave."

"You ain't no slave either, girl!" said Jazelle impatiently. "Not no more."

"There are at least two more," Valerie continued. "Craig, and another guy."

"Where they at?" asked Jazelle, alarmed. She jumped up from her cross-legged position and commenced to look this way and that in alarm.

"They're not here," replied Valerie. "Master sent them out to find the cannibals. They drew straws to see who would go, no one wanted to miss the party, but meat don't keep too long in this heat!"

"When they comin' back?" asked Jazelle, visibly relaxing her vigilant stance.

"Sundown tomorrow at the earliest, and that's only if they get lucky," she offered. "More likely the day after tomorrow. That's what they told Master."

"You're Master's dead, and you ain't no slave, no more girl," Jazelle retorted irritably. "So, stop talkin' like that. You're giving me the heebie-jeebies!"

"Twenty of them," mused Paxton to himself. "That explains why they weren't concerned about the ruckus they were causing. They must've felt pretty safe up here, with those kind of numbers to protect them."

Raising his voice, he spoke to everyone within earshot, "Listen, I know that no one feels much like partying under the circumstances, but we gotta raise some hell here, and in a hurry. Those gunshots were heard for miles around. If this camp goes suddenly silent, there's going to be scavengers comin' around here before too long to check out what went down. We gotta make some noise like we're twenty Vags havin' a knock-down, drag-out!"

"You're right, Uncle Paxton," Elizabeth said dejectedly. "No one feels like having a party."

"Let's get over ourselves, then!" encouraged Paxton, raising his arms as well as his voice. "Rachel's horse is being barbequed, there's no use wasting that bounty. And I found a couple gallons of cactus beer that's already going bad, if it was ever good! We're still alive, all of us, and that alone is a miracle worth celebrating."

"I'll take some of that rot-gut," spoke Grace for the first time. "Might help deaden the pain."

"It'll probably do us all some good," continued Paxton.

"And then some bad," chimed in Jazelle. "Let's just hope it ain't too bad."

They ate their fill of horsemeat and drank until the cactus-beer gave out. Paxton revived the fire and Jazelle and Elizabeth helped him tend to it. Paxton couldn't convince anyone to whoop it up, so he searched out his guitar and gave them a private concert, doing his level best to project his aged voice and encouraging the others to sing along. His lame attempt at a party reached a crescendo right before the cactus beer dried up, when he goaded most of the others to join him on Robbie Robertson's, *The Weight*.

Eden refused to eat or drink and didn't say a word in English all night, but continued to alternately lay her hands on all four injured women and mutter prayers in Spanish that only Elizabeth could understand. Her efforts seemed to be paying off and the injured women perked up more than they had any right to given the ordeal they had just suffered. Paxton did not know how to comfort her and he assuaged his own discomfort with a redoubled effort to get the others to join in his concert.

Jazelle left the party to spell Abraham, who proceeded to attack the remains of the horse leg like a man who hadn't eaten in weeks. When he finally stopped to take a breather, Paxton commandeered him into helping tuck the ladies into tents for the remainder of the night. He instructed Abraham to take the largest of the tents and then he walked off in the direction he had seen Jazelle take an hour ago.

She was sitting on a rock outcropping overlooking the camp and the western plain below the mountain range in which it was nestled. Paxton waved his arms and shouted out to her as he approached so as not to startle her into taking a shot at him with the rifle perched upon her lap.

"Hey," he said simply when he was close enough to her that he could speak in conversational tones.

"Hey, yourself," she returned, smiling at him briefly before her countenance returned to its usual intensity.

"We did it," said Paxton, taking a seat next to her so closely that their thighs were touching. He put his arm around her and nuzzled her neck.

"That we did," she agreed, "or Eden did. That girl is *scary*."

"Well, she was the driving force behind making us come back for the others," Paxton agreed. "She's growing more confident in her abilities."

"We never should've split up," said Jazelle.

"We had to split up," Paxton disagreed. "Elizabeth's rescue could've gone south if we had done it any other way."

"Then we should've left them at the last camp we shared together," Jazelle continued to second-guess their decisions over the past couple of days. "Bill and Barbara would still be alive."

"We don't know that," Paxton tried to comfort her. "I'm so sorry about Bill. I know how close you two were. He made a bad call to take them down into that gully, but that's all it takes in here, one bad call. We saved the rest of them."

"For the moment," she agreed, "but what's gonna happen to us up north, Paxton? You really think them Indians ain't gonna shoot us on sight?"

"Call me crazy," Paxton replied, "but I think the Comanche knows we're coming. I think he's waiting for us, up there in those hills, with open arms, and I think he's going to help us bust out of the Square."

"I knew you was crazy the first time I seen ya," chuckled Jazelle, smiling up at him. Paxton smiled back at her and then leaned in to kiss her full lips.

"Listen," Paxton said. "Why don't you go on down to the tents and get some sleep, or somethin' else, if you need it. I know how keyed up you get after a fight. Abraham's waitin' down there for you, in that big tent in the center of camp."

"He is?" asked Jazelle in surprise.

"Well, he doesn't know it yet," teased Paxton, "but I don't think he'll kick you out of the tent. Go on now, I'll take watch for a while."

She stood immediately up and stretched her arms above her head, still clutching the rifle in her right hand before passing it on to Paxton. As she was turning to leave, she instructed him, "Aw'ight, I'll go, but don't you go fallin' asleep up here, old man. I can smell the cactus beer on your breath!"

"Don't worry about me," he responded. "I'm pretty keyed up, too. I'll look for someone to replace me after a while."

He watched her saunter down the hill with feline grace before he lost her in the shadows of the small tent city below. It was only a matter of minutes before he began to hear the telltale signs of their lovemaking. Jazelle was more discrete than usual and he guessed that it was her concession to the traumatized women in the tents surrounding her. In any event, it was also over quicker than usual and a deathly silence fell over the camp while everyone but Paxton caught a few hours of precious sleep.

CHAPTER 14

VALERIE

Paxton: What is your name?

Valerie: Valerie Thompson. Citizen # 1253588192.

Paxton: Do you know your age?

Valerie: Twenty-five, give or take.

Paxton: Where are you from?

Valerie: I've always lived on the streets of Chicago, since I can remember. My mom was a street walker, that's how we lived. We slept in the cardboard shanty towns all over the city. Sometimes she'd hook up with a man for a while, and we'd have a roof over our heads, not more than a few weeks or maybe a couple of months. That usually ended in a big fight, with mom beaten up or sometimes we'd steal the poor bastard blind and get as far away from him as possible.

Paxton: What became of your mother?

Valerie: She was rounded up, same as me, in the street sweeps. They got her six months ago, or a year, I don't know. Time gets all mixed up in my head these days.

Paxton: Why is that? What's wrong with your head?

Valerie: It's the hero, man.

Paxton: Hero?

Valerie: Yeah, heroin's big brother. Like ten times stronger, and I've been a hero worshiper my whole life, until just recently. He'll keep you feelin' right, all day and all night, but he's a nasty little fucker if you ever wanna call it quits. Most folk don't survive that break-up. You don't think I look this shitty all the time, do you? You ain't got no hero in here?

Paxton: I'm sure somebody does, but we don't. Is there anything else we can do to help you?

Valerie: Water is all, I'm just so thirsty. If I don't shit my insides all out, I may yet live.

Paxton: The Vags didn't have any hero?

Valerie: Vags?

Paxton: That's what we call the people who captured you, short for Vagabonds or Vagrants. They don't have a permanent home in here but travel where they will, raiding and killing.

Valerie: They didn't have shit! Not until they took your horse. Now that was a score, and a pretty nice feast, too. Nah, those assholes weren't interested in doing anything but eatin' and fuckin'. Lucky for me, I know a little something 'bout fuckin'. Mama, god rest her soul, she taught me everything she knew and I learned the rest on the job.

Paxton: So, you think your mom is dead?

Valerie: She must be dead, unless she caught the eye of a prison guard or a soldier. That's what I did. The whole time I was locked up I was playing up a guard, young kid, didn't know what hit him. I let him fuck me through the bars, a couple of times. When it came time to go, they marched us outta there in two lines. I was in the longer one, the one for just about everybody in there. My guy snuck me into the shorter line, when no one was lookin', the one that only had a handful of ladies in it, the one that was comin' here.

Paxton: Where do you think they took the other line?

Valerie: Some of the nastier guards would talk to us at night, told us all kinds of shit to scare us and it pretty much worked, too. Most of them girls cried themselves to sleep most nights. Those guards told us that we were all bound for the firing squads. They told us after that we'd be chopped up into little bits and shipped down south as fodder for the hogs. Don't know if I believe that one, but I'm sure as shit glad I found my way into the shorter line.

Paxton: What were the Vags going to do with my friends?

Valerie: Fuck them 'til they were all but dead and then trade them to the cannibals.

Paxton: What did they hope to get in return?

Valerie: I don't know. I've only been in here a couple of weeks, I think, time gets away from me these days. They pretty much kept me chained up in the tent you found me in, since they took me, 'cept when we was on the move, then I was chained to Lonnie. They ain't fed me much, but most of it's been processed food that they get from somewhere – potato chips, crackers, Spam. There was bread when I first came here. They cooked up a couple of rabbits once, but I didn't get none of that.

Paxton: Are there any more of them I should know about?

Valerie: What do you mean?

Paxton: Were there any Vags gone off hunting or raiding when we attacked? Other than the two you already told me about?

Valerie: How many'd you kill?

Paxton: Eighteen.

Valerie: That many? I don't know how many they were all told. I tried to count 'em all once, when they took me out of the tent to shit, and I had to shout and scream and beg them for that! They was eatin' them rabbits I told you about.

Paxton: So, what was the count?

Valerie: I can't remember. Fifteen? I get so confused these days. Most of them was men. They was always comin' and goin', if you know what I mean. There were at least ten different men that come in to fuck me regularly. Lonnie was the worst one. Did you get Lonnie?

Paxton: We got them all. What did Lonnie look like?

Valerie: He was always wearin' a camouflage vest and an orange baseball cap. Mostly that cap stayed on, even when he was sleepin' if you can believe that!

Paxton: We got him.

Valerie: Thank God! He was the worst one! He was a nasty fuckin' sadist, that one. You see these burns on my breasts? He did that!

Paxton: Do you have any questions for me?

Valerie: Wanna fuck?

Paxton: No, and you no longer have to have sex against your will. We're different.

Valerie: Where have I heard that one before?

Paxton: You can make up your own mind about us in time, but for right now we just want to know if you're well enough to travel.

Valerie: You mean walkin'? I can walk, but I ain't gonna get far with no food in my belly.

Paxton: We got food, and medicine. But the Vags killed our nurse. I'm going to send Eden over here to take another look at you. She's a healer.

Valerie: Ain't no cure for what I got, 'cept time. Unless you got some hero?

Paxton: We got time, but not a lot of it. We're heading to the Guadalupe Mountains to see someone they call the Comanche. We're going to take you with us, because you'll die if we don't. We have a truck, at least until the gasoline runs out. When you heal you can decide for yourself whether you want to stay or go, we won't stop you.

Valerie: Sounds too good to be true.

Paxton: Well, where we're going is probably no picnic, but I should hope you'll fare better than you did with the Vags. Here's some horsemeat and some water, eat it slowly so you don't puke it all back up.

Valerie: You have kindness in you, I can see it in your eyes. I ain't seen any kindness in a long-ass time.

Paxton: Don't get used to it. You're not likely to find a lot of it in the Square.

GUADALUPE MOUNTAINS

It was still dark when Abraham emerged from the tent, relieved himself and searched the perimeter of their stolen camp for Paxton. He found him on a small knoll overlooking their campsite and the valley below it to their west. A taller ridge rose at his back to block the morning sunlight well beyond the early summer sunrise.

The Vags had chosen their temporary home well. It rested about halfway down the western slope of a thousand-foot ridge, hidden from all but the eagles in a depression behind a smaller ridge running down to the desert plain. One would have to climb the lower ridge most of the way to its crest before discovering their hideaway, and anyone doing that would be seen by a sentry well before they came close to the encampment.

Their tribe had been a score strong before Eden unleased her fury upon them. Without Eden they all would have died, or else they would have abandoned their rescue attempt, assuming they had they been able to retreat from the Vags unseen. With her at their side it seemed they were an unstoppable force, but there had been a significant cost to Eden. Not only had she proven she was not invincible, but Eden was exhausted after her skirmish with the Vags and her miraculous nursing of the assaulted women. Elizabeth practically had to carry her into a nearby tent when she could finally convince her to take a break.

"Paxton!" Abraham whispered forcefully, when he was close enough to discern his gun-strapped silhouette in the dim light. "Jazelle sent me up here looking for you. She says it's time for you two to head out. I'll take the next watch."

"How'd you sleep?" asked Paxton, winking at him. Abraham gave Paxton an embarrassed smile before looking down at his feet in silence. Paxton let the quiet between them linger a few moments before reassuring Abraham there were no hard feelings, "Don't sweat it, man. I can't keep up with her. Maybe you can?"

When Jazelle was keyed-up on adrenaline, the only thing that could calm her down enough to go to sleep was a vigorous fucking and multiple full-body orgasms. Paxton wasn't up to the job last night and chose to take watch instead and let the others sleep. The rest of them had split up in predictable fashion with Jillian and Grace sharing a tent, Eden and Elizabeth in another while Rachel tended to her new charge in a third tent. Paxton had been sitting cross-legged on his rock outcropping for half the night, in a hyper-aware state of meditation which probably crossed over into sleep on more than one occasion. He was startled to wakefulness when he heard Abraham unzip his tent door and relive himself.

"Not likely," Abraham conceded, pondering the boots he had removed from the corpse of the largest Vag he could find. They were still a size too small for him.

"You can see pretty well down to the west from here," Paxton continued, "or at least you'll be able to when the sun comes up. We'll signal to you from the top of that ridge over there if we see anything alarming on our way back down to get the truck. You can get this camp packed up once everyone wakes up."

"Jazelle already told me as much," said Abraham, finally looking up from beneath the boulder where the now standing Paxton was trying to work the blood back into his legs.

"God my legs are on fire!" complained Paxton. "Pins and needles!"

Abraham asked, "Do you need a hand."

"No, I'll be all right," he responded, before disappearing behind the back side of the jumble of jagged rocks. Eventually he emerged around them to stand before Abraham.

"Just need to find my feet again, that's all," he admitted. "Getting old is a bitch! But it beats the alternative!"

"So, I've heard," Abraham acknowledged one of Paxton's overused quotes.

"I've been thinking about this and I imagine we'll try to drive the truck around to this side of these mountains," said Paxton, pointing down and toward the west. "I think it'll be easier than trying to lug all of this gear up and over that ridge. It'll be all downhill from here. We'll let the truck do the heavy lifting until we run out of gas."

"It's too bad about the horse," Abraham commented.

"Yes and no," Paxton half agreed with him. "Rachel can ride in the truck and that old nag would have slowed us down. She made for a tasty dinner, though, didn't she?"

"Best meal I had since they put me in the Square," agreed Abraham. "No offense to Maggie's Farm."

"None taken," allowed Paxton. "See what you can salvage from the carcass. We'll need all the nourishment we can carry for the journey ahead of us."

Paxton reached out his hand and Abraham grasped it in a firm but brief handshake. Their eyes met briefly and Paxton nodded before saying, "I don't expect any trouble but this is the Square. Trouble has a way of finding everyone in here. If we're not back by mid-morning something went wrong. I can't tell you what to do at that point, you'll just have to wing it like the rest of us!"

"Be careful!" Abraham admonished as Paxton turned to walk away.

"You do the same," he responded, "and take care of our girls."

Paxton and Jazelle hiked slowly but steadily back to the Last Chance Ranch as the sunlight gradually grew in intensity around and upon them. They encountered no one either on their journey eastward or at the abandoned ranch and all seemed to be as they had left it in the former garage.

The truck sputtered to life at the turn of the key and Paxton drove it northward because it looked like a shorter way around the mountains that did the southerly route. Jazelle snuggled up next to him in the cab, but she kept her eyes on the roadway, searching for any signs of danger.

"Did you get any sleep at all last night, sugar?" Jazelle finally broke the long but comfortable silence that had lingered over their morning hike.

"Are you gonna be mad at me if I say, 'Yes'?" he responded, looking sidelong at her.

"When do I ever get mad at you, sweetie?" she asked, punching him playfully in the shoulder.

"Let's just say I meditated all night and leave it at that," said Paxton. "I'm sure I didn't sleep as well as you did."

"Oh, my Gawd!" she drawled back at him squeezing his bicep. "You have no idea!"

"I'm happy for you," he said seriously, "that you have Abraham. I'm not gonna be around forever. You need to look to your future, for after I'm gone."

"Hush now," she admonished, jabbing him in the ribs. "You ain't goin' nowhere!"

"Ouch!" he complained good-naturedly. "What's that up there?"

Jazelle retrieved the binoculars from the glovebox. Peering through the windshield she spotted what looked to be a dirt road traveling west, perpendicular to Route 54.

"Looks like a way through," she said. "Slow down!"

Paxton slowed down and turned left onto the secondary road. He proceeded with caution, but only after Jazelle had thoroughly scanned the desert north of the ridge they were skirting. Once again, he found the auxiliary road to be in somewhat better condition than Route 54 had been, and he cautiously applied more pressure to the truck's gas pedal with his right foot. The mountains safeguarding the rest of their posse were now to their south and the road they were traveling snaked its way between smaller hills until they were on the other side of the ridge.

"Turn there," directed Jazelle, pointing to a barely discernible dirt road which veered to the south. Paxton did as he was told and was soon crawling along the rugged trail, wishing this particular model of Dodge Ram had four-wheel drive. They continued to drive south with Jazelle scanning the ridge through Paxton's window, looking for their hideout.

They would have driven right past it had not Eden and Elizabeth jumped up and down on one of the ledges high above them as they were passing right on by. Paxton waved back at them, brought the truck to a stop and turned off the engine. He and Jazelle climbed out of the car and they both waved up at the sisters before turning to the more expedient matter of trying to get the truck in closer to the camp.

They scouted the immediate vicinity and determined that they really couldn't get the truck any closer to the ridge than to just back-track a hundred yards or so to where it looked like there was a foot trail leading upward. Jazelle took off up the trail while Paxton went back to retrieve the truck. He turned it around laboriously on the narrow road and then parked it at the trailhead. Jazelle was already so far ahead of him along the ascending trail that he resigned himself to climbing up after her solo. He scanned the western horizon for anything suspicious before pocketing the keys to the truck and taking off up the trail.

The hike up to their lair was steeper than he had given it credit for and Paxton was breathing hard and sweating profusely by the time he rejoined his friends. Elizabeth brought him some water and sat down on a flat rock with him while he caught his breath.

"You guys got everything packed up?" he asked her, between gulps of water.

"I think so," she answered, "but we're wondering what to do with the bodies."

"Leave 'em to the cannibals, or some other starving scavengers," Paxton replied. "I'd burn them but we have nowhere near enough fuel up here for that!"

"What about Bill and Barbara?" she continued.

"Oh, right," Paxton responded but then remained silent for so long that Elizabeth was just about to repeat her question when he looked back up at her and said, "We can bring them down with us to the truck. Maybe we can find enough brush down there to send off our own, but even that looks doubtful. If

I was a smarter man, I would have sent them off last night when I burned up the rest of their wood!"

"You're the smartest man I know!" Elizabeth reassured him, placing a hand on his arm. "But you can't think of everything, all the time, Uncle Paxton."

There was too much gear to get it all down to the truck in one trip. Each of the three sturdy new tents they had commandeered would give three of them all they could handle. Abraham had volunteered to carry Rachel down the mountain piggy-back. They had stripped the bodies of all of their clothing and accessories and requisitioned all of the Vags' gear, which amounted to some cooking pots and utensils, four cots, six backpacks of various sizes, a flashlight and a pair of binoculars, a rifle with no bullets that they could find and a handgun with five rounds in its clip. Each of the Vags had been armed with a machete as well and including the spares they had a pile of twenty-one of them.

Paxton stood up slowly and lumbered clumsily over to Jazelle who had been busy barking orders at the rest of their troop. Laying a hand on her arm he said, "We should bring Barbara and Bill down with us, too, and give them a proper burning."

"Are you kidding me?" Jazelle snapped back. "They're dead and they gonna stay dead no matter what we do with 'em. You burn 'em you're gonna bring every Vag within twenty miles down upon our heads!"

"We don't have to sit around and watch them burn," reasoned Paxton, "and we can speed away in the truck afterward. It's the right thing to do."

"We ain't speeding nowhere in that truck," argued Jazelle, but she had softened to the idea. "How you gonna get them down there?"

"We can make a travois with the canvas tents and wooden poles," he answered. "It'd take two of us to carry each one, though."

"That'll get two of them tents down, but there's still one more and it's too heavy for any one person to carry, exceptin' maybe Abraham," countered Jazelle. "Valerie has post-traumatic stress disorder or some such bullshit, so she's about worthless. We probably need someone to hold her hand just to get her to walk down the hill with us. We got a shit-ton of leftover horsemeat, too! Someone's gonna have to make two trips to get all of that down to the truck."

"I don't know how much room we're gonna have for all of this shit," mused Paxton. "We can take the dirt bikes out of the truck, but we're gonna need some space for passengers back there. I'm willing to make a second trip, maybe while some people prepare the funeral pyre, but let's take the essentials on the first trip just in case we need to leave in a hurry."

"So, no dead bodies?" asked Jazelle, raising her eyebrows.

"Yes, dead bodies," Paxton returned. "We can leave the third tent and the cots behind and load up the machetes and horse meat into the backpacks. You and Eden take Bill, and Elizabeth and I will take Barbara. Abraham's got Rachel. Jillian and Grace can come down with Valerie and they can stuff their backpacks with as much weight as they can carry."

"Sounds like a plan, old man," said Jazelle, slipping an arm around his waist and kissing him on the cheek. "Are you okay?"

"I'll be a lot better when we get away from all of this death," he admitted. "I don't give a shit about the Vags, but I'm sick over Bill and Barbara. We don't have time to sit around and talk about our feelings. Let's round up the others!"

It took them an hour to make their way down to the truck with the first load and Paxton was too exhausted to make good on his promise of a second trip. Jazelle, Abraham, Eden and Elizabeth turned right around and began to climb the hill once more while Paxton supervised the loading and packing of the truck. Rachel helped from inside the bed and when the heaviest objects were set in place Paxton sent the other three women out to look for combustibles.

"That wasn't right," Rachel broke the silence that had settled after the others had gone, "what the Republic did to you. Not after all you did for them."

"There are so many things that aren't right out there, beyond that fucking Wall," Paxton agreed, "not to mention the things that aren't right within these walls."

"Yeah, but you gave them anti-gravity, for Christ's sake," she continued. "You should be a national hero."

"And what did they go and do but weaponized it," commented Paxton. "I can think of at least a hundred applications that would serve humanity better than that."

"They're starting to realize it can be used as an energy source," said Rachel, as she helped to pull a rope across the back row of gear they had lined up against the extended cab. "There was even talk of pardoning you and coming in here to get you to help them with it."

"As if I would help those fuckers after everything I've been through," spat Paxton. "I doubt there's any of my family members left to hold over my head. How do you know they were going to release me?"

"Edward was on the Energy and Natural Resources Committee," she answered. "He pushed hard for your release."

"How do they even know I'm still alive?" asked Paxton.

"Are you kidding me?" she chuckled. "They have eyes all over this place. They've been watching you all with their satellites from the get-go. Edward wasn't privy to that information, except in the most general way, but they know all about your comings and goings in here."

"I suspected as much," admitted Paxton, "but I never gave it all that much thought. This does add another wrinkle to our escape from this place. Whatever plans we make are going to have to be done away from their prying eyes."

"You can't get away from their prying eyes," Rachel interjected. "They're everywhere. They've got cameras on every street corner. Republic drones fill the sky, just out of reach of thrown projectiles and it's illegal to shoot them down. The SmartHouse keep tabs on any and all human activity within its walls. They watch us every time we log onto a computer or talk on the phone. It's also illegal to cover or disable those tiny embedded cameras, the reason being that if you're obstructing their view, then you must have something to hide."

"Sounds like the RepTube on steroids," said Paxton. "I don't know why they need to watch people at their computers, I'm sure they're storing every click in some vast government database somewhere."

"RealTime, they call it, and it's just about all people watch these days," she continued. "That and the RepNews. They give out prizes if you catch someone doing something illegal, so they've got us all spying on each other. All you've got to do is log onto RepNet and choose a location. Usually there are lots of different camera angles to choose from."

"Wow," said Paxton, cinching the rope over their gear. "Things have gotten so much worse since I've been in here!"

"You don't know the half of it!" Rachel agreed. "They're not even going to the trouble of putting people in the Square anymore, not unless you've got a high profile or some political capital. Most illegals just go to the firing squads on the Range."

"And there's no resistance to any of this?" asked Paxton incredulously.

"It's there, especially in the cities, San Francisco, Chicago, New York, but it's muted, and probably futile. You're not going to like this, Paxton, but the discovery of antigravity was a game-changer. In the wrong hands…"

"How could it not fall into the wrong hands?" interrupted Paxton angrily. He had been leaning up against the truck with his elbows on the side of the bed, but he threw his hands up into the air and exclaimed, "Those fuckers will turn anything into a weapon!"

"It's worse than that," Rachel informed him. "They have a facility somewhere in Nevada where they can make people fly, but not in a good way. I saw it on my computer. That's how we know there's resistance. People are still hacking the Internet, posting pictures and videos of the atrocities committed by the Republican Guard. The images don't stay up long, not more than a day or two, and you don't want to get caught data diving for them, but they are frightening to behold. Maybe the Republic wants us to see them, to keep our fear factor at acceptable levels."

Having loaded most of the available gear into the truck, Paxton began the task of building a funeral pyre, right there in the road directly behind the truck, so that he and Rachel could continue to talk. He was glad of the distraction from her missing leg, which he could not help but gawk at every time he glanced in her direction.

"What do you mean they make people fly?" he asked.

"They have this massive coil of cables, in a circle at least at big as a football field," she began to explain. "They had to be electric wires, 'cause there were other wires feeding into them from giant transformers. The cables were elevated off the ground, at least enough for people to walk under them, 'cause they brought people in there at gunpoint, probably illegals, and then the soldiers marched outside the circle. A giant buzzing sounded and then the people in there just started to rise off the ground. They went at least a hundred feet up into the air and then the buzzing stopped abruptly and they all fell back down to earth!"

"That's horrible!" commented Paxton, even as his scientific mind began to run with possibilities. He had been able to bind gravitons in the lab, at enormous cost to the taxpayer, but to do so on such a scale was incredible, and must have cost a fortune. Then he remembered how they were testing this incredible, new technology.

"It'll save a lot of bullets," he muttered, sarcastically, before taking a deep breath and rolling Barbara over and off the tent she had been carried down upon. He dragged the assemblage of canvas and wooden poles to the back of the truck and dumped them heavily upon the sandy road. "Do you have any water?"

Rachel found a bottle in a backpack and tossed it to Paxton, who was now seated on the edge of the open tailgate with his right foot dangling over the side. He took a guarded swig of water and then tossed it back to Rachel. She caught it with the sure-handedness of an athlete and took an equally measured swallow.

"They need to save a lot more than bullets," she said, settling herself back upon the seat they had made from their own tents. "Edward used to tell me all about our dwindling resources, over dinner, or as we watched TV at night. The end of oil, the last rainforest, drinking water on the decline, food shortages directly linked to climate change, the list went on and on. He claimed that they knew all of this was going to happen years ago, the powers that be, but they wanted to keep it from the general public as long as they could to stall for time.

Hence the climate change deniers, followed by the food and water shortage deniers, and on and on. They needed time to gather up as much as they could to get themselves set up for the brave new world before the masses caught on and caused pandemonium."

"That's why they built this god-damned Wall," Paxton preached to the one-woman choir, "and they made such a big deal about immigration all those years! They took as much as they could get away with from the rest of the world and now it's time for them to close up shop and protect what they believe is theirs."

"The rest of the world isn't going to stand for it much longer," said Rachel. "Everyone's rattling their sabers at us, and at each other, but mostly at us. China and Russia are in bed with the Middle East, 'cause they still have oil. People have nothing to lose when they're already staring death in the face."

"They're culling the herd," Paxton commented drily. "We scientists have known for years that the world was overpopulated with humans, but they denied that as well. The only way to bring our numbers back into equilibrium is a massive die-off, and war is a great way to do that!"

"As long as you're on the winning side," agreed Rachel. "They think the Republic will prevail in the coming World War, now that you've given them anti-gravity."

"But who are *they*?" asked Paxton. "Who are the powers-that-be, the politicians?"

"When have the politicians ever been in power?" she returned rhetorically. "The ones with the money make the rules, until every once in a while, the people rise up and toss them out on their asses for a new set of rules. The politicians aren't even elected anymore, they're appointed by someone, but they still hold their sham elections."

"Who's the *someone*?" Paxton pressed.

"I don't think it's just one person," she guessed, "but you can bet your ass it's a boys club and they're the one percent of the one percent."

Paxton shaded his eyes with two cupped hands and glanced up the hill. Jazelle and the others were barely discernible in the harsh glare of the sun, but he counted four bodies descending toward them with their loads strapped to their backs. He jumped down off the tailgate to resume his work on the funeral pyre for Barbara and Bill.

By the time the women came back with a sorry assortment of combustibles, Paxton was mostly done with his staging. He had elevated the three ends of their makeshift travois using small boulders he found beside the road so that there was room enough to put kindling beneath it. He directed the returning women to do so as well with their armloads of brambles and garbage and then he sent them out for a second foray.

Paxton dragged Bill's travois next to his makeshift platform and began to wrestle his stiff body from one canvas to the other. Rachel jumped down from the truck on her one good leg to help as best she could. When they had positioned Bill in as comfortable a resting position as they could manage, Paxton used the travois to move Barbara into position and they hoisted her next to, and partially on top of, Bill.

The canvas was not big enough for each of them to lie fully in repose but Paxton was not going to worry over the details of the conflagration he was intent on sparking. Looking again at the meager collection of kindling the women had been able to find, Paxton realized he was going to need some type of accelerant or the funeral pyre was going to be a funeral fizzle.

Pointing to the travois on the ground Paxton asked Rachel, "Can you pack that one up as best you can? I have an idea for how we can use the motorcycles."

Rachel didn't answer him but she knelt down on one good knee before sliding onto her butt with her half-leg out in front of her. She began the process of extricating the poles from the canvas while Paxton walked around the truck to where they had unloaded the two motorcycles. Choosing the smaller of the two, he wheeled it awkwardly over the uneven terrain until its front wheel struck a side pole of his pyre. He left it standing upright upon its kickstand.

Just then Jillian staggered into their clearing dragging a log along the ground behind her. It appeared as if the effort pained her and Paxton rushed over to help her pull it the rest of the way to the pyre.

"Good job!" Paxton praised her. "Let's get it beneath them."

Having accomplished that task Paxton directed Jillian to help him man-handle the dirt bike first vertical upon its front wheel and then ass-end over handlebars onto the pyre upside-down.

Jillian's curiosity finally got the better of her and she asked, "What are you doing, Paxton?"

"I don't see how we can take these with us," he explained. "We don't have room in the truck and they've gotta be close to empty."

He loosened the cap on the gas tank and a splash of gasoline soaked the canvas between the two bodies and dripped lazily onto the log below. Paxton remarked, "See? It's just about empty. Help me shake it a little bit."

Together they shook the dirt bike back and forth and a smaller splash of gasoline greeted their efforts. Paxton continued to direct her, "Good enough. Help me with the other one."

"This is as good as I can get this tent," Rachel called from the ground. Paxton helped her up, supported her for the few hops to the tailgate and hoisted her into a seated position upon it. He and Jillian then picked up the bundled tent and deposited it onto the tailgate beside her before wheeling the second motorcycle to the funeral pyre.

"What are you doing, you damn fool!" Jazelle yelled from the hill when she was still fifty feet away from the truck. Paxton and Jillian froze with the second motorcycle still held vertical between them. He nodded to her and they let it come back down to rest properly upon its wheels. Paxton pushed down the kick stand and let the bike settle itself to wait for Jazelle to join them.

"We don't have enough wood to make a proper fire," Paxton explained when she was close enough that he didn't need to shout. Paxton felt suddenly guilty about the unadulterated wastefulness of leaving a perfectly good motorcycle in the desert. He went on to offer his feeble explanation, "And we don't have enough room to take them with us. I'm just using what's left in the tanks to get this thing blazing."

"We can still use these bikes to scout ahead of the truck," she explained, dropping her backpack heavily on the ground at Paxton's feet. "At least until they run out of gas."

"Well, I already drained the other one," he admitted. "You can have this one if you want it."

She gave him a disgusted look before confirming that she did indeed want the second motorcycle, "Yes, I want it! I'm gonna ride this one myself."

"Sorry," he offered. "I guess I'm already thinking two steps ahead of where we are. By my calculations there's not enough gas in either of the motorcycles to ride them all the way to the Guadalupe Mountains, and we barely have enough room for everyone and the rest of this gear in the truck. We'd just be leaving the bikes in the desert along the way."

"I'm sure you're right," she said in softer tones, touching his arm. "But while we still have it, I'm gonna use it."

For the next ten minutes they worked together to get the gear stowed away in the bed of the truck, while still leaving enough room for a row of passengers to sit with their backs against the cab. The four bicycles were the last to come aboard and they stacked them one on top of the other next to the tailgate and tied them down with their last remaining piece of rope.

By the time the truck was packed, the women had returned with whatever they could procure in the immediate vicinity that might possibly burn. An odd collection of tumbleweed, small sticks and garbage filled the underside of the pyre with the log Jillian had found in the center of it all. The smell of gasoline was still strong next to the pyre and Paxton could already imagine the flames bursting into life when he sparked the volatile fuel.

"If anyone has anything they'd like to say, now's the time" directed Paxton. "Once we torch this, we gotta go!"

Abraham helped Rachel down from the truck and they gathered in a circle around the pyre. Jillian and Grace joined hands and that caused a chain reaction of hand-holding until the circle was complete and it included their newest recruit, Valerie. Everyone waited expectantly for someone else to speak and when the silence became uncomfortable Paxton began to pray.

"Dear All," he spoke with his eyes closed and a tight grip on both Jazelle and Elizabeth's hands. "We commend to you the spirits of our dear friends, Barbara and William, and we thank you for the time that we had with them. Neither of them deserved to be here, and we sincerely hope that the world will be a better place when they are born again into the physical realm."

"You were a good man, Bill Nelson," Jazelle added, "and a good friend."

"We'll miss you, Barbara," stated Grace before bursting into tears and hiding her face in Jillian's embrace.

Paxton waited in the ensuing silence for almost a full minute before adding emphatically, "Amen!"

"Now get your asses into the truck!" ordered Jazelle brusquely to cover the fact that she too was getting choked up.

Paxton took a wadded-up piece of paper from his back pocket and a lighter from the front one. Squatting down next to the pyre he carefully lit the paper and then shoved it into the center of the kindling until the gasoline burst spontaneously into fire. Startled, he fell backward onto his ass eliciting a chuckle from Jazelle.

"You deserved that," she teased him, even as she was offering him a hand up, "wastin' all that gas!"

"There wasn't all that much to begin with," he defended himself. He did not let go of her hand once he stood up but gathered her into his arms for a bear hug. He whispered into her ear, "You better be careful out there, and make sure you run out of gasoline somewhere we can find you!"

"You just keep up, old man!" she whispered back, kissing him on the cheek before pushing him away. The hurried plan they had devised while they were waiting for the foragers to return involved hauling ass out of there as fast as they could safely push the truck with Jazelle riding a mile or two ahead of them to make sure they didn't fall into a sinkhole or some trap of human devising.

Paxton took a swipe at her ass as she walked away and was rewarded with a meaty slap and a surprised, "Hey!"

"I'll get you back for that tonight," she shot back over her shoulder.

"I'm counting on it," he spoke to her back. Jazelle jumped onto the bike and started it with one forceful kick. No sooner did the engine sputter to life than she had gunned the accelerator and was speeding off down the road. Paxton followed her lead and jumped behind the steering wheel of the truck, but not before he visually confirmed that all seven passengers were accounted for.

Abraham had chosen to ride in the back with Rachel, ostensibly so he could extend his large frame beyond the narrow confines of the truck's cab. Eden and Elizabeth had resumed their now familiar seats in the extended cab with Valerie sandwiched in between them. Jillian and Grace would be next to him on the front seat. Paxton closed the door, turned the key in the ignition and started off after Jazelle, albeit at a much more conservative speed. He looked into the rear-view mirror long enough to see the plume of black smoke coming off his pyre and then he turned his attention forward to their next trail and their next trial.

They didn't catch up to Jazelle for twenty miles and when they did she was walking back down the middle of the road toward them with her rifle slung across her back. Her bike had run out of gasoline and she had taken off on foot to warn them of a bad washout up ahead. Jazelle climbed into the bed of the truck and sat on the other side of Rachel as Paxton drove the truck forward at a snail's pace.

It took the better part of an hour to navigate around the washout and back onto Route 54. Since they were already pushing dinnertime, Paxton decided to take a chance on the old road and he accelerated to forty miles an hour. They saw no signs of life, except for the ever-present birds of prey circling their caravan in the hopes of carrion. Every mile they drove made El Capitan, the iconic mountain in what used to be Guadalupe Mountain National Park, loom larger and larger on the horizon.

A sense of foreboding overtook Paxton as they passed the old sign marking the entrance to the park. It was made of thick wood and Paxton marveled that the sign had not been disturbed by scavengers. It had been defaced by graffiti artists, however, and there were whitewashed letters six inches high covering the original yellowing font heralding, 'Guadalupe Mountain National Park.' The newer message scrawled across the sign read, 'All those pure of heart are welcome here.'

As if to corroborate his sense of dread, the truck chose that moment to sputter and cough in its death throes. Paxton limped along a little farther in fits and starts until the truck gave one final lurch and the engine shuddered and died for lack of fuel.

"And that's the end of our sweet ride," said Paxton, looking over his shoulder at the other cab riders. Jazelle, had taken her rightful place at his side by displacing Jillian to the bed of the truck. Having made the rounds of Eden, Valerie, Elizabeth and Grace, Paxton's eyes alighted on Jazelle and he asked, "What do we do now?"

"I guess we camp here," replied Jazelle, "but I don't like it. We're too exposed."

"The old Visitor Center can't be much farther along," Grace piped up from the other side of Jazelle.

"How do you figure that?" asked Jazelle, turning in her seat to look her friend in the eyes.

"I took a cross-country trip with my sister and my parents, when I was ten years old," explained Grace. "We never hit this park, not that I remember, but they all had Visitor Centers, usually just a couple of miles past their gates."

"What are the chances there's anything left of the Visitor Center?" asked Paxton. "I'm sure it's been picked clean by now."

"If there *is* anything left of it," reasoned Jazelle, "it could be that some Vags are using it for a hideout. Either way we should check it out, I guess. We don't want no Vags sneakin' up on us in the middle of the night."

"I guess we set off on foot, then," stated Paxton to no one in particular. "How much of this shit are we gonna be able to take with us?"

"Let's take a little ride on the bicycles and see if this Visitor Center exists and if it's not already chock full of Vags," suggested Jazelle. "Then we can decide what we wanna do after that."

"Agreed," said Paxton. "Who's gonna go?"

He was greeted with a chorus of, "I'll go!" from everyone in the cab except for Valerie. Climbing down from the driver's seat Paxton walked the few feet to the back of the truck to explain to the others what had been decided in the cab. Abraham had already jumped down on the opposite side of the bed and was relieving himself on the brown grass next to the road.

In the end it was only he and Jazelle that set off in the direction of the Visitor Center while the rest of their posse started to unpack the truck and make dinner. It was still miserably hot and Paxton was sweating profusely as they rode up the slow but steady incline on their mountain bikes.

Lucky for them, Grace had been right about the Visitor Center and it was only a couple of miles beyond the entrance to the park. It was even luckier that the big, brick building was devoid of humans, though it appeared as though some large critter had taken up residence in one corner of the big room, next to a toilet bowl that hadn't seen running water in a long time.

"It's probably a coyote," ventured Paxton.

"He won't give us no trouble when he sees how many we got in our pack," reasoned Jazelle. "I ain't seen no sign of pups."

The old Visitor Center was only one building, and in fact only one big room, but there were signs that it had once been separated with wood framed walls to cordon off several offices, closets and bathrooms. Like the ranch they had occupied the previous day, the roof was completely gone and anything remotely usable had already been ransacked from the building's shell. Still, it would provide them some cover in the event of an attack and would also serve to hide them from prying eyes while they tried to get some rest and plot their next course of action.

"This will do," Jazelle endorsed the night's lodging.

"Let's ride back and get the rest of the gang, then," Paxton directed, but instead he grabbed Jazelle from behind and wrapped her up in his embrace.

"You tryin' to get me started up, old man?" teased Jazelle. She wriggled out of his embrace just enough to turn around and plant a wet kiss on his lips.

"Just stealing a quiet moment," Paxton replied, "before the thundering horde makes their way up here."

Jazelle put her head on his chest and melted into his embrace saying, "Are we gonna be aw'ight, Paxton?"

"I can't make any promises," Paxton conceded, "but we made it this far, didn't we? You gotta have a little faith."

"My faith runnin' in short supply these days," she responded, "but I believe in *you*."

They let their intimacy linger another few moments before extricating themselves from each other's embrace and exiting the building through the gaping hole that used to contain a double glass door. The sun continued to sink inexorably toward the western horizon as they mounted their bicycles once more for the easier ride back downhill to rejoin the others.

CHAPTER 15

RICHARD

I was the leader of a cannibal tribe, for a short time, before I escaped to the Guadalupe Mountains. We called ourselves the Jackals, but that wasn't my choice. Their former leader, Leroy, was a soldier in a motorcycle club of the same name, on the outside. I was a soldier, too, in the Republican Guard before I came here, a disgraced deserter. I never thought to change our name, after I took over. What would we call ourselves, the Republicans? Anyway, the other tribes in these parts know about the Jackals and they fear us, except for the Indians. The Indians don't fear anything. Leroy had been in the Square since they cleaned out the prisons. He was serving a life sentence for murder, but he got a second chance on his life sentence, and his murdering, in the Square. He carved himself up a nice little territory in the shade of the Wall and the Guadalupes. The Square had been a boon to Leroy, right up until I killed him, in single combat, by the grace of God, else I wouldn't be here telling you this tale. I almost waited too long, to challenge him, I was so weak by then. They barely fed us in the cages, and when they did it was always and only human flesh. I refused to eat it at first, but the hunger became too painful to ignore. At least we weren't getting gang-raped every day like the womenfolk. Bobby and I were put to work instead, every day in the hot sun, carrying water or digging graves or sharpening machetes, always under the watchful eyes of our captors. Bobby made a run for it one day, but he didn't get very far. They had motorcycles, and gasoline from somewhere to put in the engines. They chased him down within the hour. They took both of his legs that evening, after dragging him back behind a Harley by his bound hands. They cut right below the hip bone and popped the ball out of its socket joint, then cauterized the cuts with a branding iron and threw him back in the cage with me. He didn't work anymore after that, didn't last much longer either. They took his arms two nights later, made him eat his own flesh just to be cruel. I ate it too, I was ravenous, but that's when I decided not to go out like Bobby did. That's when I decided to challenge Leroy to single combat, which was just about the only right we prisoners had in their world.

The odds were stacked against me, of course, and I'm not just talking about my muscles being atrophied from lack of nourishment and movement. They slipped me some acid, or something like it, in a glass of water, which I mistook for kindness, a couple of hours before our sunset brawl. I was tripping my balls off when they locked us in a cage together, several sizes larger than the one they usually kept me in, with the whole tribe surrounding us, screaming like banshees and chanting Leroy's name.

He beat the shit out of me with his bare hands, for a long time. I seemed to be moving in slow motion and Leroy was able to anticipate my every move, I was lucky if I landed a single punch. Then they threw knives into the cage, a six-inch hunting knife for me, and Leroy got a machete as long as his arm. He proceeded to carve me up slowly, enjoying every slice. He was leaving trailers out behind him as he moved and every time, I lunged I missed him completely and ran headlong into the wooden slats of our cage.

After one such fall, I crouched upon my haunches, trying to shake the cobwebs out of my head and catch my breath. Leroy was prancing around at the other end of the cage with his back toward me, inciting the crowd, clearly enjoying himself, asking them if they were ready for him to end it so they could start their feast, which I understood would be me. He turned back to me and came straight toward me without dancing left and right as he had been doing. There were no tracers then, just his shit-eating grin getting larger and closer.

He raised his machete with the intention of chopping off my head, I'm sure of it, but I sprang forward and up with every last ounce of strength left in me, the hunting knife held tightly in both hands. I caught him in his exposed throat and pushed the tip of the knife up into his skull, killing him instantly. The crowd went silent when he fell to the ground, for one astonished moment, before bursting into bedlam all around me.

We feasted on Leroy that night, though I didn't enjoy my victory, weak from loss of blood and still tripping pretty heavily. I'll never know why Leroy's second-in-command, Allen was his name, didn't just end me that night, it would have been easy. It has to do with their code, apparently even cannibals have a code, or at least the Jackals did. Instead, my wounds were tended to, the worst of them cauterized, and I became king of the Jackals.

It was a short-lived reign; my heart wasn't in it. Their world was too incredibly brutal and I could never get past the fact that I was eating another human being. I resolved to escape, and I got the chance early on. It was easy, actually, being the king has its privileges. I was soon riding Leroy's, now my, Harley all over their territory, mostly accompanied but sometimes alone. One morning I found myself alone, near the eastern border of our territory, and I just kept riding east, into the Guadalupe Mountains.

The Indians captured me right away, I'm sure I was making a hell of a noise out there in the desert, out in their desert. One of them put a steel arrow right through the spokes of my front wheel. I wasn't moving too fast at the time, lucky for me, but I still went head-over-handlebars and they were upon me instantly. They bound my hands and blind-folded me, but they left my feet free for what turned out to be a long fucking walk.

That was the night I met Mukwooru, and he peered into my soul. I didn't understand what was happening at the time. I didn't know that it was a test of my moral fiber, a test that would decide my fate, that would decide whether I lived or died. They just sat me down, cross-legged, and removed my blindfold. It was already dark and there was a small fire burning, and on the other side of the fire sat the oldest man I had ever seen.

He didn't say a word, but just smoked his long pipe, slowly savoring each puff of what smelled like ganja, all the while staring right into my eyes. There was a hand on each of my shoulders keeping me from moving too much and one of my captors told me not to say a word, in perfect English, but to just keep looking at the old man. I don't know how long this went on, it felt like an hour or more, but eventually the old man nodded, almost imperceptibly and they finally let me stand up and untied my hands.

I didn't know it at the time but that sit-down was a test, and had I failed it I would have been sent back out of the Park to walk the gauntlet of cannibal tribes, which is how the Tribe keeps the peace with the cannibals, by supplying them with fresh meat. That and we kick the shit out of them whenever they get too close to the Park.

I was lucky, or blessed, or the old man must've seen some humanity in me that I thought was long dead, because there aren't a lot of people who pass that test. We don't have much of anything to share here in the Park, just like the rest of Megiddo, and we don't take on new members very often. There have only been three more since I got here, until Paxton and his crew showed up. Now it seems they're letting everybody in.

That's how I became a soldier in another army, but I got no qualms about my role here. They're not asking me to shoot live rounds into crowds of American citizens, or eat human flesh. We defend ourselves, to be sure, and I done my fair share of killing for the Tribe, but it don't keep me up at night, not like it did when I was killing for the Republic.

THE TRIBE

"Well, what do we do now?" asked Jazelle. Their rag-tag group was seated haphazardly across the cement floor of what used to be the display room of the Guadalupe Mountain National Park Visitor Center eating a breakfast of stale biscuits, smashed green tomatoes and half-cooked horse flesh. Only Jillian was missing as she was currently keeping watch on the north side of their hideaway.

They had passed the night uneventfully, taking turns at watch every hour on the hour. Paxton had a hard time falling asleep on the cold cement floor with an infinitude of stars to examine in the desert night sky. He had tried to wake Jazelle when the meteor shower, he was witnessing seemed to be peaking. He only succeeded in becoming the brunt of a string of expletives for his efforts, as soon as Jazelle realized there was no emergency which required her to rouse herself to full wakefulness.

"I don't know," admitted Paxton, grinning sheepishly. "Jonas said that the Indians are nomadic and they could be anywhere in the Park. I have no idea where to even begin to look for them and it's not like they're passing out maps of the place anymore. I guess I just thought that they would find us."

"That's your plan?" asked Jazelle skeptically. "Sit tight and let them come to us? It's brilliant, Paxton, simply brilliant!"

"Do you have any better ideas?" he asked, smiling at how pleased she was with herself. "What did you and Abraham discover on your reconnaissance?"

"I don't think we want to take the road," Abraham answered for the both of them. "It exits the Park a couple of miles east of here."

"No, you're right," agreed Paxton. "I think we should be heading into the interior, into the mountains."

"Which one?" asked Jazelle. "We found an old wooden sign, down by the trailhead, right where three trails were comin' together. Guadalupe Peak, El Capitan or something called the Devil's Hall."

"There was another trail leading off toward the north," said Abraham.

"Don't know what that one's called," added Jazelle, "but it starts climbin' right off."

"We want the Devil's Hall," interrupted Elizabeth.

"I don't wanna be in no devil's hall, girl!" scoffed Jazelle. "That's the only trail not headin' into the mountains."

"It's the one we take," Elizabeth continued. "I saw us, in a narrow canyon, with steep walls on either side. They were watching us, painted Indian warriors."

"Shit!" interjected Jazelle. "That's the last place I'd ever lead you into. Didn't you learn nothin' from what happened to Bill and Barbara? You hearin' this shit?"

This last question was directed at Paxton who sat listening to their conversation with a mouthful of biscuit. When he had swallowed enough to be able to speak, he answered, "Beth's been right about things time and time again. I think we should hear her out."

"There's not much more to say," Elizabeth admitted. "My vision ended in that narrow canyon, with the Indians looking down on us."

"Gettin' ready to pounce on us, more'n likely," offered Jazelle.

"That's just it," said Elizabeth excitedly. "I can't speak to the Indians' intentions, but it felt like we were doing the right thing, that everything was going to work itself out, somehow, everything was going to be alright."

"It *felt* that way?" asked Jazelle incredulously. "You as crazy as your sister. You know what's at the end of the Devil's Hallway, girl? Hell itself!"

"Well, we don't wanna use what precious water we have left climbing the wrong mountain," Paxton surmised, "let alone carry all this shit farther than we have to."

"So, you wanna go catch a glimpse of the Devil?" scoffed Jazelle. "Is that it?"

"Under normal circumstances I would yield to your strategic advice, Jazelle," said Paxton, "but these are not normal circumstances. Usually, we would be trying to avoid contact with anyone and anything out here in the desert. But in this instance, we're trying to be found. I say we follow Beth's vision and hope for the best."

"You the boss," muttered Jazelle.

"Really?" Paxton teased her. "Since when?"

"Let me just say," continued Jazelle, ignoring him, "that I don't like it, not one little bit. It's called the Devil's Hall for a reason."

"Your criticism has been lodged and recorded," Paxton returned, pantomiming the writing motion with his index finger on his open palm. "You can reserve the right to say, 'I told you so,' if things don't work out for us."

"Only if we're alive to tell the tale," said Jazelle, getting in the last word for the moment.

Just as soon as breakfast was shared and their gear put away, they left the scant shade that the eastern wall of the Visitor Center had afforded them for the already intense heat of the midmorning Chihuahuan Desert. They cached some of the Vags' gear, a tent, pots and pans and some clothes, in a hole beneath a desert willow in an effort to travel as efficiently as possible. They all knew where to find the gear if a future need precipitated the occasion. Paxton had reluctantly left his guitar in the cab of the truck the night before and he doubted that he would ever strum it again.

Jazelle took her usual grey mountain bike to scout ahead of their party. Paxton agreed to ride another bike in their rearguard. Once a course had been set, Paxton and Jazelle lapsed into journey mode with Paxton content to let Jazelle lead so that he need only follow her orders.

Eden and Elizabeth walked on either side of a third bicycle, upon which straddled Rachel in obvious pain. She tried to push herself up on her one good leg as much as possible so as not to have to sit on the unforgivingly narrow bike seat. Eden and her sister took turns alternately and awkwardly leading the bike by its handlebars or just walking and talking to keep the other two distracted. The going was slow on the thin and uneven trail, which had only a slight but steady incline.

Jillian and Grace were almost too sore to walk let alone ride a bike, so they trudged along after Rachel, their eyes downcast from the sun and searching the ground for serpents. Valerie was able to keep up with them, even though she appeared in some ways worse for the wear. Her eyes were gaunt and her skin clung to her bones. She took water when it was offered to her but she rarely ate. Eden had done her best to soothe her but she seemed to be increasingly skittish about being touched and especially resistant to Eden for some reason known only to her subconscious.

Abraham was leading the last bicycle laden with as much gear as they could drape upon it and still not interfere with its wheels. Even under this heavy load he was moving faster than the women and he had to continually stop to let them catch up to him. Paxton and Jazelle were for the most part invisible, except when one or the other popped up to check on their progress.

At the three-way junction they chose the trail indicated on a small wooden sign which pointed north toward Devil's Hall. Here there was more vegetation than the prickly pear cacti, yucca and ocotillo they had seen on the desert floor. Junipers and stately madrone trees had once been supported by the seasonal river and some of them were still clinging to life.

The only wildlife they saw were lizards and centipedes. Although they were ever on the lookout for rattlesnakes, they were causing too much commotion to come upon one unawares. There was scat from some larger mammals, but they must have been nocturnal because there were no sightings of anything warm-blooded. The carrion birds circled overhead, waiting for someone to take a fatal misstep.

It was noticeably cooler as they rose ever so slightly into the mountains, following the twisting course of a long-dried riverbed. Eventually the path led right into the riverbed and it became harder to use the bicycles. There were short rock climbs in which they needed to dismount and carry the bikes. Abraham managed to stay ahead of the pace, even with the constant loading and unloading of his bicycle.

They had been plodding along in the brutal sunshine for more than an hour, moving slowly but steadily along the course of the riverbed, when Grace finally looked up from her feet and asked, "Has anyone seen Paxton lately?"

"No, come to think of it," answered Eden. "Not for a while, now."

"I haven't seen Jazelle, either," confirmed Abraham, just as they were catching up to him. "Not for a half-hour at least."

"Should we be worried?" asked Jillian.

"We should always be worried," instructed Grace. "Anyone who lets their guard down in this place is cannibal fodder."

"Well, what do you want to do?" asked Abraham.

"It's not much farther," said Elizabeth. "Whatever is going to happen to us is just up ahead. Do you see those cliffs up there? That's where they are, the Indians. We might as well leave the bicycles and continue on foot. We can always come back for them."

"Are you crazy?" asked Jillian. "Why would we abandon all of our food and gear? You really are a Newt."

"Suit yourself," countered Elizabeth. "I'm sure the Indians won't let any of it go to waste. Let's help Rachel down from this bike."

Rachel swung her half-leg over the crossbar and Eden laid the mountain bike gently down upon the dusty ground. The two sisters continued to help Rachel balance with her arms draped around each of their shoulders. Abraham tried to set his load down gently as well, but the top-heavy mass eventually reached a critical angle and the whole load came crashing to the ground.

"Let's just leave it for now and take a break," offered Eden. "How much water we got left?"

"Not much," confirmed Grace, stooping down to retrieve a half-full gallon jug from the outskirts of the fallen load. She took a quick swallow and passed it around. Valerie guzzled more than her fair share but no one had the heart to stop her as she looked like she needed it more than they did. Grace and Jillian set their backpacks down as well, but Valerie made no move to do the same with her smaller pack.

"That's the Devil's Hall," Elizabeth informed them, "right below those cliffs. It's just the way it looked in my dream."

"Nooo!" screamed Valerie, clawing at the air. "I don't wanna see the Devil!"

"Hush up!" spat Jillian, covering the woman's mouth with her hand. "It's just a fancy name for a slot canyon."

"It'll be suicide to go in there," commented Grace.

Jillian looked daggers at her and said under her breath, "You're not helping matters, here."

"Sorry," Grace replied before helping Jillian to quiet Valerie down to muffled sobs. Abraham looked over them all toward the cliffs towering above them.

"The Indians are probably going to take us anywhere and anyway they want to take us," he said. "This is their land and they know it best. In any event, they know we're here now. We might as well walk on up ahead and take a look."

Jillian and Grace helped steer Valerie forward even as Eden and Elizabeth did the same for Rachel. When the ground got rough, they made a seat for her butt with their interlocked arms. Abraham took point with a two-handed grip upon the cocked rifle resting on his hip. He scanned up toward the rim of the deepening canyon as they trudged slowly forward.

Soon they reached a natural rock-shelf staircase and they climbed step by step up toward the mouth of the slot canyon. Still there was no sign to indicate that they weren't alone. They trudged ever onward between the high walls and it was only as they were nearing the other side of the canyon that they heard a piercing bird call from behind them and they all turned around to see what had given rise to that shriek.

When they finally turned back to continue their exploration, they found their way blocked by five Indian warriors, their naked torsos glistening in the sunlight. Abraham raised his rifle to his shoulder and took aim at the foremost Indian.

Elizabeth put her hand gently upon his shoulder and directed him to lower his rifle saying, "Don't do it, Abraham. Look up!"

There on the cliffs above them were twenty or more Indian warriors pointing spears, arrows and rifles at their compacted group. Another bird call came from behind them and they turned to see six more warriors in the slot canyon blocking their retreat, all of them armed with a combination of machetes, bows and guns.

"Lay down your weapons and you will not be harmed," a voice with a Texas twang spoke from in front of them. Abraham immediately bent down and deposited his rifle on the rock floor of the canyon. The women did the same with their machetes. Just as soon as they stood back up the Indians were upon them.

Working with incredible efficiency, the warriors lashed their arms to stout, wooden poles as if they were going to be crucified. Grace tried to complain and was immediately gagged with an old T-shirt and bungie cord. The others were gagged as well, with an odd assortment of rags and ties. Jillian looked daggers at Elizabeth, who was unsuccessful in the attempt at shrugging her shoulders.

They were directed back down and out of the canyon the way they had come into it, with two warriors flanking each of them in case they stumbled and needed assistance. The two on either side of Rachel were supporting her pole on their own shoulders so that she was mostly being carried but also helping to navigate the boulders in their path with her one good leg.

When they had returned to their pile of gear, the bikes were gone but everything else was the way they had left it. Their captors used rope and bungie cords to lash all of their possessions onto the poles supported by their shoulders so that all of them, except for Rachel, would be forced to carry his or her own things. Once this task had been completed, they began walking again, exiting the dry river bed on the north bank and climbing a ridge on an imperceptible path known only to the Indians.

Upon closer inspection, most of the Indians weren't Indians at all but a mixture of races. They looked the part, with their bronzed and painted skin, long braided hair and bows slung upon their backs, but a few of them were blonde and there were at least two with black skin. Only three were women, but they appeared to be just as formidable as the men in their war party.

They had not trekked very far up the ridge before they were reunited with Paxton and Jazelle, both of whom were trussed up in a similar fashion, except that Paxton wasn't gagged. Instead, he was speaking to the man who had addressed them in the slot canyon with his thick, Southern accent.

"Is this really necessary?" asked Paxton, upon seeing the rest of his posse trudging up the hill beneath their burdens. "We've come here to see the Comanche, we're not going to try to escape!"

"Protocol," answered the muscular man with a map of crisscrossed scars all over his torso. Raising his voice so that everyone could hear him he continued, "Y'all won't be harmed, not by us, and not before you've had a chance to meet the old man. After that your fate is in his hands."

"So, the Comanche is still alive?" asked Paxton excitedly.

"Barely."

"How long of a hike do we have?" asked Paxton.

"Couple of miles," the man answered perfunctorily, "mostly uphill."

"Can't you at least take their gags out?" pleaded Paxton. "They can't breathe properly, and they're going to need water."

The man nodded his head slightly and each of their gags was removed but left dangling about their necks in case of future need. He addressed them all in a loud voice, "I don't wanna hear a peep from any of y'all or they go right back in! Now march!"

March they did, step after step, climbing steadily upward into the Guadalupe Mountains. They were given small sips of water, every hour or so, but they did not stop to rest. When Grace buckled under the weight of her load, the backpacks hanging from her poles were removed, but not the pole itself.

Once they had attained the top of the ridge, they started immediately down the other side, descending only until they crossed a more obvious trail running east-west along the contours of the ridge. At the direction of their captors, they turned toward the setting sun and then continued their ascent. Here in the mountains, there was a slight breeze which tempered the desert sun, but they were nevertheless drenched in sweat and unable to wipe it off their brows.

Most of the warriors they had seen in the show of force in the Devil's Hall had disappeared into the desert. Paxton still counted one guard for every prisoner, plus their leader, who was definitely not an Indian. Not that numbers really mattered with his crew all tied up, nor did Paxton have a strong desire to fight, even with the ignominy of the walking crucifixes. It was a fitting end to their pilgrimage, no matter how it turned out in the end.

"Of course, it's going to work out," thought Paxton to himself. *"Surely the Comanche will recognize Eden for who she is."*

Emboldened by the thought Paxton turned to the warrior next to him and asked, "Can we please have some water?"

She turned a full circle while deftly removing her bow from the catch at her back and she brought it down on Paxton's back in a blow that sounded worse than it was. Paxton cried out in surprise and a little pain that dissipated quickly. Jazelle rushed to his defense from right behind them.

"Leave 'im alone!" she shouted angrily, advancing toward the dark-haired woman. This time she turned only a half-circle and swung her bow in a backhand that caught Jazelle's calf and brought her to one knee.

"What the fuck?" shouted Jazelle, which earned her another blow to the back of her shoulder.

Their leader turned around and said, "That one needs to be gagged."

"No. Please," Paxton pleaded. "We're just tired and thirsty. Can we please just rest five minutes, to catch our breath?"

The warrior raised her bow as if to strike Paxton again when their leader shook his head and surprised Paxton by saying, "Five minutes. Everyone, take five minutes, but no talking."

"Can I ask you something?" asked Paxton, ignoring his last order. When he received a slight nod in answer he continued, "How much farther is it?"

"A couple of miles," came the repeated answer from earlier.

"That's what you said a couple of miles ago," Paxton complained. "We are injured and tired and hungry. I don't think we can go on much longer."

"If you'd rather stay here, we could put you out of your misery," he replied with an underlying menace which belied his genteel manner.

Paxton was about to respond when a movement in the sky behind and above the man's head caught his eye. A dark speck came hurtling downward, growing larger with every passing second. Flapping wings gave away the bird of prey, but it was flying erratically, as though it was hurt. The man with whom Paxton had been conversing turned around to follow Paxton's gaze skyward as did most of the others around them.

As it got closer Paxton could see that it had something in its talons, something nearly as big as itself. The two creatures were turning somersaults in the air as the unforgiving ground rose to meet them. Just as it seemed that impact was a foregone conclusion, the red-tailed hawk let go of its prey, unfurled its wings and glided swiftly over the spectators' upturned faces. Its prey righted itself as well, using mechanical engines and propellers to bring it to a hovering stop not five feet from the ground.

The drone lingered there a few seconds before it began to rise again with a high-pitched whirring of blades. Paxton watched it climb to ten and then twenty feet above the ground before he heard a twang from behind him and an arrow bounced off the drone's underbelly. A second arrow entered the radius of one of its propellers, effectively stopping its motion. The loss of a propeller coupled with the extra, lop-sided weight of the arrow proved too much for the small aircraft and it came to an awkward landing on the slope of the mountain directly above them.

Immediately the Indians were upon it, covering it with a blanket. One of them flipped it over and set to work with a screwdriver, removing the bottom panel and extracting the lithium battery that served as the drone's power source. Next the arrow was removed and the blanket tied into a carrying sack that was slung over the shoulder of a tallest warrior in their group. The whole endeavor took less than three minutes.

A young warrior who was providing water to the captives had just reached Paxton when their leader stated, "All right, show's over. Time to get moving."

He held the water bottle to Paxton's lips and emptied the last small sip onto his eager tongue. Paxton barely had to swallow the meager rations, but he was grateful for the warm liquid in his parched mouth nonetheless. With a supreme effort Paxton leaned forward and straightened up, rising from the boulder he had been resting upon. He took a quick look at the tired expressions on his friends' faces before forcing his legs to begin trudging up the mountain pathway once again.

The sun had long since disappeared behind the mountain ridgeline to their west as they continued their forced march. Paxton had been grateful for the sunset and the slightly cooler temperatures, but as the twilight deepened, he found himself stumbling more often upon the increasingly rocky trail. Each trip brought new pain to his tied and chafing wrists and aching shoulders. He was also more than a little concerned about scaring up a sidewinder in the dusky light but he reasoned that the front of the column was more likely to come upon a snake before he did, if they even took up residence at this altitude.

The warriors on either side of them did not seem to be bothered by the darkness at all. They stepped lightly and quickly over the familiar path and communicated with each other using different animal calls, mostly birds. Paxton searched for a pattern in their chirps and growls but couldn't decide if each warrior had his or her own personal call or the different calls were used to signal specific commands and responses.

Eventually Paxton began to hear bird calls off in the distance in front of them and the leader of their column called a halt. He stopped in his tracks but Jillian kept right on walking until her head collided with his spine.

"Oops! Sorry, Paxton," she said aloud and was immediately shushed by someone off to Paxton's left. A whooshing sound came from behind his head, followed by a smack and a grunt of pain from Jillian.

"Are you okay?" he whispered to her.

"I'm fine," she whispered back through gritted teeth, "but when they untie my hands, I'm gonna snap that fucking bow in half!"

Another swoosh was followed by another slap and another grunt from Jillian. She complained just loud enough for Paxton to hear her curse, "Mother fucker!"

"We're nearly there," came an explanation in the classic Texas drawl from Paxton's right side. "We're just waiting for an escort."

Paxton searched the horizon in front of them and thought he saw an anomaly in the darkness, a faint and flickering orange glow that could only be a campfire. When they started moving again, they took a tack straight toward the source of this light, which grew more distinctive with every passing step.

The closer they got to the campfire, the more half-naked men, and a few women, pressed in on them from both sides. They formed a gauntlet which opened into a semi-circle as they emerged from the darkness into the bright light of a rather large bonfire. The blaze was composed of six-inch diameter cottonwood logs stacked in the shape of a teepee just large enough to accommodate a human, though no one in their right mind would take up residence in that intense heat.

On the opposite side of the fire, two old Indian men sat facing the captives, cross-legged with knees touching and one each of their hands clasped. They were both old men, but there was a difference in their ages that was apparent at first glance. The one on the right was an old man, past the age of retirement, probably in his late sixties or seventies. The man seated next to him was ancient, his skin wrinkled and hanging off the bones of his arms as if he hadn't eaten in weeks.

The older man smiled up at them as they were ushered into a circle around the fire which included the two old Indians. Paxton made eye contact with him and he could not look away. He stood mesmerized by the depth of understanding he felt coming from behind those black eyes and he reasoned that this old man must be none other than the Comanche himself.

The man who had been leading their party all afternoon walked right up to the two old Indians and said, "Da'anzho."

"Da'anzho, Richard," said the younger of the two old men, and then he invited him to join them on the ground with a wave of his hand.

Richard took a cross-legged seat on the other side of the old man, taking his gnarled hand in both of his own. He whispered something in his ear which made the old man chuckle, but his eyes never left Paxton's eyes. Richard then turned to look at Paxton as well and said expansively, "This is Mukwooru, Chief of the Tribe."

CHAPTER 16

MUKWOORU

My name is Mukwooru, which means 'spirit talker.' I have always been able to talk with the sprits of my ancestors. I am the great-grandson of Peta Nocona, who led the Quahadi Comanche during the Texas-Indian Wars more than a century ago. That was before I was born, but not by much. I am one-hundred and twelve years old.

They call me the Comanche, as if I am the only one left. There are still a few of us left, but there used to be so many more, scattered across the plains like the buffalo. And like the buffalo, white men hunted us to the brink of extinction. When we were at our peak, there was no tribe more respected and feared than the Comanche. Here I am, getting nostalgic. It's an old man's vanity.

What's left of the First Nation is gathered here in Megiddo, in the Guadalupe Mountains. There are probably a few more of us, hiding in the modern world, part of the modern world, but the rest of us are here. Comanche, Apache, Cheyenne, Lakota, Hopi, Navajo, Natchez, Kickapoo and Tiwa and a handful of loners, a Chicksaw, a Crow, an Ute.

The white man has almost succeeded in wiping us from the face of the Earth. They forced us off our land. There is no more land for them to take. They've even taken the casinos, now. The land which was given to us, promised to us for all future generations, has been rescinded, another in a long line of broken promises. Chief Red Cloud, of the Lakota Sioux once said, "They made us many promises, more than I can remember, but they kept only one. They promised to take our land and they took it."

Now we live in the Guadalupe Mountains, in the Chihuahuan Desert. This place is sacred to our people, to all the tribes who lived here but especially to the Apache. The white men liked it so much they made it a National Park, sometime after they took what they wanted from the land, which was sometime after they took the land from us. They told us they could steward the land better than we could, better than we had for centuries, for millennia.

The white men have overrun the land. They have taken everything the land had to give them and then they defecated on what remained. The land will no longer support them. They will go the way of the buffalo, hunting each other until only a handful remain. Maybe the ones that survive will respect the land. Maybe they will build something better than what their ancestors left behind. Maybe they have learned something from their history. Maybe.

Chief Crazy Horse, also of the Lakota Sioux, once said, "Treat the Earth well. It was not given to you by your parents. It was loaned to you by your children." He was stabbed in the back by a soldier while under a flag of truce at Camp Robinson in Nebraska.

I traveled to South Dakota once by car, to see the image of Crazy Horse being carved into a mountain. A tribute to the spirit of his people, of my people. There is only a face, and the outline of an arm, pointing out over the lands that once belonged to his people. They planned to carve part of his horse into the mountain as well, but I don't think they will ever finish it, not now. The white men already have their own heroes carved into a mountain in South Dakota.

The Lakota land was so different from ours, more bountiful, more forgiving. Ours could be bountiful, too, if you knew what you were looking for. My brothers and I used to ride all over this land, living off the desert, back in the distant past, when I was just a boy. We had to cross some of the white man's borders, but that didn't stop us from our explorations.

We knew the land well back then, it was our land, or it used to be our land. We can't get back to Comanche land now, not with the Wall between here and there. The Guadalupe Mountains were claimed by the Apache. My brothers and I would steal their horses to prove our courage, back in the day, but we never came this far south.

Peta Nocona told me to come here, in a dream. I have always trusted my dreams. I have lived my life based upon the wisdom they convey, and I am not about to question my visions this late in my life. My great grandfather told me to come to the Guadalupe Mountains, that I was to prepare the way for a great teacher, a great warrior that would avenge the Comanche for all of the injustices we have endured at the hands of the white men. I heard and I obeyed, even though the journey almost killed me.

We came in two pick-up trucks, from our reservation in Oklahoma. We had to leave the trucks on the other side of the Wall. It was finished where we climbed over, where they carried me over, but there were no guards posted there yet. We came straight to the Guadalupe Mountains, looking for the cave I had seen in my vision. We found it on the southeastern slopes of the tallest mountain in Texas, the one they call Guadalupe Peak.

Most of the tribes around these parts feature caves in their stories of the creation of the world. Humans emerged from caves in the ground into the light and life of the world above. Carlsbad Caverns was sacred to my people, the Comanche. They took it from us when they took the land, and again when they made it a National Park that we are not permitted to visit. If it were up to me, I would be buried in the Caverns.

In the Apache stories, the moon was called Changing Woman, and she lived in a cave on the side of the highest mountain peak in Texas, maybe the very cave we found. Every time she gave birth, Big Owl came to eat the child.

Finally, she gave birth to a boy whom she hid from the Owl. She taught the boy to shoot a bow and arrow. The boy grew into a man and he was now able to defend himself from the Owl. This boy, the son of the moon, Changing Woman, became the father of the Apaches.

The great Apache chief, Geronimo, wished to be buried here in these mountains, long after he had surrendered this land to the soldiers. He said, "It is my land, my father's land, to which I now ask to be allowed to return. I want to spend my last days there, and be buried among those mountains. If this could be I might die in peace, feeling that my people, placed in their native homes, would increase in numbers, rather than diminish as at present, and that our name would not become extinct."

Now we are all in danger of becoming extinct, both red and white men alike. The buffalo, or the elk or the deer will die off in great numbers, usually in winter, when their numbers are so great that they fall out of balance with the land. Humans have now become too numerous for the land to support. We too will have a great culling of our herd. We may become extinct too, if we cannot find our balance, but I don't believe that will come to pass.

It is said that Crazy Horse was also a visionary. He predicted, "I see a time of seven generations, when all the colors of mankind will gather under the sacred tree of life and the whole earth will become one circle again. Upon suffering beyond suffering, the Red Nation shall rise again, and it shall be a blessing for a sick world, a world full of broken promises, selfishness and separation, a world longing for a light again."

I believe that light has now come, in the form of a woman, a woman to lead the Tribe of humanity back into the circle of life, back into the circle of light. That is why Peta Nocona asked me to come to the Guadalupe Mountains. That is why I obeyed his summons, though I am an old man. This is my last gift to the children of the Earth, before I go to meet my ancestors and the Great Spirit that watches over us all.

(Translated by Nantan. Transcribed by Paxton Stephens.)

THE COMANCHE

Immediately upon hearing the name, Paxton bent his head down in respect for a few moments and then lifted his chin and said simply, "We need your help."

The two old men whispered to each other in a language Paxton could not understand until the younger of the old men raised his arm, patted the air down a few times and barked in English, "Kneel!"

Eden had been amongst the last in line and she suddenly burst forward through the crowd of other prisoners and their guards. Before anyone could stop her, she walked up to within two paces of the seated men and got down on her knees. She immediately bent forward to prostrate herself before Mukwooru. The rest of her party followed suit, at least insofar as getting to their knees. Some of them had to be forced down by the guards behind them with heavy hands upon their shoulders.

A guard whose face and torso were painted in garish black and red streaks now stood directly behind Eden. He looked at Mukwooru, who shook his head back and forth almost imperceptibly and the guard relaxed into a spread-legged stance. Eden looked up and shuffle-crawled on her knees to Mukwooru as quickly as she could. He opened his arms in welcome and she fairly flung herself into his lap, causing the old man to chuckle happily.

The man beside him smiled broadly as well as he addressed their assemblage, "You are welcome to share our fire. Untie them and bring them water and nourishment."

The warriors worked deftly at the knotted ropes binding the captives' hands to the poles upon their shoulders and soon freed all nine of them. Eden was last as her guard waited for a sign from Mukwooru before interrupting their awkward, one-sided embrace. It was the man they had called Richard who finally gestured that it was okay to do so and he quickly stepped forward and sliced through the thin ropes binding her wrists with what looked like a very large, very sharp hunting knife. Eden's arms immediately came up and around the frail, old man.

"Please, have a seat," the other old Indian offered with a sweep of his hand. "This is Chief Mukwooru and I am Nantan, his war general and his interpreter."

Eden made no move to get up from Mukwooru's lap but she had shifted most of her weight back upon her legs so that they could rest their foreheads together. They seemed to be unaware of the rest of the camp as they stared deeply into each other's eyes.

Richard had already taken the seat to the right of Mukwooru and he motioned for Paxton to come sit next to him. The others were herded into a loose circle and then told to sit down around the fire. The warriors stood in an even looser circle surrounding them. Two large metal water bottles were started on either side of Mukwooru and everyone but he and Eden took a sip from each one as they passed around the circle and came back to the servers.

Nantan raised his voice a notch to once again welcome them, "Welcome to the Guadalupe Mountains. We will break bread together now and then pass the peace pipe."

Paxton realized that Nantan was speaking literally when several large loaves were introduced to the circle and they each broke off a piece before passing them along. Paxton and Nantan began a conversation that became an interrogation while several other conversations started piecemeal around the fire.

"What brings you here, Paxton?" asked Nantan.

"Wait!" Paxton returned, "How do you know my name?"

"Your fame precedes you," answered the old man, "even in here."

"We're here to see the Comanche," Paxton answered his original question. "What did you say his name is? Mook…woo…"

"Mukwooru," corrected Nantan. "What business do you have with Mukwooru?"

"This business," answered Paxton with a shrug of his shoulders and a nonchalant, open-handed indication in Eden's direction. "We had to bring Eden to meet Mukwooru. She is the one from the prophecy, from his prophecy."

They both looked over in Eden's direction just as she leaned in to whisper something in the old man's ear which made him giggle with glee.

"Then it seems you have accomplished your purpose," Nantan decreed with ominous undertones. "What more have you to offer the Tribe?"

"We don't want to join the Tribe," Paxton replied. "We want to know how to bust out of this place. Eden is needed elsewhere and everywhere; we have to get her out into the world!"

"To have made it this far," Nantan explained, "to the very heart of the Guadalupe Mountains, your choices have become somewhat limited, I'm afraid. You can join the Tribe, or you can be cast off our lands."

"I would very much like to join the Tribe," Eden contradicted Paxton, turning around to look at him. "What do I need to do?"

"You're already doing it," commented Nantan, "and I do not doubt you will pass the test based upon how smitten Mukwooru seems to be with you. Let's not get ahead of ourselves, however, first we must smoke together."

Just then a long pipe was handed to Nantan. Taking a lighter from his shirt pocket he brought the end of the pipe to his lips and then fired up the bowl. He puffed out a few small clouds of smoke as he stoked the chamber and then a larger one as he emptied his lungs of the soothing vapors.

He held the pipe for Mukwooru to drag from it. The old man seemed to be merely holding the pipe in his teeth for the longest time before he exhaled a huge cloud of smoke that smelled strongly of marijuana. Then Nantan slowly rose to his feet and held the pipe out in front of him.

"Each of you will now smoke from the peace pipe and then you will come kneel before Mukwooru. He will judge whether or not you are worthy of joining the Tribe."

"What happens to us if we are not found worthy?" asked Abraham from across the fire.

Nantan had just passed the pipe to a very frightened Valerie and as he turned back to them, he said without emotion, "You will be banished from the Guadalupe Mountains, never to return."

Eden twisted around on the balls of her feet to face them and volunteered with enthusiasm, "I'll go first!"

She reached over to grab the pipe from Valerie in one hand while the other sought out the lighter from Nantan. Eden took a drag from the pipe and exhaled a voluminous cloud into the fire where it was quickly thrust skyward in the updraft of the flames. She immediately doubled over in a coughing fit before passing the pipe and the lighter back to Valerie. Once she had recovered her breath, she turned back to Mukwooru and the two of them were soon once again locked in mental embrace with their foreheads touching.

Valerie took a long, practiced drag from the pipe and exhaled a thick, white plume of smoke from her nostrils before passing the pipe to Jazelle. She waited patiently for Eden to finish commiserating with the old man before taking her place at his feet. Each of them took turns, first with the pipe and then on their knees, holding Mukwooru's gnarled fingers and staring into his fathomless eyes. He said not a word to any of them, but just nodded when their turn was over and they found their seats once again in the ring around the fire.

Paxton was the last to smoke from the pipe. It had reached him long before it would be his turn to sit with the Comanche because the meetings were taking longer than the smoking. He held it in his hands a few minutes while he watched his friends' encounters with Mukwooru. What would he do if some of them were rejected? What if he was rejected? It seemed clear that Eden would be accepted, and that was all that really mattered. He was not so overconfident in the cleanliness of his own soul that he could be sure of the outcome of his evaluation, but Eden was above reproach, surely.

When Grace rose to her feet beside him, he finally put the pipe to his lips and lit what was left in the chamber. He immediately registered the unmistakable taste of marijuana, but there were other flavors and smells at work which were not as familiar. He let out a small puff of smoke with an abbreviated exhale and then gathered himself for a long pull on the pipe.

The second drag went right to his head and he was high in an instant. He thought to himself, "*This is some good shit!*"

Paxton broke into a fit of giggling which was completely incongruous with the gravity of his situation and all eyes turned to him, except for Grace and Mukwooru. He mumbled an apology and shook his head to try to clear his thoughts, but it only left him feeling more muddle-headed. He continued to have a conversation with himself in the confines of his own head.

"*There must be something besides pot in this pipe!*" he reasoned. "*How can it be affecting me this quickly?*"

He suddenly had the urge to tell the truth, his truth, from the beginning, and it seemed he would get the chance to do just that as Grace arose from her kneeling position and Nantan beckoned him forward. Paxton crawled the few feet to Mukwooru and then planted himself upon his knees before him. The old man reached out his arms to take Paxton's hands and when they touched Paxton felt a jolt through his whole body as if he had just grabbed a live electric wire.

His whole life played out in his mind, on fast forward and unfiltered by his selective memory. He had experienced this playback once before with Thorn, on Bald Mountain in Maine, when they examined his past and future lives from within a deep meditative state. This did not feel the same, however, but rather felt like his life playing itself out upon his consciousness in preparation for death.

"*Oh God*," he thought, "*does this mean I'm not going to pass the test?*"

"You have nothing to worry about, Paxton," came the response in his head, and the words carried the familiar timbre of Thorn's gravelly voice. "You have done well."

"*Thorn?*" he called out with his mind. "*Thorn? Is that you?*"

His earnest entreaty went unanswered and indeed the trance that had formed between he and Mukwooru was suddenly broken and Paxton was recalled to his surroundings. Mukwooru continued to hold his two hands, but he looked over at Nantan and said something in a language Paxton assumed was Comanche.

Nantan then stood up and addressed the group in a loud, clear voice saying, "You are all welcome here!"

Several of the warriors gasped and Richard's mouth dropped open in astonishment but no one seemed ready to contradict the old man's assessment. Paxton's group visibly relaxed and started side conversations amongst themselves as Nantan continued to speak.

"You must be tired from your journey," he allowed. "Space will be made for you in the longhouses. There is food if you are hungry."

"We have horse meat to share," Paxton offered, dropping Mukwooru's hands and standing up to face Nantan. "It won't last much longer and we would like to share it with you and your people."

"We don't eat horse meat," Nantan informed him.

"Neither do we," countered Paxton, "normally, not even in the Square, but we met with some trouble on our journey. Our supplies and gear were stolen and our horse was cooked by a bunch of Vags due south of here. We took it all back, but it was too late for the horse, and two of our party."

"What happened to the Vags?" asked Richard from his seated position on the other side of Mukwooru.

"We killed them all," answered Paxton simply. "All that were there at the time, anyway, except for her."

"I ain't one of them!" Valerie said in her own defense.

"Valerie was captured by them, at the Intake," Paxton explained. "The rest of us came from the McDonough clan, except for these three Newts. We took them at the Intake a week ago."

"Then let us feast and we will thank the Great Spirit for this gift of sustenance!" decreed Nantan.

All of their gear was brought forward to the outskirts their circle and everyone in Paxton's party set about finding their personal effects and making sure everything was accounted for. The fire was stoked and what was left of the horsemeat was placed upon skewers draped across two horizontal logs where it could be turned over the open flames. The captives were served some type of thin corn chowder in earthen bowls and Paxton continued to converse with Richard and Nantan as he devoured two bowlfuls of the rich-tasting broth.

Mukwooru spoke in a gravelly voice which was no more than a whisper and Nantan leaned in to listen. When the old man was finished, he translated, "Mukwooru wants to know if the chief of the McDonough clan still lives."

"He was alive until a few days ago," Paxton answered, choosing his words carefully. "He died when the Mexicans attacked the Rockin' M."

"So, the war has begun," stated Richard, looking over at Paxton.

"Begun and ended for all I know," Paxton responded. "The battle was just getting started when we escaped, but the Mexicans had superior numbers. I don't think the McDonoughs survived that fight."

"And you're sure their chief is dead?" asked Nantan.

"I saw him killed right in front of me," replied Paxton, "so yes, he's dead."

Nantan translated Paxton's words for Mukwooru, who merely nodded his head once to indicate he understood.

"Mukwooru has been waiting a long time for the woman you brought here," said Nantan. "I think it's the only thing keeping him alive."

"How old is he?" asked Paxton

"He is one hundred and twelve years old," Nantan responded.

"And one half," said Mukwooru in perfect English, smiling at Paxton.

"You know English?" asked Paxton. "Then why the interpreter?"

"He doesn't often speak English anymore," explained Nantan, "or speak at all for that matter. I believe your send-off will be his last hoorah."

"Our send-off?" repeated Paxton.

"You're going to want to break out of the Square, are you not?" asked Nantan. "That's what he thinks. We've been preparing an army to help you do it."

"It's a damned suicide mission!" scoffed Richard, joining their conversation.

"Perhaps," agreed Nantan, "and yet still a worthwhile endeavor. I trust Mukwooru with my life."

"What about the lives of every member of the Tribe?" countered Richard, in what sounded like an argument they were not having for the first time.

"We have come up with a plan to blow a hole in the wall," continued Nantan, "but everyone in the party that starts that explosion will most likely be incinerated."

"And we don't even know if it's going to work!" interjected Richard.

"It will work," said Elizabeth, walking up to the edge of their foursome. "I've seen it, in my dreams. A huge explosion, obliterating everything at ground zero and radiating shock waves outward for miles, shock waves that flatten anything taller than a cactus."

Mukwooru held out his open palms to her and Elizabeth kneeled down next to him, holding his two hands in her own.

"I think the whole thing's a bunch of bullshit," said Richard. "All I know is that I sure as shit ain't gonna be anywhere near ground zero if it comes to that."

"Richard joined the Tribe quite recently," said Nantan, by way of apology.

"It's been a year!" Richard corrected him.

"Recently in Mukwooru years, then" returned Nantan. "We rescued him from the cannibals."

"I rescued myself, thank you very much," said Richard.

"And then he was lucky enough to be accepted into the Tribe," explained Nantan, "instead of sent right back out there to the cannibals."

"Mukwooru saw my value," said Richard as though he were trying to convince himself as well as Paxton. "He must've seen somethin' in you, too. I ain't never seen him take in so many at one time, nor never a whole group like yours."

Elizabeth leaned in just then and whispered conspiratorially, "He says not to trust Valerie. Says he would have sent her away on a normal day but since she was with us, he gave her the benefit of the doubt."

"How do you know he said all that?" asked Paxton. "I haven't heard him say anything at all since you got here."

"I'm somehow connected to him," shared Elizabeth, "through our minds. Kind of like the way we communicated with Thorn."

"You still remember that?" asked Paxton, surprised.

"Of course, I do," she answered. "You don't forget something like that."

"What's wrong with Valerie?" asked Paxton.

"She's not right in the head," answered Elizabeth, after a moment's pause where she appeared to be deep in thought.

"She's comin' down from the hero worship," interjected Richard. "That's plain enough and it don't look like she's gonna make it. She'd take another dose right now if I had one to give her!"

"She's not really with the rest of us," admitted Paxton. "It just didn't feel right leaving her to die out there in the desert. Don't you have any medicine you could give her?"

"We'll do what we can for her," offered Nantan, "and for the rest of you. If she's strong enough, she'll pull through."

"What about the one with half a leg?" asked Richard. "What's her story?"

"She hasn't been with us for long either," answered Paxton. "She escaped the Intake only to be captured by cannibals. Then she escaped the cannibals and ran into us."

"How did she run anywhere with one leg?" asked Richard.

"She took their horse, the one that's roasting on that spit over there," said Paxton. "I'm not worried about Rachel. She's probably stronger than all of us."

"Well, she ain't gonna be good in a fight," Richard pointed out. "How's she gonna contribute to the Tribe?"

"The Tribe's not going to survive this fight," allowed Nantan. "Our purpose is to get that woman, what's her name?"

"Eden," Paxton and Elizabeth answered simultaneously.

"Our purpose is to get Eden out of the Square," Nantan continued. "She's the only hope we got at saving some semblance of humanity!"

"According to him," said Richard, pointing at Mukwooru with his thumb. "What if he's wrong?"

"When have you ever known him to be wrong?" countered Nantan. Mukwooru continued to smile through this exchange, focused upon Elizabeth more than the men.

Just then a warrior appeared from the shadows behind them and offered Paxton an earthen jar full of liquid. One whiff of its contents confirmed that it was alcoholic. Paxton took a tentative sip. It tasted like cactus beer, but stronger. If it was cactus beer it was better than any cactus beer they had managed to ferment upon Maggie's Farm. He took a longer swig of the hoppy brew and passed it along to Nantan.

"What's your plan?" Paxton asked, wiping his frothy lips with the back of his hand. "How do you propose we get Eden out of the Square?"

"They wanna blow the Dump!" stated Richard emphatically.

"What dump?" asked Paxton.

"There's a spot in the northeastern corner of the Square," explained Nantan, "where the Republic dumps their radioactive waste. We don't go near it as a rule."

"Damned straight!" interrupted Richard. "Anyone that goes near it gets messed up!"

"The thing is," continued Nantan, "the Guard doesn't go near it either. They probably got their side of the Wall lined with lead, and they do still have soldiers in Hazmat suits on patrol there, but not near as many as they have elsewhere on the Wall. It's the last place they'd expect us to target."

"That's because it's a suicide mission," repeated Richard.

"We've got a scientist of our own," Nantan said, "a Chinaman. You don't see too many of them in here."

"Ain't no Chinese getting past the death squads these days," added Richard.

"He's been in here since the beginning," Nantan resumed his storytelling, "like a lot of the Tribe. He was working on that old army base, Fort Bliss, outside of El Paso. Got himself walled in with a bunch of others the Guard didn't want anymore. They damn sure didn't want the rest of the world to know what they were doing on that base. Probably thought they were doing them scientists a favor, not killing them, but they were all civilians and ill-equipped for what this place has become. I'll let Shi Li tell you that story sometime, it's his to tell."

"Powerful shit!" Richard chimed in. He and Nantan exchanged a knowing look and Paxton could almost see a smirk on Nantan's stoic countenance. Richard continued, "He thinks he can blow that stockpile. He thinks he can blow a fucking hole a mile wide, right through the corner of the Square!"

"I'd like to talk with this … Shirley," said Paxton, pronouncing it like a girl's name.

"Shhh … Lee," Nantan corrected him. "I'm sure he'd like to talk to you as well, but he's out on patrol at the moment. Everyone in the Tribe is first and foremost a warrior. We all contribute in other ways as well, based upon our abilities, but everyone is prepared to fight and die in the protection of the Tribe."

"For the moment, let's suppose his plan works," said Paxton, "and he creates a hole in the Wall. What happens after that? They aren't going to let us just waltz through there and back into the Republic."

"That's where the army comes in," Nantan replied.

"What army?" asked Paxton.

"We've been cultivating an army," said Nantan. "We've been at this endeavor a long time, now."

"How many soldiers do you have in this army?" asked Paxton.

"A thousand, maybe more," he answered. "It's hard to say because we are scattered throughout the Guadalupe Mountains, in clans no larger than fifty. We don't want the Eye in the Sky to see too many of us gathered together until we're ready."

"Ready for what?" asked Elizabeth, causing Paxton to remember that she was still privy to this conversation.

"Ready to escort Eden out of the Square," said Nantan as though that was all they needed to know.

"What's not to like about this plan?" asked Richard. "There's the nuclear explosion to avoid, though we don't really know the size of the blast zone. If you survive that, there's the battle of one-thousand Indian warriors armed with bows and arrows and rifles against a high-tech defense behemoth that can obliterate us using only drones. Survive that battle and you had better run your asses off if you hope to escape the second nuclear blast!"

"Second blast?" asked Elizabeth.

"They're going to drop a nuclear bomb on the Square," explained Nantan. "Mukwooru has seen this in multiple visions. It's what his prophecy foretold in the first place."

"But everyone in here will die," Paxton stated the obvious.

"Everyone must die," Mukwooru spoke softly in English. "Not everyone gets to choose the manner of their death."

"Would you rather stay in here indefinitely?" asked Richard. "It was my understanding that you wanted our help to break out!"

"Yes," agreed Paxton, "and that has always been a part of the prophecy, but now that the time has come, I'm beginning to realize what that will mean. Will everyone die?"

"Pretty much everyone, I expect," answered Nantan. "Whoever survives the initial blast will have earned themselves a slow death by radiation poisoning."

"And you're all okay with this?" asked Paxton.

"It's not a matter of being okay with it," Nantan translated Mukwooru's words, which had reverted back to Comanche, Paxton presumed. "All of this shall come to pass, and we all have our parts to play. Some of us will continue the struggle, like you and Eden, and this lovely girl beside me. Others will continue in some other form."

"It's a lot to take in," admitted Paxton, "but I believe that we need to get Eden out of here, whatever it takes. Let's just hope it'll also be the end of the Square, and they won't just start again with a fresh set of prisoners."

"It will end the Square," prophesied Mukwooru, after Nantan had translated Paxton's words. "It will end the Republic too, once Eden is finished with them."

"Now we're talking!" said Paxton. The cactus beer had just made its way around their smaller circle and back into his hands. He took a long draught of it and the alcohol went straight to his head, reminding him that he had eaten almost nothing all day during their forced march to Mukwooru. As if in answer to his unspoken need, a plate full of horseflesh was suddenly dropped into his lap from above and behind him. He upended the mug of beer he was holding until the last dregs were gone and then set it aside to concentrate on the feast before him.

"We've certainly been having a lot of parties since you and your sister showed up in the Square," Paxton said to Elizabeth. "This is not normal in here. Most of the time we're struggling to feed all the mouths we've got, while also trying to not get killed by something more swift and decisive than starvation."

"Really?" asked Elizabeth with a sly grin, "but you seem so good at it, Uncle Paxton."

"Back in the day, I was," Paxton responded, also grinning, "but not so much anymore."

Paxton looked over at Jillian and Grace who were dancing cheek to cheek in movements incongruous with the drum beat which was coming from outside the circle of firelight. Eden was swaying to the beat as well, though she looked lost in some world of her own which had taken her far away from them. At a sign from Mukwooru, several warriors joined the girls in a stomping, jumping dance more aligned with the staccato beat of the drums.

"We have been preparing for this day for many years," said Mukwooru, as translated by Nantan. "Tonight, we celebrate your arrival. Tomorrow there is much work to do."

Paxton ate and drank his fill before Jazelle pulled him into the ring of dancers and began to gyrate against his body most provocatively. Paxton felt very alive and very much in the present moment, enjoying the sensations of lightheadedness from the beer, a belly full of horsemeat, the heat of the bonfire upon his skin, the primordial rhythm of the drums and the movement of the dancers all around him. He suddenly wanted Jazelle more than anything else in the world and he told her as much.

They left the firelight in search of an empty longhouse but there were none to be found. When they had reached the fourth and last one in the row and found it half full of sleeping men and women, Jazelle just shrugged her shoulders and pulled him inside the cowhide flap that served as its door. They fumbled at each other's pants as they tumbled down upon an empty sleeping bag between an intertwined couple and a heavily snoring man who was being continually kicked by his neighbor and told to, "Give it a rest!"

They removed only their pants in their impatience and Paxton sported an erection like he hadn't felt in years, if not decades. Jazelle was both surprised and pleased to find it with her hand and she immediately climbed on top of him and guided his turgid shaft to the entrance of her moist folds. She sat down hard upon him, taking his full length inside of her with one smooth motion.

Jazelle let out an animalistic growl of pure pleasure that prompted Paxton to reach up with his right hand and put his index finger to her lips in a silent entreaty for her to be quiet. She bit his finger playfully instead, causing him to cry out in surprise and a little pain and prompting a few sleepers to admonish them with a chorus of, "Shhh!"

She did not seem to mind being shushed and she certainly didn't let their close quarters prevent her from moving up and down upon him, seeking out the exquisite friction that brought them both to orgasm in a matter of minutes. Paxton came quietly but Jazelle was not to be denied the expression of her pleasure and she gasped loudly as she came, causing another round of shushing. She giggled as she fell down upon Paxton's chest and Paxton wondered to himself if he had ever heard her make such a childishly gleeful sound.

He held her tightly to his chest until their breathing returned to normal and then she rolled off him and onto her side so that he could spoon her as they fell asleep. They were so exhausted in both body and mind from the crazy flight from Maggie's Farm over the past couple of days, and the longhouse they shared with the other members of the Tribe felt so completely safe and secure, that they were both deeply asleep in a matter of minutes.

CHAPTER 17
SHI LI

I have a very powerful name in my native Mandarin, Shi Li. My surname Shi means 'rock' and my given name Li is 'strength' or 'power'. Chinese is a tonal language, so the words need to be pronounced correctly or they mean something completely different. Li can mean 'pear' or 'profit', amongst other things, and shi is the verb 'to be' as well as 'lion', and one of its tones means 'shit'.

I made the mistake of trying to explain the nuances of the Chinese language to Richard one night over too many cactus beers and he took to calling me, 'powerful shit'. I'm still trying to decide if this is any better or worse than what he was calling me before that, the English girl's name, Shirley.

I am not supposed to be in the Square. I did nothing illegal or immoral, unless you consider the anti-gravity gun, I helped to create an aberration. I never had any moral qualms about its applications until I discovered the atrocities the Republic was prepared to commit with it. I was too focused upon the physics of antigravity and what had now become possible with Dr. Stephen's Unified Field Theory.

What Dr. Stephens contributed to particle physics was even more significant than Einstein's Theory of Relativity. In fact, Einstein worked on Unified Field Theory himself for the second half of his life without ever resolving it. It has been the holy grail of physics ever since and many scientists have spent their careers seeking for it.

In a nutshell, Unified Field Theory resolves all of the known forces - gravity, electromagnetism and the strong and weak quantum forces that hold an atom together – under a single theoretical framework. The mathematics involved is both incredibly complex and elegant at the same time and involves string theory and 8-dimensional space.

What's more important than Unified Field Theory itself is what the theory has now made possible – antigravity, nuclear fission, teleportation, and possibly time travel. I have no idea what else they're working on, now that I am out of the scientific loop, so to speak, but the possible applications are endless. I would love to be back in a proper lab again and working with all of the new technology, but that sort of thing is hard to come by in the Square. Everything is hard to come by in the Square. Sometimes I wish I had never left my homeland to come to the Republic, but life was no picnic in China either.

I was a child prodigy, back in Beijing. I graduated from Tsinghua University at eighteen years of age with a double degree in mathematics and physics. My parents were extremely proud that I had been accepted to graduate school at Stanford. The Republic has a very limited quota on foreign students studying in its universities and almost no Chinese nationals are accepted anymore, what with first the cold war and now an actual war.

I went through extensive training and trials by the Chinese government before they ever allowed me to leave, and it was only with the understanding that I would be bringing back all of the knowledge and information I could access from the Republicans. I went through just as many trials when I arrived in California, debriefings and psychological profiling, probably intended to ensure I wasn't a spy for the communists. It was understood that the Republicans were keeping a close eye on my comings and goings and monitoring all of my electronic and cell phone activity.

Even so, I felt several degrees more freedom in California than I had ever experienced in Beijing, even with the constant surveillance. Beijing's population had grown to forty million people when I left, and all anyone in China ever talked about was overpopulation. There were shortages of everything, and long lines to wait in for the basic necessities of life.

People disappeared all of the time, either carted away by the police or commandeered for work parties that never returned. My family was more insulated than most, with my parents working for the military and my academic achievements singling me out for special treatment, but even a single misstep could lead to one's displacement from society.

My years at Stanford were the happiest of my life. I had friends for the first time, now that I wasn't in constant competition with my classmates. I even had a girlfriend, a Vietnamese girl named Linh. She was very smart, and beautiful and kind. She was there studying chemical engineering. We enjoyed our forbidden love for as long as it lasted, knowing that neither of our families or countries would permit us to get married.

After I received my PhD, I was offered a research post-doc at an army facility in Texas, and it was made clear to me that it would be the only opportunity I would have to stay in the Republic. Beijing was probably salivating over the new military technologies to which I would have access, so I got the blessing from the Party. Just like that, not even a week after graduation, I was taken from the comfort of southern California and Linh's arms to the west Texan desert and an army outpost that might as well have been a prison for all of the chances I had to escape from it.

I was put to work immediately as part of a team that was developing a gun that could project antigravity at a military target. There were more than a hundred scientists in the facility, most of them from countries outside the Republic, and we did little else but eat, sleep and work. Every Friday night they would allow us to sit together in the mess hall and watch a movie or two, but that was the extent of our entertainment and diversion from our only purpose in life as far as they were concerned. Anyone that complained too loudly was removed, and we didn't dare ask where they had gone.

Our work stretched out into years before a sense of urgency to finish our various projects came down the chain of command. My team had already engineered several working prototypes for an antigravity gun that could create a local suspension of the gravitational forces acting upon its target. Our superiors appeared to be pleased with our progress and the Guard packed up our lab equipment and materials. There was a great deal of apprehension amongst my team as to what was going to happen to us, but no one would give us a straight answer.

We found out one Friday night when they had scheduled a movie for us after months without one. We were all in the mess hall and one of the Transformers movies was playing at a volume loud enough to mask the sounds of the departing troops and trucks. When the movie was over, we discovered that we had been locked inside the mess hall. They had left us with food, so there was no need for immediate panic, although there was a great deal of it in the first few hours after we had discovered our predicament. With the collective brainpower enclosed in that room we made our escape the next day, only to discover that the Guard had completely abandoned their base.

Our first few days inside the Square were governed by fear and confusion. We could get no cell phone or RepNet signal so we had no idea what was going on. We found some viable vehicles in the garage and several parties were sent off in different directions to ascertain what the hell was going on. Most of those parties never came back.

One of the cars that returned spoke of bedlam in El Paso and the impenetrable Wall running right through the city to our west and also north of the base. We had heard rumors of the Wall, even with our limited Wi-Fi on the base, but it always seemed far-fetched and far-off and we never dreamed we'd be enclosed within it. Over days and weeks, the rumors were confirmed by everyone that came our way, both the friendly and the not-so-friendly.

One guy that came onto the base killed six of us before we could kill him, and it was then that I knew we'd have to find a way to protect ourselves in here. I know what happens when there are too many of any creature living in close proximity with limited resources. Others would come to take the supplies left to us by the departed Guard. I resolved to not let that happen.

We had all kinds of spare parts, not only in my lab but elsewhere in the facility. Most importantly, they had left behind a small quantity of U-235 in the lead-lined vault. To this day I don't know why they did it. Was it an oversight? Did they not want to bother with its containment in their hasty retreat, or did they leave it here on purpose hoping we would somehow blow ourselves up with it? Scientists are a notoriously curious lot.

I and several others set about building an antigravity gun to defend ourselves from marauders. We had to jerry-rig a few things for lack of parts but we found most everything we needed. I made a few modifications to the gun that allowed me to change the frequency modulation so that the gun could also be used to suspend the subatomic forces holding together individual atoms. This made it a much more effective gun, and it works reasonably well, but it is just one gun.

When the Tribe came to the compound they captured us, and our one antigravity gun, relatively easily. There were only six of us left by then and Martha was killed in the skirmish. We took one of theirs as well. Only myself and one other passed Mukwooru's test and were allowed to remain with the Tribe and we have been with them ever since.

I'm pretty much in charge of the antigravity gun for the Tribe. We almost never fire it up. We have no reason to fire it this far into the interior of the Park because the Tribe is perfectly capable of defending itself using the other weapons at our disposal. I have other duties for the Tribe, and warrior training as well, but they have given me a small laboratory and lots of time off to use it. The problem is that I don't have anyone to bounce ideas off since Harold is a chemist and seems to have embraced the life of a warrior without looking back at his former life as a scientist.

I didn't have anyone to talk to until Dr. Stevens showed up, that is. What are the odds that the one person in the world I would most want to talk to would knock on my laboratory door, right here in the Park, in the Square? It's a rhetorical question but I'll answer it – astronomical. I am grateful and honored to have met him, face to face, even though our introduction comes at the end of my life.

ANTIGRAVITY

Paxton walked behind Richard through the dimly-lit longhouse between rows of sleeping bags and pillows toward a door at the far end. The sleeping quarters were completely empty at this hour, but Paxton guessed that the room at the back of the longhouse was not. When they reached the door, Richard knocked on it in a practiced pattern. Knock-knock-knock-pause-knock-knock. There was movement from within the room followed by the metallic sound of a lock being disengaged.

As soon as the door was pulled inward, light came pouring through the widening crack from a single LED bulb which hung from the roof by a short wire. There was no one in evidence as Richard and Paxton passed through the portal, but once they stood in the center of the small room the door swung shut and a short man with jet black hair emerged from behind it.

After relocking the door, he turned back toward them and Paxton could immediately distinguish not only his Asian features, but his surprising youth. The man smiling back at him looked to be no more than twenty-five years old and certainly not old enough to be the nuclear physicist with a plan for blowing a hole through the Wall.

Paxton extended his hand and said, "I'm Paxton…"

He was interrupted immediately by an overenthusiastic handshake as his introduction was completed by the young man, "Dr. Paxton Stephens, I know who you are! The whole world knows who you are! It's an honor, sir. I can't believe you're here!"

"And you are?" asked Paxton, extricating his hand from the continuing handshake.

"Dr. Shi Li," came the reply, and it sounded nothing like the girl's name, 'Shirley.' The first syllable was the same as the admonition to be quiet, 'Shhh' and the second syllable sounded like the last name of the famous kung fu master, Bruce Lee.

"You can call me Lee," the man continued, still beaming at him. "We heard rumors that you had come to the Square, but I never imagined I would get to meet you in the flesh. I still can't believe this is happening!"

"Get over yourself, Lee," said Richard. "This is not a social call. Your hero, here, wants to know more about this plan of yours. Specifically, is it going to work?"

"Well, there's no telling that until we try it," answered Lee, "but here, have a seat, both of you."

Lee pointed to a small table covered in papers and two folding chairs which were tucked neatly in under it.

"I'm not staying," said Richard gruffly. "I delivered him to you, like I was asked to. Now I got better things to do than listen to a bunch of scientific mumbo-jumbo that's way above my pay grade."

"And what pay grade is that?" asked Lee, a smile playing at the corners of his mouth.

"Room and board, as always," groused Richard. "Room and board."

Richard made a move toward the door and Lee reached over to unlock it for him. Looking back at Paxton he said, "Nantan wants to see you when you're done here. I expect he'll be wherever Mukwooru is. He don't much leave his side anymore."

"Got it," Paxton replied. "Thanks, Richard."

Richard stopped in his tracks as he was passing through the threshold and turned back to face Paxton saying, "Thanks for what? You don't much hear that word around here, *thanks*."

"Thanks for bringing me here to meet Shi Li," explained Paxton. "Thanks for not killing us on sight two days ago. Thanks for all of the help you're giving us to break out of here!"

"I'm not doing it for you," Richard responded truthfully. "It's the old man, there's something about him, something otherworldly, like he's some kind of prophet or holy man. I can't seem to refuse him any request, even this suicide mission he's hell bent sending us on."

"Well, thank you anyway," Paxton repeated.

"You're welcome," Richard said before turning around and disappearing through the open doorway. Shi Li closed the door behind him and locked it.

"Please, sit down," he offered to Paxton again with a wave of his hand. "Would you like some tea?"

"You have tea?" asked Paxton amazed.

"Well, it's not good tea, but it's tea nonetheless," said Lee with almost no trace of an accent. He crossed over to the wall where a water pot sat on an electric burner and he poured a cup of tea.

"Where are you getting your electricity?" asked Paxton.

"We scavenged some solar panels from somewhere," Lee responded. "We don't have any batteries, though, so we only get juice during the daytime."

"We had the same problem on Maggie's Farm," offered Paxton, "but it was better than no juice at all, which is what we had after our panels were stolen."

"We studied your work extensively at Stanford," said Lee, changing the subject as he passed the cup of tea across to an already seated Paxton. "Your work on Unified Field Theory was worthy of Einstein himself!"

"I was Einstein, in a past life," offered Paxton in a serious tone, but Lee was all smiles.

"Yeah," I've read your fiction, too," said Lee. "You're a real Renaissance man, Dr. Stevens, just like Leonardo Da Vinci."

"I don't think I was Da Vinci," joked Paxton, taking a sip of the warm brew. "It tastes pretty good to me. I can't remember the last time I had real tea, a couple of years at least. Where did you get it?"

"Who knows?" answered Lee with a shrug of his shoulders. He poured himself a second cup of tea and sat down next to Paxton, saying, "We all put in requests, from time to time, for the things we'd like to procure. Then when we're out bartering, we look for the things on the list. Sometimes they turn up but most times they don't."

"Who do you barter with?" asked Paxton with genuine curiosity.

"The Outlaws, when we can find them. You would probably call them Vagabonds," guessed Lee.

"We call 'em Vags," confirmed Paxton.

"But most of the time we trade with the cannibals, I'd guess," Lee continued. "They bring us things they've scavenged and we give them fresh meat, enough to keep several tribes satisfied. We like the competition; it increases our bargaining power."

"Doesn't it bother you?" asked Paxton. "Turning all of those people over like lambs to the slaughter? Literally."

"It did at first," admitted Lee, "but the analytic part of my brain, coupled with the basic biological instinct for survival, went into overdrive the moment I found myself in the Square. Any moral qualms I might have had about the choices I've had to make in here have long since been buried. We're at a very precarious balance in here. We have to limit the size of our population if we are to continue to live on the meager resources available to us.

"The Tribe doesn't take on new members very often. Most of the people who wander in here become fodder for the cannibals. Everyone sits and smokes with Mukwooru, and they say that he can peer into your soul and deem if you're worthy of joining the Tribe, but I don't buy it. If someone has some skill or knowledge the tribe needs, they are permitted to join. If not, they are cast out and one of the cannibal tribes picks them up."

"It sounds pretty Draconian," commented Paxton, "but it doesn't surprise me, given what I've already seen, and done, in the Square. They can't toss us all in here, refuse to provide us the basic necessities for life, and expect that we aren't going to go all *Lord of the Flies* on each other!"

"This whole place is a grand experiment," Lee agreed, "like creating the penal colony that became Australia, but instead of surrounding us by ocean we have been surrounded by impenetrable walls. Oh, and then there's the part about the ever-increasing inhabitants having to fend for themselves with ever-decreasing resources."

"Kind of like a microcosm of what's going on out there," commented Paxton wryly, "on the rest of the planet."

"Exactly," agreed Lee, "and you can bet they're looking at what happens here like a petri dish of bacteria under a microscope. Only they're using satellites and drones to keep tabs on us. The Tribe calls it the Eye in the Sky, and it sees all."

"One of Richard's men shot a drone right out of the sky, on our hike in here," offered Paxton, "with a bow and arrow!"

"We can do amazing things with a bow and arrows," explained Lee. "It's all part of our training. Every member of the Tribe is a warrior at heart, even Mukwooru. We've been raising an army, for a long time. We can't all be together in the same place at the same time because of the Eye in the Sky, but we've been training and living in small groups all over these mountains. In theory we can all be assembled together in a couple of hours when the need arises."

"And how will you call on them to assemble?" asked Paxton. "The airways must surely be monitored."

"Smoke signals," answered Lee, "if you can believe that shit, but they really work."

"Who are you raising this army to fight?" asked Paxton.

"The Mexicans are looking to take over this whole place," Lee responded. "That's what we tell the soldiers to give them a reason to train and prepare. You and I know the real reason we're raising an army, and it's not to defend ourselves from the Mexicans. We're going to war with the Republic. Mukwooru plans to bust out of this place."

"War is as viable a population deterrent as cannibalism, I suppose," Paxton ruminated out loud.

"Exactly," agreed Lee. "In order to keep the balance, we have to limit the size of our population, in the Square as well as the Republic. Somebody's finally starting to see the writing on the wall. The Wall, that's funny, get it?"

"I get it," stated Paxton sardonically.

"If I were going to worry about my morality," Lee commented, returning to an earlier thread in their conversation, "or my mortality for that matter, I would worry more about the explosion I'm hoping to detonate at the Dump and what it'll do to anyone in close proximity to the blast, than I would worry about the fate of the walking meat we release to the cannibals. If my calculations are right, everyone within a ten-mile radius of that blast is going to be incinerated!"

"Well let me help you check those calculations," offered Paxton. "It never hurts to have a fresh pair of eyes. What exactly is your plan?"

"As you know," began Lee, "nuclear waste has already spent most of its usable fuel. It's not like we have a cake of Uranium-235 to work with here, but there is a lot of spent fuel in the northeast corner of the Square. The Republic has been dumping their waste there since before the Square was completed."

"You're not going to be able to get an accurate estimate of the power of the explosion you're hoping to create," reasoned Paxton, poring over the pages of mathematical equations on the myriad of disheveled sheets of paper spread out all over the table before him. "You need a better estimate of the mass of depleted uranium you're working with."

"We've tried to get one, but the whole region is so hot we can't get anyone close enough without putting their lives in danger," Lee explained. "We had a drone I was able to repair and repurpose, a couple of months ago, and we got some images from that, before the Guards on the Wall realized it wasn't one of theirs and shot it down. That's how I got my upper and lower estimates for the mass of depleted uranium you can see there."

"I'm not even sure what's out there for waste," continued Lee. "Unified Field Theory has opened up countless possibilities and technology is advancing in leaps and bounds on the other side of the Wall. For all I know, they found a better way to split the atom, or maybe they've perfected nuclear fission, but that wouldn't explain all the waste they continue to heap on us."

"You don't get too many rocket scientists in here, do you?" asked Paxton, "Not any that make it through the Intake and Initiation, I'll wager. I've been hungry for news of what's going on out there as well."

"You're the first one I've seen in years," agreed Lee. "That's why I was so excited to have you here."

"This is a staggering amount of radioactive waste," commented Paxton, "but how are you going to get the last of the spent fuel rods to fizz?"

"You've provided the key for that," answered Lee. "I'm going to break apart the nuclear bonds using an anti-gravity gun I perfected for the Guard before they entombed me here. You've proven that all of these forces are essentially one and the same thing, so I've surmised that a concentrated electromagnetic pulse can be used to start a chain reaction which I hope will continue throughout the entire stockpile."

"Where are you going to get an anti-gravity gun?" asked Paxton. "Is such a thing even possible?"

"I have one!" answered Lee excitedly. "My team designed the gun for the Guard, and then I built a reasonable facsimile of one from the spare parts they left behind when they abandoned us in the Square to die. My gun actually has two different settings, a modification I never shared with the Guard. One frequency creates a localized field of anti-gravity and a second frequency negates the subatomic forces holding ordinary atoms together!"

"Can I see it?" asked Paxton eagerly.

"I don't have it here," admitted Lee. "It's safely locked away in our armory."

"Well, how does it work?" Paxton continued to interrogate the younger scientist.

"The gun creates a strong, electromagnetic field which negates all of the other forces in its path, from gravity to the atomic forces keeping electrons in orbit around their nuclei," explained Lee. "It can be aimed at the feet of an enemy combatant, causing them to be lifted right off the ground."

"But that's not the most effective way to use the gun." he continued. "The anti-gravity anomaly it creates is so localized that the best you can hope for is to throw the enemy off balance or lift them high enough to break a bone when you turn off the gun and they come crashing back to Earth. If you use a shorter frequency and aim my gun directly at a person's body, however, the individual atoms in the path of the electromagnetic field split apart spontaneously. I have seen crows and coyotes disintegrate before my very eyes when they are caught in the beam of my gun."

"That's just great," exclaimed Paxton sarcastically. "Of all of the miracles we can now perform because of Unified Field Theory, we've decided to use it to create better ways to kill each other!"

"Hey," Lee defended himself, "I didn't have any choice in the matter. It was kill or be killed, ever since I was impressed into the service of the Guard."

"What do you mean you were *impressed* into the service of the Guard?" asked Paxton.

"One minute I'm starting a research post-doc and the next they've taken my passport and revoked my visa and interred me in an army base in West

Texas. The Chinese were told that I had defected, so I'm sure my family must have suffered for the news of that alleged treason. I could have killed myself, I suppose, but I don't have it in me, and besides, the work was just so fascinating. The possibilities are endless. You really have opened Pandora's Box, Dr. Stevens."

"Please, call me Paxton," he offered. "Indeed, I have opened Pandora's Box, and the new technologies at our fingertips are exciting, if only we humans can stick around long enough to develop them. For some reason I can't quite understand, we seem to be hell bent on annihilating ourselves."

"Hasn't that always been the case?" asked Lee. "It's just that now we have the means at our disposal."

"Well, we also have the means of our salvation," countered Paxton, "right here in the Square."

"You're talking about this woman you brought with you," surmised Lee. "Everyone is talking about this woman. Is she the one foretold in your books?"

"She is," answered Paxton, "and I believe that she has the power to save us from destroying ourselves, but not if we stay in here."

"Which is where I come in," guessed Lee. "I'm happy to help. The Tribe has been good to me, and I have lived a lot longer than I ever expected I would when I first found myself in the Square. I would ask a favor of you Dr. Stephens…Paxton. If you do succeed in breaking out of here, I have a message I'd like for you to send to my family, back in China, if such a thing is still possible."

"You can come with us and send it yourself," offered Paxton. "You're certainly not going to want to stay in here when all is said and done."

"Someone has got to pull the trigger to start the chain reaction," said Lee resignedly, "and if Richard is right about one thing, he's right about that. Whoever pulls that trigger is not getting out of here alive. I'll not send someone in my place to initiate a nuclear explosion of my own design."

"Can't you rig a timer and shoot the gun from a remote location?" asked Paxton.

"We don't have that kind of tech in here," admitted Lee. "And even if we did, we're only going to get one shot at this. If it doesn't work, or the plan needs to be adjusted, we'll need a human intellect to make those decisions on the fly."

"There's something I don't quite get about this gun of yours," said Paxton, shifting the direction of their conversation away from Lee's sacrifice. "In order to create an electromagnetic field capable of suspending gravity, you'd need a huge influx of energy. What is the power source for this gun of yours?"

"That's almost the best part of the technology!" said Lee, jumping out of his seat excitedly. He crossed the small room to retrieve the tea kettle, filled both of their cups with the still tepid brew and then sat back down next to Paxton. "There is a mini-reactor in the base of the gun, similar to the ones they're using to power their SmartHouses. It's encased in lead, of course, to protect the one who wields it."

"It must be heavy as hell," commented Paxton.

"It is," agreed Lee. "The engineers had a hell of a time trying to design a way for it to be carried by a single soldier. They can manage it with a shoulder harness but the guns can't be carried for long distances."

"Can I see this gun of yours?" asked Paxton again, draining the last dregs of his teacup. "Is it somewhere close?"

"Not too far away," said Lee. "We'd have to clear it with Nantan. He's in charge of the day-to-day operations around here. He's defers to Mukwooru, of course, but the chief doesn't seem to concern himself with much other than eating barely enough to keep himself alive, and smoking his pipe."

"What about Richard?" asked Paxton.

"I guess you could say he is second-in-command," Lee answered. "Or third, if you count Mukwooru."

"Well, I'm supposed to go and see them after this," Paxton offered. "Do you have time to come with me?"

"Why not?" asked Lee. "I'd love to see the look on your face when you witness what Unified Field Theory has made possible!"

"Oh, I know what's possible now," countered Paxton, "and I don't know why it should still surprise me that the warmongers have been so industrious, but in my mind, I still hold humanity to a higher standard."

"Your mistake," commented Lee.

"I guess so," said Paxton with a far-off look.

"Let's go then," stated Lee, rising from the table and Paxton followed suit.

They found Mukwooru and Nantan in essentially the same spot they had been sitting the previous evening, though the fire had long since gone cold. Eden and Elizabeth sat on the other side of Mukwooru. A four-pole awning had been erected over their heads to keep the worst of the sun's rays at bay.

They were sharing a pipe between them and Nantan immediately offered it to Paxton when he sat down next to him. Paxton took a long drag and savored the taste of tobacco and marijuana on his tongue before exhaling a cloud of white smoke. He felt the head rush almost instantaneously and smiled at the old man who had been studying his face intently since he sat laboriously down and folded his legs beneath him.

"I'd like to see the anti-gravity gun Lee told me about," he said to Nantan, though he was looking at Mukwooru. He couldn't seem to pry his eyes away from the unfathomable depths of the old man's penetrating gaze.

Nantan translated and Mukwooru acceded with a slight nod of his head. Lee nodded as well and then turned around and retreated from the direction they had come. Paxton took a second hit from the pipe when it was returned to his hands.

"How did you sleep, Uncle Paxton?" asked Eden.

"Pretty well, all things considered," he answered.

"Wait," interrupted Nantan. "You're the girls' uncle?"

"Not really," admitted Paxton. "It's a long story. I was a friend of their parents once, a long time ago. Where are the others?"

"They've all been given a job to do," Elizabeth volunteered.

"No one in the Tribe is ever idle for very long," instructed Nantan.

"Except for you four, apparently," Paxton pointed out.

"We're plotting strategy," allowed Nantan, grinning sheepishly. Mukwooru winked at him as if he understood their conversation completely. "Now that you've heard the plan, do you think it will work?"

"It's hard to say until I see this gun of yours," Paxton answered. "Nuclear waste is not typically recycled into nuclear bombs for a reason. The fuel has already been spent. I suppose anything is possible."

"You learned that from Thorn," interjected Elizabeth.

"I guess I did," agreed Paxton. "If it does work, there's no telling how big of an explosion it will produce. It's not like we can perform a test run. We could produce anything from a slow meltdown to a full-on thermonuclear explosion, or anything in the spectrum between those two extremes. Are you really sure you want to do this?"

"Can you think of a better way to break out of here?" returned Nantan. "How badly do you want to get out?"

"Pretty badly," admitted Paxton, "and I wouldn't mind getting back at the bastards that put us all in here, but all of those lost lives!"

"There will be lives lost no matter how you decide to bust out of here," pointed out Nantan. "At least this way the soldiers on the Wall will go quickly and painlessly. I'm sure you're aware of the prophecy."

"That a virgin will bring about the destruction of the Square?" Paxton responded as a question. "Everyone associated with the McDonough clan was well acquainted with the prophecy. Jonas brought it back from Mukwooru himself."

"Haven't you ever wondered how the Square would be destroyed?" he pressed. "Mukwooru has seen a nuclear explosion, in his visions. That's how he knows the Square will cease to be."

"Isn't there some other way?" pleaded Eden.

Mukwooru made a terse statement in Comanche and Nantan translated, "This is the way it must be."

Just then they heard the sound of movement from somewhere to the west of their awning, but it was several minutes more before a makeshift cart was pushed into the space on the other side of last night's dead fire. Lee had commandeered help from a burly man with a big, black beard and the two of them seemed to be exerting a fair amount of effort to move what looked from the outside to be nothing more than a large, brown box on wheels.

Once they had ceased their efforts and the box stood still, Lee inquired of Nantan, "Can we borrow your shelter for a few minutes? We don't want the Eye to see what we've got under here."

Nantan nodded his head and then reached behind Mukwooru's back to retrieve the hat which was dangling there by a string around his neck. He fixed the hat firmly upon the old man's head and then covered his own head with a similar hat. Paxton realized that he didn't have the faintest idea what had become of the hat he had worn for most of his time in the Square. He missed it sorely when he stepped out from beneath the shade of the awning and into the midafternoon heat of the desert.

Paxton stood next to one leg of the awning and Lee and his helper each took another leg. Seeing an unattended corner, Elizabeth stood up and took her place to help the men lift and move the light but bulky, temporary shelter. Only when it was fixed firmly atop the rolling box did Lee remove the cardboard cover to reveal its contents.

Paxton could tell at first glance that he was looking at a gun, but it was unlike any gun he had ever seen. The stock was unusually short but the barrel was twice as long and wide as his own, favorite rifle. Three baffled rings were attached to the end of the muzzle, spaced about three inches apart from each other. The whole thing was jet black, including the twelve-inch cube it was mounted upon, which Paxton could only assume contained the gun's power source.

"It looks heavy," was all he could muster to say as he stared at the gun made possible by Unified Field Theory.

"Try and lift it," offered Lee. Paxton stepped forward and grabbed the gun by the stock and barrel. His first attempt barely budged the thing, but when he gathered himself for a second attempt and got his legs under him, he was able to lift it an inch or two off the cart. He could not hold the awkward position for long and he let it fall somewhat heavily back to its original resting place.

"Jesus!" he exclaimed. "How do you expect someone to carry that thing?"

"I told you," Lee responded, "it can only be carried with a shoulder harness, and not for very long. I imagine the Guards mount them to something more mobile, and less crude than the cart we built for this one."

"What can we aim it at?" asked Paxton.

"That depends," Lee responded. "Do you want to make something levitate or dissolve?"

"What about that cactus over there?" suggested Paxton, pointing to a small, brownish prickly-pear cactus about twenty feet from the gun, and even farther from the spectators now seated in the still fierce, afternoon sunlight.

"Dissolve it is," exclaimed Lee. "The cactus wouldn't float anyway, rooted to the Earth such as it is."

"Don't float *anything* out in the open like that," admonished Nantan.

"Get behind me," Lee directed Paxton. "You too, Barnabus."

Paxton looked over Lee's shoulder so he could see what steps he was taking to fire up the gun. Lee flicked a switch and although the gun made no sound, the air around them changed subtly, as though it was somehow electrically charged. The hair on Paxton's arms stood straight out and he was filled all of a sudden with a feeling of foreboding.

Lee looked through the gun's sight and turned a couple of cranks on the underside of the mechanism to adjust the aim. Stepping back, he looked over his shoulder and asked, "Is everybody ready?"

"Should I put my hands over my ears?" asked Paxton.

"Not at all," answered Lee. "You won't notice any difference in the gun when I fire it. Just concentrate your attention on the cactus."

Lee looked through the sight one more time and then pulled the trigger. There was no difference in the gun, but Paxton gazed in astonishment as the cactus was slowly erased from existence. It did not explode as with the impact of a projectile, nor did it melt as though it was being cooked by microwaves, but it slowly disappeared as if someone was using a giant eraser and working on the cactus from the edges inward.

By the time Lee turned off the gun, not only had the cactus disappeared but there was a circular depression which penetrated five or six feet into the dirt and sand where the cactus had just stood rooted to the ground.

"What happened to the cactus?" asked an astonished Elizabeth.

"I temporarily negated the atomic forces which kept the electrons spinning around the nuclei of the cactus' atoms," Lee explained, "and any other atoms in the path of the gun's beam. Without those polar forces of attraction, the subatomic particles were free to disperse and later reform as other, or potentially the same, types of atoms."

Paxton walked closer to the hole and peered inside. The only thing left of the cactus were some severed roots which were now tan circles at the edges of the darker brown, earthen hole. Squatting down he reached into the opening to touch the still moist end of one of the roots.

"Fuck me!" he mumbled under his breath. Standing up Paxton turned back to Lee and asked, "How long has this technology existed?"

"Not long," guessed Lee. "They left most of us to die in the Square after we had developed a working prototype. That was about a year ago, give or take."

Looking over at the still seated Nantan Paxton asked, "Do the guards on the Wall have these guns?"

"Some of them do," confirmed Nantan. "We've seen them using the cannibals for target practice. Mostly they still carry standard issue semi-automatic rifles."

"What kind of range does one of these have?" Paxton asked.

"Depends on the power source," Lee responded. "You can see where the hole stops in the ground here. That's as far as this one can shoot, roughly ten meters."

"Thank the All for that!" exclaimed Paxton. "They've gotta get in close to use one of these."

"Unless they have a bigger gun," Lee interjected.

Lee's words hung in the air as everyone pondered over the implications. Paxton looked at the perspiring women seated next to the two old Native Americans and asked, "Do you want us to move the awning back?"

"No, no," answered Nantan, standing up slowly. "Leave it right where it is and put the box back over that damned thing! We need to prepare the sweat lodge."

Nantan reached downward to grasp the older chief by his elbow and bicep in order to help him to his feet and Eden did the same on his other side. They lifted him bodily and he unfolded his legs so that he could rest his weight upon them. Neither of them removed their grip from his arms as he tried to find his balance.

"What is a sweat lodge?" asked Paxton.

"Our warriors need to purify themselves before going into battle," explained Nantan. "A sweat lodge is like a sauna only more intense. In the sweat lodge we will seek visions to guide us through the coming struggle."

Mukwooru leaned almost imperceptibly toward Nantan and whispered something so softly that Paxton could not even tell what language he was using. Nantan nodded but did not otherwise offer to translate the chief's words.

Paxton asked, "Well? What did he say?"

"He said," translated Nantan finally, "'*It is time to prepare for war.*'"

CHAPTER 18

EDEN

I am no longer the same person who wrote in this book a week ago. Can it really be only one week? I have killed another human being. I have killed a lot of human beings, and I will kill many more before I am through. You could argue that the Vagabonds deserved it, that the killing was somehow justified, but it still makes me sick to my stomach. I killed all of those people, just by wishing them dead. And that's not all I can do.

I can make things happen, just by thinking them. When I look back, I can see that I've been doing it for years, probably my whole life. The things I wanted just materialized and events always seemed to turn out in my favor. Now I can see that I made them happen that way, by just wishing it to be so. Paxton would say that thoughts create reality, but I don't think he means it literally. Maybe he does.

And then I met Mukwooru and it was as if I was greeting an old friend, one that I haven't seen in years. We conversed together using only our minds. He saw right through me, right away, and he made me to see right through myself. He helped me to remember that I am a prophet, in a long line of prophets, most of whose lives didn't end so well. He knew I was the virgin from his own prophecy, the minute he laid eyes on me. My coming has been foretold by many peoples and many religions over the millennia. Mukwooru's foresight is merely the most recent prediction.

All of the prophesies are pretty similar, when you think about it. 'A Savior will come to rescue humanity from the brink of destruction.' Why is it that humanity always needs saving? No matter how many times I return to enlighten them, they seem to be singularly intent upon their own annihilation, almost as if they revel in it.

Why do I even bother to keep coming back? I love them, that's why, I love them all. We all have our parts to play in the cosmic dance. Mine is turning out so much different than I could ever have imagined back on the farm with Mom and Pop in Argentina. That seems like another lifetime to me now, especially after Mukwooru took me back through so many of my past lifetimes in the sweat lodge.

It sounds too incredible to be true, but I have been a prophet for most of the religions in the world, except for Satanism. Old Nick can have that one. I was Jesus, of course, but I was also Buddha, Mohammed, Baha'u'llah, Sonam Gyatso, Quetzalcoatl, St. Francis of Assisi, Mansur-al-Hallaj, Ramanuja, Lao-Tzu, Joan of Arc, Parshva, Confucius, Zarathustra, Elijah, Krishna, Plotinus, Pythagoras, Solomon, Maximilla, Saul, Hui-Yuan, Socrates, Bodhidharma, Shankara, Merwyn, Meister Eckhart, Guru Nanak, Mary Anne de Paredes, Ba'al Shem Tov and an oak tree named Thorn, in my most recent incarnation.

The Christians speak of the Second Coming of Christ, but it's misleading to call it my 'Second' Coming. It's more like my Thirty-Second Coming. For anyone who's counting, the above was not meant to be an exhaustive or chronological list. I failed to mention many other lives as less well-known personas. They wait for my Second Coming as though it is a good thing, when in truth I return to them now during a time of great suffering. I hope I can be their Savior again, but I really don't know how many I can save this time, certainly not all of them. It's going to get much worse on this planet before it gets better.

Now that I know who I am, or at least who I was, I'm can feel the power surging throughout my being. I'm beginning to understand it and I'm learning to control it. Who am I that I should be given all of this power? What have I done to deserve this destiny, to be the Savior of a world? I am tempted to ask the All to take this cup away from me, as I did on the cross on Golgotha two thousand years ago. If such a thing were even possible, could I really abandon them to their fate? Is it better to let them go extinct and start the whole process of evolution all over again?

Who exactly would I be asking for this respite? My father? My mother? I've never much talked with God, before now, and I've certainly never received an answer from Him, or Her. Mom and Pop were pretty much hands-off when it came to religion, so I have no formal training in any of the world's religions. Is it me? Am I the one they all pray to, hoping for a better life? That's much too weird to contemplate, but I'm beginning to feel powerful enough to be a god!

I cannot leave them to their own devices, even if I wanted to do so, because Lucifer is already meddling in their affairs once more. He has also taken physical form again and has begun to manipulate global affairs in his favor. He has been subtly, and sometimes not so subtly, pushing this planet toward destruction, mayhem and chaos for millennia, the yin to my yang. If I were to do nothing, he would end this little experiment called humanity.

But I am getting way ahead of myself here. I need to fight one battle at a time. First, we must put an end to the Square. It's not enough to escape, we need to end this place, and the irony is that the Republic is going to do it for us. Hopefully we'll be long gone before that comes to pass. I feel quite capable of protecting myself, even from a nuclear explosion, but will I be able to protect the others? Lizzie? Paxton?

I'm not infallible, nor all-powerful. That's the thing about coming back into the physical realm. This body around me is alive, which means it can also die. All of my other incarnations ended in death, why should this one end any differently? But why do I keep coming back? Where would I be if I chose not to be reincarnated?

Could I really fix all of this with a wave of my hand? For some unknown reason, I don't think that's the way this is supposed to go down. My destiny is to help them help themselves, not to solve all of their problems for them. I have tried to teach them, time and again, with some degree of success here and there, but by and large they are at best apathetic and at worst openly bent on destroying themselves and everything they have built here.

I need them to transcend the limitations of what they deem to be reality so that I might transcend the limitations of my spirit and move on from this place. I'll certainly not abandon them to Lucifer. He is bound by the same universal laws and just as stuck here, but he won't be free unless he can devolve this system into the chaos from which it was born. He can't do it with a wave of his hand either, but must help them to destroy themselves.

This is the battle we must undertake and Earth is the battleground. The fate of humankind hangs in the balance. It's not a battle I intend to lose, but win or lose, I feel like this will be my last entanglement with my old friend. Humans will either be headed toward extinction or they will take a quantum leap in their awareness and collective spirituality and rebuild a better world from the ashes of the coming conflict.

Either way, it's time for me to move on. It's a great big cosmos and I have tarried here long enough. I have loved my time here amongst them, but I am not one of them, and it's time for me to move on.

SWEAT LODGE

Paxton shared a picnic table with both old and new friends as the last rays of the mercifully setting sun were being blocked incrementally by the Guadalupe Mountains to the west of their encampment. Jazelle and Lee sat on either side of him, while Eden sat across the table flanked by both Elizabeth and Abraham. They were eating the last of the horse meat and a surprisingly tasty stew that had been cooked over an open fire for most of the afternoon.

"What's in this stew?" asked Elizabeth. "It's delicious!"

"Prickly pear," answered Lee. "I think there's also some sotol in there. You would be amazed what the Tribe can scavenge for food from the desert."

"It's not that surprising," Paxton countered. "The Apache were living off this land long before we showed up."

"Just about everything you see growing out here can be used for something," Lee continued. "We eat the fruit and flower buds from the cholla and yucca, berries from the juniper and algerita and the acacia seeds and pods are ground into flour for pinole."

"How do you know so much about the desert plants?" asked Eden.

"It's just my scientific mind trying to find things to keep it occupied in here," admitted Lee. "I can only spend so much time thinking about particle physics with no lab and no colleagues. I've been writing a field guide to desert flora and fauna in my spare time.

"The Apache have a wealth of knowledge which gets passed down as oral history from generation to generation. It's even more invaluable in here in the absence of the RepNet. You can learn a lot if you're interested and you ask the right questions."

"Last night I saw one of the warriors make a poultice for Grace out of crushed up roots," commented Elizabeth. "What plant was that?"

"Probably ocotillo," answered Lee, "if it was used to bring down swelling. Or possibly algerita. Was it being applied on open sores?"

"Yes," confirmed Elizabeth. "He was putting it on the welts on her back."

"Algerita, then," said Lee with conviction.

"Now you're just showing off," teased Paxton.

"It's all right there in my field guide," said a beaming Lee, "if you care to read it. They have uses for everything out here. Fibers from yucca and sumac are woven into ropes, mats and baskets. The wood from juniper and desert walnut is used for bows and fuel. They make dyes from…"

"Maybe some other time," interrupted Paxton. He was genuinely interested, but at the moment they had more pressing matters to discuss and he said as much to Lee by way of apology.

"Tell me again," said Jazelle, taking advantage of the opening, "what you gonna do to this dump."

"The easiest way to describe it," said Lee patiently, "is that I am going to shoot a ray of antigravity at the heart of that stockpile of spent fuel in the hopes of starting a chain reaction nuclear explosion that will blow a hole in the corner of the Wall."

"This is nuts!" exclaimed Jazelle. "Y'all be killed instantly, if the damned thing even works. If it don't work you'll die a slow, horrible death from all that radiation. Do you even have one of them suits, you know, that blocks out the radiation?"

"We have several, actually," answered Lee, "taken from the military base where I used to work for the Guard. But hazmat suits won't protect us from a nuclear explosion!"

"And you have one of these guns?" asked Abraham. "Here in the Square?"

"He does," Paxton answered for Lee. "He gave us a demonstration this afternoon. He melted a cactus with it."

"It was more like he erased it from existence," interjected Elizabeth.

"Not quite," corrected Lee. "The subatomic particles were still there; they were merely set free from their bonds to form other atoms and molecules."

"Well, why don't you melt a hole in the Wall so we can all just walk on out of here?" asked Jazelle.

"Have you ever been up next to the Wall?" asked Lee.

"Not since my Intake Day," admitted Jazelle.

"They have an electromagnetic field around the whole thing," he continued. "They know if anyone is getting too close and when that happens, they use us for target practice. We'd never be able to get through undetected and if we managed to somehow duck under their fire then we'd have to deal with the Guard on the other side. No one in here knows what that will entail, we're too far removed from the Republic at this point, but I would guess that they'd be taking no prisoners."

"Ain't you gonna have that same problem at the dump?" asked Jazelle, ever the tactician.

"We don't think they keep as good a watch at the Dump as they do over the rest of the Square," answered Lee. "No one wants to go near that place, from either side of the Wall. I only need to get one clear shot at the center, or as close to the center as I can get, and that will be the end of it, assuming my theory holds true."

"It'll be the end," agreed Jazelle, "one way or another."

"How many people are you going to take with you?" asked Eden earnestly.

"I'd do it alone if I had my say," grumbled Lee, "but Nantan thinks I might need someone to cover me from the Guard. I'm going to have to get in pretty close to the Wall for my best shot at this. I'm only going to take a handful of warriors with me."

"Who's going to join you on this fool quest?" pressed Jazelle.

"Most everybody at this camp has already volunteered," Lee replied. "We're going to have a lottery to decide who will accompany me. I don't want to make that decision."

"I want to go," said Eden decisively.

"What?!" asked Paxton and Elizabeth in unison.

"If this is our best plan," Eden spoke confidently, "then our best chance of success is for me to lead it."

"No way!" said Paxton excitedly, rising from his chair. "Absolutely not!"

"You've seen what I can do, Uncle Paxton!" she responded, rising to Paxton's level of enthusiasm, even as she also rose out of her chair. "I think I can block the harmful radiation, from everyone. I'm feeling so powerful now, like I can do anything I set my mind to do. Watch this!"

Eden held out her hands, palms upward and the silverware on the table began to rise slowly in front of their eyes. The cups and plates followed suit until everything that had been sitting on the table hovered a few inches above its plastic tablecloth.

"What the fuck?" exclaimed Lee, despite his usually cool and collected demeanor.

Next the table began to shake and it too rose a few inches upward so that the dinnerware returned to sit in its rightful place on the tabletop, however everything was now three or four inches off the ground. Soon their chairs began to lift off the ground as well so that only Paxton and Eden were still rooted to the Earth.

"You *spooky*, girl!" Jazelle said, making the sign of the cross. "Stop that!"

In answer to Jazelle's instructions Eden snapped her fingers and just like that the tables and chairs all came crashing to the ground, shaking a few spoons over the edge and upsetting at least one glass of water.

"How did you do that?" asked an amazed Lee.

"I'm just tapping into Paxton's antigravity," Eden said simply, as though it were the easiest thing in the world she could do. "He can tell you all about the science behind it."

"But to cause a local gravity disturbance this strong you would need a tremendous amount of energy," surmised Lee. "Where's all that energy coming from?"

"I can't tell you anything about that," admitted Eden. "I just concentrate hard upon a particular thought and it happens. I told you I'm feeling powerful, but this is all just so new to me. I'm still learning how to control it."

"Who are you?" he asked, the astonishment still plain upon his face. "Really?"

"She is the reason we need to bust out of the Square!" Paxton answered for her. "She is humanity's last, best hope for salvaging a world on the brink of environmental collapse!"

"You're so melodramatic, Uncle Paxton," chuckled Eden. "I'm just a woman trying to find her way in the world, same as everybody else."

"Well, I can't do what you just did," Lee admitted. "So, I'd say you are not the same as everybody else."

"And you really think you could shield everyone from the radiation?" pressed Paxton. "What about the nuclear explosion we hope to create?"

"I don't know," she admitted. "I'm feeling so strong, but I don't know for sure if I'll be strong enough, right there at ground zero. But I feel like I have to try."

"You have to *try*?" asked Paxton sarcastically. "You don't try this one, Eden, you either do or you die. And we all know you can bleed now."

"What, this?" she returned, holding up her arm in his face. "It was nothing."

Indeed, he could scarcely make out what had been a long red gash across her bicep three days ago. Still, he continued to admonish her, "I don't like it, not one little bit. I've got to agree with Richard on this one! It's a suicide mission!"

"How can I expect anyone else to make the ultimate sacrifice if I'm not willing to do the same?" reasoned Eden.

"Yeah, but they're willing to make the ultimate sacrifice to free you from the Square!" he shot back at her. "It will all be for nothing if you die right along with them!"

Eden was about to launch a rebuttal when their argument was interrupted by a blonde warrior with very tanned skin showing everywhere except for his loincloth. He came right up to Paxton and announced loudly, "The sweat lodge is ready. Mukwooru would like you all to join him there."

Everyone who was still seated joined Paxton and Eden on their feet and they fell into line behind the blonde warrior. Paxton was directly behind Eden in line and he craned his neck forward so that he could whisper in her ear, "This discussion is not over, Eden. I won't risk losing you to a nuclear blast."

"It's not really your decision to make," she responded over her shoulder, but she winked at him to let him know she was being cheeky, not insolent.

They followed the blonde warrior to the outskirts of camp until they came to what looked like a large desert tortoise. A closer inspection revealed a hemispherical edifice about twelve feet in diameter which was covered in old blankets. Mukwooru and Nantan sat beside a small fire next to the lodge and Nantan beckoned the six of them to sit around the fire, which had already burned down to a good set of coals.

No sooner had they sat down than Nantan lit another peace pipe and passed it around their circle. Several warriors used the slight gap between Abraham and Lee to place mostly round, soccer ball-sized stones onto the bed of coals at the center of their powwow. When the pipe was passed to Paxton, he took a long drag of it and felt immediately light-headed. He passed it along to Jazelle on his left and looked over at Nantan.

"I can taste the ganja," he guessed, "but there's something in that pipe I just can't place."

"Peyote," said Nantan simply. "It'll help with your vision in the sweat lodge."

The pipe passed around the circle three times before it was announced that they were ready to move into the interior of the lodge. No one spoke during this time but they could hear drumming and chanting in another language from just far enough away that the musicians could not be seen from their cross-legged positions around the fire.

As they started to rise and stretch out their limbs, the warriors returned to retrieve the round stones from the smoldering fire using more of the dirty blankets from a pile outside the lodge. They carried their burdens through a flap that was being held open by a young, female warrior and when they reemerged from the lodge, they were empty-handed.

Mukwooru and Nantan were the first to enter the lodge, but not before they were helped out of their clothing by attending warriors. Mukwooru's naked body was mostly wrinkled skin and bones, but he shuffled slowly forward under his own power. He disappeared through the open flap without even having to duck, so stooped was his ancient frame. Nantan entered behind him, carrying his still-powerful body and not-as-wrinkled skin with him.

When it became self-evident that nakedness was expected of everyone entering the sweat lodge, Paxton's group began to disrobe as well, albeit more self-consciously than either of the Indian chiefs had been. They followed the two old men into the dimly-lit lodge in single file, stooping through the doorway which continued to be held open for them.

Eden entered first, followed by Paxton, Jazelle, Elizabeth, Abraham, Lee and two members of the Tribe who were as yet unfamiliar to them. Lee whispered to Paxton as he passed him that the two warriors invited to join them had been chosen to accompany him on the mission to blow up the Dump.

It was stiflingly hot and almost pitch-black inside the lodge, especially after the flap had been closed behind them. Paxton and Eden took seats in the center of the lodge around the pile of fire-warmed rocks that had been deposited there. They sat in the North-South positions while Mukwooru and Nantan took the East-West. The other six sat in a second circle surrounding their square, with their backs up against the sides of the lodge.

When Paxton's eyes adjusted to the dark, he could see that the framework for the lodge was made out of sapling trees, bent over and lashed together into a hemispherical configuration. A hodgepodge of blankets were draped over the pliant poles with only a small hole at the very apex to let a faint light into their man-made cave. The chanting they could hear got somehow louder after they had taken their cross-legged seats on the dusty floor and Paxton guessed that the voices were coming from right outside the lodge.

Paxton joined hands with Mukwooru and Nantan and Eden did the same on the other side of the rocks, completing their circuit. Everyone behind them joined hands as well and created a second circle encompassing the first. The two old men began to chant in what Paxton could only assume was Apache and they were joined by the two warriors on either side of Lee.

Paxton closed his eyes and concentrated upon his breathing. When the chanting stopped, he was already in a light meditative state, exacerbated by the peyote. Mukwooru took a ladle from somewhere and began to drizzle water from a bucket onto the hot rocks. The phase change from water to vapor was immediate and intense and the lodge was soon full of steam.

Paxton's lungs filled with the hot air and he had a momentary panic attack when it became hard for him to breathe and he felt like could not sit there in that dark, enclosed space for another moment. As if they sensed his anxiety, both Mukwooru and Nantan gripped Paxton's hands a little more tightly and

Paxton willed his racing heart to slow its beating. He concentrated once again upon the air entering and leaving his body through the portal of his nostrils.

There was silence both inside and outside the sweat lodge, except for the hiss of the water still being ladled upon the hot stones. Paxton felt as if he were perspiring from every pore in his body. He was light-headed and probably would have collapsed onto his back if the two chiefs did not have hold of his hands. He became less and less aware of his body and his consciousness seemed to float somewhere near the top of the lodge, directly above the heat of the stones and rising water vapor.

After what could have been several minutes or several hours, Paxton's reverie was interrupted by a sudden movement from within the cramped space. He was displaced and disoriented and became even more so when he heard Thorn's familiar voice in his head for the second time in two days.

"*I'll bet you never saw yourself doing this*," his former teacher commented. "*High on peyote and sweating your balls off in the middle of the Chihuahuan Desert.*"

Paxton's eyes flew open at the intrusion into his thoughts but he could see nothing through the thick fog. He called out with his own thoughts, "*Thorn? Where are you?*"

He received no response but the air inside the lodge seemed to clear almost imperceptibly until he could see Eden smiling down at him from across the source of the steam. She had risen to a standing position, which was just barely possible in the lodge, even with her small frame.

"*Which voice do you prefer? This one?*" Eden asked, although her lips did not move. The next thing Paxton heard in his head was the deeper voice of his mentor, "*Or this one? We are one and the same.*"

"*Does this mean....?*" Paxton's thoughts trailed off as he contemplated the implications.

"*Yes, Uncle Paxton,*" Eden answered him in her own voice. "*I have discovered my true self and I know now, what must be done.*"

"*What is that?*" asked Paxton, still just thinking the questions at her.

"*It's not going to be easy,*" she answered, evading his question, "*but we still have a chance to rescue humanity from extinction. Many humans will die in the transformation. You may even need to take some lives yourself. Can you do that, Paxton?*"

"*I've killed before,*" Paxton defended himself. "*Just the other day I shot a Vag to save your ass!*"

"*You winged him in the shoulder,*" Eden corrected. "*I finished him off. I ended them all.*"

"*My intent was to kill him,*" said Paxton in his head. "*I would do anything to protect you, Eden!*"

"*I'm going to hold you to that,*" returned Eden. "*It won't be enough for me to lead by example this time around. This time, it'll be all out war!*"

"*I'm ready,*" confirmed Paxton.

"*So has it been prophesied,*" continued Eden, "*so shall it be.*"

With this last pronouncement Paxton could feel her drawing away from him and indeed the steam in the lodge got suddenly thicker and Eden's face disappeared behind its veil. Paxton was recalled to his physical form and he felt the ache in his back for having sat so long with his spine held erect over his crossed legs.

Some of the others were getting up and exiting the lodge and Paxton decided to do the same. His legs were asleep and he wouldn't have been able to rise without Abraham's firm grip upon his arm. They shuffled stoop-shouldered through the break in the blankets and out into the desert twilight.

Paxton was amazed that they had been in the lodge for so long and his naked body shivered at the relative cool of the evening air outside the stuffy lodge. He retrieved his clothes and put them on, but they did little to relieve the shock to his system. He gratefully accepted the proffered blanket at the end of a muscled and painted warrior's arm and he gathered it around his shoulders and torso in an attempt to retain his body heat.

Paxton looked away in embarrassment when Eden and Elizabeth emerged from the sweat lodge, although he had no problem with Jazelle's naked form. He helped her into her clothes and then shared his blanket and his embrace to quell her shivering. Once the girls were dressed Paxton tried to catch Eden's eye but she was deep in whispered conversation with her sister.

"Did that really just happen in there, Eden?" Paxton directed the question to her with his thoughts in an attempt to determine if their telepathic connection was still intact. She ignored him completely but continued to whisper in Elizabeth's ear.

Other warriors were filing into the sweat lodge to take their places. Lee emerged from the slit in the blankets, followed by Nantan, but there was no sign of Mukwooru. When they had retrieved their own clothing, they joined Paxton's huddled group outside the lodge.

"Many of you have been granted a vision from the Great Spirit," said Nantan. "This gift was meant for you alone, but there is no taboo against sharing your vision should you choose to do so."

"What if we didn't see nothing?" asked Jazelle. "I just sorta fell asleep in there."

"I wouldn't worry too much about it," answered Nantan. "Some people are more receptive to these things than others. These visions are meant to give us guidance. Perhaps the Great Spirit is already content with the direction of your path. For my part, I have been told that I must lead the mission to the Dump. There will be five of us on this quest – myself, Lee, Tarak, Kuruk and Eden."

"That can't be right!" interjected Paxton. "I thought the whole idea was to break Eden out of the Square, not to blow her up!"

"It's going to be okay," said Eden, touching Paxton's arm in a soothing gesture. "I was given the same vision. It's our best chance for ending this place."

"It's your best chance for getting yourselves blown up!" Paxton returned. "What if Lee's chain reaction doesn't materialize? You'll all get a heavy dose of radiation, let alone what the guards on the Wall will do to you!"

"We will succeed in blowing a hole in the Wall," confirmed Nantan. "This I have seen. I don't know what happens after that, but we're going to cause one hell of an explosion."

"I don't like it," complained Paxton, "not one little bit. There has to be another way."

"This is the way," Lee joined the others in the attempt to convince Paxton. "We've been preparing for this day for a long time. This has always been our plan."

"Well, what do we do now?" asked Paxton testily.

"Now we get some sleep," instructed Nantan. "There will be much to do tomorrow."

"Tomorrow?" asked Paxton.

"We won't blow the Dump until tomorrow night," continued Nantan, "under the cover of darkness, but we have to prepare for what comes after. We need to have the army in readiness to fight our way out of here once the Wall is breached."

"I still don't like this plan," groused Paxton, "but I guess my vote doesn't count for much."

Eden pushed herself up on her tiptoes to kiss his cheek and whispered in his ear, "It's all right, Uncle Paxton. I will protect us all."

Paxton looked deeply into her eyes for some acknowledgement to the conversation that had taken place in the sweat lodge but Eden merely winked at him and then turned away to gather her sister and head for one of the longhouses. Jazelle tugged upon his arm to distract his intent gaze at her retreating form.

"Come on, sweetie," she said. "Let's go to bed."

On the way back to the longhouse they had shared the previous evening, Paxton pressed her about whether or not she had experienced anything extraordinary in the sweat lodge. He asked, "So you really didn't see or feel anything in the sweat lodge?"

"I felt every damn ounce of water leave my body," she answered cagily. "I felt dizzy and nauseous. I felt like it was a waste of my god-damned time!"

"I still feel like you're holding something back, hon," he pressed her. "What did you see that you don't want to tell me about?"

"Fine," she said, stopping in her tracks and turning to face him. "If you really wanna know, I saw a nuclear explosion, and we were too damned close to it for my comfort."

"Really?" asked Paxton. "That can't be right. All of this would be for nothing."

"That's what I saw," she confirmed. "After that I wasn't gonna close my eyes again, that's for damn sure!"

"Come here," Paxton said, gathering her into his arms. "I can't tell you why you saw what you saw, but I have to believe we're doing the right thing. If we fail here, then the world is lost."

"Then let's make sure we don't fail," she said, wriggling out of his arms and continuing their walk toward the longhouse and their bedrolls.

Paxton had to jog to catch up to her. When he was once again beside her he said, "You think this is a suicide mission."

"Don't matter what I think," she said gruffly. "It's too late to put the brakes on this one."

"It matters to me," said Paxton, grabbing her forearm, forcing her to spin around and face him. "Tell me what you really think."

"We're all gonna die!" she shouted louder than she had intended. "You're banking we can outrun a nuclear explosion, and let's say you're right. Then we gotta fight our way out of the Square with bows and arrows against the full might of the Republic. If we somehow manage to do that, we'll be on the run in a foreign country that plays by a different set of rules, let alone that you've got one of the most recognizable faces in the world!"

"But we have Eden!" countered Paxton. "You've seen what she can do. She's the world's next Messiah!"

"Well, I ain't never gone in for that voodoo shit and I ain't about to start now," she said, turning away from him and resuming her walk to the longhouse.

"She'll make a believer out of you," Paxton spoke to her back.

He followed her in to the mostly empty longhouse and they found their sleeping bags where they had left them in the morning. Jazelle climbed into hers and turned her back to him. Paxton had been anticipating an end of the world romp with her before their exchange on the walk back, but now it seemed as if she was upset enough to put her out of the mood, which was rare for Jazelle.

He climbed into his own sleeping bag and sidled up to her back to spoon her, half expecting her to shrug him off. Instead, she grabbed his hand and pulled it around her flat abdomen in a gesture of forgiveness. Paxton nuzzled her neck with his nose and lips.

"I love you, Jazelle," he whispered in her ear before kissing her cheek.

"I love you too, old man," she returned. She wriggled closer to him so that she was cocooned in his embrace and they were both asleep in a matter of minutes.

CHAPTER 19

NANTAN

My name is Nantan. In my former life, most people called me Danton, except on the Reservation. The Mescalero know that Nantan means spokesman in Apache, and I was their spokesman, for many, many years. I still am, after a fashion, although it's mostly for the old man these days. And the irony is that our ancestors were bitter enemies, the Comanche and the Apache.

I didn't even know where Mukwooru came from until just now, when I read his entry in Paxton's book. He never volunteered anything about his own story, just the oral histories from his people and their struggles with the God-Damns. That's what the Mescalero called the white men who came to our land because they were so fond of the saying. We had struggles of our own with the God-Damns. They dirtied our water, and water is the most precious of resources out here in the desert.

I have been struggling with the God-Damns my whole life. I was a lawyer before they walled us in, when it was still possible to fight for my people in a court of law. Not that we ever much won. The game was rigged against us just as soon as the white men came to this land. We had our chance to rig the game against them, for a short while, in our casino on the Rez, which didn't really belong to us either as it turned out. They took that away from us just like they took everything else.

I tried to sue the Republic, for the Tiwa peoples, down in Ysleta del Sur Pueblo in El Paso, when we first heard about the Wall on the RepNews. No one even gave them a heads-up, nor did they offer any compensation for their reservation lands. My case was filed, or thrown in the garbage for all I know, but it never saw the inside of a courtroom. Some of the wealthier Tiwa bought their way into the Republic, the others became Megiddans.

The Mescalero Reservation was north of the Wall, in New Mexico, but we had problems of our own with the God-Damns. Someone in Washington decided that we had been given too much land, back in the day, when the Reservation was established. Someone came up with the bright idea to carve up our land for the ranchers they were displacing in the Square.

At first, they just took half, the better half, of course. I sued the Republic, and lost. They were using Eminent Domain as a defense in more places than just the Square. They took half again and the judge dismissed my lawsuit as frivolous before we had even gotten to argue our case. We saw the writing on the wall, so to speak.

Some of us decided to sneak into the Square, just before they finished it, in the chaos of the evacuation of East El Paso. The Wall ran north-south, just east of, and parallel to, Route 54. The West Gate was built on the Fort Bliss Airfield, so even the Guard had to give up some land to the Square. They let most of the residents of East El Paso come through the gate before they finished it, if they had the proper documentation.

We posed as construction workers, that's how we got in. Most of them were Mexicans and the God-damns can't tell us apart on a good day, let alone in all of that confusion. There were more than a hundred of us in the first wave, and we picked up some of the Tiwa on our way through the city.

We reasoned that the Republic was going to put us in the Square eventually anyway, after they took away the rest of our land, so we thought we'd get a head start on claiming a territory of our own on the newly vacated land. We could either stay on a shrinking reservation in a country that despised us, or we could form our own country, free of the Republic. That was before any of us knew what this place would become, and that we'll never be free of the Republic.

We had our eyes fixated upon the Guadalupe Mountains, which were sacred to my people. The whole National Park was being enclosed in the Square, so no one already inside would have a claim to it. All of this land used to be part of the Apaches' territory, before the God-Damns forced us off it, not that we ever claimed ownership of the land like they do.

It was a romantic notion, akin to the back-to-the-landers movement of the 1960's and 1970's. I was a young man back then, but I remember the allure of the hippies and their promise of a better world governed by love and freedom. They came onto the Reservation, trying to learn some of the old ways from the tribal elders. We were just as naïve as they were, coming back to the Guadalupe Mountains and believing we could live off the land like our ancestors had done more than a century ago, as if such a thing were still possible. The world has moved on.

For one, none of us really remembered the old ways in any practical sense. They were just stories passed down to us in our oral histories. The buffalo are long gone, as well as most of the other wild game. We used to be able to forage in the desert for food, but the desert has grown hotter, a lot hotter, and the things that used to grow and live here have moved on as well. Everything that lives needs water, and there is so very little of that to be found here now.

Mukwooru and a small band of Comanche were already here when we arrived, but they welcomed us to their tribe. Or we welcomed them to ours, we certainly outnumbered them. We were a motley crew, ill-equipped to survive in this harsh land, certainly not without each other, and we called ourselves simply the Tribe. I was elected chief, but in the coming months and years I deferred to Mukwooru more and more often.

There is something about him, something otherworldly, something completely ethereal and spiritual. He doesn't speak very often, but when he does his words carry a weight of their own, a conviction rooted in the past but also stretching toward the future. Mukwooru can see into the future. His visions have proven right time and again. He is the real chief of the Tribe, but he doesn't concern himself with the day-to-day decision making. That falls squarely upon my shoulders. Or it used to. I don't think I am long for this world. I don't think any of us are long for this world.

We welcomed outsiders in the beginning, taking in anyone who wandered into the Park and cared to join us. We were losing members all the time to accidents, illness and malnutrition, and later human predation. That was before we fully understood how many of us the land was capable of supporting. That's before the Reservations were being emptied and our brothers and sisters were joining us in ever larger numbers.

We became much more discerning about who was granted membership into the Tribe after that, even though the influx of Native Americans fell off when the serious ethnic cleansing began and it was easier to send them to the firing squads that to put them in the Square. Now we make a show of letting Mukwooru decide the supplicants' fate, but he rarely speaks up for anyone. Most of the unlucky bastards we catch wandering into our territory are traded to the cannibals for the supplies we need. It's another in a long line of harsh realities which govern our lives here in Megiddo.

I've lived a long life and for that I am thankful. It has never been easy, but I have seen love and beauty as well as tragedy and sorrow. I buried my wife of forty years and two children before I ever set foot in Megiddo. I don't know what became of my eldest. Last I knew he was in Chicago. I fought in the Vietnam War, which makes me a veteran, I guess, though I never self-identified as one.

I was a lawyer, and a damned good one, before the courts were infiltrated by the Republic. I won my fair share of legal battles, lost some too, but I defended our way of life right up until the end of my life. That will be tomorrow, or the day after, most likely. I don't see myself winning this battle. The odds are evermore stacked in the Republic's favor. I don't know who can stop them now.

Mukwooru thinks Eden can. We've only just met. I can't speak to her mettle, but I know Mukwooru. I trust Mukwooru. If there's any chance at all to bring the God-Damns to their knees, it's worth taking that risk. It's worth any sacrifice, even the ultimate one.

I've lived a long life and for that I'm thankful.

SUICIDE MISSION

"You're sure about this?" Paxton asked Eden. They were seated around the table in Lee's laboratory with an old road atlas opened up to the map of Texas, spread out on the table between them. Richard and Lee were also seated at the table while Jazelle, Nantan, Tarak and Kuruk stood looking over their shoulders.

"Absolutely!" Eden answered enthusiastically. "I can protect our party from the radiation and the explosion. You just worry about your end of things, Uncle Paxton."

"The army will assemble here," Nantan said, reaching over Richard to place his finger on a wavy blue line between route 652 and the New Mexico border. "The Delaware River used to run through here from the Pecos. We should be able to gather our forces in the dry river bed, unseen in the darkness."

"How are we going to move all of our warriors over there without being seen by the Eye in the Sky?" asked Richard.

"They'll see us," answered Nantan, "if anyone is paying attention, but we're taking care to approach in small groups from different directions. The smoke signals were sent yesterday. Our troops have already been on the move for a full day, now. In the end it won't matter what they see, because we're going to hit them full force at the Wall and knock their teeth out!"

"What about the cannibals?" asked Richard.

"They've been informed of our plans," said Nantan. "Some have even pledged to join us, though not as many as I had hoped."

"Even they know this is a suicide mission," scoffed Richard.

"I expect that they'll hang back at the periphery," continued Nantan, "waiting to take their bounty from the carnage. They wouldn't dare attack us, not with the kind of numbers we're going to have."

"What kind of numbers will that be?" asked Paxton.

"Close to one-thousand warriors," answered Nantan, "give or take. Not enough to storm the Republic but hopefully it'll be enough to get you out of here."

"That still puts us forty to fifty miles from the Dump," Paxton reasoned, measuring with his finger in relation to the key upon the map. "How much of the Wall do you figure you can take out?"

"You know as well as I that we can't make that calculation exactly," answered Lee. "There are too many variables involved. We don't know the exact amount of waste at the dump, nor do we know its potency. And as far as I know, no one has ever attempted to fire an anti-gravity gun at a smoldering pile of radioactive waste."

"What's your best guess?" pressed Paxton.

"At worst, it'll fizzle out and I won't get the kind of chain reaction I am hoping for," explained Lee. "Best case scenario the blast will obliterate everything within a ten-mile radius."

"Yourselves included!" exclaimed Paxton, eyeballing Eden.

"We've already been over this, Uncle Paxton!" she returned.

"The army will be forty miles from the breached Wall," calculated Paxton. How are we going to cover that ground quickly enough?"

"We don't need to cover it," answered Nantan. "The explosion Lee hopes to create is merely a diversion. While the Guard scrambles to plug the hole in the Wall, we're going over the Wall here, where the Delaware used to cross the border from New Mexico."

"With the uncertainty involved," continued Lee, "we don't dare take the army too close to the blast zone. The last thing we need is to blow our whole army up with my experiment!"

"After Lee blows a hole in the Wall," explained Nantan, "We'll hightail it directly north through the desert to the Wall as fast as possible."

"What if there ain't no explosion?" Jazelle chimed in for the first time, "or it's much smaller than y'all are hoping for?"

"We're going to be prepared to scale the Wall regardless," answered Nantan. "At that point we'll be out in the open and committed to our breakout. If Lee fails then we'll just have to hope our frontal assault on the Wall will be successful regardless."

"It can't be done!" Richard chimed in.

"It never *has* been done," Nantan corrected him. "That doesn't mean it can't be done. No one has ever attempted a full-fledged assault on the Wall."

"It won't come to that," Lee reassured them. "We'll blow the Dump, just as the arc of the moon rises over the eastern edge of the Wall. What happens after that is anybody's guess."

"But what *does* happen after that, for you guys?" asked Paxton. "Let's say that Eden is able to protect you all and you survive the blast. How are we going to meet back up with you?"

"We're going to haul ass out of there," said Lee, "and find you on the Wall."

"You don't sound convincing," commented Paxton.

"I'll admit that I never expected to survive that blast," said Lee.

"You won't!" interjected Richard.

"I haven't given much thought to what comes after," Lee continued. "If we still have a working truck, we can drive right up route 285 to within a couple of miles of where you'll be going over the Wall."

"That could take a couple of hours," reasoned Paxton, "in the dark, on those shitty roads."

"Then you'll just have to hold the Wall until we get there," said Eden. "I have every confidence in you, all of you."

"I'd feel much better if you were with us," said Paxton, looking directly at Eden.

"Then you really would be sending the others on a suicide mission," she countered. "Besides, they might need my help to pull this thing off."

"I don't think…" Paxton began, but he was interrupted by Nantan.

"Good, it's settled then. Time for us all to get moving. We have preparations to make and miles to travel, and before that Mukwooru wants a word with all of us."

As they stood up and backed away from the table, Jazelle commented sarcastically, "Well by all means, let's not keep the old man waiting."

All of the remaining members of Maggie's Farm sat in a loose circle around a small fire, in the shade of the portable awning. Mukwooru sat with them while Nantan, Lee, Kuruk, Tarak and Richard stood behind them, clumped together at the western edge of their group to catch what limited shade the awning had to offer.

It was the first time all eight of them were together since they had been brought before Mukwooru two nights ago. Only Valerie was missing, though it could be argued that she wasn't really a member of their group. She hadn't emerged from the longhouse in two days and no one was really sure if she was alive or dead.

Mukwooru was holding a few sprigs of sage which he had lit in the fire and the sweet smell was wafting over the group as the smoke made its slow path in and around them in the absence of even the slightest breeze. Nantan handed Mukwooru a long, wooden pipe which Paxton had not yet seen, and the old man lit it as well, taking a long drag and exhaling the smoke through his nostrils. The distinctive smell of marijuana intermingling with the burning sage had an overall calming effect on Paxton, and he relaxed into his sitting bones, a smile spreading across his face.

"We invite all of you to join the Tribe," Mukwooru began in Comanche, with Nantan translating. "We offer you our protection, our sustenance and our friendship. In return we expect you to contribute to the life of the Tribe, each according to his or her capacity. You must put the life of the Tribe above all else, even your own lives. If you agree to these terms and you wish to join the Tribe, you need only smoke from the ceremonial pipe when it is passed to you."

"What if we decline?" asked Jillian, ever suspicious of answering to a higher authority, especially since the Tribe's population was predominantly masculine.

"Under normal circumstances," Nantan fielded her question himself, "you would be cast out into the lands controlled by the cannibals. But nothing that has become normal for the Tribe will likely remain by sunrise tomorrow. If you choose not to join us, you are free to go and may the Great Spirit bless you."

"Oh, I'm not going anywhere," returned Jillian. "I can't wait to take some revenge on the Republic. I'm just not a joiner, that's all."

Eden, who was seated to the left of Mukwooru, reached for the pipe and it was deposited in her two palms. Before taking a pull from it she said, "I join the Tribe of my own free will. If we are to save humanity from destruction and extinction, then we must learn to live on this planet in harmony with, rather than in struggle against, Mother Nature. I can think of no better way to remake the world than to model it after the First Nation. I plan to gather all that remains of humanity into my Tribe, starting right here and right now with this Tribe, who were kind enough to take me in and aid me in this quest."

She relit the bowl at the end of the long pipe and inhaled so deeply that she burst forth into a fit of coughing that caused the other members of her group to smile and snicker.

"You had me there, sis," laughed Elizabeth. "Right up until you hacked up a lung!"

"I'm not used to all of this smoking," said Eden good-naturedly as she passed the pipe along.

No one else had much to say but they all took the requisite drag from the peace pipe, even Jillian. When it had almost come full circle back to Mukwooru, there was a commotion at the perimeter of their circle and two warriors appeared supporting the gaunt Valerie between them. She was seated upon their interlocked forearms with both arms up and around the neck of the shorter man, her head resting upon his chest. They set her down gently between Jazelle and Paxton and she immediately transferred her head to rest upon his shoulder.

Jazelle had been about to pass the pipe to Paxton and she looked over at him quizzically, unsure what she should now do with it. Paxton leaned in to whisper in Valerie's ear, "We've been invited to join the Tribe. To accept the invitation, you need to take a hit from the pipe."

At Paxton's words, Valerie raised her head from his shoulders and swiveled it around their circle in an apparent attempt to focus her hollow eyes upon someone she recognized. Failing this she looked up at Paxton and asked hopefully, "Hero?"

"Not hero," he answered gently. "It's just a little pot."

"You sure she should be doin' this?" asked Jazelle.

Paxton shrugged his shoulders as if to say that he didn't know, or didn't care, but Mukwooru nodded his head once in ascent and Jazelle handed the pipe to Valerie's practiced hands. She took a long drag from it, her eyes suddenly wide with anticipation, but as she exhaled her body seemed to deflate and the vacant look came back to her face.

"Not hero," she said disappointedly, but she took a second hit from the pipe nonetheless. Paxton had to pry it from her clutching hands and this time she slumped against Jazelle as he prepared to complete the circle.

"I would like to take this opportunity to thank Mukwooru and the Tribe," Paxton began with raised voice so that everyone gathered around them could hear him. "We did not know what would become of us when we crossed the border into the Park, nor did we expect to be accepted so readily among you.

"We came here seeking advice and you offered us assistance. I know that most of you have agreed to take part in this fool's errand based upon your trust in Mukwooru, and for my group's part, probably because they are willing to put their trust in me. I thank you all for your trust in us and I pray to the All that your trust is not misplaced.

"Many of you have seen what Eden can do. Some of you can feel her vibration, the subtle energy coming from her aura, and it's a good energy. It's the same energy you can feel from Mukwooru and it somehow just feels right. That's why we choose to follow them. They are your prophets, our gurus. I guess I am a prophet, too, but I tap into just a small part of the boundless energy they enjoy. It's worth it to me, to try to perpetuate that energy, to help it grow, even in the face of insurmountable odds.

"For some of us, that will mean the ultimate sacrifice, this very day, and I thank you all for that. But I suspect that many of you share my feeling that the path we're on is the right one, that we're working for the greater good, that..."

"Fuck that!" Jillian interrupted his long speech. "I just wanna kick the Guard in the balls and get out of this shitty place!"

There was a general murmur of agreement from those gathered and a few outright verbal assents, though whether they were uttered for Jillian's words or an end to Paxton's soliloquy was anybody's guess.

"There's that, too," Paxton agreed good-naturedly. He raised the pipe above his head and said ceremoniously, "To the Tribe!"

"To the Tribe!" came a plethora of staggered, enthusiastic responses. Paxton raised the pipe to his lips, set the flame to the bowl and drew a long, slow inhale into his lungs. Another general huzzah was launched skyward as Mukwooru accepted the pipe from Paxton. He took another puff from it before passing it along to Nantan behind him so that the standing members of their group could partake as well. Then the old man closed his eyes and began to chant in Comanche, his body swaying ever so slightly in a small circle around his anchored buttocks.

"Mukwooru is asking the Great Spirit to bless tonight's venture and to watch over the Tribe," explained Nantan. "He is also offering thanks for all of our blessings, for our lives and for this chance He has given the Tribe to rescue Eden and help her escape into the world. He's asking Eden to save us, to save all humanity from self-destruction."

"Ura," Mukwooru finished and opened his eyes.

"The correct response from all of us is the same, 'Ura'" offered Nantan.

"Ura," they all said, though not in unison.

Those on the perimeter of the circle began to depart immediately as Paxton's crew rose slowly to their feet. Nantan and Paxton helped Mukwooru to rise and he immediately took Eden's elbow and whispered in her ear. They departed the circle together in the direction of the longhouses and the center of camp.

"Say your goodbyes to her," Nantan directed the rest of their group. "We leave for the Dump within the hour."

Once all of the preparations had been made all five of the Suicide Squad, a nickname coined by Richard but adopted by most of the Tribe, said their goodbyes to their friends and loved ones. Nantan sat on the ground behind the truck's tailgate, deep in conversation with Mukwooru in Apache, or Comanche, but certainly not English. Tarak had a wife or girlfriend in his thick embrace while Kuruk was surrounded by half a dozen male warriors. Lee and Richard argued back and forth from the bed of the truck where the antigravity gun had just been loaded and secured.

Eden stood in the center of the remnants of Maggie's Farm and accepted hugs and advice from everyone. Abraham held on to her for a long time, whispering in her ear. Paxton could see she was telling him no, and the way she gently put her hands on his chest and pushed him away gave the appearance of a lovers spat. Paxton was pretty sure they were not lovers, but it made him wonder what relationship they did have.

Eden finally came up to the trio of Elizabeth, Paxton and Jazelle. Her sister hugged her and would not let go for a long time. When she finally did, she said with teary eyes, "I know you're going to be okay. I'll see you on the other side of the Wall."

Jazelle gave her a hug, too, albeit much shorter. She told the younger woman, "Don't let any of these jackasses push you around, you hear me? You're a strong, independent woman and you can follow your own counsel."

"Whatever happens, take care of Paxton," she whispered in Jazelle's ear. "You're the One for him and he truly loves you."

"I'll try to keep the old fool from harming himself," she joked in low tones and Eden giggled and looked over at Paxton. "It's a full-time occupation. I love him, too."

"I know," she said. "Enjoy what time you have left together."

"Shit, girl!" exclaimed Jazelle, pushing her playfully away. "You gonna have to tell me what you mean by that."

"Nothing specific," Eden responded. "Lizzie's the psychic. I just mean that life is short and time is precious, especially with what's about to go down on this planet. I hope you both live long and happy lives together."

Finally, Eden stood in front of Paxton and they began a staring contest that lasted the better part of a minute. The others didn't understand what was going on, and became somewhat alarmed by the time it ended, but Paxton and Eden were in their own little world conversing quite freely from within the privacy of their connected minds.

"*This isn't goodbye, you know,*" she said from within his mind and without moving her lips at all. "*So don't go all maudlin on me.*"

"*Let me come with you then,*" Paxton thought back to her. "*Surely I could be of some service.*"

"*Not on this mission,*" Eden returned. "*You'd only be in the way. Besides, you're going to have your hands full getting over the Wall. Our crew look to you for leadership, even if the rest of the Tribe seems quite capable on their own.*"

"*I still don't like this,*" Paxton offered his opinion one last time. "*I have a bad feeling about you going to the Dump.*"

"*Ye of little faith,*" Eden responded in Paxton's head with Thorn's deep masculine tones. Paxton's eyes widened momentarily but only Eden noticed. "*Don't worry so much about your bad feelings, concentrate on the good ones. Your thoughts create your reality. Did you learn nothing up there on Bald Mountain? If you believe this plan will work, it'll work.*

"*Of course, you're going to feel a little queasy,*" Eden continued in Thorn's voice. "*Lee is hoping to create a thermonuclear explosion not too far from here as the crow flies. That's your survival instinct kicking in and I'd be surprised if it didn't.*"

"*Thorn!*" he called out with his thoughts. "*I knew that was you, back in the sweat lodge.*"

"*You've known it was me ever since Eden first set foot in the Square,*" Thorn replied.

"*You can call it my survival instinct all you want,*" countered Paxton, "*but I'm not okay with nuclear warfare. There have already been whole cities obliterated by nuclear bombs. What's going to be left for humanity if we turn this planet into a radioactive wasteland?*"

"You make a good point," Thorn conceded. *"Let's make sure that doesn't happen. As for today, this is the opening salvo in our bid to take back the Republic. We need to knock them off their game. The real war will be waged against the forces Lucifer is amassing in Asia. We will need the Republic's war machine if we have any hope of defeating him."*

Just then Nantan walked up behind Eden and put his hand on her shoulder, effectively ending their staring contest. He said, loud enough for them all to hear, "Time to go."

Eden stepped forward and hugged Paxton, whispering in his ear in her normal, feminine voice, "See you on the other side, Uncle Paxton!"

She kissed him on the cheek and winked at him, then turned quickly away and followed Nantan to the truck. Paxton shouted at her back, "What's that supposed to mean? Eden!"

She was already climbing into the cab and Nantan loaded in right behind her. Tarak was seated behind the steering wheel while Lee and Kuruk had taken positions in the bed of the truck with the antigravity gun. Each of them also clutched rifles in their hands, just in case they needed to fight their way through to the Dump.

The truck shuddered to life and Nantan stuck his hand out the window in farewell as they took off east. Paxton grabbed Jazelle's hand and they watched the departing truck kick up clouds of dust for a full minute before Richard was in their midst shouting out orders of his own.

"All right, people!" he yelled. "Chop! Chop! We're getting the hell outta here, too! Don't just stand around, gather your weapons and your packs and meet me back here in five minutes! Five minutes!"

He wandered off barking orders at other members of the Tribe and Paxton bent over slightly to kiss Jazelle lightly on the cheek. He told her, "So it begins."

"So it begins," she agreed, kissing his lips briefly before disentangling her fingers from his and moving off in the direction of the longhouse they had been sharing with the members of what was now their Tribe.

CHAPTER 20

NICHOLAS

My nam is nicholas needmore. I was a soldur asined to the wal. It was a prety easy asinment up until about a wek ago. Thats when the injuns blu a hole rit thru the wal and excapd. I was thar prisner but it dont fel like that nomor. Im not tid up. I cud of excapd many tims over if Id a wantd to. Only problem is I cant think a nowar to go. I cant go bak to the wal. If I go bak to the army they wil probaly send me to the war in china. I cant go home to iowa. I cudnt wat to lev that plas. Mayb I wil sta with thes pepol for a wil and se how that gos.

I no im not the smartest soldur in the army, but im not the dumest ether. I stad in skul up til I was 12. My mama and papa wer law abidin pepol. My bruther fred wantd to kwit skul wen he was 10 but they mad him sta until he was 12 to. Thats wat the law says, everywuns got to go to skul until thar 12. If they pas thar tests at 12 they can sta in skul or not. I wasnt gona pas no tests so I sind my plej of alejins to the republic and was dun with skul.

They dont let nobody join the army until thar 16, so fred and me, we got to work on the bisickls maken lectrisity. 6 days a week. On sundays they let us go hom to church and visitin with our moms and dads. I was most productiv pedler 3 months wil I was thar. Fred got it twis. Thar musta bin mor than 100 ridrs, so thats saying a lot.

Fred was older than me by 2 yers. He sind up for the army on his 16 birthday. Got hiself kild in sawdi arabica. After fred did, I didnt want nuthin to do with the army, so I watd until I had to go at 18. I got put on the wall, rit after but camp. That was down in misisipi war its hotr than hel. Mabe not, but its a heluva lot hotr than iowa or even texas. I bin her on the wal ever sins, until about a wek ago. Now I dont no if thar stil is a wal.

I didnt want to sta in the army, wen my to yers was up. I sind all the papers, I thot they was discharg papers. Then my sarjent told me I sind up for to mor yers. I crid that nit, soft lik, so no wun els cud her. The next tim I sind bak up on porpus. Wat els cud I do. I hav no skils exsep ridin a bisickl. My famly stopd calin yers ago dont no if theys aliv or ded. War wud I go. Lest her we get 3 mels a day and thar aint no wun shutin at us, up until last wek.

I hop they let me sta with them. I dont mind bein thar prisner. I cant go bak in the army. They wil shut me as a desertr. I can be usful to the injuns. I no thins about the republic how to get a rownd how to by fud. Thar gona ned my help. I wil thro myself at thar fet. They wont hurt me, I no it. Don't ask me how I no it, but I just no it.

I had a drem, the first nit after they tuk me. I saw this butiful garden, ful of hapy pepol. She was thar. She lukd like mother earth. She sed it was wat the world wud be lik wen she was dun with it. I belevd her, it all felt so rel. It shur lukd to be a hol lot beter than the world is rit now, I can tel yu that.

Im sory Paxton but I cant rit in her no mor. My hand is tird. My bran is tird. I nevr cud spel wurth a dam. Plez dont send me bak to the army. I can help yu. I promis to be gud and help yu al.

GROUND ZERO

Paxton, Jazelle and Elizabeth rode to the rendezvous point in the back seat of a battered Jeep Wrangler with Mukwooru in the passenger seat and Richard at the wheel. Valerie sat cross-wise in the small bed behind them, hugging her knees to her chest and muttering to herself unintelligibly. She was too frail to travel any other way but she had insisted on coming with them to the Wall.

In an effort to disguise their movements, all of the members of their portion of the Tribe had been split into groups that left the park at staggered times and used varied modes of transportation. Those on foot began the journey the previous evening, under the cover of darkness. None of Paxton's group had as yet been initiated into the Tribe, so they were spared that forced march.

Jillian and Grace rode two of the bicycles they had brought from Maggie's Farm in a group of other cyclists that left base camp almost as soon as they had partaken of Mukwooru's peace pipe. Abraham rode an old Honda dirt bike with Rachel straddled behind him and holding onto him for dear life. They traveled in Paxton's caravan with another tandem dirt bike and a rusty old pickup truck loaded with weapons and climbing gear beneath a dusty-brown tarp.

Their plan was to cut across the desert from the Park to old route 652, because the road leading out of the Park from Pine Springs would take them too close to the Wall and cannibal territory. Route 652 would take them to Orla, which wasn't even really a town before the Square, although it had once boasted a post office. From Orla they could travel in a straight shot to the Wall, though they would have to turn west at some point to meet up with the rest of their army in the washout from the once seasonal Delaware River.

"Eden seemed somehow different to me, before she left," said Paxton, looking across Jazelle to Elizabeth, who had been staring out the window since they began their journey. "Did she say anything to you?"

Elizabeth turned slowly toward him, as if she hadn't quite heard the question but she somehow knew Paxton was talking to her. Paxton was just about to repeat his question when she said, "She *is* different now, more confident, maybe a little over-confident. I had a bad dream, about their mission at the Dump."

"What?" exclaimed Paxton. "Why didn't you say something before now?"

"It's not about Eden," she clarified, "or their mission. I fear for the people with her. Eden may be invincible now, or at least she believes herself to be, but the others are merely human."

"The others have prepared themselves to meet the Great Spirit," Mukwooru's gravelly voice came from the front seat. Neither he nor Richard had spoken since they had climbed into the Jeep, nor did he follow up this exclamation with an explanation.

A vague sense of foreboding overcame Paxton and he turned his head slightly to catch Jazelle's eye, raising his own eyebrows in a questioning gesture.

"Don't look at me!" she told him. "I done told you this is a fool's errand from the start. Ain't nobody gonna listen to me."

Jazelle's complaining was suddenly irresistible and Paxton leaned over and kissed her on the lips before she could say anything more. She chuckled when he came up for air and said, "That's one way to get me to shut up, old man."

They stopped briefly in Orla to consult with a scout who looked the part of an Indian brave except for the red hair braided halfway down his back. He directed them to a water source just off the road so that they could fill every container they had full of the precious liquid. There was no telling where they would next get the chance to rehydrate.

Jazelle and Rachel traded seats before they headed north on the last leg of their journey to the Wall. Jazelle was going stir-crazy in the cramped back seat and Rachel was tired of the bumpy, windblown ride behind Abraham's broad back and the necessity of leaning her body this way and that to help balance the bike over the uneven ground. Jazelle insisted on driving so Abraham had to maneuver his large frame onto the seat behind her.

They stashed the Jeep at an empty weapons cache just as the Wall came into view on the northern horizon. Paxton did not think they would ever come back for it, but it did not hurt to have a contingency plan. Jazelle and Rachel exchanged places on the dirt bike and Richard would take Mukwooru on ahead on the back of the second motorcycle while the rest of them walked. They would appear to be a roving Vagabond band to any watchful eyes on the Wall, until they reached the cover of the dry river bed. Then they would follow its meandering course to the rendezvous, even though it would add length and time to their march in the still, scorching glare of the mid-afternoon sun.

Paxton felt safer in the crevice produced by millennia of running water, but Jazelle was skittish and continually searching the rim of the slight canyon over which they could see nothing but sky. Paxton assured her that the Tribe had it covered, that their approach had already been well-surveilled, but that did little to assuage her nervousness at traveling blind through a winding canyon that only allowed them a hundred feet of visibility both ahead and behind them. Jazelle pointed out that it was just such a crevasse that put an end to Bill and Barbara.

In any event, they reached the rendezvous point without incident, though they were all drenched in sweat and tired from their long walk. One minute they were trudging alone in the natural corridor and then they turned around a bend, which looked no different from the many other bends they had encountered that afternoon, and they stopped in their tracks, amazed at the teeming mass of bodies all huddled together in the now shaded corridor in front of them.

The painted warriors moved to either side of the riverbed at their approach and did little to hide their astonishment at their first glance of the woman they believed to be the one from Mukwooru's prophecy. Richard and the old man must have given the Tribe a heads-up that they were trailing behind them, because everyone seemed to know exactly who they were. They whispered to each other and pointed as they walked by, and many of the warriors reached out to touch Elizabeth as if to verify that she was a flesh and blood woman and not some kind of apparition.

Elizabeth was good about it, smiling at them as she passed and holding hands briefly with those that reached out to her. It reminded Paxton of what the scene must have looked like as Jesus rode into Jerusalem on a donkey during the Passover, on what modern Christians now referred to as Palm Sunday, less than a week before He was tried and crucified. Paxton prayed that this procession had a happier ending for Elizabeth than its counterpart had for her sister some two-thousand years ago.

Paxton figured that they must have passed through most of the army before they reached Mukwooru and Richard, but he couldn't be sure because there were still warriors crowded into the gully ahead of them. Most of the soldiers looked the part of Indian braves complete with painted faces and bodies, but as they had progressed through their ranks, there were others scattered amongst their numbers, mostly men dressed in plain clothes, some wearing traditional cowboy hats. Paxton tried not to speculate which ones were cannibals but found it increasingly hard not to do so.

Mukwooru sat in a small circle with Richard and three others, two men and a woman. He invited Paxton and Elizabeth to sit with them. They were smoking his peace pipe and Paxton wondered briefly about the wisdom of getting stoned before a battle. He nevertheless took a drag from the long pipe when it was passed to him. The smoke calmed his frayed nerves immediately and he decided that it was just the thing he needed after all.

Richard explained that the other three in the circle were akin to generals in their army and introductions were made all around. Paxton did not get the reception from them that he had gotten from Lee, but they seemed to know who he was. The man sitting next to him called him Dr. Stephens and shook his hand. They were much more interested in talking to Elizabeth and began to rapid-fire questions at her.

"Will your sister succeed in blowing up the Dump?"

"Will she survive it?"

"What's gonna happen to us on the other side of the Wall?"

"Will we be successful in breaking out of the Square?"

Mukwooru must have told them about her powers of prophecy and they were looking for an edge before the battle. Elizabeth answered all of their questions patiently, explaining that the outcome of the battle was unclear from her dreams, but a great many people were going to die. She said that she had a vision of a great explosion which briefly turned night into day and the bedlam and chaos that came afterwards. She told them that in her heart she knew they would be victorious, but that she didn't have any concrete vision which had pointed to that conclusion.

"I already told them as much," said Mukwooru in English, winking at Elizabeth. "They wanted a second opinion."

They sat there together for the better part of an hour as the shadows deepened and the first stars began to appear in the sky. The generals talked tactics for storming the Wall, while Elizabeth and Paxton spoke of her life with Claire and Tucker in Argentina. Jazelle and Abraham eventually joined them and they formed their own smaller circle, sometime after the pipe was put away. Mukwooru did not participate in any of these conversations but rather rocked back and forth slightly on his sit bones and chanted softly in Comanche.

Their brief respite was interrupted by a warrior carrying a drone and a laptop computer into their midst. One of the male generals stood up and said, "It's time for us to get some eyes on the Wall."

Before heading off to the Dump with Eden, Lee had repaired and repurposed the drone the Tribe had recovered when they captured Paxton's party in the Devil's Hall. The warrior set the drone down on the ground and then dropped himself down beside it in a cross-legged position with the computer on his lap. He began to type and the drone's rotor's whirred to life. Soon it was hovering above them and then it took off on a beeline toward the Wall, ascending as it traveled northward.

Paxton moved behind the seated warrior so that he could see the computer screen better. The resolution was surprisingly good and he watched their little group get smaller and smaller as the drone pulled away from them. Soon enough it was hovering again, this time directly above the Wall, about a half-mile from their hideaway. The drone's controller had chosen a point halfway between two guard towers, and there was only one guard in evidence, making his way slowly toward the east with a rifle strapped to his back.

Just then an excited murmur took hold of the camp and the energy changed noticeably from an air of waiting around to one of readiness. Elizabeth tugged at his shirt, pointed eastward and said, "Look! It's the moon! The moon is rising!"

Everywhere people were strapping on backpacks and grabbing guns and machetes and strapping them down somewhere on their persons. When everything was prepared for a quick sprint to the Wall, they recommenced their waiting, but now they were poised to launch themselves into motion as though they were a thousand coiled springs.

From the corner of his eye Paxton caught sight of Grace and Jillian walking toward him and he turned his head to greet them. Grace smiled and said, "There you are! We were hoping to find you before the battle so we could fight side by side."

Paxton was about to answer when the women's faces were lit up from an intense, white light which emanated from somewhere behind him. The sound of the massive explosion followed some seconds later and he couldn't help but flinch as they waited expectantly for the aftershocks. This far away from the blast all they could feel was the rush of wind above their heads and a slight rumbling in the ground beneath their feet.

The warriors assembled in the riverbed stared at each other expectantly as though they were asking each other in silence, "What do we do now?"

Richard held his arm up and this gesture was repeated by others down the line of warriors in a prearranged signal that told their horde to wait a moment before storming the Wall. Paxton looked back down at the computer screen which was still balanced on its operator's lap.

In the few minutes it took the soldiers on the Wall to recover from their initial shock, they must have received their marching orders because it seemed as if every available guard was being shuttled toward the blast zone in black jeeps and troop transports. The reinforced doors at the base of each tower stood wide open to let the speeding vehicles pass through unhindered. It took ten minutes for the bulk of that parade to pass their section of the Wall and in the end, they had to wait for one last straggling jeep to pass by before Richard finally lowered his arm and they launched their attack.

They scrambled up the steep sides of the riverbank and sprinted toward the Wall as fast as they could run with the gear, they each carried upon their backs. Paxton looked around him as he ran to verify that his small group was still together. Everyone was accounted for except Rachel and Abraham, whom he hoped were following behind the initial wave of warriors on the dirt bike, or at the very least one of the mountain bikes they brought from Maggie's Farm.

They reached the Wall without incident but they tripped a proximity alarm as they gathered themselves beneath it and two very loud sirens began to herald their arrival from the two towers on either side of their position. Despite the unsettling noise, the warriors set about their tasks and several grappling hooks were thrown up onto the battlements. Others had carried ladders made out of wooden poles lashed together with rope. No sooner were these ladders placed vertically against the Wall than their warriors were scrambling up the rungs, even as others took the harder route of scaling the Wall with the ropes now anchored at the top.

Paxton waited his turn for a ladder and then ascended it quickly behind Jazelle. They reached the top and jumped down the few feet to what looked like a road running straight between the two tunnels of the adjacent towers which still had their gates wide open for the passage of the eastward troops.

"We've got to take those towers!" he said to no one in particular. A party of a dozen warriors were already heading toward the western tower and beginning to draw gunfire from the soldiers left behind to man it. Paxton took off toward the eastern tower and was followed by most of Maggie's Farm plus a handful of warriors who were closest to him. The rest of their army continued their unhindered ascent of the Wall.

As they closed the distance to the tower, Paxton heard gunshots from above them and he even felt a bullet zing by his right cheek. There was no cover to be had in their mad dash for the tower so there was nothing for it but to run like hell and hope for the best. Paxton was soon outdistanced by everyone but Jazelle, who ran by his side, glancing over at him periodically as if to verify that he wasn't having a heart attack.

One of the warriors ahead of them went down with a gunshot wound to his head and they ran right by him as it was abundantly clear there was nothing that they could do for him. The runners up ahead were just reaching the gates as they started to close inward upon their hinges. A guard was standing in the doorway, unloading his rifle at them as the doors closed, but he went down with an arrow in his chest, shooting the last of his bullets up into the sky as he fell. Two of their warriors jumped into the closing aperture just before the gates clanged shut.

They heard gunshots from inside the tower as they reached the closed doors, and then Paxton could only hear the sound of his own labored breathing as he struggled to catch his breath. In another minute the gates began to swing inward and one of their own stood in the widening slit with his arms up to quell the tension.

"Hold your fire!" he yelled above the creaking of the iron gates. "The tower is secured!"

Paxton took a good look around him for the first time since the tower guards began shooting at them. Jazelle and Elizabeth were beside him, the former with her rifle still ready at her hip. Grace and Jillian were looking out over the edge of the Wall on the Republic side.

Two warriors came limping up to them, one of them half-carrying the other one, who was bleeding profusely from his leg. He set the man gingerly down upon the ground and Elizabeth rushed to his side. She put pressure on the gunshot wound with the palms of her hands, all the while murmuring platitudes to the surprisingly young man.

"Anything over there?" Paxton asked the women looking over the Wall.

"Same as on our side," Jillian answered. "Just god-damned desert!"

"No soldiers over here yet!" Grace provided him with more useful information.

Paxton nodded his head once and turned into the entrance to the tower. He saw a staircase to his left and he immediately began to ascend it, stepping over a fallen Guard at the first landing. Another dead Guard had been shot coming out of the main room at the top of the stairs. Inside the control room, the second Tribe warrior pointed a rifle at a scared-shitless Guard on his knees, with his hands behind his head.

"Please don't kill me! Please don't kill me!" pleaded the prone Guard in earnest.

"We're not here to kill you," Paxton placated the young man. "We're just passing through. If you cooperate with us, you won't be harmed. Put your hands behind your back."

Paxton lowered his own rifle and nodded toward the other Tribe warrior, who lurched forward and tied the soldiers hands roughly behind his back with rope he pulled from somewhere at his side. Paxton pulled up a chair and sat upon it while still maintaining his bead upon their prisoner.

"I need information and I need it quickly," Paxton said. "Are you going to help me?"

"Yes! Yes!" agreed the man, who looked to be not much older than twenty, but Paxton was no longer a good judge of the passage of time at his own advanced age.

"What's your name, son?" Paxton asked him with as much kindness as he could muster.

"Nick," the soldier stuttered, "Nicholas. Nicholas Needmore."

"Okay, Nick," Paxton began his interrogation. "Why did the Guard speed eastward a few minutes ago?"

"There was an explosion," the boy-man explained, "somewhere east of here. Some soldiers were saying there was a breakout at the Containment Center."

"You mean the Dump?" asked Paxton.

"The Containment Center," Nick repeated, "where they store all the nuclear waste, so it doesn't hurt nobody."

"Store my ass!" scoffed Paxton, but he immediately brought himself back to the task at hand. "What is the protocol for a mass breakout from the Square?"

"They're gonna nuke the Square," Nick replied. "Mickey called it in, just as soon as we heard the sirens. We didn't see you comin' at first 'cause we was all lookin' east. He told Command there were hundreds of you climbing over the Wall."

"Thousands," lied Paxton. "Where will they drop the bomb?"

"Right in the center of the Square, if they can," said Nick. "I think they called it the *incenter* in our drills. They said they would preserve the Wall and keep all of the radiation inside the Square. We're supposed to shoot anybody that comes scurrying toward the Wall to escape the nuclear holocaust."

"We gotta get on the other side of the Wall!" said Paxton, jumping to his feet. "Now!"

"What do you want to do with him?" asked the warrior still pointing his gun at Nick's chest.

"Let's take him with us," Paxton decided after a slight hesitation. "He may yet prove useful."

"Yes, I can be!" enthused Nick, clearly relieved that he would be allowed to draw breath a while longer. "I can be very useful!"

They made Nick walk down the stairs ahead of them, through the half-opened gates and into the night beyond them. The others were startled by Nick's black uniform, but not so much that they opened fire upon him at first sight. Paxton's companion had taken the time to gag him so that his status as a prisoner would be readily apparent.

"We gotta get down off the Wall!" Paxton announced to the small assemblage. "They're going to nuke the Square!"

Immediately those carrying ropes began to secure them to the steel handrails on the north side of the Wall. Paxton ordered one of the warriors to run back and warn the others still climbing the Wall. A glance in that direction led Paxton to believe that more than half of their group had already made it to the top and a crowd of warriors were already gathered upon the ground inside the Republic.

First Jillian and Grace scaled slowly down the north side of the Wall and Paxton was chomping at the bit for them to pick up their pace. Next, he and one of the Tribe's warrior's lowered Nick down with the rope secured beneath his armpits and his hands still tied behind his back. Having had success with this maneuver they did the same for Elizabeth and Jazelle. They were going to lower the injured warrior in the same way but when Paxton checked his pulse, he realized that it was already too late, he had bled out from his severed femoral artery.

Paxton let the two warriors climb down next while he surveyed the horizon in all directions for any sign of Eden or a massing of the Guard. When he saw neither he untied one of the ropes and tossed it down to their small group huddled at the base of the Wall. Walking back inside the guard tower he located the button which worked the gates, pushed it and hurried through the closing aperture.

When he climbed down the remaining rope, he realized that it was a lot harder to do so than it looked while watching the others from above. His forearms were cramping by the time he reached the bottom and several pairs of arms caught his short fall to the ground at the end of his escape. There was no retrieving the last rope so their group gathered themselves and began to trot westward along the Wall to rejoin the bulk of their army.

When they were still a quarter mile away from the edges of the growing horde of warriors, they began to see explosions detonating right in their midst and painted bodies flying helter-skelter as a result. They stopped in their tracks a moment and looked questioningly at each other as there was still no sign of the Guard and no clear source for the origin of the missiles, they could now see headed toward their army from the trails of exhaust they left behind in their flight paths.

Paxton wheeled on Nicholas, grabbed him by his biceps and shouted in his face, "What's going on? Where are those missiles coming from?"

"Prob...probably shot from drones," stuttered Nicholas, after Paxton had pulled the gag out of his mouth. He was clearly terrified of Paxton's wrath.

"They're small but they pack a punch. It's what the Guard uses before they mount an assault."

Paxton turned back to the slaughter and sure enough, a black mass of soldiers and vehicles were now advancing toward the Tribe from the north. They were also launching artillery shells at the assembled warriors, who seemed to be sustaining heavy losses.

"What do we do now?" asked Grace in Paxton's ear.

"We join the fight!" answered Paxton. "What other choice do we have?"

Even as he answered the two painted warriors in their midst had already taken off at a run toward the bulk of their army. Paxton was just about to launch himself in the same direction when Jazelle put a hand on his forearm and pointed toward the east.

"What is that?" she asked. Paxton squinted his eyes in the moonlit duskiness and he eventually saw what Jazelle was pointing at, a cloud of dust low on the horizon speeding directly toward them.

"Run!" Paxton yelled, and they took off after the warriors in the direction of what now appeared to be a heated battle between the Tribe and the Guard. Paxton glanced over his shoulder as he ran to verify that the cloud of dust pursuing them, which now appeared to be caused by a single vehicle, would soon overtake them. He called a halt, wheeled around and sank to one knee with the butt of his cocked rifle anchored upon his shoulder and pointing at what now appeared to be a battered old pickup truck.

He jumped to his feet and screamed, "Don't shoot! Don't shoot! It's Eden!"

The truck drove right into their midst and shuddered to a halt, its braking tires kicking up a final dust cloud which washed over them and made Paxton sputter and cough. When the dust cleared, he could see that Eden was indeed in the passenger seat of the Dodge Ram with a stranger behind the wheel.

The driver, who looked to be a middle-aged Mexican man, rolled down his window and barked at them, "Get in!"

Everyone jumped into the bed of the truck, except for Nicholas who had to be hoisted in by Paxton and Jazelle. When Paxton was sure they were all safely aboard he opened the passenger door and motioned for Eden to move over and make room for him. No sooner had he climbed in beside her and slammed the door than the truck took off again in the direction of the battle.

Paxton gave Eden a spontaneous hug and said in her ear, "You're alive. Thank the All you're alive. Where are the others?"

"Dead," said Eden with sadness. "I couldn't protect them after all."

"Never mind," said Paxton urgently. "There's no time. We should turn around. The battle is lost."

"Where's Abraham?" asked Eden.

"I don't know," answered Paxton. "We got separated."

"We have to rescue Abraham," stated Eden as though that was reason enough to enter the fray. The truck showed no sign of slowing down and soon they had reached the edges of the fighting. Paxton could hear shots being fired from the bed of the pickup, as well as the bullets striking the metal sides of the truck.

He struggled to extricate his rifle because the strap was now trapped behind his back. He had forgotten to take it off his shoulder when he jumped in the cab. He finally succeeded in getting it between his knees with the butt resting on the floorboard and he was about to roll down his window so he could bring it to bear when Eden laid her hand on his and said, "Don't bother. Just help me look out for Abraham."

Just then a projectile flew past the windshield and exploded south of the truck. It jolted them from their chosen course but did no damage to the truck or its passengers. Jazelle came close to being flung off the back of the truck and she screamed at them, "Keep this mother fucker on course, goddammit!"

"Wait!" said Eden squinting intently forward through the windshield. "Isn't that Mukwooru?"

A man sat on a blanket on the ground in full feathered headdress, seemingly oblivious to the heated battle taking place all around him. They couldn't see his face, but the long pipe he was smoking was a dead giveaway. Richard was fighting hand-to-hand with a Guard directly in front of the old man and succeeded in stabbing his opponent in the gut with his machete. Another Guard was aiming at Richard from behind him but he crumpled to the ground, taken down by a timely bullet from someone in the bed of their own truck. Richard turned around at the sound and the surprise was evident upon his face when he saw the familiar truck skid to a stop a few yards from the seated Mukwooru.

Paxton rolled down his window and Richard put his hands on the hot metal, leaned in and shouted, "Get the old man outta here! He ain't even trying to defend himself!"

Paxton jumped out of the truck and he and Richard manhandled Mukwooru into the bed. Paxton was about to get back in when he noticed that Eden was missing. Wheeling around he saw that she was standing a few yards away, supporting Rachel on her one good leg. Paxton ran to help them and they were able to heft her into the back of the truck as well. As Rachel flopped down into the truck, she pointed at the sky to a lone airplane flying directly above them and headed for the Square.

"That'll be the nuclear bomb!" stated Paxton. "We gotta go!"

"Rachel said she saw Abraham go down back there," Eden said, pointing back toward the Wall. "I'm going back for him."

"Eden, no!" Paxton screamed, clutching at her arm, but she wriggled free. The chaos of battle raged all around them and the noise from the gunshots and exploding artillery was deafening. When Paxton turned toward the truck, Jillian and Grace had already jumped down and were following Eden back toward the Wall. Jazelle was about to do the same but Paxton laid a hand on her arm to stop her.

"You stay here!" he yelled directly into her ear. "Keep this truck running! We'll be right back!"

Paxton took a moment to retrieve his gun and then he also took off running after the women. The battle was less heated the closer they got to the Wall. There were dead bodies everywhere, mostly fallen Tribe but also a few of the Guard. Eden ran zigzag over the battlefield peering at the bodies on the ground for any sign of her new friend.

Paxton follow behind her, scanning left and right for enemy soldiers, his rifle at the ready. Suddenly Eden stopped and bent down behind some sagebrush and he momentarily lost sight of her. Paxton sprinted up to her in alarm and as he rounded the clump of sand sage, he saw Valerie seated on the ground and hugging her legs to her chest. She seemed unharmed but she was muttering to herself hysterically as she rocked backward and forward, nodding her head.

"Don't let him take me! Don't let him take me!" she repeated with every forward movement of her torso.

"Don't let who take you?" Paxton asked, getting down on one knee and grabbing both of her arms to force her to look at him.

"The Devil!" she screamed into his face, interrupting her mantra. "He's here! I saw him!"

"Shhh," soothed Eden, grabbing the frail girl into her embrace. "We're here now. We won't let him take you."

"We're looking for Abraham," Paxton said to her urgently. "Have you seen him?"

"He's dead," she sobbed into Eden's chest. "Shot in the gut."

"Where?" asked Paxton. She pointed toward the Wall and then broke into a thin wail that was only partially muffled by Eden's breast. Just then Jillian and Grace caught up to them and Eden motioned for Grace to take her place on the ground.

"We'll be right back!" she shouted above the noise of the continuing battle. She grabbed Paxton by the elbow and they took off at a jog toward the looming Wall. They found Abraham lying face-down on the dusty ground with a gory exit wound on his lower back where his kidney should have been. Eden pushed him onto his back and put her face next to his, trying to shake him awake. Paxton knelt beside her and checked his wrist for a pulse.

"He's gone, Eden," Paxton said. "We've got to get back to the truck!"

"Not without Abraham!" she screamed back at him as she tried unsuccessfully to lift him off the ground by his limp arm. Paxton slung his rifle on his back and grabbed Abraham's other arm. Together they pulled him up into a sitting position. Paxton took advantage of all of the adrenaline he could muster and with one huge pull he hefted Abraham's body up and onto his left shoulder. He staggered under the big man's weight but his legs held true and he turned back around to look for the truck, which was nowhere in sight.

"Follow me!" said Eden, and Paxton staggered after her with his burden. Jillian and Grace fell into step on their flanks, the latter half-dragging the stumbling Valerie in her wake. The weight of Abraham's lifeless body was too much for Paxton and he was sure that he would stumble and fall, but he continued to put one foot in front of the other, concentrating upon Eden's back as the beacon which would lead him to the truck.

Paxton was relieved when the truck's headlights finally came into view through the smoke of the many explosions that had already rocked the field of battle. He stopped in his tracks, however, when he noticed the group of five or six Guard soldiers that were moving steadily toward them from the east to cut off their escape route.

With an unearthly scream Jillian launched herself at their squad, rifle blazing in the dusky moonlight. Grace let go of her burden so she could follow her lover into the fray and Valerie slumped back down upon the ground. Together they pushed forward into the midst of the soldiers and mowed down one, two, three, and then four of the enemy soldiers.

Jillian reminded Paxton of a berserker in battle and it looked like she and Grace were going to make a clean sweep of the soldiers between them and the truck when an artillery shell landed in the midst of that fracas and decimated everyone within its blast radius. Even Paxton was blown off his feet and he dropped Abraham on the ground.

He was disoriented and his ears were ringing when he got to his hands and knees and tried to remember in which direction he had been headed before the blast. Suddenly Jazelle showed up at his elbow and pulled him to his feet. Eden did the same for Valerie and then Richard and the truck driver were beside them as well. Together they lifted Abraham by his armpits and feet and shuffled him over and into the bed of the truck.

Jazelle screamed into his ear, but he could barely hear her above the ringing. She repeated herself and Paxton got the gist of it by reading her lips, "Move your ass, Paxton! We gotta get the hell out of here or we're all gonna die!"

His leaden feet began to move and he allowed her to lead him to the truck, picking up speed with every footfall. She guided him back to the passenger seat and he fell into it beside Rachel. Jazelle slammed the door shut behind him and then jumped over the side and into the bed of the truck. She was still in midair when the truck's tires began to spin wildly through the sand, kicking up clouds of dust that effectively hid them from the soldiers closing in all around them.

They accelerated toward the west, picking up speed quickly and soon they were on the edge of the battle. The truck struck an enemy soldier full force before they were seemingly in the clear, although Jazelle and Richard continued to shoot at any targets, they could see behind them in the growing darkness.

Only when the noise of the conflict had died down did Paxton begin to take stock and count the number of survivors who had managed to escape that bloodbath in the old, beat-up Dodge Ram. There were eleven of them in total, including the soldier they had taken prisoner, the man that had come from the Dump with Eden and was still driving the truck and Abraham's lifeless body.

Because Paxton was turned around in his seat, he was momentarily blinded by the intense flash of white light which briefly turned night into day as the center of the Square disappeared in a ball of flame.

CHAPTER 21

EDEN

I couldn't save them. Paxton warned me about being overconfident. He was right, of course. I didn't count on being knocked unconscious, but that's exactly what happened. I also didn't expect to see my old friend, Lucifer, right there in the middle of everything, all that waste, but I'm pretty sure that was only in my head. Anyway, if I'm going to try to tell this story, I guess I should start at the beginning of it.

We drove all afternoon in the heat and the dust. Nantan said it was one-hundred miles to Kermit and we were only going twenty-five miles an hour for most of the way. All Nantan wanted to talk about the whole ride was death. He was convinced he would die at the Dump and I kept trying to tell him that I would protect us all, from the radiation and the explosion, which turned out to be a lie after all.

In Kermit we met an operative for the Tribe named Nine-Finger Martín. He's a Mexican man who was with Xavier's crew before he escaped to the Guadalupe Mountains. They're the ones who took his finger, but that's not my story to tell. He directed us to an old tool shed north of town where we stayed a couple of hours to wait for dusk. That's where he told me his story, in Spanish, even though his English is very good.

The sun was low on the horizon when we started north for the Dump. There's a railway next to the road that's still intact, the railway not the road, but they both run right into the Dump. Martín had gotten hold of an old railroad hand-cart from somewhere and it was already up on the tracks waiting for us.

I asked Lee why we didn't just drive the truck up there and he said we were trying to avoid the heat signature from the truck that would alert the soldiers on the Wall that we were coming. It was a long, slow trip on that crowded cart. We took turns at the push handle and when we weren't pumping, we sat on the edge with our legs dangling over the side to make room for the antigravity gun.

We stopped about a mile from the Dump to put on lead-lined, hazmat suits. We only had four of them so Nantan and I volunteered not to wear one, for completely different reasons. He was convinced of his impending death and I was still confident I could protect us all. After that we proceeded even more slowly in the ungainly suits, one squeaky lever push at a time.

It was dark when we got our first glimpse of the massive pile of fifty-five-gallon drums stacked haphazardly one upon the other, but the eastern sky was already lighting up from the rising moon. The tracks ended abruptly at the foot of that hulking mass and we were barely able to stop our forward momentum before we came crashing off them.

The built-in Geiger counters in the hazmat suits started going crazy just as soon as we set out on foot with Tarak and Kuruk carrying the antigravity gun between them, a strap upon each of their shoulders. Lee discovered almost immediately that the radiation readings diminished significantly when they stood close to me. The whole group huddled around me while we advanced cautiously forward, as if they were protecting me instead of the other way around.

Our close formation lasted only for a few meters, until we were caught in a hail of machine-gun fire from the soldiers on the Wall. Tarak fell face-down in the dust and the antigravity gun clattered to the ground awkwardly, pulling Kuruk down with it. We all dove for cover wherever we could find it, huddling behind containers which were dented and, in some cases, busted open from whatever method they used to deposit them in the Square.

I decided it was time to flex my newfound strength and I thought the word, "Stop!" in the direction of the Wall, flinging my arms out and away from my body. The gunfire ceased immediately and I told Lee it was time to do what he came here to do. He and Kuruk picked up the antigravity gun and carried it onto the pile for a better shot at its core. We followed behind them as close as we could but it was not an easy climb on the shifting drums.

Just as Lee prepared to fire the gun from above us, a strange feeling of weightlessness enveloped me and I began to feel myself lifting up and off the pile. Nantan was rising right next to me and we grabbed each other's hands just to have something to hold onto. Soon I was on my belly looking down at the ground receding below me. We went up two meters, then four, then six. The last thing I remember was Lee shouting, "Shit! They've got an antigravity gun, too!" It was the last thing I ever heard him say.

I play this moment in my mind over and over again. If only I would have caught myself when they turned the gun off, I could have floated gently back to the ground. I could've negated their antigravity gun from the start and stayed standing on that pile with the rest of them. I was disoriented and upside down by the end of it, and then it just stopped and I plummeted to the ground in an instant, too fast for me to think up a different outcome.

Everything went dark for me then. Everything else I know about the next half hour comes from conversations with Martín after the fact. Apparently, I was knocked unconscious and Nantan broke his leg. Lee began firing into the heart of the biggest peak of nuclear garbage with Kuruk at his side, unloading his rifle at the soldiers on the Wall.

Nothing happened at first, but soon the canisters in Lee's beam began to turn red hot and liquefy. Lee shouted to Martín, "Get them out of here!" Nantan's tibia was protruding through a hole in his shorts and he told Martín to go on without him, to save me. Martín put me on his shoulder and carried me back down the mound of waste. He says he sprinted as fast as he could carry me to the railroad cart, tossed my limp body down so he could climb aboard himself and just started pumping the handle up and down as though his life depended upon it. I suppose that both of our lives did.

I think it was the noise from that squeaking handle that woke me up, or at least that was the first thing that I heard when I came to. Immediately I scrambled to my feet, threw my hands in the air and screamed, "Nooo!"

Just then the world turned brilliant white for an instant, followed by a deafening boom and a rumble in the ground. I just continued to hold my hands in the air and screamed for Martín to keep pumping. He needn't have bothered as we began to accelerate beyond his capabilities from the shock wave we seemed to be surfing upon. It was if my mental shield acted as a sail that propelled us forward using the energy of the explosion in place of the wind.

Miraculously we never left the rails completely but were borne on down the tracks and eventually back to our truck, although the last part of our trip did require some pumping from both of us, with the whole world burning down around us. The truck was intact, even though the garage that had been hiding it had been blown down and incinerated around it. We cleared the rubble and the truck started on the first try.

Martín drove the truck along the pock-marked road as fast as we could safely go, but the road was headed due west and I told him to turn off it and head straight north through the desert instead. I didn't know how big of a hole Lee had managed to create in the Wall, but I thought it best to get ourselves through it before worrying about meeting up with the others. Whatever the outcome of the battle at the Wall, it made more sense to approach the rendezvous point from the other side because at least we would be free of the Square.

The Wall was in ruins, some of it still scattered chunks of concrete and steel but other places it was just not there at all, until it spontaneously burst back into existence somewhere off to the northwest. We didn't want to get too close to the part that was still intact because of the soldiers that must surely be amassing there. To the east it was all scorched earth with at least three visible fires burning and black pillars of smoke billowing upward.

There was nothing left alive in that wasteland, at least not on the surface of the desert. We were both so focused on navigating the ground directly in front of the windshield that we were a kilometer through the Wall before either of us realized we had busted out of the Square. We drove a couple more kilometers north, keeping the Wall within eyesight but not close enough for anyone to get a shot off at the dirty, old pickup truck escaping the blast zone. Then Martín took a ninety-degree turn to the left and began to accelerate.

It took the better part of an hour for us to reach the others, and they were battling for their lives when we got there. Abraham gave his life, but I couldn't let that stand. I had failed to protect Nantan and Lee, Kuruk and Tarak. I could not fail Abraham, too, not if I could resuscitate him. He wasn't completely gone, nor was Lazarus all those years ago for that matter, but he was a few breaths away. I held him in the back of that pickup truck, and I prayed for him and wished for him to be healed. You can still see the nasty scar, but I think Abraham will make a full recovery, minus one kidney, of course.

I have been agonizing over the others we lost, ever since that night, second-guessing myself and wondering what I could have done differently. I could have negated the antigravity if I had only been prepared for it. If I had my guard up, they never would have been able to lift me off the ground and dump me upon my head.

And then there was Lucifer, perched on top of that pile of nuclear waste just looking down at me and laughing his ass off. I guess he thought he had gotten the better of me, but that's never going to happen. He wants me to give this world up to him, but that's not going to happen either, at least not without a fight.

My dad had a saying that he repeated all too often, mostly when he was losing at cribbage, a card game he brought to South America from Maine. He taught Lizzie and I how to play just as soon as we could hold the cards in our little hands, and once we understood the game, he didn't stand a chance against two girls who could read him like a book. We loved to taunt him when we had the lead, to which he would invariably reply, "He who laughs last, laughs best."

ON THE ROAD

Paxton awoke as the first rays of the rising sun filtered through the thin nylon walls of the tent he was sharing with Jazelle, Eden and Elizabeth. It seemed that the women were content to sleep longer so he unzipped his sleeping bag and gathered his clothes as quietly as he could. When he emerged from the tent, he had the sinking feeling that he was back in the Square. The desert looked just the same and the three tents huddled together could easily have been the posse he led to the West Gate for Intake Day just two weeks ago.

When he realized that they were on the other side on the Wall he decided that the alternative was somehow more frightening. They were back in the Republic illegally, with no documentation, no allies and the Republican Guard no doubt scouring the desert for any survivors of the hellfire and brimstone they had rained down upon the Square.

Paxton emptied his bladder upon the desert, even though the need wasn't pressing. He scanned the perimeter of their camp for any sign that something was amiss. He appeared to be the only one awake but he knew there must be a sentry out there somewhere. Paxton zippered his jeans and began to move cautiously toward the small ridge that he would have chosen for sentry duty. It was Martín he encountered, just this side of the ridge and gazing eastward in the direction their pursuers were most likely to spawn. He was awake but it seemed just barely so, and Paxton offered to take his place so that he could catch a few winks.

"I'm up now," Paxton said. "You might as well get a little shut eye while the rest of them are still sleeping."

"You don't have to tell me twice," Martín responded, letting a languid yawn escape his open mouth as he stretched his arms skyward.

"I'd don't plan on traveling too far in the daylight," Paxton allowed, "but we at least need to find some cover, someplace the drones can't see us. And before we can do that, we'll need a group discussion to think through our options and figure out where the hell we're going to go from here. As long as no one is chasing after us, you got time for some sleep."

"I ain't seen nothing in the past four hours except for a couple of night hawks and a fox," Martín reported, "and the planes, of course. You can see their lights through this haze. Seems to be a lot of planes in the sky tonight."

"Looking for us, no doubt," Paxton commented, "and anybody else that made it out of there alive. Let's hope we'll be okay here a little while longer. Eden promised she would keep us hidden from the Eye in the Sky, but I'd feel safer in an abandoned house or gas station."

"You ain't gonna find any of those this side on the Wall, man," Martín commented. "This here's the land of milk and honey."

"Shit!" Paxton interjected as quietly as he could. "I keep forgetting. Even so, I don't see much milk and honey flowing around here. We'll find something."

"I wouldn't sweat it, man," said Martín. "After what I seen her do, if Eden says she can shield us, I believe it."

"What exactly happened out there at the Dump?" asked Paxton. "You were pretty quiet last night when Eden told us the story."

"It happened just like she said," he answered after a pause, "but she didn't tell y'all how it felt. I was sure I was gonna die, first at the Dump and then on the railroad cart. I just kept pumping that handle up and down, up and down. There's only so fast you can go.

"Eden was kneeling there, facing forward, with her hands out on either side of her. We started picking up crazy speed, and everything around us was burning, but we were unharmed. It was like we were in some kind of bubble, man."

"It's good to have her on our side," Paxton said. "We're going to need all the help we can get."

"You ain't lyin', man," agreed Martín. "Alright, then, I could use that sleep. You sure you're alright up here?"

"Go on," instructed Paxton. "I'll be okay. It's already getting light."

Paxton watched the sun rise over the eastern horizon but it took longer for it to reach the tents in the natural depression they had chosen to set up their campsite. The sun's rays warmed his skin immediately and soon enough his body began to perspire to offset its rising temperature. Paxton knew the tents would start to bake as the angle of the sun's rays increased, and that soon enough his sleeping companions would be forced out of their ovens.

Paxton scanned the horizon in all directions for any signs of danger before he closed his eyes to meditate while he still had a few moments of solitude. He rested his upturned palms upon his knees and concentrated upon the rhythm of his breathing for a few minutes before opening a one-sided dialogue with the god of his imaginings.

"*Thank you, All,*" he thought to himself, "*for getting us this far. We are the first people to ever break out of the Square, and hopefully the last, now that they've blown it up. For all of us who still draw breath after that ordeal, I offer my gratitude.*"

"*Thank you for sending us, Eden,*" he continued. "*We wouldn't be here without her. We wouldn't have any hope for the future without her. I know that *there is so much more we still need to accomplish, but with Eden by our side, anything seems possible. I am confident that by your grace we can take back our world and save it from destruction.*

"Thorn once told me that I would be a prophet for Eden, and that it would get me killed. I'm an old man, not as old as I look, but an old man nevertheless. I thank you for the amazing life you have given me, but if it must come to an end, as all lives do, then I am content to lay down my life in service to Eden. Her legacy is the only one worth protecting, for without it, we will all die."

Paxton's prayers were interrupted when he heard a tent door zip open and a camper emerge from its mouth. He opened his eyes to verify that it was Eden who had awoken and was now waving up at him. He returned her wave as she started to walk toward him.

"Speak of the Devil," he thought to himself and it caused a wide smile to spread across his face. *"Or should I say God?"*

"You look awfully pleased with yourself," said Eden when she stood in front of him. "Did I miss something?"

"I was just thinking about you," he admitted. "Please join me."

Eden sat on the dusty ground next to him so that she could share in the viewing of the sunrise. Neither one of them spoke for a long time until Paxton finally said, "We have a long way to go, don't we?"

"We do," she agreed. "But I once said, a long time ago, that 'the journey of a thousand miles begins with a single step.'"

"But which direction should we take that first step?" asked Paxton.

"I don't know," she answered truthfully. "We need to consult with Mukwooru."

"One thing's for certain, we can't stay here," said Paxton. "I'm sick to death of this All-forsaken desert!"

Others were now emerging from the tents as well. First Abraham came out, then Rachel from the same tent. When they caught sight of Paxton and Eden, they immediately headed in their direction with Rachel leaning on Abraham for support. Their awkward gait reminded Paxton of a three-legged race and he supposed that's exactly what they were doing, although they didn't seem to be in much of a hurry this early in the morning.

Elizabeth was next, followed a few minutes later by Jazelle, who was wearing a Life is Good T-shirt and nothing else. She squatted next to the tent to relieve herself and then went back inside to retrieve the rest of her clothes. When Richard finally came out of his tent, he dragged Nicholas out with him. The corn-fed Iowan boy looked formidable enough to take on the grizzled, old biker in a fair fight, which wouldn't be happening anytime soon with his hands tied behind his back. Valerie emerged after them and the three of them came up the small hill to join the others, leaving only Martín and Mukwooru still asleep in their tents.

Valerie had a haunted look about her, and she was furtively scanning the desert this way and that as she trudged slowly up the hill. Eden scrambled down the hill to put her arm around her shoulder and help shepherd the wayward sheep back to their flock. They were speaking so softly that Paxton couldn't understand what they were saying until they were almost upon him.

"What did he look like?" asked Eden.

"He had brown skin," Valerie stammered, clearly shaken up, "and black hair. But he had blue eyes, beautiful blue eyes, until he smiled. When he smiled there was nothing beautiful about him."

"What did he say to you?" Eden pressed her.

"Mostly he just sat on the edge of the Wall and laughed and laughed," she replied, "but then he was right by my side, in an instant. He told me he might have a job for me, later on."

"What kind of job?" asked Paxton.

"I don't know," she sobbed. "After that he just disappeared."

She broke down crying and Eden gathered her into her arms and whispered things into her ear that were between just the two of them. Whatever she said to Valerie must have helped because when they disentangled themselves, Valerie looked relieved and even managed a brief smile before the two of them sat side by side next to Paxton.

When the whole group was seated in a rough circle at the top of the hillock, Paxton began, "Well it seems as if we're all here, except Martín and Mukwooru. How's the old man?"

"Still old," answered Richard sarcastically, "and sleeping. You want me to wake him up?"

"Let them both sleep a little longer. Mukwooru must be exhausted, and Martín pulled sentry duty right before sunup. If they can sleep in this heat, more power to 'em!"

"We need to talk," he continued. "We need to figure out our next move, and what to do with our captive."

"Only one thing to do," Richard stated emotionlessly. "He's seen all of our faces; he knows where we are. He could easily turn us in to the Guard."

"He doesn't know where we're headed," Elizabeth pointed out.

"Do *we* know where we're headed?" asked Rachel.

"What we gonna do, Paxton?" asked Jazelle. "Now that we done the impossible, where we gonna go? Do you even know?"

"I'm still working on it," Paxton replied with a grin. "I want to talk to the old man. In the mean time we need to get off this ridge and find someplace to hole up for the day. I think we should do our traveling by night."

"Damned straight!" agreed Jazelle. "But what are we gonna do with him?"

"The safest thing to do would be to put him out of his misery," Paxton replied, "or we could just cut him loose once we're ready to go. We'd have a pretty good head start by the time he finds his way back to civilization."

Nicholas was mumbling crazily into his gag with wide eyes and flared nostrils. Paxton nodded toward Richard and said, "Let him speak."

Richard moved to loosen his gag but whispered into his ear loud enough for Paxton to hear, "If you scream, I will end you right here and right now. Understood?"

Nicholas nodded his head frantically and Richard removed the T-shirt that had been stuffed into his mouth. Nicholas immediately offered them a third option.

"Take me with you!" he said hurriedly. "I can help you. I have a RepubliCard. I can pay for things. I can get you through the toll booths on the highways."

"Hold on a second," Paxton interrupted him. "Why should we trust you? You'd turn us in to the Guard the first chance you get!"

"No, I won't!" Nicholas defended himself. "I don't wanna be in the Guard no more! All I was gonna do was my two years mandatory, but they tricked me into staying on. There ain't no more Wall to guard, no how. If I go back now, they'll shoot me for a deserter."

"Just tell 'em you were captured," offered Jazelle. "They ain't gonna punish you for gettin' captured."

"You don't know the Guard," Nicholas countered. "Failure is not an option. Even if they don't shoot me, they'll ship me off to the War. I'd rather be here, with her."

He looked pointedly at Eden as he finished and all eyes turned to her as well. She stared at him hard for a few moments as everyone waited to hear her opinion on the matter.

"Nic poses no threat to us," she said finally. "I think he is right; he can be useful as we navigate through the Republic. I say we take him with us. I say there's been enough killing for the time being."

"How do you know my name?" he asked her incredulously.

"I was just inside your head," she said as if it were the easiest thing in the world to do. To the rest of the group she said, "There is no guile in him. I believe him that he won't betray us to the Guard."

"Well, I don't like it," said Richard. "He ain't part of the Tribe. He sure as shit ain't got no reason to be loyal to the Tribe, or any of us, for that matter."

"The Tribe is gone, man," Abraham spoke up for the first time. "You saw what the Guard did to us back at the Wall. Anyone who survived that bloodbath is scattered to the winds."

"The Tribe lives on in us," grumbled Richard. "That's what Mukwooru would say."

"He can identify each and every one of us to the Guard," Jazelle pointed out. "If we let him go, everyone in the Republic will be looking out for us."

"Everyone in the Republic will be looking sidelong at us anyway," offered Paxton. "We're eleven people traveling together in an old, pick-up truck. Two of us are black, we've got a Hispanic and a Native American, and one of us has half a leg. It's going to be hard to fly under the radar with this motley crew."

"So, what are we gonna do about 'im?" asked Jazelle, poking her finger at the still trussed-up soldier.

"I don't know what they do in the Tribe, but on Maggie's Farm we'd put it to a vote," said Paxton. "Martín and Mukwooru are still sleeping, so we'll count them out, which leaves eight of us. A simple majority will win. All those in favor of letting him live, raise your hand."

All but Richard and Jazelle raised their hands. Richard said, "This is crazy and not at all how we do it in the Tribe. The highest-ranking member of any party is the leader of that party and their decision is final."

"Then who is our leader?" asked Rachel.

"I'm now second in command after Mukwooru," said Richard, "and it was really Nantan who made all of our day-to-day decisions. With him gone and Mukwooru sleeping, that makes me the leader."

"Like hell, you are!" exclaimed Jazelle. "Call us what you want, you and Martin and Mukwooru are the only surviving members of the Tribe. The rest of us come from Maggie's Farm and Paxton is our leader."

"Technically, the four of us only joined Maggie's Farm two weeks ago," Rachel pointed out, "and Valerie was new to the Square as well, so there are just as many Newts here as anybody else. I think Abraham should lead."

"Eden should be our leader," interjected Abraham.

"Yes," agreed Elizabeth. "She's the Messiah. She should be our leader." "I will lead when the time comes," agreed Eden, "but I know nothing of the Republic, nor how to survive in a hostile environment like you all have been doing in the Square. I'm content to be a follower for the time being."

"If I were to lead, I would still put all of our important decisions to a vote," explained Paxton, "which is exactly what I think we should do now. Are there any other nominations for who should lead our little band of misfits?"

When no one offered up any more alternatives Paxton put it to a vote. Everyone but Richard voted for him. Even Valerie, who was looking so much better that Paxton thought she just might survive her detox, voted for him. Nicholas couldn't raise his hand for either candidate as they were still tied behind his back.

"Even allowing that Martín and Mukwooru would vote for you, Richard," said Paxton, "that still makes it seven votes to three. Are you willing to concede leadership to me?"

"What other choice do I have?" groused Richard.

"It's settled then," Paxton closed the matter and reopened another. "What about our prisoner. What did you say your name was?"

"Nicholas Needmore," he replied. "My friends call me Nic."

"Let's take another vote," offered Paxton. "Do we take Nic with us, or set him free? All those in favor of taking him with us raise your hand."

Eden, Elizabeth and Rachel raised their hands immediately while Abraham, Richard and Jazelle showed no signs of doing the same. Paxton waited a long moment for anyone to change his or her mind before he said to Valerie, "Are you gonna vote?"

When she shook her head no, he continued, "I guess the decision falls to me after all."

"What decision?" asked Mukwooru, who was now standing at the edge of their circle. No one had seen him coming up the hill and those nearest to him were visibly startled by his presence.

"Good, you're awake," Paxton acknowledged him. "We're trying to decide what to do with Nic, here."

"And who should be leader of the Tribe," interjected Richard.

Abraham and Eden helped the old man into a cross-legged, seated position between them and he sat there with his eyes closed for a minute or more. Paxton thought he might have fallen back asleep and was just about to address him when he opened his eyes and spoke in his gravelly, century-old voice.

"Eden is your leader," he spoke with confidence.

"Eden has declined for the moment," Paxton informed him.

"Then it should be Paxton," Mukwooru continued, "after I'm gone."

"Where are you going?" asked Richard.

"I want you to take me to Carlsbad Caverns," he answered, "to die."

"What? No!" yelled Richard before he could stop himself.

"This body has held on longer than most," he explained. "I have played my part. Now that Eden is in the Republic, I can finally rest. I think I have earned that much."

"Of course, you have," agreed Eden, crawling the short distance to him so that she could take his hands in her own. "Thank you for all you have done for me."

"But there is still so much to do," argued Paxton. "I don't even know where to start…"

"All in good time," Mukwooru interrupted him. "I leave you in good hands."

"Why Carlsbad Caverns?" questioned Paxton.

"The caves are sacred to my people, and not far from here," explained Mukwooru. "I would like to leave this body in the belly of the Earth and let my spirit join my ancestors, wherever they may be."

"What about him?" asked Richard, gesturing toward the still bound soldier. "We were just talking about what to do with him when you came up here."

"Bring him to me," ordered Mukwooru.

Richard and Paxton picked Nic up by his elbows and helped him maneuver into the space directly in front of Mukwooru. Eden scrambled back to her original spot on the circle's perimeter to make space for him. Mukwooru stared into his eyes for a long minute before addressing the young man directly.

"Would you like to be in the Tribe?" he asked him simply.

"Yes," answered Nic, just as simply.

"He is now one of us," Mukwooru said in a louder voice.

"Really?" asked Richard. "Just like that?"

"First we must smoke," acceded Mukwooru, and he reached inside the light jacket draped upon his shoulders for his pipe.

"Not the god-damned pipe!" grumbled Richard. "We need to keep our wits about us."

"It's not for you," Mukwooru replied, smiling up at his lieutenant and friend.

"We're going to take you with us, Nic," Paxton spoke to him from just behind his right ear. "Untie his hands, Richard. You should be aware that we'll be keeping a very close eye on you. If you do try to betray us, we won't hesitate to put a bullet in your skull."

Richard fiddled with the ropes binding Nic's wrists behind his back and soon he had them loosened and off. Nic commenced to rub his sore wrists and he half-turned to look up at Paxton.

"Thank-you," he said, offering his hand for Paxton to shake. "You won't regret it."

"My name is Paxton," he introduced himself, sharing in Nic's vigorous handshake. He then proceeded to introduce the rest of the Tribe.

"Well, it sounds like we have a tentative plan," said Paxton, as Mukwooru lit the bowl he had just packed full of ganja. "Subject to change at a moment's notice, of course. Let's get something to eat and then get those tents packed up and into the truck. We gotta put some more miles between us and the Wall."

Jazelle was the first one to her feet and she immediately started barking orders at the slow to rise, grumbling misfits all around her. Now that they had a clear direction, Jazelle was all action and she exhorted them, "Get up off your asses! You heard the man. We got work to do."

An hour later the truck was packed with the last of the Tribe and its possessions. Elizabeth and Eden rode with Abraham, Martín, Nicholas and Valerie in the bed, Rachel and Mukwooru sat in the cramped second row of seats and Richard was behind the wheel. Paxton and Jazelle stood arm in arm outside of the open passenger side door, looking out over the already-too-hot desert vista.

"Now that we're leaving this desert," said Paxton in her ear, "I can admit that it's beautiful, in its own way."

"Are you shittin' me?" asked Jazelle, elbowing his ribs as she turned toward him. "Ain't nothin' beautiful about it. You wanna see beauty, let me take you down to the Bayou. Now that's beautiful. This here's the Devil's playground. I don't care if I ever see it again, tell ya the truth."

"Maybe you can do that someday," Paxton agreed. "Take me down into the deep, dark swamp, where it's probably even hotter than it is here. You probably want to feed me to the alligators."

"You wouldn't be nothing but a morsel to them," Jazelle teased him. "I might find a better use for you."

"Before we can do that," said Paxton, removing her hand from his crotch, "we have work to do. If we fail in the coming struggle, if Eden doesn't prevail, this whole planet will be the Devil's playground!"

"So melodramatic," she said before kissing his cheek gently. "You know, sugar, one good thing did come out of this fuckin' desert. I met you. I love you, Paxton Stephens."

"I love you, too, Jazelle Porter," he replied, before leaning in for a lingering kiss. The passengers in the truck started making catcalls and Richard held his open palm out and above the steering wheel, poised to honk the horn at them before he decided better of it.

Instead, he said, "Alright, already! Do you two lovebirds wanna saddle up and ride?"

"We're coming!" said Paxton, kissing her one more time on the nose before turning to the staring group. "We're just saying goodbye to the desert."

EPILOGUE

PAXTON

We fucking did it! We busted out of the Square. We busted the Square. They said it was impossible but we fucking did it. Those evil motherfuckers nuked the place. I still can't believe it. Let me have this celebration for a couple more moments before reality reaches up to slap me in the face.

We're headed to Carlsbad Caverns to lay Mukwooru to rest, unless I can talk him out of it. Eden says I shouldn't bother, that we have already asked enough of him, but I feel like we're on a rudderless ship as it is. Where are we supposed to go? What's going to become of us if we jettison the captain? Pick a new captain, I guess. They want it to be me, but I haven't a clue where to begin or how we're possibly going to be able to overthrow the Republic.

If we by some miracle succeed in taking control of the vast war machine of the Republic, we will need to use it to defeat the forces of the Devil himself which are already massing against us. Let's say we come out on top of the battle of Armageddon, whatever that might mean, we will need to emerge from that bloodbath and reorganize the remains of humankind to clean up our mess and learn how to adapt in an environment that has changed in fundamental ways. I'm usually an optimist, but I can't seem to wrap my head around the odds of pulling this thing off.

We do have our ace in the hole, Eden, who is at the very least a prophet of God and at best God herself. That's got to tip the scales in our favor. She's still flexing her muscles, but hopefully she'll get her act together in time to save us all. There's that optimism rearing its cheerful head. Eden is amazing, but can she clean up the oil spills, radioactive fallout, greenhouse gases, fire damage and chemical pollution in our land, water and air?

Our world is overpopulated, but a great many people are going to die in a very short period of time, so that problem should take care of itself. But how do we make sure we're not amongst the ones that don't make it? There's the rub. Survival of the fittest, but what does that mean in this modern world? The fittest are no longer the strongest and fastest. I'd like to think that the fittest are the ones with the highest intelligence, the ones who know how to avail themselves of modern technology, but the cynic in me suspects it'll be the ones who already hold the most wealth and power.

Speaking of modern technology, I am morbidly curious as to what applications they've put antigravity. Are they using it for travel, transport or the lifting of heavy objects? Or is it all just war machines? We've always been so damn good at war machines. And to what other uses have they put Unified Field Theory besides antigravity?

I haven't been away that long, but a lot could have happened in those two years with our big brains working collectively. If only we could have put all of that brainpower toward the preservation of our environment, all those years, while our elected officials continued to deny there was a problem, we might not be in these dire straits. Or maybe it was inevitable.

Maybe this showdown between good and evil, order and chaos, yin and yang, God and the Devil, was inevitable since the creation of the universe. Certainly, Armageddon has been prophesied many times over, which is part of the problem. When these predicted deadlines come and go and the world doesn't end, we become inured to the notion that we will be held accountable for our actions. Everyone thinks that they will live forever, until one day they don't.

As for me, I know my days are numbered. I may still have some small part to play in the coming struggle, and I will play it to the best of my ability, but I fear I am not long for this world. I grow older and more tired every day, as do we all, but when you get to be my age you begin to lose the illusion of immortality and face the reality of the deterioration of this physical vessel for the soul. And I'm already living on borrowed time. Thorn brought me back from the dead many years ago. He said my life's work wasn't finished yet. It's got to be nearly finished by now.

I have been dreaming of Thorn lately, stress dreams really, because he's always telling me things I should be doing, or should already have done, to save the planet. Haven't I already done enough? As far as I'm concerned, I have one purpose left to me and that's to keep Eden alive so *she* can save the planet! My planet saving days are over. I'm a tired, crotchety old man.

What I really want, truth be told, is to sit on my porch in Farmington, Maine, drink a few beers as I watch the sunset, maybe strum out a couple of songs on my guitar. It doesn't sound like much, but right about now, it seems to be just as unobtainable as saving the planet. Here's hoping Eden has some insight into the latter because I am fresh out of ideas.

gramcontent.com/pod-product-compliance
g Source LLC
e TN
0312070526
LV00069B/6459